HELL OR HIGH WATER

A DEEP SIX NOVEL

JULIE ANN WALKER

Published by Sourcebooks Casablanca an imprint of Sourcebooks, Inc.
P.O. Box 4410, Naperville, Illinois 60567-4410
(630) 961-3900
Fax: (630) 961-2168
www.sourcebooks.com

Printed and bound in Canada.
MBP 10 9 8 7 6 5 4 3 2 1

To all the fans who have followed me through each adventure in every story, who have encouraged me to keep writing, and who have cheered me on since the first sentence of the first book I ever published. This one's for you!

As the son of a son of a sailor, I went out on the sea for adventure...

—Jimmy Buffett

Prologue

May 26, 1624…

The end is near…

The words rang through Captain Bartolome Vargas's mind with the ominous clarity of a death knell. The seas…the wildly capricious seas had turned against him just as they had done many times before. But unlike all those earlier hard-fought, hard-won battles, something inside him—a premonition, perhaps? Or maybe simple intuition?—told him this day there would be no escaping the watery jaws that waited to swallow his beloved ship and the 224 souls aboard her like a giant blue whale gulping down a gullet full of krill. This day neither Christ nor cannon could protect his precious galleon from the huge, frothing waves rushing up against her hull.

"Take in the main sails! Make haste!" he bellowed to the crewmen crawling in the rigging and scrambling and sliding across the Santa Cristina's waterlogged deck. His first mate blasted the command through a whalebone whistle, the three-note trill nearly lost when the ferocious wind caught it and whipped it out to sea. Raking the rain and salt spray from his eyes, Bartolome wrestled with the big wooden wheel, looking toward the east and the roiling wall of clouds that heralded his doom. When he'd awakened that morning to the eerie glow on the horizon, his sailor's instincts had warned him they were in for one hell of a storm. But so early in the season, he had not been prepared for this...

Un huracán—*a hurricane. There was no doubt in his mind.*

With a violent curse, he swung his gaze to the north, hoping his sister ship, Nuestra Señora de Cádiz, *had made it to Bone Key in time to ride out the fury on the leeward side of the island. Upon seeing the tumultuous red sky at sunrise, he and Captain Quintana, his counterpart aboard the* Cádiz, *had made the decision to split the armada sailing for Spain. Quintana would continue on, taking refuge along the way at Bone Key if need be. And Bartolome would turn back to their home port of Havana—and if he could not make that, he would shelter near the ringed island halfway between. Their thinking had been that if worse came to worst, at least one ship would survive the tempest. But* un huracán... Un huracán *could very well see them both at the bottom of the sea.*

Just like Eustacio...

With a grimace, Bartolome thought of the man he lost overboard midmorning along with six of his bronze deck cannons when the Santa Cristina *took a rogue wave broadside. It should have been his first clue this was no mere summer squall. He should have sought shelter then.*

He had not.

"God help them." Bartolome quietly whispered a prayer for both Eustacio and his sister ship. Then he included a prayer for himself and his remaining crew, "God help us all," before turning his attention to the south.

The merciless wind whipped his hair from the clasp at his nape, plastering it against the stubble on his cheeks and chin. He paid it no mind as he strained and wished with his whole heart to see the glittering, welcoming lights of Havana. Unfortunately, with the city still so far away, that sight was no more substantial than a memory. It was impossible to fight the wind and the tides to sail back to her now.

As if to prove his point, he watched, stricken, while the San Andrés *and the* San José, *the two gunships tasked with protecting the* Santa Cristina, *each fell victim to the monster waves crashing over their decks. First one, then the other quietly slipped beneath the surface of the teeming water. Their demises rendered even more horrific by the seeming banality, the simplicity, with which they were dragged to the bottom.*

The end is near…

Those words once again rose up to taunt Bartolome, and he had just enough time to send up an invocation for the lost souls aboard the gunships when—sploosh!—the Santa Cristina's *yardarms plunged into the angry ocean as she rolled violently to her side. The deck heaved beneath his feet. He gripped the wheel with one hand and the slick rail with the other, holding on so tightly his fingers ached. The mighty masts groaned and creaked in dire warning, and the bitter smell of silt and kelp, stirred up by the swirling currents, added to the sharp bite of electricity burning through the air.*

Boom! A burst of lightning, only found in the most turbulent and unpredictable hurricanes, sizzled through the sky overhead, highlighting the determined faces of

Bartolome's crew as they battled for the life of the ship, and ultimately their own salvation.

They had only one chance: the ringed island he'd left behind just a short time ago when he was still arrogant enough to think it was possible to reach home port…

"We are coming about!" he yelled to his first mate.

Nodding jerkily, the young officer lifted his whistle to his lips. Bartolome saw the man's cheeks puff out, but no sound emerged from the small instrument. With a shouted curse, his first mate shook as much of the sea spray from the whistle as he could before trying again. This time, two short, clear notes pierced the blustery air, followed by one long, melodious trill.

Bartolome watched through the blinding screen of rain as his valiant crew struggled to do his bidding. When the rigging was ready, he spun the wheel, his muscles burning from the long hours of desperately working to control the big ship. The Santa Cristina *moaned mightily, the wood of her hull straining as she fought to make the turn in the heaving seas. But the instant the secondary sails caught the force of the gale, lifting the ship sharply before plunging her to her side, it became obvious it was too late. She could probably hold together long enough to take them back to the ringed island, but she was far too cumbersome to make the maneuvers needed to safely sail them around to the leeward side.*

"She is too heavy, sir!" the cook's son yelled, clinging desperately to the railing of the quarterdeck. The fear in the young lad's wide eyes was as stark as the choices that lay before Bartolome. "We must relieve her of her cargo if we want to live!"

Her cargo…the tons of gold and silver coins, the barrels of jewelry and uncut gems the Santa Cristina *carried in her big belly. It was a treasure King Philip desperately needed to fund the ongoing fight against the English, French, and Dutch—those scurvy bastards determined to see Spain's empire burned to ashes. A treasure the king had entrusted to Bartolome, Quintana, and the twin ships they captained, the prides of the Spanish fleet.*

Bartolome knew what he must do. King and country first.

Yanking the wheel hard left, he struggled to follow the currents and pilot the ship from the deceptive safety of the deep water to the certain perils of the shallows.

"What are you doing?" the boy screeched as the ship plowed up a mammoth wave, the deck going nearly vertical before cresting the swell and plunging down the other side. "You will run us aground!"

And that was exactly Bartolome's plan. If he stayed out in the fathomless depths of the straits and liberated the Santa Cristina *of her precious cargo before sailing around to the north of the island, they stood a chance against the wrath of the storm. However, half of the wealth of his nation, the wealth his king was counting on, would forever be condemned to a black, watery grave.*

"We will steer her toward the reef line!" he yelled to the lad as another wave crashed over the decks, sending his crewmen sliding and grasping for handholds, and momentarily blinding Bartolome with a face full of foul, briny water. "There will be a chance for salvage!"

"But you will kill us all!" the cook's son screeched,

and Bartolome once again viciously swiped the salt spray from his eyes, sparing the thirteen-year-old boy a quick, pitying glance.

So young to be facing the inevitability of death. Likely has not yet tasted his first woman…

The idea gave Bartolome momentary pause. But then he shook his head and pushed the thought aside, returning his attention to steering the ship through the treacherous seas. The life of a sailor was uncertain at best, and the lad had been well warned of the dangers before signing on to join his father on this voyage with the royal fleet.

"Please do not do this, Captain!" the boy pleaded, choking on his tears and the water that continued to deluge the ship as the shadowy outline of a small island appeared off their bow.

Bartolome paid the youth's cries no heed. And forgoing the whistle of his first mate, he bellowed to his crew on deck, "Away the anchors, boys!"

If he could catch part of the approaching reef, the galleon would be assured to sink in shallow, salvageable waters and he would have done his duty. Giving his all, his life most likely, for his country and its cause.

For a split second following his order, all activity aboard the galleon came to a halt, the crew realizing his intent. He wondered if perhaps his men would mutiny. Then his heart swelled with pride when one of his midshipmen—Rosario, perhaps?—began calling out orders and the brave sailors aboard the Santa Cristina *once more raced to do his bidding.*

Boom! Another burst of lightning flayed open the blackened sky like a wound, spotlighting the chains on the anchors as they raced over the side of the gunwale, disappearing into the frenzied waters.

And now all that was left to do was hang on.

"Lash yourself to an empty water barrel, lad!" Bartolome shouted to the sobbing youth, keeping a firm handhold on the wheel as the anchors dragged against the sandy bottom, searching for the ridge of coral and causing the ship to list precariously as waves continued to beat against her squealing hull like giant, angry fists.

And then it happened. The anchors found purchase a mere heartbeat before a breaker lifted the Santa Cristina *and hurled her against the exposed reef. Crash! The galleon split in two, water pouring into her ruined hold. Bartolome could do nothing but watch as the cook's son, strapped precariously to the water barrel, was dragged overboard.*

Good luck to you, my boy, *he thought as he closed his eyes and lifted his face to the furious sky, the screams of his terrified and dying men filling his ears. Seconds later, a swell overtook him and the great ship, dragging them both beneath the raging surface of the sea…*

Chapter One

"AND THE *SANTA CRISTINA* AND HER BRAVE CREW AND captain were sucked down into Davy Jones's locker, lost to the world. That is…until now…"

Leo "the Lion" Anderson, known to his friends as LT—a nod to his former Naval rank—let his last words hang in the air before glancing around at the four faces illuminated by the flickering beach bonfire. Rapt expressions stared back at him. He fought the grin curving his lips.

Bingo, bango, bongo. His listeners had fallen under a spell as deep and fathomless as the great oceans themselves. It happened anytime he recounted the legend of the *Santa Cristina*. Not that he could blame his audience. The story of the ghost galleon, the holy grail of sunken Spanish shipwrecks, had fascinated *him* ever since he'd been old enough to understand the tale while bouncing on his father's knee. And that lifelong fascination might account for why he was now determined to do what so many before him—his dearly departed father included—had been unable to do. Namely, locate and excavate the mother lode of the grand ol' ship.

Of course, he reckoned the romance and mystery of discovering her waterlogged remains were only *part* of the reason he'd spent the last two months and a huge portion of his savings—as well as huge portions of the savings of the others—refurbishing his father's decrepit, leaking salvage boat. The rest of the story as to why he was here now? Why they were *all* here now? Well, that didn't bear dwelling on.

At least not on a night like tonight. When a million glittering stars and a big half-moon reflected off the dark, rippling waters of the lagoon on the southeast side of the private speck of jungle, mangrove forest, and sand in the Florida Keys. When the sea air was soft and warm, caressing his skin and hair with gentle, salt-tinged fingers. When there was so much…*life* to enjoy.

That had been his vow—*their* vow—had it not? To grab life by the balls and really *live* it? To suck the marrow from its proverbial bones?

His eyes were automatically drawn to the skin on the inside of his left forearm where scrolling, tattooed lettering read *For RL*. He ran a thumb over the pitch-black ink.

This one's for you, you stubborn sonofagun, he pledged, flipping open the lid on the cooler sunk deep into the sand beside his lawn chair. Grabbing a bottle of Budweiser and twisting off the cap, he let his gaze run down the long dock to where his uncle's catamaran was moored. The clips on the sailboat's rigging lines clinked rhythmically against its metal mast, adding to the harmony of softly shushing waves, quietly crackling fire, and the high-pitched *peesy, peesy, peesy* call of a nearby black-and-white warbler.

Then he turned his eyes to the open ocean past the underwater reef surrounding the side of Wayfarer Island, where his father's old salvage ship bobbed lazily with

the tide. Up and down. Side to side. Her newly painted
hull and refurbished anchor chain gleamed dully in the
moonlight. Her name, *Wayfarer-I*, was clearly visible
thanks to the new, bright-white lettering.

He dragged in a deep breath, the smell of burning
driftwood and suntan lotion tunneled up his nose, and
he did his best to appreciate the calmness of the evening
and the comforting thought that the vessel looked, if not
necessarily sexy, then at least seaworthy. *Which is a hell
of an improvement.*

Hot damn, he was proud of all the work he and his
men had done on her, and—

His men…

He reminded himself for the one hundred zillionth time
that he wasn't supposed to think of them that way. Not
anymore. Not since those five crazy-assed SEALs waved
their farewells to the Navy in order to join him on his
quest for high-seas adventure and the discovery of untold
riches. Not since they were now, officially, *civilians*.

"But why you guys?" The blond who was parked
beneath Spiro "Romeo" Delgado's arm yanked Leo
from his thoughts. "What makes you different from all
those who've already tried and failed to find her?"

"Besides the obvious you mean, *mamacita*?" Romeo
winked, leaning back in his lawn chair to spread his arms
wide. His grin caused his teeth to flash white against his
neatly trimmed goatee, and Leo watched the blond sit
forward in her plastic deck chair to take in the wonder
that was Romeo Delgado. After a good, long gander, she
giggled and snuggled back against Romeo's side.

Leo rolled his eyes. Romeo's swarthy, Hispanic looks
and his six-percent-body-fat physique made even the most

prim-and-proper lady's panties drop fast enough to bust the floorboards. And this gal? Well, this gal might be prim and proper in her everyday life—hell, for all Leo knew she could be the leading expert on high etiquette at an all-girls school—but today, ever since Romeo picked her and her cute friend up in Schooner Wharf Bar on Key West with the eye-rolling line of *"Wanna come see my private island?"* she'd been playing the part of a good-time girl out having a little fun-in-the-sun fling. And it was the *fling* part that might—scratch that, rewind—*did* account for the lazy, self-satisfied smile spread across Romeo's face.

"I'm serious, though." Tracy or Stacy or Lacy, or whatever her name was—Leo had sort of tuned out on the introductions—wrinkled her sunburned nose. "How do you even know where to look?"

"Because of this." Leo lifted the silver piece of eight, a seventeenth-century Spanish dollar, from where it hung around his neck on a long, platinum chain. "My father discovered it ten years ago off the coast of the Marquesas Keys."

Tracy/Stacy/Lacy's furrowed brow telegraphed her skepticism. "One coin? I thought the Gulf and the Caribbean were littered with old doubloons."

"It wasn't just one piece of eight my father found." Leo winked. "It was a big, black conglomerate of ten pieces of eight, as well as—"

"Conglomerate?" asked the brunette with the Cupid's-bow lips. Tracy/Stacy/Lacy's friend had given Leo all the right signals the minute Romeo pulled the catamaran up to Wayfarer Island's creaky old dock and unloaded their guests. It'd been instant sloe-eyed looks and shy, encouraging smiles.

Okay, and confession time. Because for a fleeting moment when she—Sophie or Sophia? Holy Christ, Leo was seriously sucking with names tonight—sidled up next to him, he'd been tempted to take her up on all the things her nonverbal communications offered. Then an image of black hair, sapphire eyes, and a subtly crooked front tooth blazed through his brain. And just like that, the brunette lost her appeal.

Which is a good thing, he reminded himself. *You're gettin' too old to bang the Betties Romeo drags home from the bar.*

Enter Dalton "Doc" Simmons and his nearly six and a half feet of homespun, Midwestern charm. He'd been quick to insert himself between Leo and Sophie/Sophia. And now her gaze lingered on Doc's face when he said in that low, scratchy Kiefer Sutherland voice of his, "Unlike gold, which retains its luster after years on the bottom of the ocean, silver coins are affected by the seawater. They get fused together by corrosion or other maritime accretions. When that happens, it's called a conglomerate. They have to be electronically cleaned to remove the surface debris and come out looking like this." Grabbing the silver chain around his neck, Doc pulled a piece of eight from inside his T-shirt. It was identical to the one Leo wore.

"And like this," Romeo parroted, twirling the coin on the chain around *his* neck like a Two-Buck Chuck stripper whirling a boa.

Their first day on the island, Leo had gifted each of his men—*damnit!*...his *friends*—with one of the coins, telling them their matching tattoos were symbols of their shared past and their matching pieces of eight were symbols of their shared future.

Leo tipped the neck of his beer toward Doc. "Maritime accretions, huh? You sound like an honest-to-God salvor, my friend."

Doc smirked, which was as close to a smile as the dude ever really got. If Leo hadn't seen Doc rip into a steak on occasion, he wouldn't have been all that convinced the guy had teeth.

"But even a conglomerate of coins wouldn't be enough to guarantee the ship's location," Leo added, turning back to the blond. "My father *also* found a handful of bronze deck cannons. All of which were on the *Santa Cristina*'s manifest. So she's down there…*somewhere*." He just had to find her. All his friends were counting on that windfall for various reasons, and if he didn't—

"But, like you said, your dad tried to find this Christy boat for"—Leo winced. Okay, so the woman seemed sweet. But the only thing worse than mangling the name of the legendary vessel was referring to it as a *boat*— "like twenty-some-odd years, right?"

"And Mel Fisher searched for the *Atocha* for sixteen years before finally findin' her." He referred to the most famous treasure hunter and treasure galleon of all time. Well, most famous of all time until he and the guys made the history books, right? *Right*. "In shallow water, like that around the Florida Keys, the shiftin' sands are moved by wind and tide. They change the seabed daily, not to mention after nearly four centuries. But with a little hard work and perseverance, you better believe the impossible becomes possible. We're hot on her trail." Her convoluted, invisible, nonexistent trail. *Shit*.

Doc slow-winked at the woman by way of agreement, twirling the toothpick that perpetually stuck out of his mouth in a circle with his tongue. It must have dazzled poor Sophie/Sophia, because she sucked in a breath before batting her pretty lashes and sidling her lawn chair closer to him. Throwing an arm around her shoulders, Doc turned to wiggle his eyebrows at Leo. Just like the others, Doc was never one to pass up an opportunity to feed Leo a heaping helping of shit. Par for the course considering Leo was…*fuck a duck*…*used* to be their commanding officer, a prime target for all their ass-hattery.

Yeah, yeah, Leo thought, quietly chuckling. *So, I pulled the Roger Murtaugh, I'm-gettin'-too-old-for-this-shit bit. And you think I screwed up royally when I turned down what she was offerin'? So, go ahead. Rub it in, you big corn-fed douche-canoe.*

"Why do you need to find that old treasure anyway?" the blond asked. "You have a private island." She motioned with her beer toward the rippling waters of the lagoon, tipsily splashing suds into the fire and making it hiss. "Aren't you r—" She hiccuped, then covered her mouth with her fingers, giggling. "Rich?" she finished.

"Ha! Hardly." Leo rested his sweating beer bottle against the fabric of his swim trunks. Here in the Keys, shorts and swim trunks were interchangeable—unlike his possible bed partners, apparently.

Come on, now! Why can't you get Olivia Mortier out of your head?

And that was the question of the hour, wasn't it? Or more like the question of the last frickin' *eighteen months*. Ever since that assignment in Syria…

"But if you're not rich," the blond insisted, "then how can you"—*hiccup*—"afford to own this place?"

No joke, Romeo had better double-time her up to the house and into his bed. One or two more brewskies and she'd be too many sheets to the wind for what the self-styled lothario had in mind for her. Romeo may be a horndog extraordinaire, with more notches on his bedpost than Leo had sorties on his SEAL résumé, but like all the guys, Romeo was nothing if not honorable. If Tracy/Stacy/Lacy was too incapacitated, Romeo would do no more than tuck her under the covers with a chaste kiss on the forehead. And as their SEAL Team motto stated: *Where's the fun in that?*

On cue, Romeo turned to Leo, snapping his fingers, a worried frown pulling his black eyebrows into a V. Leo hid a smile as he reopened the cooler and dug around inside until he found a bottle of water. He tossed it over the fire, and Romeo caught it one-handed. Then Mr. Slam-dunk-ovich made quick work of exchanging the blond's beer with the H_2O. "Try this, *m'ija*," he crooned, really laying his accent on thick before leaning over to whisper something no doubt highly suggestive into her ear.

The blond giggled, obediently twisting the cap off the water bottle to take a deep slug.

"We don't own the island, darlin'," a deep voice called from up the beach. Leo turned to see his uncle coming toward them. The man was dressed in his usual uniform of baggy cargo shorts and an eye-bleeding hula shirt. His thick mop of Hemingway hair and matching beard glowed in the light of the moon, contrasting sharply with skin that had been tanned to leather by the endless subtropical sun.

Bran Pallidino, Leo's best friend and BUD/S—Basic Underwater Demolition/SEAL training—swim partner, had once described Leo's uncle as "one part crusty sea dog and two parts slack-ass hippie." Leo figured that pretty much summed up the ol' coot in one succinct sentence. "My great-great-I've-forgotten-how-many-greats-grandfather leased the island for one hundred and fifty years from Ulysses S. Grant."

"*President* Grant?" the brunette squeaked, coughing on beer.

"The one and only," Uncle John said, plunking himself into an empty plastic deck chair, stretching his bare feet toward the fire, and lifting a tumbler—filled with Salty Dog, John's standard grapefruit, vodka, and salted-rim cocktail—to his lips. Ice clinked against the side of the glass when he took a healthy swig. "You may not know this, Tracy," he said—*Tracy*. Leo snapped imaginary fingers and endeavored to commit the name to memory—"but ol' Ulysses smoked 'bout ten cigars a day. And my great-great"—Uncle John made a rolling motion with his hand—"however-many-greats-grandpappy happened to be the premier cigar-maker of the time. In exchange for a lifetime supply of high-quality Cubans, Great-Grandpappy secured the rights to make a vacation home for himself and his descendants on this here little bit of paradise for a century and a half." Uncle John's familiar Louisiana drawl—the same one Leo shared, though to a lesser extent—drifted lazily on the warm breeze.

The Anderson brothers, Uncle John and Leo's father, James, originally hailed from the Crescent City. Like their father before them, they'd trained to be shrimp-boat captains in the Gulf. But a chance discovery during a simple afternoon dive off the coast of Geiger Key had changed everything. They'd found a small Spanish gunboat equipped with all manner of archeological riches, from muskets to daggers to swords, and the treasure-hunting bug had bitten them *hard*. The following year, when Leo was just five years old, the brothers moved to the Keys to use their vast knowledge of the sea to search for sunken riches instead of plump, pink shrimp.

Unfortunately, they never found another haul that could compete with that of the gunboat. Uncle John gave up the endeavor after a decade, settling in to run one of Key West's many bars until his retirement six months ago. But Leo's father had continued with the salvage business, splitting his time between jobs and hunting for the *Santa Cristina* until he suffered a heart attack during a dive. Leo took solace in knowing his old man had died as he'd lived, wrapped in the arms of the sea.

"Ulysses S. Grant? So that had to have been, what? Sometime in the eighteen seventies?" the brunette asked.

"You know your presidents, Sophie." Uncle John winked, taking another draw on his cocktail.

Sophie, Sophie, Sophie. Leo really should have paid more attention to the introductions. I mean, seriously? What was his problem? If a woman's name wasn't Olivia Mortier, it just went in one ear and out the other? *For shit's sake!*

"I teach history at the Girls' Academy of the Holy Saints High School in Tuscaloosa." She hooked a thumb toward her friend. "Tracy teaches home ec."

Leo nearly spewed his beer. It wasn't high etiquette, but it was damn close.

"Ah." Uncle John nodded sagely. "Well, that explains it. And you're right. It was in the eighteen seventies."

"So then"—Sophie's lips pulled down into a frown— "you're kicked out in, what? Five? Ten years?"

"Eh." Uncle John shrugged. "We can't really get kicked out because it was never really ours to begin with. Besides, this crew will have found the *Santa Cristina* by then." John had moved out to Wayfarer Island under the auspices of "helping" Leo search for the ship. But really Leo suspected the old codger was just bored with retirement and looking to take part in one last hoorah. "And," he continued, "they'll have enough money to buy whatever house or island they want. Am I right, or am I right?"

"Hooyah!" Doc and Romeo whooped in unison, lifting their beers in salute.

Leo didn't join in. He wasn't a superstitious man by nature, but the ghost galleon brought out the avoid-the-black-cat, throw-salt-over-my-shoulder in him, and he didn't want to jinx their chances of finding the wreck by treating it like it was a foregone conclusion. He also didn't like to think that in a few short years he and his uncle would lose the lease on the island that had seen generations of Andersons for spring breaks and summer vacations, for Fourth of July weekends and the occasional Christmas getaway. It wasn't until Leo arrived with his merry band of Navy SEALs that anyone had attempted to live on the island permanently; it was just too isolated.

"And speaking of the crew…" Uncle John said. *Crew.* Leo rolled the term around in his head and figured *right. I reckon that's a label I can work with.* "The other half of 'em just called on the satellite phone."

Because when Leo said isolated, he meant *isolated*. The nearest cell tower was almost fifty nautical miles away. Which begged the question: What the ever-lovin' *hell* had Tracy and Sophie been thinking to let Romeo sail them out here? They were damned lucky Romeo was a stand-up guy and not some ax murderer. Had Leo felt more obliging, he'd have given the women a well-deserved lecture about the ill-advisedness of hopping onto a catamaran for a four-hour sail with a dusky-skinned gentleman sporting a too-precisely trimmed goatee. But right now, he had more important things to discuss.

"What'd they say?" he asked his uncle, referring to his three friends who'd spent a week across the pond in Seville, Spain.

"They said they finished photocopyin' and digitizin' the images of the documents in the Spanish Archives yesterday afternoon and sent all the data to What's-his-name, that historian you've been talkin' to online."

Online via the Internet connection Leo had established using the satellite he mounted to the top of the house. Because while he and the guys might've been fine to forgo cellular signals, there would have been serious mental and emotional fallout had Mason "Monet" McCarthy not been able to watch his beloved Red Sox play on their lone laptop or Ray "Wolf" Roanhorse not been able to Skype with his bazillion loving relatives back in Oklahoma. And the satellite was one *more* reason Leo's savings account and the savings accounts of the others were barely in the black.

God, we need a salvage gig. A big one. Because they only had enough funds left to fuel the search for the

Santa Cristina for two, maybe three more weeks. And that wasn't going to be enough.

Of course, before they could start advertising their services, they needed to actually incorporate their fledgling business. Which meant paperwork and opening accounts and coming up with a *name* for their company. Leo was not happy with Romeo's suggestion that they should call themselves Seas the Day Salvage. I mean, he enjoyed a play on words as much as the next guy, but, come on now, that was just *bad*.

Pushing his cash problems and the long list of things he still needed to accomplish aside, Leo got back to the point at hand. The historian he'd been emailing.

"Like I've told you twenty times before, the guy's name is Alex Merriweather," he scolded his uncle, not pointing out that John had no trouble remembering the names of Sophie and Tracy, two women he'd just met— *the lecherous old fart.* "And he assures me that if there's anything new to discover in those documents, he's the man who'll find it."

Treasure hunters die old and broke. It was a saying Leo sure as shit didn't want to see come true for him and the guys, which meant he was exploring every possible avenue he could. Including hiring an overpriced historian to go through all the old documents that pertained to the hurricane of 1624 and the fate of the Spanish fleet.

"Hmmph." His uncle made a face. "I doubt some library nerd is goin' to be able to tell you anything more than—"

"So what else did they say?" Leo interrupted, not willing to engage in that argument. *Again.* "After receivin' the digitized copies, did Alex gave 'em any indication that—"

"Hold on there, Leo, my boy." Uncle John raised the hand not wrapped around his cocktail glass. "Don't let your mind go runnin' around like a gnat in a hurricane. First of all, they didn't go into any detail with me. Second of all, I don't think they've *got* any details. The sorry sonsofbitches have been stuck on a transatlantic flight all day long. They just landed in Key West a little while ago. They're goin' to rack out there for the night and head here first thing tomorrow mornin'. You'll have to hold your questions until then."

Leo sat back in his chair, frustrated by the delay but comforting himself with another long pull on his beer.

"I need to run to the little girls' room," Tracy suddenly announced. "Want to"—*hiccup*—"come with me, Sophie?"

After a quick look at Doc, Sophie pushed up from her lawn chair. "Of course," she said, giving the back legs of her Daisy-Duke-style jean shorts a quick tug. It didn't do a damn thing to cover the lower curve of her ass cheeks peeking from beneath the frayed denim.

"I'll show you the way." Romeo bolted up from his chair. The guy knew an opportunity to move things along when he saw one. "You coming, *vato*?" he asked Doc, one black brow raised meaningfully.

"Be there in a sec," Doc said. The three of them still seated around the fire watched, heads tilted, as Romeo herded the women across the sand toward the house. *What?* They were all healthy, red-blooded, heterosexual males, and the sight of long, tan legs and sweet, heart-shaped derrieres was not something to be missed.

"Hey, LT," Doc said, taking the toothpick from his

mouth, "if you've changed your mind about Sophie, I'll gladly hara-kiri myself."

"You'll what?" Leo turned away from the view.

"You know," Doc snickered. "I'll fall on my sword so *she* can, uh, fall on *yours*."

Maybe he really *was* getting too old, or maybe he just had other things on his mind—*not Olivia, not Olivia… okay, probably Olivia*—but Leo just couldn't force himself to feel any enthusiasm about the prospect of another meaningless one-night stand. "Thanks for the offer, even as distasteful as you just made it sound." He grimaced. "But believe me when I say she's all yours if you can get her."

"Don't you worry." Doc winked, pushing up from his seat, throwing the toothpick into the fire, and turning toward the rambling old house. "I'll get her."

Yes, sir, Leo figured Doc probably would. After all, a woman had once told him that Doc was the spitting image of some big French actor. And though Leo hadn't the first clue who she was talking about, he figured from her dreamy expression that the comparison was meant to be a compliment. "Me and Uncle John will hang out here. Give you all some time to do your wooin'."

"If that's the case, you may be here all night," Doc boasted. "My wooing has been known to last—"

"Yeah, yeah." Leo waved him off. "Get lost, will you? I'm tired of lookin' at your smug face." And sure enough, Doc's expression became even more…well… *smug*. Leo grinned because he knew just what to say to get rid of it. "Besides, you stay here too much longer and you may give Romeo time to convince dear, sweet Sophie that a little two-for-the-price-of-one action could be lots of fun."

Doc's grin melted away as he called Romeo a foul name beneath his breath. But to Leo's surprise, Doc didn't hightail it up to house. Instead he angled his head, his eyes searching Leo's face over the glow of the fire.

"Well?" Leo asked. "What are you waitin' for?"

"It, uh…" Doc lifted a hand to scratch his head.

"What's up, bro?" And, yes. More than his *men*, or his *friends*, or even his *crew*, the five guys who'd hitched their wagons to his mule were his *brothers*. In every way that counted.

"You know, the, uh, the way I see it," Doc said haltingly, "part of our pledge included no more pussyfooting around when it comes to going after the things we really want." Leo watched Doc unconsciously rub the tattoo on the inside of his left forearm. "And it's been obvious since day one that you want Olivia Mortier."

Damn. Just hearing her name spoken aloud made the hairs along the back of Leo's neck stand up.

"So, why don't you send her an email, huh? See if she'll take some time off from The Company to come down here for a little visit." And now that smug smirk was back on Doc's face. "Maybe after she's wobbled your knob a time or two, you'll stop mooning around like a lovesick teenager."

Sonofa—Sometimes it sucked ass living in such close quarters with a group of men trained and tested in the fine art of observation. "Wobble my knob? What are you? Thirteen?"

"Avoiding the question?"

Damnit. "For the record," Leo growled. "I don't *want* her to wobble my knob, as you so eloquently put it."

A voice inside his head warned him his nose would be growing Pinocchio-style any minute now.

All right. So, if he was totally honest, he *would* have liked to see where things with Olivia were headed. He would have liked to know if all those not-so-subtle flirty looks and that one ball-tightening kiss could have turned into something more—knob wobbling included. Unfortunately, Fate had intervened in the form of the goatfuck of all goatfucks, which had precipitated his exit from the Navy and negated all chances that he'd ever again work in the same arena as one oh-so-tempting Olivia Mortier.

He was a civilian now. And civilians and CIA field agents weren't exactly known to find themselves in a position to mix it up. So even if he *could* convince her to take a vacation from missiles and mayhem, it's not like there was any real chance at a future for them. After all, the woman was all about the adrenaline high, and he was…well…*retired*.

Chapter Two

3:21 a.m....

"WE NEED TO HAUL LEO ANDERSON'S ASS OUT OF retirement," Olivia Mortier told her supervisor over the phone as she hastily threw T-shirts and shorts into an overnight bag, admonishing herself for not already being prepared to go. Then again, her part in this mission was *supposed* to be finished. She was *supposed* to have a night off because Morales was *supposed* to be running the show from here on out.

But nothing is certain except death and taxes. Okay, and yeah. There was *that*.

Blood rushed through her veins until it pounded in her ears, and her adrenaline was spiked way past the red line. She chalked up both afflictions to the fact that she'd just found out their scheme to root out the CIA mole or *moles* had officially and finally failed spectacularly, and not the fact that she might get the chance to work with Leo again.

Big, world-weary Leo "the Lion" Anderson.

A recollection of the last time she'd seen him blew through her brain like a mortar round, making her forget where she was in her packing. He'd been climbing into the back of a CH-47D heavy-lift Chinook helicopter, and when his dusty combat boots hit the ramp, he'd turned to look back at her, grabbing her hand and squeezing.

Holy shit, you better believe the moment was crystalline in her memory...

The wash from the rotors caused his sandy hair to riot around his head, and the shaggy beard covering his comic-book-hero-esque jaw had been matted with blood and dust. She'd wanted to tell him so much, *too* much because...well, because in the three months they'd been stationed together, she'd grown not only to like and respect him, but to *care* for him in a way she'd never cared for anyone.

Of course, she'd done her duty and kept her mouth closed despite knowing that his hawk-like gaze was searching her face from behind the mirrored lenses of his sunglasses. And his expression in that moment? *Sweet baby Jesus*, even now, all these months later, it still made her sick to her stomach. It had been the look of a soldier who had crossed long miles on short rations. The look of a leader who had just seen one of his most loyal men loaded into a body bag.

He didn't know it—and a part of her, a *cowardly* part, hoped he'd never find out—but that body bag was all her fault...

As it happened any time she thought about that catastrophic mission, a wave of unremitting guilt washed over her, the force of which was almost enough to drop her to her knees. Then Director Morales spoke up. "Why Anderson?" he asked, and she was able—just barely—to focus on the question and the problem at hand while pushing the paralyzing remorse to the back of her brain.

Compartmentalization. It was a handy skill. One just about every CIA field agent learned to master lest one day they find themselves eating a bullet from their own service weapon. And considering her background, she was better than most at keeping things locked away in safe, separate emotional cubicles.

What had she been doing? *Oh yeah*. She snapped her fingers. *Underwear*.

Turning toward her dresser while balancing her cell phone between her shoulder and her ear, she told her boss, "Because he's the best deep diver on the planet. And considering that the pressure gauges on those tracking devices say the package is sitting almost two hundred feet below the surface, we can't take a chance with anyone but the best. Plus"—she sweetened the pot—"Leo is already in Florida with his very own salvage boat." So sue her; she'd kept tabs on him.

"By my calculations, he can reach the package in four hours once he pulls anchor, which might be faster than we could find other divers and scramble the equipment they would need to go down and do the retrieval. And if all of that doesn't convince you, how about this? By using Leo, we can still maintain radio silence within government ranks. And *that* just might let us get out of this mess without alerting the traitor or traitors to the fact that we're on to them. It might give us a chance to set another trap."

She figured that last bit was just the impetus her supervisor needed to give her the go-ahead. And cue the music…

"What makes you think Anderson will agree to this?" Morales asked.

"You mean besides him being a patriot, and that turning down a request for help from his country goes against his very nature?"

"Yes"—Morales's tone was skeptical—"besides that."

"He needs money." And, okay, so she'd really, *really* been keeping tabs on him. That was *her* nature. She was a spy, after all.

If that's what you have to tell yourself…

For the love of—*Fine*. So, the truth was she couldn't seem to forget about him or what had happened on that arid plateau. And even if she hadn't realized it before now, she'd been looking for a way to help him. Looking for a way to—not make up for it; she could never make up for it—maybe balance the scales a bit. Put some providential change back into her karma bank. And put some *actual* change back into Leo's *real* bank.

See? It's win-win!

"Money for what?" Morales asked.

"To pay for equipment, fuel, and all the other expensive crap that I suspect comes with searching for a four-hundred-year-old sunken ship."

There was silence on the other end of the line, and Olivia held her breath. Then, finally, "How much do you think it'd take to convince him?"

Hip-hip-hooray! And since the CIA was in the business of carting around briefcases full of cash to pay off warlords, rebels, and mercenaries, she didn't feel the least bit hesitant to tell her supervisor, "Half a million dollars would probably do it. Keep them in the black for a year or so."

Without missing a beat, or likely batting a lash, Morales said, "Fine. I'll have the cash waiting for you…where?"

She shot an imaginary fist in the air. "Reagan National

Airport. As soon as I hang up with you, I'll request that one of my local assets have a private jet waiting for me on the runway there."

"You and your assets." She could almost hear Morales shaking his head. He liked to tease her and say she collected informants, snitches, and sources the way a squirrel collected nuts.

"You know me, sir. I figure it's better to have a bird in hand *and* two in the bush."

He snorted. "I'll meet you there and bring along an additional signal locator, as well as a secure satphone."

"Sounds like a plan," she said, checking the time on her glowing digital alarm clock. "With drive time to the airport and flight time to Key West, I figure I'll be on the ground in sunny Florida around daybreak. If you could have a floatplane ready to take me out to Lieutenant Anderson's family's island—"

"Done," Morales interrupted her, never one to use ten words when one worked just fine. She was in the process of shoving clean bras and panties into her go-bag when he added, "But I'm only giving you twenty-four hours. After that, I don't care that we'll blow the top off this operation"—and likely blow the top off their reputations and careers—"I'm calling in The Company big guns and doing whatever it takes to get back those chemicals."

"Roger that," she said as she threw her toiletry kit into the black duffel.

"And, Agent Mortier?"

"Yeah?"

"Be careful. We don't know what happened out there. It's entirely possible you could find yourself surrounded by unfriendlies. Since I can't use the satellites to track you, I'll be flying blind."

"I hear you, sir." She shivered at the thought of floating out in the middle of the endless blue ocean, surrounded by members of the offshoot al-Qaeda faction. "But don't worry. You can count on me." *And Leo Anderson*. Because if it came to holding off a group of militants at sea, she could do a lot worse than the big SEAL nicknamed "the Lion." But she probably couldn't do much better.

"I know I can," Morales said. "Now, the question is, do you want me to have the A-Team meet you in Key West?"

Olivia thought about arriving on Leo's doorstep with a group of private contractors in tow and grimaced. "I think, given all parties involved, it would be better if I go it alone. But I wouldn't be opposed to the apprehension team joining us out at the package."

"Done," Morales agreed. "See you at the airport." As was typical, the line went dead without her supervisor first signing off.

Typing in the number for her asset at Reagan, she quickly made arrangements for the private jet. Then she opened the top drawer of her bedside table and pulled out her trusty Sig P228. When she first joined the CIA, she'd come to terms with the unsavory idea that at some point during her career, she would probably be forced to use her sidearm for more than simple dissuasion. But as the years dragged on, and the occasion for violence never presented itself, she'd begun to think perhaps Fate had thrown her a bone, kept her out of harm's way so she would never have the weight of a lost life anchoring down her conscience.

Of course, Fate wasn't known to be a fickle bitch for nothing. True to form, all Olivia's good fortune had ended in the most inconceivable way that day in the high desert when somehow, someway—she'd since come to suspect the mysterious CIA leaker's involvement—her cover had been blown, and she was forced to end a man. It had been awful. Worse than she'd imagined. Particularly since that death had resulted in a blowback that claimed the life of one courageous American warrior.

Not for the first time since that disastrous mission, she questioned whether she wanted to continue working for The Company. The stress she could handle. The danger and the intrigue? Piece of cake. But the killing and the death… Those were whole other ball games, weren't they?

"Sonofabitch," she cursed, shaking her head at herself. "Get it together, Mortier." Forcing some steel into her spine, she straightened her shoulders and took a quick look around the tiny loft she kept in Washington, DC.

A full-sized bed with a drab, gray coverlet took up most of the space. It was flanked by two nondescript bed-side tables she'd purchased five years earlier from IKEA. Not one piece of art graced the brick walls. Not one photo sat on a shelf. And rounding out the whole antithesis of *Better Homes and Gardens* decor was the uninspiring desk and chair she used on those rare occasions when she was home and needed to work on her laptop.

As she turned toward the kitchen, the yellow wash of the overhead light revealed that the ivy plant she'd impulse-purchased a month ago—or had it been two months ago now?—had shriveled up and died in its pot on the windowsill. Its once-glossy leaves were brown and brittle. They seemed to mock her in death. Apparently she couldn't even keep one hardy little vine alive. And that was just…something. Sad, maybe? Pathetic? *More like typical.*

"Not leaving much behind, are you, old girl?" The words seemed to echo around the cramped space, circling back to slap her in the face.

There had been a time, not so long ago, when she would have laughed at the melancholy turn of her thoughts. After all, the only thing she'd wanted since she was fourteen, sitting under the big oak tree in the orphanage yard and reading Tom Clancy novels, was to be a spy. Aloof. Unattached. Indifferent.

But something had changed in the last several months. Something was…*missing.*

A place to really call home? People to care about? People who cared about *her*?

Sh'yeaaah, as if. She'd never had that. Never needed that. Never *wanted* that.

But maybe it was recently reaching the milestone of her thirtieth birthday, or perhaps it was some sort of sadistically ticking biological clock thing, because the words sounded hollow even though they were banging around inside her own head.

Okay, so if she wanted to be completely honest, the truth was that ever since Syria, ever since meeting Leo, ever since that kiss…

Holy hell! That kiss!

Even now, anytime she thought about it, she got all soft and gooey inside. All estrogen-y and womanly and not at all CIA agent-y, which was…not exactly something she was proud of, but there you go.

"Sheesh, Mortier. You're a sad piece of work. You can't let one little smooch—" Wait...*little*? That kiss hadn't come anywhere close to being *little*. In fact, in the *Guinness World Records*, you could probably find it under the title "Deepest and Hottest Lip Lock of the Century." Because it'd been a *long* time coming. Three months to be exact, ever since they first locked eyes on each other. And just when she was beginning to think the man would *never* make a move, he did.

They'd been standing in front of a weapons locker checking their inventory, of all things, when he suddenly turned to her, placed a warm, callused hand beneath her jaw, and lowered his head. His hot breath had whispered across her lips the second before his mouth landed atop hers. And when his tongue slowly, languidly pushed inside? Well, like a pin pulled from a grenade, her passion had exploded and her knees had buckled beneath her. Actually *buckled*. Which she'd thought only happened in sappy rom-coms and cheesy romance novels, but she'd learned that afternoon that fiction really did mirror fact.

Well, whoopty-friggin'-doo! Good for you! Not.

She squared her shoulders and tried again. "You can't let one kiss throw a wrench into your entire life plan."

There. Done. She'd said it. And it was sound advice. Unfortunately, she knew it was advice she'd be hard-pressed to heed. Because she was mere hours away from seeing Lieutenant Leo "the Lion" Anderson again...

—✹—

7:34 a.m....

Everything inside Leo's skull—gray matter, blood,

cerebrospinal fluid, what have you—had congealed into one giant throb of hangover pain. He lay motionless in the hammock strung up between two palms. The shrill *cock-a-doodle-doo* of the rooster that had stowed away on the catamaran during one of their many supply runs from Key West to Wayfarer, and the fact that Meat was bathing the fingers of the hand he had hanging over the hammock in rancid doggy slobber, made Leo seriously consider the possibility that he might be doing himself and everyone else in the world a giant favor if he tied a load of rocks around his waist and chucked himself into the ocean.

Why? Why had he thought it would be a good idea to polish off the last of the beer with his uncle after Doc, Romeo, and the ladies turned in for the night? He was a reasonable, rational, grown-assed man. So, repeat, *why* had he done this to himself?

Oh yeah. That's right. Because without the benefit of his friends' ribald conversation to distract him— and probably owing much to Doc's knob-wobbling comment—his mind had shot like an arrow from a speargun straight to Olivia and that god-awful mission. To dull the memories, one still so painful it made it hard for him to breathe and the other so damned hot it made him hornier than a forty-year-old virgin, he'd chosen door number two when his uncle asked him, "So, you want to talk about it, or you want to drink about it?"

Bad idea. Really, really *bad idea.*

A dull *shnick*-ing sound told him his uncle had just pressed Play on the bright-yellow boom box circa 1980-something that sat on a small wrought iron table on the front porch. The thing ate D batteries by the half dozen and came equipped with exactly three cassette tapes: Bob Marley, Harry Belafonte, and Jimmy Buffett. Just those three because his uncle's musical tastes were embarrassingly limited, and because the rest of the guys wouldn't have the first clue how to contribute to the selection of tunes because, you know…*cassette tapes*. Enough said.

Leo had a brief moment to wonder which song his uncle had chosen to start off the day when—*ah, Christ, I should have known*—Bob Marley started crooning in his Jamaican accent to *smile wit dee risin' sun*!

"Shit," Leo groaned as he carefully lifted the hand not being bathed by Meat's big, wet tongue. He pressed it to his forehead as he slowly, gingerly pushed into a seated position, careful to keep his eyes slammed shut against the merciless rays of *dee risin' sun* already hanging hot and heavy above the eastern horizon.

Unsteadily climbing from the hammock, he stood and concentrated on sucking in deep, steadying breaths. The pungent aroma of Uncle John's favorite chicory coffee tunneled up his nose. "Shit," he muttered again as he slowly peeled open one eyelid.

Woof! Meat barked happily, licking his ridiculous underbite as his wrinkly back end wobbled in the English bulldog version of a tail wag.

"I should've made Mason take you with him to Spain, you flea-bitten mutt," he grumbled, gingerly taking the warm mug of coffee his uncle held out to him. "Thanks, Uncle John," he managed. Because even though the smell turned his stomach, he knew if he could just choke down the tart brew, it'd go a long way toward mitigating the effects of the brown bottle flu he'd stupidly allowed himself to contract last night.

"Yep," his uncle replied monosyllabically, leaning back against the trunk of a palm. He was humming softly and tapping his foot in rhythm to Bob's jam.

When Leo glanced over, he was disgusted to discover the sea dog seemed none the worse for wear after last's night overindulgence. "Just looking at that shirt makes my head hurt," he groused.

"Now, don't you go blamin' your skull-pounder on me, son." Uncle John adjusted the collar of his shirt and smoothed it over his chest. "Besides, you only *wish* you looked this good."

Despite himself, Leo grinned. That is until—*woof!*—Meat barked again. It occurred to him that instead of chucking himself into the ocean, he might be better served by giving Meat the heave-ho.

Woof!

Cock-a-doodle-doo!

"Oh, for the love of *Christ*," Leo growled at the damn dog and his damn rooster companion. "I swear, it's like we're living in a motherfrickin' zoo. I thought Romeo said he was takin' that noisy-assed rooster back to Key West with him on his last run." The island at the end of the chain of the Florida Keys was swarming with wild chickens, happily referred to by residents as feral fowl or jungle fowl.

"He did," his uncle told him.

In the bleary, confused way only a jug-bitten man can pull off, Leo glanced down at the rooster pecking in the sand at his feet. The bird's brilliant plumage was as much of an assault on his eyes as his uncle's hula shirt. "Huh?"

"Romeo said the winged shithead—Romeo's words,

not mine—refused to stay in Key West. He just kept hoppin' back on the catamaran." Uncle John shrugged. "So I suppose that means we're keepin' him."

"Keepin' him?"

"Yep."

"Sonofa—"

Cock-a-doodle-doo!

"Shut up, you little bastard, before I turn you into fried chicken!" Leo shouted. Taking a quick sip of the coffee, he winced at its bitterness and swished the liquid through his furry teeth and over his fuzzy tongue before spitting it on the ground. *Fuck a duck.* Thank God he didn't have a mirror. Because he didn't think he'd like to see the thing staring back at him.

Raking in a deep breath, he steeled his woozy stomach against what was about to enter it before he upended the mug and downed the remaining contents, welcoming the burn in his throat because it distracted him from his other maladies. His uncle liked to brag that his coffee was strong enough to walk into a cup all on its own, and Leo figured that pretty much hit the nail on the head. *Come on, caffeine. Work your wonders.*

"And that's what I've decided to call him, by the way," Uncle John added.

Again, Leo went with the spectacularly witty rebuttal of "Huh?"

"Li'l Bastard. That's what you and the others are always hollerin' at him, so I reckon that should be his name."

Leo once again lowered his gaze to the rooster. The annoying bird was obviously ready to let loose with another one of its ear-piercing crows. "Don't you even *think* about it," Leo snarled, stomping his foot in the sand. The rooster flapped its wings and let out a resentful squawk.

Woof! Woof! Woof!

"Oh, for cryin' out loud. I'm goin' to need a lot more coffee," he warned his uncle. And as bad as he felt, he didn't hesitate to take the half-empty mug when it was offered to him. Chugging what was left of his uncle's coffee, he handed over both earthenware cups before squatting next to Meat. He'd promised Mason he'd look after the mutt. And even though scooping foul-smelling dog food from the sack they kept under the kitchen counter was something he looked forward to with about as much enthusiasm as a root canal, he was nothing if not a man of his word.

Besides, he knew one way to shut the silly dog up was to give him something to put in his mouth. "Are you hungry?" he asked the big, furry lunkhead, scratching the row of fat wrinkles that passed for Meat's neck.

The bulldog immediately licked his chops, brown eyes sparkling with zealous canine fervor.

"Yeah? So what else is new?" Because as far as Leo could figure, Meat had three stomachs. The first was used for kibble. The second was used for Milk-Bones and the occasional morsel of human food the cunning mongrel managed to steal. And the third was used for any rank-ass smelly thing Meat happened to come across. In Leo's estimation, each stomach had a limitless capacity.

"Come on, then," he told the dog as he shuffled toward the house. The bracing effects of the coffee were beginning to take hold, making him feel almost human again. In fact, if the growling of his stomach was anything to go by, he might just be able to keep down some breakfast.

"What do you say to banana pancakes?" he asked his uncle as they trudged up the stairs leading to the pine-plank porch that wrapped around the bottom half of the old house. The whole structure needed a fresh coat of paint, but that was way down on Leo's list of Shit That Needs Doin'. If it *ever* got done, that is, considering there was no real financial incentive to pretty up the place.

"You cookin'?" his uncle inquired.

Leo shot him a look as he reached into the breast pocket of his T-shirt. Snagging his pack of Big Red and quickly unwrapping a single stick, he folded the piece of cinnamon-flavored chewing gum into his mouth and said, "Are you tellin' me you don't know how to make banana pancakes?"

"It ain't a matter of knowin' how." Uncle John shook his shaggy head. A lock of stark white hair flopped over his brow. "It's a matter of effort versus pleasure. Is the pleasure I'm goin' to get from eatin' the pancakes worth the effort of me standin' over a hot stove and flippin' the suckers? I suspect not."

Slack-ass hippie, indeed...

"Fine." Leo opened the screen door, wincing when the hinges screamed in rusty agony. *Item number one million and one on The List: oil the hinges.* That one he *would* get around to eventually, if for no other reason than to mitigate any unnecessary noise on mornings like this. And on the subject of unnecessary noise, Meat raced by him, doggy nails scrabbling on the waxed wooden floor in his mad dash toward the kitchen. "I'll cook. But only if you promise to turn that shit off, or else find some new music to torment us—"

His words were cut off when he heard the low buzz of the Canadian-built de Havilland Otter floatplane that was Romeo's pride and joy. Romeo had purchased the single-engine, propeller-drive aircraft under the auspices of *we need a faster way than the catamaran to get back and forth to Key West*. But Leo figured Romeo just flat-out *wanted* the aircraft, considering his time behind the throttle was cut short due to the fact that they were now, you know, *C*-words. And even though it hadn't *really* been in the budget, who was Leo to tell a guy he couldn't spend his hard-earned cash the way he wanted? Plus, the plane *had* come in handy more than a time or two.

Of course, it had irked Romeo to no end that Wolf— the only other guy in their group with a pilot's license— had gleefully requisitioned the aircraft for transportation preceding and following the trip to Seville. When Romeo objected, Wolf had simply said, his black eyes flashing, "Letting me take the Otter just makes plain good sense, and arguing about it is as useful as wrestling with shadows."

Ray "Wolf" Roanhorse could play the quiet, resolute, impeccably *logical* card better than anyone Leo knew. And when he combined that with the colorful Cherokee-isms he'd picked up from his wise, old grandmother, none of them could naysay him. Not even Romeo, who usually had a smart-alecky comeback for everything.

Unhooking his aviators from the collar of his T-shirt, Leo slid the sunglasses onto his face and stepped toward the edge of the porch. The little Otter was coming in for a landing in the lagoon, but just before its pontoons cleared the ring of choppy water that heralded the presence of the treacherous underwater reef, the left wing dipped once—the flyboy equivalent of *hello*. It was then that Leo realized the catamaran was no longer tied to the dock, but motoring through the break in the reef line toward open water. Squinting against the glare of the sun, he could see the main sail on the twin-hulled boat unfurling. It caught the wind with a loud *snap* that echoed back to him a moment before the *sploosh-hisssss* of the Otter touching down drowned out all other sounds…even ol' Bob, who had switched from singing about three little birds to singing about a buffalo soldier.

"Romeo and Doc are sailin' the ladies back to Key West," his uncle informed him, seeing the direction of his gaze. Leo walked over and clicked off the boom box and…silence. Blessed, sweet silence. "They said they'll be home by dinner. But, hey"— his uncle clapped a hand on his shoulder when he returned to lean against the porch rail—"this is an auspicious arrival, ain't it? I suspect you can talk Bran into makin' us some banana pancakes."

Despite the rough start to his morning, Leo felt his lips curve. His best friend loved cooking like most men loved beer, brats, and reruns of *Baywatch*, and Leo had no doubt that all it would take for Bran to don his ridiculous apron—the thing actually read *Mr. Good-Lookin' Is Cookin'*; *I mean, for chrissakes*—would be for Leo to mention in passing that banana pancakes would just about hit the spot. Of course, all thoughts of breakfast vanished like smoke on the water when the Otter motored toward the beach, its pontoons kissing the edge of the sand, and Leo counted not three but *four* silhouettes in the little floatplane's windows.

Now, who is that? he wondered.

Wolf throttled up until the bird was secure on the beach, then cut the engine. The back cabin door popped open and Mason McCarthy hopped out. Mason was their resident underwater demolitions expert and ace electrician. And when you combined those terribly macho talents with his big, burly, Black Irish facade and his South Boston propensity for using the work "fuck" in all its glorious variations, the fact that he liked to paint landscapes in his off time seemed a bit...well...contradictory. Then again, any hobby that could quiet the cacophonous mind of a former fighting man was A-okay in Leo's book.

He watched Mason fist both hands into the small of his back before arching into a stretch. At 5' 11", what Mason lacked in height compared to the rest of the guys, he more than made up for in sheer muscle mass. And the interior of the Otter was a squeeze for even an average-sized man, much less one who looked like he could be John Cena's stunt double. After working out the kinks, Mason turned to offer a hand up to their guest.

Long, tan legs emerged from the plane. *Smooth* legs.

Wrinkled khaki shorts soon followed. *Short* shorts.

A ribbed, black tank top came next. *Tight* tank top.

And then...

Olivia Mortier.

What the hell? Leo's chin jerked back at the same time his pulse jumped into overdrive. *What's she doing here?*

And then it occurred to him that the guys must have

taken it into their fool heads to do what he'd been refusing to do, namely, contact Olivia.

Stupid, interfering sonsofbitches!

He was all set to rip the assholes some new assholes
when he saw Bran open the copilot side door and jump
down from the plane carrying a huge black duffel. After
skirting the nose of the aircraft, he tossed the bag to
Mason before slinging a muscular arm around Olivia's
shoulders. And, no. *No, no.* All thought of ripping *anyone*
a new *anything* flew out of Leo's head quick as a whistle,
replaced by a surge of possessiveness so strong he knew,
then and there, and without a doubt, that his life had just
gotten a lot more complicated. Because if there was one
word in the entire English language to describe Olivia
Mortier, it was certainly, unequivocally "complicated."

Shit!

"Ahoy, the house!" Bran called, a skip in his step and
a goofy grin plastered across his face.

Leo wondered if the two affectations were due to
Bran having just spent a night carousing in the bars
on Key West—the place was like the holy Mecca for
a drifting, shiftless, unattached guy just looking for a
one-night stand—or the shoulders of one black-haired,
blue-eyed CIA agent that were supporting his arm.

Can you say, "All of the above," boys and girls?

Shit!

All right, Leo was definitely sensing a theme for
the day.

"Who do you suppose she is?" his uncle inquired
from beside him, leaning against the porch rail and
squinting at the new arrivals as they made their way up
the beach toward the house.

Trouble with a capital T. *Temptation on two legs. My wildest fantasy come to life.* "Olivia Mortier," Leo managed, his voice coming out all scratchy and rough, like he'd been swallowing fistfuls of sand or some other such equally asinine thing.

He felt his uncle turn quickly toward him, but couldn't take his eyes off the woman coming his way.

"*The* Olivia Mortier?" Uncle John asked. "As in the woman Doc was talkin' about last night?"

"That's the one," Leo admitted, still not quite believing his eyes. "And I think some serious ass-kickin' is in order. Because I told 'em I—"

Woof!

Having lost patience in the kitchen, Meat had his snout pressed against the screen door, his bark the doggy equivalent of *What's the holdup?* Then he spotted Mason and his very manly sounding *woof* turned into a series of terribly girly-sounding *yip-yip-yips!* Leo managed to peel his eyes away from Olivia long enough to turn and see Meat spinning in circles behind the screen door, unable to contain his doggy excitement upon the return of his beloved owner.

Then Leo's neck jerked around so fast it was a wonder he didn't give himself whiplash when four pairs of footsteps pounded up the porch's wooden steps. Olivia was suddenly standing in front of him in that oh-so-confident way she had, all while wearing…*that.*

Woot-whooooo!

If he wasn't mistaken, that was the wolf-whistle sound that was supposed to accompany his tongue unfurling from his mouth to hang down to his knees. He'd only ever seen her in baggy, desert-drab cargo pants and scuffed-up combat boots. Which meant all the skin now on display was enough to give him an eye-gasm.

"Hello, Leo," she murmured in that smoky, Stevie Nicks voice that just…*holy Christ*… It *got* to him. And, as if that wasn't enough, her subtle perfume drifted on the balmy morning breeze, causing his nostrils to flare wide.

He remembered that smell all too well. How the hell could he forget it when it haunted his dreams at night? And damned if he could ever figure it out, but even after twelve hours under the baking Syrian sun, she'd still managed to exude that tantalizing aroma. Like wild jasmine, all things sweet and exotic.

"Olivia." He nodded, giving himself major points for playing it cool when cool was the dead-last thing he was feeling. He was on fire from head to toe. "What brings you here? Wait"—he held up a hand—"let me guess. It's thanks to five Navy SEALs. And as soon as I get 'em alone, I can assure you their asses will be grass."

For such a small movement, the lifting of one perfectly arched black brow packed quite a punch. "Your men don't have anything to do with why I'm here."

"They don't?" He looked around at the faces of some of the men in question, quickly noting their amused, slightly quizzical expressions. "You don't?" he demanded of them, a sense of foreboding scratching at the back of his brain.

"We found her at the airport, LT. Swear on my mother's grave," Bran vowed, his bastardly arm *still* around Olivia's shoulders. Leo had never before begrudged Bran his wavy dark hair or lithe swimmer's physique. But right now, he couldn't help but wish the guy looked a little less like he belonged in underwear commercials and a little more like he belonged under a bridge.

"She was about to hop on the Seaplane Charters' Otter when we spotted her. And, can you believe it? She was headed this way. Says she has something she needs to…uh…*discuss*"—Bran wiggled his eyebrows meaningfully—"with you. So, I guess it's a classic case of ask and ye shall receive, eh, *paisano*?"

All right, and now the least of Leo's worries was Bran and his too-friendly embrace of Olivia. Because all of his foreboding instantly morphed into dark dread. He turned back to her, ignoring the cheap shot her pretty, heart-shaped face always delivered. "So then what the hell *are* you doin' here, Olivia?"

And though he hadn't meant for it to be, he could tell by her expression he'd just posed a loaded question, loaded six ways from Sunday. He knew deep in his gut he wasn't going to like her answer.

"I'm here to call in all those IOUs," she told him, her laser-blue eyes gleaming in the dappled morning light cutting through the palm trees and lighting up the front porch.

"What IOUs?" He lowered his chin, regarding her over the tops of his Ray-Bans. He didn't remember filling out any IOUs.

"Okay, you got me." She smiled, flashing him that slightly crooked front tooth, the one so sexy it made his bare toes curl against boards of the porch. "So, the truth is, I'm here to ask you for a favor."

Uh-huh. And suddenly he knew why his sixth sense was screaming and running around in circles like its hair was on fire. Because when a CIA agent came begging for favors, you knew it was time to bend over, put your head between your legs, and kiss your ass good-bye.

He didn't want to ask, but, "What kind of favor?"

She glanced over at his uncle, and Leo remembered his manners. "Olivia, this is my uncle, John. And whatever you have to say to me, you can say to him. Now, what kind of favor?"

She seemed hesitant to talk turkey in front of a full-on civilian. That was the closed-mouth, mum's-the-word CIA agent he'd grown to know and…um…*know*. Then she shrugged. "The kind where you help me retrieve three capsules of sunken chemical weapons my supervisor and I inadvertently gave to an al-Qaeda faction."

Shhhiiiiit!

And the theme for the day was definitely holding strong…

Chapter Three

7:46 a.m....

LEO DIDN'T JUMP BACK OR GASP AT HER WORDS. HE just got very still. Which Olivia suspected was the hardened operator's equivalent of both of those reactions. And as mottled sunlight caught in his sandy locks—burning and brooding and laughing at her and the temptation she felt to take a step forward to run her fingers through the thick mass—she watched the jaws of the other four men sling open in horror, as if they were attempting to swallow the bomb she'd just dropped. Of course, since she was in the business of dropping literal and figurative bombs, their impersonations of Pez dispensers didn't much faze her.

What *did* faze her was the fact that if propriety and professionalism hadn't stopped her from giving in to the urge to reach for Leo, his acidic stare would have. *Holy hell*, even partially concealed behind his aviator sunglasses, that stare still threatened to melt the flesh from her bones. Okay, so she hadn't exactly been expecting party hats and a welcome banner but—

"I have a question." Leo's deep voice sounded rough, like boulders crunching beneath the tracks of a tank.

A question? Well, all right, a question was good. Better than him yelling at her to get the hell off his front porch. "What's that?"

"Do the other three Horsemen of the Apocalypse know you've arrived safely on earth?"

"Ha-ha." She blew out a breath, frowning up at him. Way up. *Has he always been this tall?* "Very funny. But I'm serious, Leo."

"So am I, Olivia. Christ, what will you think to do next? Provide Pakistani warlords with long-range missiles tipped with nuclear warheads?" The way he thrust out his chin highlighted the scar there, the one that marred the perfection of his short-cropped beard. He had others, she knew. Scars. Like those on his knuckles and that big, puckered one on his arm.

Is that one new? She didn't remember him having that back in Syria. And, yeah, maybe she was being whimsical, or maybe she was totally in over her head where he was concerned, but all those scars, all those reminders of a life lived on the edge, seemed to enhance rather than diminish his blatantly male appeal.

Sheesh, Mortier. You're here for his help, not to ogle his abs.

Although, with him dressed in nothing more than low-slung swim trunks that emphasized the leanness of his waist and a tight, V-neck T-shirt that unapologetically delineated the bulging muscles of his chest and shoulders, ogling was pretty much a given. Still, she straightened her spine and did her best to push off her hormonal-woman hat so she could make room for her CIA-agent cap—which seemed to slip straight off her head anytime Leo was in the same room with her, the fickle, exasperating thing.

"Well," she said, lips twisting, "let's just say I won't equip them with missiles and nuclear warheads unless I have a really, *really* good reason to."

He glared at her, his jaw grinding so hard she fancied she could hear his teeth creak. "I half hope you're kiddin'," he growled in that delicious Southern accent of his. And, *oh goody*. There was nothing sexier than Leo going all big and badass... *Whoops*. There went her CIA-agent cap again. *Damnit!* "Scratch that." He shook his head. "It's a whole hope, because if you're not, then I—"

"Cool your jets, sailor," she assured him. "Neither I nor The Company have any plans to start selling hardware to Pakistani warlords. Hopefully, we learned our lesson about that back in Afghanistan in the eighties."

"But givin' chemical weapons to the folks who brought down the Twin Towers is okay?" He made a rude sound of disbelief that, had she not been looking at him to see his lips vibrate, would have made her wonder which end of him it had come from.

Okey dokey. So this was not going at all as planned. She knew she needed to take a step back and start over. Perhaps change tactics from brash and demanding to demure and pleading. Unfortunately, stepping back wasn't something she did well. And demure and pleading? *Sh'yeaaah. As if*. Especially since the look on his face—the one that clearly telegraphed his belief that somehow this was all her idea and all her fault—lit a match under the kindling of her temper. Okay, so asking for his help *had* been her idea, but that's as much as she was taking credit for.

"Yes, it's okay," she declared righteously, mirroring his stance and placing her hands on her hips. Bran dropped his arm from around her shoulders, backing away like perhaps *she* was one of the deadly chemical weapons they were discussing. "Especially considering we did it to catch a much bigger and, so far, largely elusive fish that has been threatening our national security for *months* or, more likely, *years*. And taking into account that if we *didn't* do something fast, then—"

"Whoa, whoa," Bran cut in, patting the air in the universal signal for her to slow her roll. "Let's all take a T.O. here. We can go inside, maybe take a load off, and—"

Ignoring the man, she continued to face off against Leo. "For the love of all that's holy, Leo, you know as well as anyone that when it comes to espionage, sometimes the wrong methods elicit the right results. So why don't you stop busting my balls and let me explain what happened and how you can help me?"

One corner of his mouth twitched before he reached up to pull his sunglasses down his nose. He slid a slow, considering look up the length of her body. "Balls, huh?" he murmured, all deep and throaty and, holy hell…chill-inducing. Her antagonism leached out of her like radioactive waste from a dirty bomb. "And here you had me convinced that all you were packin' in your pants was a firearm."

She disregarded the heat that skittered through her veins when his hazel eyes skimmed over her skin. "I was trying to make a point," she said. "And since I'm working on a short clock here, I'd like to get to it."

"You mean you've got *more* information with which to blow our mindholes?" Wolf Roanhorse, who'd moved to stand beside Leo, lifted one dark eyebrow. Leo and all the SEALs of Alpha Platoon were warriors. But Wolf really *looked* like one, like something out of

an old spaghetti Western. Of course, he didn't dress like
one—he was wearing shorts and a frayed T-shirt—and
he certainly didn't *sound* like one when he continued,
"Good God Almighty, woman, I don't think I want to
hear it."

Yeah, well, in a perfect world, she wouldn't want to
hear it either. But theirs was *not* a perfect world. Case in
point: the missing chemical weapons. "Would it change
your minds…er…*mindholes* about listening to my story
if I told you there was half a million dollars waiting for
you at the end of the tale?"

7:54 a.m.…

Leo didn't realize he'd unconsciously let his gaze drift
down the length of Olivia's body, noting the soft flare
of her hips, the tiny turn of her ankles, and the graceful
length of her unpolished toes revealed by her plastic dime-
store flip-flops until his eyes returned to her face and he
was waylaid by her flinty, tough-as-nails expression.

"Were you paying *any* attention to what I just said?"
she demanded, leaning against one of the kitchen's old
Formica countertops. They'd done as Bran suggested,
retiring inside the house to stop Meat's incessant bark-
ing and because Leo hoped more of his uncle's hot,
strong coffee would be enough to make even the most
harebrained CIA scheme sound plausible. "Or were you
too busy giving me dirty looks?"

Oh, he'd been giving her dirty looks, all right. But
he suspected her definition of "dirty" and his definition
of "dirty" were light-years apart. Although he reckoned

it was better all around to let her go on believing his heated perusal of her body had been derisive rather than desirous.

"I heard you," he assured her. "I heard you say you began suspectin' there was a mole or group of moles inside the CIA after that catastrofuck in Syria. I heard you say you've spent almost a year and a half tryin' to draw them out. I heard you say that somethin' suggested to you they might have contacts in Cuba."

"Not *might* have contacts in Cuba. *Do* have contacts in Cuba," she insisted. "As you well know, the photos taken of the prisoners from inside the detention center"—the ones that had been splashed across the news websites showing the prisoners shackled and chained, the ones that had outraged the international community—"were leaked to the press by a group of al-Qaeda extremists living and working in Cuba. But what you don't know, what *nobody* knows is that those photos were proprietary to The Company. The only way those guys could've gotten their hands on the pictures is if someone inside the CIA *gave* them the digital files."

"Okay, fine," Leo relented. "So, since you and your supervisor were convinced the double agent had connections in Castro-ville, you all decided to cook up this crazy, idiotic plot to plant a too-good-to-be-true bit of Intel in a Company memo with the hopes that said double agent would take the bait." He glanced around the kitchen at his friends. "Is it just me," he asked the SEALs, "or does this reek of a case of the Mondays?"

"What's *that* supposed to mean?" Olivia demanded, looking around the room.

"There's a saying the Teams like to use," Mason

explained, which surprised Leo since Mason lived by
the motto, "A quiet man is a thinking man." It was
usually a miracle if they could get two sentences out
of the guy. "It goes a little something like: You tell me
our intelligence community is fuckin' shit up, and I'll
tell you it's Monday." His quintessential South Boston
accent made "our" sound more like "ah."

"Lovely." Olivia's flattened expression broadcast
quite clearly how much she enjoyed *that* little anecdote.
"The point is…" she said, impatiently tucking a strand
of hair behind her ear. Leo remembered the texture.
Spun silk that was cool to the touch. "Even though I
can't take credit for the idea—it was Director Morales's
brainchild—I wholeheartedly approved of it. And it
may've been crazy, but it certainly *wasn't* idiotic.

"They *did* take the bait. They passed along the Intel
to their assets just the way we hoped they would. And
last night the cameras in the warehouse—which were,
in fact, in perfect working order despite us alluding otherwise in the memo—recorded those very same assets
breaking in." When it became clear that no one had anything to say to Olivia's little monologue, she jutted out
her stubborn chin and finished with, "So, how's *that* for
a case of the Mondays, huh?"

Despite himself, Leo felt one corner of his mouth
twitch. Even though she had an exterior that looked no
more threatening than a vanilla cupcake, her inner core
was made of pure, tempered steel.

"Question," Uncle John said from one of the wooden,
ladder-backed kitchen chairs. Other than the times when
his fingers seemed as if they wanted to dance toward
the closed zipper of that big, black duffel sitting in

the middle of the table—talk about an elephant in the room—he was casually sipping his coffee and looking for all the world to be completely unruffled by the presence of a CIA agent talking about moles, terrorists, and missing chemical weapons. But, like always, Leo wasn't sure if his uncle's placid expression had more do to with the fact that the guy was imperturbable by nature, or the fact that he liked to partake fairly regularly of the crop of Mary Jane he had growing out behind the house.

For my glaucoma, his uncle insisted, though Leo was pretty sure the old man didn't *have* glaucoma.

"Shoot," Olivia said, downing the last of her chicory coffee. Leo couldn't help but admire the smooth, delicate arch of her neck, and wondered what it would be like to kiss that spot just above—

"If you and your boss were workin' alone," Uncle John said, "outside CIA channels because you have no idea who the mole is or how high up in the chain he or she or they may be, then how did you coordinate with Guantanamo?"

The question quite effectively ripped Leo's wandering brain back on track. *Thank Christ!* He poured himself the last few swigs of coffee from the pot, lifted his mug, and downed the tart brew like it was a shot of cheap whiskey. It burned just about as well and tasted about half as good.

"Morales is old friends with the general there," Olivia said, her tone all about the easy-peasy-lemon-squeezy.

"Ah"—his uncle nodded—"okay, I'm beginnin' to get it."

Well, that made *one* of them.

"So, why the hell didn't you and Morales have the

Gitmo guys apprehend the radicals then and there?" Leo demanded. "Why let 'em load the weapons on a boat and set sail?"

"That was the *plan*." She threw her hands in the air. "But a riot broke out in the prison, and the guards around the warehouse were called in to help subdue it. In the mix-up and chaos, the radicals were able to grab the case with the chemicals and escape."

"You reckon the riot was the mole's doin'?" his uncle asked. "A distraction?"

"Morales says no." Olivia shook her head. "He thinks it was just bad friggin' timing and worse friggin' luck. A true-blue case of Murphy's Law."

Wow. This entire plan was rating a ten out of ten on Leo's Fucked-Up scale. And something in his demeanor must have told Olivia as much, because she frowned up at him. "I know what you're thinking," she grumbled.

"Now, darlin', don't you go accusin' me of thinkin'."

She ignored his attempt at levity. "You're already sticking the knife of judgment in me and twisting. But I'm telling you, it's not as bad as it sounds. Morales covered his bases and his ass. He had the general at Gitmo attach tiny tracking devices to the underside of the chemical capsules in the event that worse came to worst and the radicals were able to escape. Morales was keeping an eye on them, monitoring their every move.

"As soon as it looked like they were going to make landfall, he planned to board their boat in a blaze of glory, seize every last one of them before they had a chance to make a Mayday call or alert the traitor or traitors, and then interrogate them until they gave up the identity of the double agents or told us where we could find the fuckers." She winced, glancing surreptitiously over at Leo's uncle. "Um, excuse my French, sir."

"Is 'fucker' French?" Uncle John's eyes widened theatrically. "Well, I'll be damned. I never knew."

She grinned, her slightly crooked tooth winking at Leo as surely as a Duval Street hooker. *What* is *it about that tooth, anyway*? Why did it *do* things to his boy parts?

"Well, now *I* have a question." Bran spoke up for the first time since they'd retired to the kitchen. He was leaning against the softly humming refrigerator, arms and ankles crossed, his usual jovial expression devoid of any sign of humor. Despite all the years Leo had worked alongside Bran, he'd never gotten over how quickly the man could go from cutup to cutthroat. It was as if he had an internal switch. Right now, that switch was flipped to the Badass Navy SEAL position.

"Considering you and Morales were working alone on this deal, flying completely under the radar, how did you expect to apprehend eight… You did say the warehouse footage showed there were eight radicals, right?" Olivia nodded. "Okay, so how did you guys plan to take on eight men all by yourselves? Are you both *pazzo*?" He circled a finger around his temple to illustrate the word.

"Not us," Olivia assured him. "When the radicals escaped on the ship, Morales contacted one of his many civilian sources and enlisted the help of hush-hush private contractors to come in and do the heavy lifting."

Contractors. Leo knew the type. Former spec-ops guys who'd decided there was more fun to be had—and *definitely* more money to be made—hiring out as nonmilitary-affiliated operators.

"You aren't talkin' about Black Knights Inc., are you?" he asked, referring to the group of guys, some of whom were Navy SEALs from his old platoon, based in Chicago and operating what was *supposed* to be a custom motorcycle shop. In reality, the big warehouse on Goose Island was just the front for their covert government-defense firm. For chrissakes, it was like Hells Angels meets 007 up there.

"Who?" she asked, frowning.

"Never mind," he told her. "Forget I asked." And he should have realized Director Morales would not have tapped Black Knights Inc. for this mission. Morales was avoiding all government channels so as not to alert the mole or moles, and given that BKI reported directly to the president and his Joint Chiefs… Right. Probably not a good idea to get them involved.

"The guys we hired work for Titan Corp."

"Never heard of 'em."

"Doesn't matter," she continued, waving a dismissive hand through the air. "They were in New Orleans waiting for Morales to give them an approximate heading when the signals on the tracking devices suddenly stopped moving. Ten minutes later, the pressure gauges indicated the capsules were sitting in nearly two hundred feet of water. So either the terrorists chucked the CWs overboard for some reason, which isn't likely. Or the boat sank, which is what we suspect."

"Isn't it possible the tangos simply tossed the tracking devices overboard?" Wolf asked, falling back into old habits and using military slang to refer to the terrorists. "The simplest answer usually being the right one?"

"Nope." Olivia shook her head emphatically. "If they'd screwed with the devices or removed them from the capsules, we'd have known."

"How's that?" Leo asked, trying really hard not to notice how the sunlight cutting through the kitchen windows bathed her in a warm, golden glow, picking up the subtle auburn highlights in her otherwise black-as-midnight hair.

"Those tracking devices are the latest to come out of the science and technology department back at Langley. Not only do they have heat sensors, pressure gauges, and the ability to connect to all satellites everywhere—foreign and domestic, civilian and military—but they're also about the size of one grain of rice."

Uncle John whistled, and Leo looked over to find the old man's hands now resting ever so casually on the big duffel bag. "You really *are* James Bond, aren't you?" his uncle said. "Or Jamie Bond. You know, since you're a girl and all," he added unnecessarily.

"But that's not the real kicker," Olivia continued, wiggling her eyebrows at his uncle, "because all of that technology is pretty standard in today's spy market. What *isn't* standard is the adhesive on these tracking devices. It's embedded with nanotechnology that trans-mits a warning signal if the apparatus is tampered with.

"So far, we haven't received any such signal. So the weapons were tossed or the whole damn boat sank. Either scenario sucks, and have I mentioned how much I hate that guy Murphy?" She blew out a breath and shook her head. "But regardless of what happened, we have to get those CWs back. We can't leave three capsules of chemicals lying around on the ocean floor that, if combined and aerosolized, could take out the population of a small city."

"Sonofabitch," Wolf cursed. "Just what kind of stuff are we talking here?"

"Methylphosphonyl difluoride, cyclohexylamine, and cyclohexanol." She rattled off the list of tongue-twisting agents like a bona fide chemical engineer.

Leo wondered if it were possible for a person to shit their own heart. "Cyclosarin?" he demanded. "You let these sonsofbitches escape with the mixture for cyclosarin?" It was one of the most deadly nerve agents ever to come out of a German laboratory. He thought he'd been *joking* when he named her one of the Horsemen of the Apocalypse. "Jesus H. Christ, Olivia!"

"Why am I picturing you with your pinky held to your lip while you stroke a hairless cat in an ominous fashion?" Bran asked her, eyes hard as stone.

"Huh?" She frowned at him.

"You know, Austin Powers?" When her face remained blank, Bran added, "Dr. Evil? How long has it been since you watched a movie?"

"Look," she said, her tone defiant, "if we could've planted fake capsules, we would have. But these types of weapons have elaborate QR codes etched into their casings. Those QR codes can't be duplicated with any sort of precision. The OPCW made sure of that."

"The Organization for the Prohibition of Chemical Weapons," Wolf clarified for Leo's uncle's sake.

"If the mole or moles wanted to," Olivia continued, "they could have had the tangos snap a picture of the code for verification, and it would have been easy to check that code against the OPCW's online manifest."

When no one said anything to that, she continued to plead her case. "Was it a risk using the real chemicals as bait? Yes. Undoubtedly. But catching the traitor or traitors, plugging the leak in the Intelligence Community, and potentially saving the necks of agents and civilians alike made the reward worth the risk. We just…"—she sighed and threw her hands in the air—"we just didn't bargain for all of *this*."

Bran glanced around the kitchen as if he was expecting to see someone other than the six of them and Meat who, after finishing his kibble, had immediately retired to the doggy pillow shoved beneath the freestanding, farmhouse-style sink. The big, furry dope was sprawled on his back, legs spread wide, cock and balls all on display, and snoring loud enough to rattle the windowpanes.

"Okay, I get it," Bran said. "So you and Morales saw an opportunity and you took it. But then where the hell are these contractors you were talking about? Why aren't you with those *spostatas*"—the New Jersey Italian in him came out when he got worked up or tipsy, and it was like being in the middle of a *Sopranos* episode— "instead of here with us?"

She squinted at the clock on the wall. Like everything else, patience was finite, and Leo could tell she had just about reached the limit of hers. He couldn't blame her, of course. I mean, she'd allowed frickin' *chemical weapons* to be stolen and then sunk to the bottom of the ocean. Her and Morales's asses were definitely in a bind here.

"None of the contractors are dive specialists," she admitted, slicing her hand through the air like a karate chop. She used the gesture as punctuation. A physical exclamation point. "But don't you worry, Morales has already had them transfer to Key West and rent a boat. They'll meet us out at the, uh, the code name we're using during transmissions is 'the package.'"

"Clever." Bran snorted, and Leo watched Olivia's lips curve into a frown as her eyes glinted with... What was that emotion he saw on her face? Derision? Determination? Or desperation, perhaps?

Well, whatever it was, it made his heart clench and the deep breath he dragged into his lungs burn. Then again, maybe that last part was due more to the fact that the air inside the kitchen smelled strongly of chicory coffee mixed with the rather pungent aroma of the tuna casserole his uncle seemed to live on.

"Anyway," she continued, "if we pull anchor *now*, we should arrive at the capsules about the same time the contractors will. Which is good since we have no idea what we'll be dealing with out there. I'm hoping that if the boat sank, it pulled the terrorists down right along with it. But since Morales can't take the chance of accessing our satellites to search the area without potentially alerting the moles to our little operation..." She let the sentence dangle, shrugging.

Leo sensed Bran and Mason's gazes landing on his face. Carefully, feeling as if everything he'd worked so hard for during the last two months was on the line, and that Fate, in the form of one curvaceous female, was slicing at the rope, he said, "So you're tellin' me that not only do you want us to dive down and recover your lost capsules, but you also think it's possible we'll only be able to do that after a firefight with eight card-carryin' al-Qaeda militants?"

"It's not out of the question." She met his gaze head-on.

Any other time he would have appreciated her no-bullshit approach. Not today. Because today she was attempting to involve him in a mission that would put an indefinite hold on his search for the *Santa Cristina*. Bad enough. Worse still was the fact that said mission might just be enough to get him and his men...his *friends*...killed. And *that* would pretty much obliterate any chance they had of keeping their promise.

Right. The thought sucked so hard he figured there was a hickey on his brain.

Looking around at his crew, Leo made a decision that went against everything he'd stood for since the day he attached his Budweiser, the pin of the Navy SEAL brotherhood, to his dress whites. "I'm afraid you've wasted a trip, Olivia," he said, the words threatening to slip backward from his lips to lodge in his throat. "We weren't jokin' when we bugged out. We're done. Finished. Kaput. Which means this is now a case of not my circus, not my monkeys. I suspect you and Morales can find a team of contractors with divin' credentials that'll allow you both to continue to keep this whole thing on the down-low while keepin' us out of it."

Olivia's eyes rounded. Yessir. She hadn't been expecting *that*. Leo was even a bit shocked himself. But before she could open her mouth to utter a word of protest, the sound of Wolf pushing back from the table, the legs of his chair scraping against the linoleum floor, interrupted her.

The man stood to his full six-foot, one-inch height

and looked Leo square in the eye. "You know I've always followed your lead, LT. And this whole thing stinks like a jackass festival, for sure. So even if we hadn't made that promise—"

"Promise?" Olivia asked. "What promise?"

"I would understand why you'd want no part of it," Wolf continued, ignoring Olivia's interruption. "But before you go making any decisions, there's something you should know."

Wolf's words, as well as his troubled expression, had Leo's stomach dropping to the floor of the kitchen so hard he was surprised he didn't hear a resounding *splat*. "What's that?"

"That historian, or translator, or whatever you want to call him, emailed and said he hadn't been prepared for the sheer volume of documents we sent his way." Oh right. The documents from Seville. How could Leo have forgotten about *them? Two words*—he answered his own question—*Olivia Mortier*. "If we want him to translate all of them, he says he'll need another two weeks and another ten grand."

"Ten *grand*?" Leo bellowed, causing Meat to hop up from his pillow. In sleepy confusion, the silly mutt let loose with a loud *woof!*

Cock-a-doodle-dooooooooooo!

Leo winced, turning to see the rooster—Li'l Bastard, apparently—perched on the porch railing right outside the kitchen window. The multiple cups of coffee might have taken care of his headache, but that fat chicken's ridiculous vocal stylings were enough to send a hammer-strike of pain smashing into his skull.

Or perhaps the throb in his temples had less to

do with the rooster and more to do with the fact that the universe was seriously screwing him over and leaving him standing there holding double handfuls of shit.

Unable to contain himself a moment longer, Uncle John unzipped the duffel bag, pulling the edges wide. The *scriiiiiitching* sound of the zipper seemed particularly loud in the sudden silence of the kitchen, but not nearly as loud as his uncle's exclamation of, "Well, cut off my legs and call me Shorty! Would you look at that!"

And there it was in all its greenback glory. Half a million dollars. Olivia had certainly delivered after blowing their mindholes with her tale.

Leo's heart was pounding so hard it was a wonder his T-shirt wasn't fluttering. He turned to her and watched one black brow slowly slide up her smooth forehead.

"So," she said, jutting out her stubborn, adorable, *irresistible* chin, "shall we go retrieve my missing chemical weapons, Lieutenant Anderson?"

Chapter Four

His name was Banu az-Harb.

At least that's what it *secretly* was now…ever since he opened his eyes to the one true faith and threw off the identity of Jonathan Wilson. Ever since he realized his Caucasian ethnicity, degrees in criminology, and unassuming white-bread background made him perfect to infiltrate the CIA. And ever since Allah revealed that if he was patient, if he was smart and cunning, he could be one of the most useful and celebrated soldiers in the great and terrible holy war raging around the globe.

For nearly ten years he'd kept up Jonathan Wilson's gun-toting, Mickey D's-eating, rootin'-tootin', American good-ol'-boy facade. Going to barbecues and football games. Wearing Polo shirts, loafers, and khaki slacks. Working his way up the ranks of the CIA, watching his security clearance rise higher and higher, and all the while amassing contacts the world over.

He grinned, thinking about the time The Company was poised to catch the leader of the AQAP—al-Qaeda in the Arabian Peninsula. He'd been able to warn the man minutes before the operation went down, and the revered commander had escaped. His smile widened when he remembered coming across a bit of Intel regarding the transportation of nearly two dozen decommissioned Soviet tanks. The convoy had been due to pass close to the Lebanese border, and his quick actions in contacting the Hezbollah fighters active in the region meant that now their righteous group had ten IS-4 heavy-duty battle tanks on their list of armaments.

There had been other instances, of course, when he'd dropped the right piece of information into the right ear at the right time. And he was proud of each and every act of treason against the nation that was his birthplace but that he no longer considered his home. Unfortunately, to date he had yet to find The One Thing guaranteed to rain down death and destruction the likes of which the country hadn't seen since 9/11. The One Thing that would ensure his name would be splashed across the headlines and live on into eternity.

Then, yesterday morning while reading a Company-wide memo, his eyes had alighted on one line item near the bottom. Almost like an afterthought. Apparently, a small chemical weapons shipment, taken from the al-Assad regime, was being stored at a warehouse right on the water in Guantanamo Bay. Due to remain there a mere twenty-four hours before it was slated for transport to the mainland where it would be destroyed.

According to the memo, the warehouse's security system had suffered a major malfunction—alarms, cameras, *everything* was down. But the powers-that-be had decided to take a hope-for-the-best stance. They surmised that nothing too nefarious could happen to the shipment in such a short time.

Fools! he'd thought, staring wide-eyed at his computer screen and nearly hyperventilating with excitement. His cock had hardened just like it always did when he came across something of interest, something that could help him forward the cause and make a name for himself. *You're leaving a cache of chemical weapons right there for the taking. And so close to the American coast, too. This is it! This is The One!*

Time had been of the essence, of course. And he'd wasted none of it before contacting his sources in Cuba. Following his precise instructions, those holy fighters had managed to locate the chemicals, spirit them from the base to the boat they'd purchased, and set sail for the backwaters of south Florida where Banu had agreed to meet them.

Unfortunately, halfway into their journey, disaster struck…

Apparently, the vessel his contacts had acquired was sixty years old and full of poorly patched holes. *That's Cuba for you.* And since the men weren't exactly sailors, they hadn't realized there was a problem until it was too late. Their boat had sunk beneath them like a lead weight, taking one of his assets with it while the remaining seven escaped in a dinghy.

When Nassar, Banu's point contact, had called via satellite phone to give him the news of the vessel's unexpected end, he'd punched a hole in the wall of his DC apartment and thrown the bag he'd been packing clear across the room. But Nassar had quickly informed him that he'd taken a GPS reading just before the boat went down. He knew the coordinates of the wreck.

Fat lot of good that does us had been Banu's initial thought. But then an idea occurred to him…

A quick Google search of the underwater topographic maps of the area had assured him that all was not lost.

Glory to Allah! All the knowledge he'd gleaned during those family vacations to the Virgin Islands, all those diving expeditions his father insisted he go on where he'd learned about neutral buoyancy and absolute pressure, the Rimbach system and outgassing, were finally going to come in handy for something more than simple self-indulgence and entertainment. Sure, it would be dangerous. A dive that deep was *always* dangerous. But he'd read the literature, knew the right gear to use and the right gases to mix and—

"I have programmed the coordinates into the GPS, brother," the guy sitting beside him in the rented fishing boat said. His English was amazingly good. And with his shaved face, floppy fisherman's cap, and T-shirt printed with a picture of a stick figure on a boat holding a rod and reel that read *Go Deep*, one would never know by looking at him that he was anything other than what he was pretending to be. A captain taking a handful of tourists out for a little deep-sea fishing. Unfortunately, playing a part was apparently where the man's aptitude ended. Which was why Banu was just now embarking on the mission to retrieve the weapons a whole flippin' *five* hours after he arrived in Miami.

At first, the man—his name was Ahmed—had brought him dive tanks with the right mixtures but the wrong concentrations. Then the guy forgot to include the high-performance buoyancy controller Banu needed, even though Banu had asked for it *specifically*. And to top it all off, poor clueless Ahmed had rented the wrong size boat. The original vessel had neither the horsepower nor the fuel capacity to get them where they needed to go, much less bring them back again.

But now, *finally*, Banu had his equipment and the right boat, even if it did come with the ridiculously sophomoric name of *Breaking Wind*—*I mean, who does that?* Some fat, pompous, ill-witted American, no doubt—and he was ready to set sail.

He slid on a pair of Oakley sunglasses and glanced around the various fishing rods at the four dark-skinned men Ahmed was bringing with them. Banu was pretty sure they didn't speak a lick of English, though they were dressed like any other American tourist in T-shirts, ball caps, and cargo shorts. Of course, the Russian AK-47s they'd stowed beneath the bench seats on deck were about as far from the red, white, and blue as you could get.

"How long will it take us to get there?" he asked, his gaze skimming over the turquoise water beyond Miami's Rickenbacker Marina. Dragging in a deep breath that brought with it the smell of fish and sun-warmed salt water, he found himself anticipating the rest of the day. A day that would end with him being hailed as a hero.

"It is approximately one-hundred-and-fifty nautical miles to the sunken trawler," Ahmed answered. He made the word "approximately" sound one syllable too long. "At twenty knots, and depending on wind and current, we should be there in…six, maybe seven hours. Of course, it could take longer since we must pick up the others." The others being Banu's assets, who'd run out of fuel trying to maintain their position near the downed vessel. They were now floating aimlessly in the middle of the ocean.

"But the tide is pushing them toward us. So it should not take us too far out of our way." Ahmed clapped a large, brown hand on Banu's shoulder. And when he leaned close, the scent of chai tea lingered on his breath. "Then you will go down and retrieve the chemicals, and you will finish this thing you began all those years ago. It will be as Allah intended. You will strike a great blow for our cause. Until then, relax, enjoy the ride, and let your mind be at peace, brother."

Peace?

His name was Banu az-Harb. Loosely translated, that meant "child of war." *Peace* wasn't part of his makeup, nor would he want it to be. Peaceful men didn't end up in the history books…

———

12:14 p.m.…

"What do you think?" Madison "Maddy" Powers asked as she peered through the binoculars at the small boat…no, more like a rubber dinghy, really…bobbing haphazardly on the glistening waves. Had there not been bright-orange fabric on the sides of the little boat, Captain Harry, the skipper of the *Black Gold*, her father's hundred-thirty-foot motor yacht, might have sailed right by without ever seeing the—she did a silent head count—seven men who were crammed onto the tiny vessel.

"Cuban refugees?" the captain suggested. "Trying to make their way to America?"

"I suspect you're right," Maddy agreed, swinging her binoculars to the boat's single outboard engine. "They're not under any power. I think they must've run out of fuel."

"We should call in a Coast Guard cutter. Let them

deal with these men." He reached for the satellite phone sitting on a charger atop the bridge's main console.

Maddy lowered the binoculars and turned to face the captain. His long, quintessentially English face was full of lament though his jaw was clenched resolutely. She placed a gentle hand on his sleeve, keeping him from pressing the button that would connect them to the authorities.

"Surely there's another way," she told him. "You know if we call in the Coast Guard they'll repatriate those men to Cuba quicker 'n you can say 'Hail to the Queen.'"

"It *is* their home, is it not?" Captain Harry insisted, his accent making the word "not" sound more like "nawt." Between her thick Texas twang and his high-falutin inflections, it was a wonder they were able to communicate with one another. And, to be really honest, when she'd first hopped aboard the *Black Gold* in Bermuda, she'd had some trouble understanding him. But it hadn't taken long for her ears to attune themselves to the particular diction and phraseology that he shared with his two English crewmates—Nigel, the deckhand, and Bruce, the engineer. And theirs to hers, she figured. Which was good. Since she had an earful of an answer to the captain's last question.

"Their *home*?" She made a face. "I know the U.S. has made moves to lessen sanctions and reform diplomatic ties with the country, but have you *been* to Cuba lately? The people there still aren't allowed to own property. They still can't own their own businesses. Their sweat and toil brings them no hope of a brighter future. It simply allows them the means to scrape by day after day. There's still no freedom of the press. Still no freedom of religion. I don't know about you, but that doesn't sound like *my* definition of a home I'd want to go back to. Besides, these men could be political dissenters tryin' to escape communism and the Castro regime."

"Or they could be convicts."

"I think political dissenters *are* convicts in Cuba."

Captain Harry's expression turned even more sour. "What would you have me do?" he asked. "If we leave them out there, they could float out to the Atlantic where they will die of dehydration or starvation, or both. But if we take them aboard the *Black Gold*, we will be forced to report the rescue to the authorities. And then they'll be in the exact same boat." He shook his head when he realized what he'd said. "There was no pun intended there, I assure you, Miss Madison."

"How many times do I have to ask you to call me Maddy?" she said, softening her tone and her expression.

"Your father hired me for my unblemished record and my professionalism," Captain Harry said, puffing up like a game hen. She figured now was not the time to inform him that the only reason her roughneck father had hired him was because he got a Texas-sized hoot out of English accents and thought it would be more fun than you could shake a stick at to have a stuffed-shirt Brit captaining his boat. Her father was nothing if not full of piss and vinegar mixed with a heaping helping of whimsy. "It wouldn't be right for me to address you by a pet name."

She punched the captain in the arm. The move caused his eyes to go round. "Lighten up, Harry."

He cleared his throat, adjusting his navy-blue double-breasted captain's jacket. "I am English, Miss Madison. I do not *lighten up*."

She snorted, shaking her head at him. There was a sense of humor buried somewhere under that thinning coif of salt-and-pepper hair and that stiff upper lip. She was sure of it. And before they docked in Houston, she was determined to find it. But for right now...

"Can't we just...I don't know...give them some fuel and food and send them on their way? If they make it to the Keys—"

"Yes, I am well aware of your country's wet-foot, dry-foot policy," he interrupted, referring to the 1995 amendment to the Cuban Adjustment Act. It stipulated if a Cuban immigrant placed one foot, just *one* foot on U.S. soil, then he or she was allowed legal permanent-resident status and the opportunity for citizenship.

"Well, then?" she asked, tightening the sash on her knee-length terrycloth robe. She'd just hopped out of the shower when Captain Harry summoned her with a sharp knock on her cabin door after spotting the little boat. And given the circumstances as he'd explained them to her, she hadn't taken the time to do more than throw on a robe over her bra and panties, which didn't bother her a lick. Having grown up with four nosy and rambunctious older brothers, there'd been no opportunity for her to develop any sense of modesty. However, considering the way Captain Harry quickly glanced away from her bare feet and legs, her state of dishabille obviously discombobulated him.

Stuffy-O fart, she thought with affection.

Of course, some of that affection waned when he said, "I may be overstepping my bounds here, but are you sure you aren't letting your bleeding heart influence your head in this decision? It would be far better to—"

"Just because I oversee the charitable enterprises of my father's businesses"—her old man was one of Texas's wealthiest oil tycoons—"doesn't mean I'm a bleedin' heart. There's a difference between folks who genuinely need a helpin' hand and those who are just lookin' for a handout. Believe me, I've gotten real good at spottin' the difference over the years. And these guys?" She gestured out the window at the turquoise ocean. A golden ray of sun happened to catch the dinghy just right, spotlighting the heartbreaking plight of the men. "These guys need a helpin' hand."

Captain Harry seemed to hesitate a second more, then said, "We mustn't tell anyone we did this. Ever."

She pantomimed zipping her mouth shut. "My lips are sealed, oh captain, my captain."

"And we mustn't involve Nigel and Bruce in this business," he continued. "I'll tell them to remain below-decks. They'll know something is off, of course. But they have enough training not to ask what it is."

"You're the boss," she told him, winking saucily.

"Hmph." He frowned at her, his cornflower-blue eyes narrowing. But he grabbed the *Black Gold*'s throttle and pushed it up without further argument. The yacht's big engines responded with a well-tuned purr, and they soon halved the distance to the men in the boat.

Maddy kept an eye on the dinghy through the binoculars until they were close enough for her to make out the black hair and dark skin of its inhabitants—*definitely Cubans, poor souls*. Captain Harry hailed the two deckhands via their shipboard walkie-talkies. Just as he'd claimed, the men didn't make a peep of protest. They simply replied with a couple of *Aye, aye, Captains* and headed to their cabins.

"Former Royal Navy men like myself," Captain Harry boasted. "Very disciplined. Very stoic."

"So I see." Maddy curled her lip, knowing she was neither of those things. Lifting the binoculars again, she could now make out the holey T-shirts and grubby appearance of the men. "I don't suppose you speak Spanish, do you?" she asked.

"I speak French."

"Well, that won't do us a piddlee-O bit of good," she grumbled, setting the binoculars on the console and turning for the door.

"Where do you think you're going?"

"Out on the back deck," she called over her shoulder. "I've picked up a little *español* here and there. Hopefully I know enough to get across the point that we're friends and not foes."

"I—"

Whatever Captain Harry's objection might have been was lost when she let the bridge's rear door slide shut behind her.

The afternoon air was warm and welcoming. It smelled of salty sea and the stainless-steel polish that Nigel used on the yacht's endless metal accoutrements. Lifting her face into the breeze, Maddy breathed deeply, letting the wind tunnel through her hair to caress her scalp. Then she turned to make her way down the stairs to the back deck, reaching up to twirl a strand of her ponytail and realizing, quite shockingly, that it was gone. On impulse she'd had her stylist give her a pixie cut—her father wasn't the only one given to whimsy— right before she hopped the plane to Bermuda. She was having trouble getting used to the new 'do.

Make me look chic and super cute, she'd told her hairdresser. *Like Pink or Michelle Williams*. Unfortunately, after having studied her reflection in the mirror a time or two over the last few days, she was a little worried that her stylist had missed that whole Pink and Michelle Williams mark and instead saddled her with the Justin Bieber.

"Serves you right for leapin' before you looked," she scolded herself as she pulled the two halves of her robe closer together and skipped across the deck as the *Black Gold* sliced through the seas like a greased torpedo, all sleek and sure. She chided herself for not taking her father up on his offer of some time spent alone on the yacht before now. But for the last seven years she'd needed all of her waking hours—and some of her should-be-sleeping hours—to get to the point where Powers Petroleum Company's myriad charities were staffed by good, upstanding folks and running smoothly enough for her to take a break.

And what a break it's turnin' out to be!

Her heart beat with happiness at the thought that she was here this morning to help these unfortunate men. And even though she didn't believe in destiny or kismet or any of that other woo-woo hoopla-hoo, she couldn't help but think it awfully coincidental that *she*—a bona fide professional philanthropist—happened to be making the ocean crossing with Captain Harry the one time he came upon a boatful of stranded would-be immigrants.

Captain Harry pulled back on the throttle when the dinghy was still a good way off the bow, deftly maneuvering the big yacht parallel.

"*Hola!*" she called when the men were within ear

reach, leaning over the rail and trying to see into the bottom of the dinghy. She hoped they carried fuel cans that she could fill with gasoline from the *Black Gold*'s mammoth tanks, because the only other containers she could think to use were the pots from the yacht's kitchen. Unfortunately, the men were still too far away and the angle wasn't right for her to see inside the little boat.

"*Me llamo* Maddy! Uh…we…have *la gasolina* and…I mean *y*…uh…" She made a face and murmured to herself under her breath, "Damnit, Maddy! What's the word for 'food'?" She snapped her fingers and started over. "*La gasolina y la comida! Sí?*"

The men blinked at her, then glanced around at each other. They were bone-thin with scraggly beards, and she couldn't help but wonder if, in fact, they *were* escaped convicts, just like Captain Harry had said. They certainly had the air of a group who'd been on the run or in hiding for a while.

A niggle of apprehension skated up her spine, but the sensation was short-lived because one of the men yelled back in broken English. "Thank you! Please throw rope!"

"You speak English!" she hollered delightedly, the smile returning to her face. Common Cuban street thugs surely wouldn't know English, would they? Maybe *she* was the one who was right before. Maybe these men were political dissidents. *How cool would* that *be*?

"Yes!" the man yelled again. "Rope?"

"Of course!" She ran down the edge of the deck until she came to one of the bright-white life-preserver doughnuts attached to the railing. Pulling the floatation ring off its peg, she took a step back, wound up, and threw the sucker with all her might. The attached rope sailed out after the ring, creating a pristine alabaster arc over the turquoise water.

Much to her surprise, she actually got fairly close to her target. Within a couple feet of it anyway. The men were able to lean over the rubber raft and paddle until two of them could reach the life preserver. After they got a firm handhold, she grabbed her end of the rope and walked toward the aft of the yacht, pulling the dinghy closer and closer with every step. By the time she descended the stairs to the teak swim deck, the men in the rubber boat were already securing the rope to one of the *Black Gold*'s glistening stainless-steel cleats.

Shoot. No gas canisters. Just a couple of weird-looking metal tubes. Well, no matter. She'd make do.

"It's a good thing we saw you—" That was all she managed before the yawning black mouth of a gun barrel was shoved in her face.

She blinked twice, stumbling back as her entire body flashed hot and cold. The hair on her head tried to crawl off her scalp, the traitorous stuff, and she opened her mouth to scream. But when the man drawing down on her saw her gearing up for a bloodcurdling yell, he quickly jumped from the boat onto the deck. He punched her straight in the throat, and that was the end of that. The only sound to issue from her open mouth was a wheezing, *"Uhhhhh! Uhhhhh!"*

The pain and shock of the blow played second fiddle to the fact that she could…not…breathe. She clutched at her paralyzed neck, falling back another step. Her eyes watered; her chest ached from lack of oxygen.

This can't be happening!

The remaining six men crawled from the bobbing dinghy onto the deck, each of them shouldering what looked to be a machine gun. She couldn't be absolutely sure of the make of the weapons since her only experience with firearms was limited to the shotguns and rifles her father and brothers used to hunt pheasant and white-tailed deer. But she'd seen *Black Hawk Down* and *Apocalypse Now*, and the lethal black weapons clutched so casually in these men's hands certainly *looked* like machine guns.

"Do not speak," the first guy said, spinning her around so he could snake an arm around her neck and shoving the barrel of his gun into her right kidney.

Do not speak? Holy shitfire! As if she *could* with a crushed windpipe!

The man turned to say something to one of his compatriots in a language that didn't sound a thing like Spanish.

This can't *be happening!* her mind yelled again, unable to get its ass in gear and come to terms with the harsh reality of her situation. *It's a nightmare. You're having a nightmare. Wake up, Maddy! Wake up!*

"Move!" the man holding her hostage hissed in her ear. His breath smelled like something had up and died inside him. And that was better than any pinch to the arm, because even *her* wild imagination couldn't have conjured up *that* stench. She *wasn't* dreaming. This *was* happening. Which meant that all that darkness edging into her vision was real, all those prickling sensations along her nerve endings were genuine, and if she didn't get some oxygen to her brain in about five seconds, she was going to pass out flat.

"*Uhhhhh! Uhhhhh!*" Her lungs worked to expand her ribs, even though her crippled neck refused to let one drop of life-sustaining oxygen through. But just as her vision tunneled down to a single dot, just as her legs began to crumple beneath her, her throat chose that exact moment to open itself up. *Praise be to Jesus and all his followers!* She sucked in a burning, desperate breath and was disgusted to discover that her captor's rancid mouth wasn't the only thing that could stand a good, solid scrubbing. The air around her was filled with the smell of tangy sweat and nauseating body odor. So strong she could almost taste it.

Who the hell are these men? Not Cubans. The man's accent was decidedly…*off.*

Terrorists.

The idea bloomed in her mind like a poisonous flower, but she refused to pluck it. Terrorists? No, surely not. Surely she was just predisposed to labeling them as such because of all the stories in the news. Because *why* in the world would terrorists be floating in a dinghy out in the middle of the Florida Straits? It didn't make a lick of sense! Though the racing of her heart and the throbbing of the blood in her brain told her that, sense or no sense, terrorists or no terrorists, she'd allowed her father's yacht to be boarded by a group of very nasty men.

"Move!" the man behind her hissed again, his foul breath making her gag. And when he punched the barrel of his machine gun into her side, causing her to cry out, she was left with no recourse but to do as she was told.

Someone had replaced her kneecaps with jelly. Which didn't do a damn thing to make her journey up the stairs to the back deck any easier, especially not with the man's arm secured around her neck.

"Miss Madison?" Captain Harry's posh accent drifted around the corner. "Do you want me to pack a box with foodstuffs, or would you prefer—"

"Run! Lock yourself in the engine room!" Maddy screamed. A sweaty hand clamped over her mouth, and her kidney took another blow from the barrel of her captor's weapon.

Three of the gunmen raced passed her before Captain Harry could act on her shrieked instructions. They grabbed the captain by his arm and yanked him into view. Harry's eyes popped out of his head and his face flashed florid when he realized a couple of brutal-looking machine guns were aimed under his jaw.

"How many more on boat?" the man behind her asked, removing his hand from her mouth to once more snake his hairy arm around her abused throat. She could taste the sweat clinging to her lips. The sweat and the grime. It took everything she had not to double over and retch like the time she was four and her mama had dosed her with ipecac after she'd gotten into the bathroom cleaner beneath the sink.

Instead, she gritted her teeth and shook her head, refusing to answer. Even though the *Black Gold* was a sturdily built ship, sound traveled far on the water. It was possible Nigel and Bruce had heard her scream and were, even at this moment, making their way to the engine room where they could lock themselves behind the heavy steel door and use the satellite phone down there to alert the authorities to their…er… she supposed this was a hijacking? And if that was the case, she was determined to give the two crewmen as much time as she could.

"How many!" the man bellowed, smacking her upside the head with the heel of his hand and causing stars to dance before her eyes. "Talk, bitch!" *Bam!* Another blow had the stars going supernova. The only thing that kept her from stumbling sideways was the fact that he had her in a choke hold.

"Two!" Captain Harry answered for her, his voice raspy and broken. "There are two belowdecks. Please don't hurt her!"

More, Maddy couldn't help but think. Hurt her *more*. Because she'd already sustained a blow to the throat and two to the head. The thought of suffering more abuse at the hands of these vile men should have filled her with paralyzing fear. But she'd often been accused, usually by her brothers, of having more balls than brains. Which meant the fear she *should* be feeling was replaced by boiling rage.

Chapter Five

12:24 p.m....

"NEVER THOUGHT WE'D BE DOING *THIS* AGAIN,"
Wolf said.

Bran Pallidino glanced across the table bolted in the
middle of the computer room aboard *Wayfarer-I* to find
Wolf checking the firing mechanism on his M4 rifle.
They'd each taken one of the sawguns with them when
they waved sayonara to the Navy. And even though,
technically, they were supposed to return Uncle Sam's
hardware—after all, there was a law against civilians
owning full automatics—their commander had understood their desire to keep the Colts that'd put a whole
hell of a lot of rounds downrange.

Most guys had a lucky pair of socks or a lucky set
of golf clubs. SEALs had lucky sidearms or full autos,
or both.

"Welcome back, Kotter," Bran replied, adjusting the
M203 grenade launcher—simply called a 203—that was
attached to his M4. He didn't know if it was awesome
or awful, but the gas-operated, magazine-fed assault
rifle felt like an extension of himself. And he hadn't
realized he'd been bereft without it until he once more
held it firmly in his grip. The metal was...familiar. The
weight...*comforting*. "Shoulda known ol' Uncle Sam
wouldn't let us get away that easy."

Mason looked up from fiddling with a hose on one of their dive tanks. He'd already readied his weapon and was now preparing their gear for the deep dive. "Don't go blaming this fuckfest on anyone but those chowder-heads at Langley."

Bran grimaced, nodding. "Yo, is it just me, or do you guys feel like any time they take the lead on something we get bent over and screwed without first being kissed?"

"It's not just you," Wolf agreed.

For a few minutes, nothing more was mentioned. The steady hum of *Wayfarer-I*'s big engines and the occasional beep or buzz from the wall of computers and sonar equipment were the only sounds to breach the silence of the room. Bran breathed deeply of air that was ripe with marine anti-fouling paint and gun black. One odor reminded him of the future they were all trying so hard to grab onto, while the other brought back memories of the past they all shared.

Glancing around, he made a quick perusal of the room. This cabin was where they were supposed to map the ocean floor around their salvage site. This table was where they were supposed to lay out the old documents and charts that would hopefully lead them to the final resting place of the legendary *Santa Cristina*. These chairs were where they were supposed to sit and count their gold coins and uncut emeralds.

Instead, what were they doing? Well, just like the not-so-good ol' days, they were cleaning weapons and readying ammo. *Bada-bing, bada-boom. Here we go again.*

"Did you see the look on LT's face when he realized we had Agent Mortier with us?" Mason murmured.

Bran flicked his gaze to the ceiling. Above them, Leo
was in the pilothouse, doing what Leo did best. Namely,
taking charge, leading the way, and getting them where
they needed to go.

And though Bran would never tell anyone this, there
was a time back in BUD/S when he'd been green with
jealousy over Leo's rank of officer, furious at the military's custom of putting guys like him in charge just
because he had some college courses and a couple of
bars on his collar. But that had only lasted a week.
Because it soon became obvious that Leo Anderson was
born to command.

That was why Bran hadn't hesitated to agree when
Leo reluctantly said, back in the kitchen on Wayfarer
Island, *I reckon if we have any hope of keepin' our
promise, of cleanin' up this mess the CIA has caused and
keepin' innocents safe, and of havin' better luck findin'
the* Santa Cristina *than my ol' man did, we should take
Agent Mortier up on her offer of a big bag of cash.*

"Yeah, it looked like he was seconds away from
swallowing his tongue," Wolf said. "I don't know why
he hasn't tried to contact her since Syria. Maybe it's a
case of 'From passion arises fear.'"

"And what's that?" Bran frowned over at the guy.
"Some more Buddhist bullshit?" Wolf prided himself
on being a student of the religions of the world and, as
such, was always quick with an esoteric quote—much
to the irritation of the rest of them.

"It's the truth," Wolf said simply.

Bran begged to differ. "Dude, the only thing that arises
from my passion is centered directly behind my fly."

"Maybe he hasn't called her because this transition

has been hard as fuck for him," Mason speculated, ignoring their exchange. He tapped the gauge on another tank before setting it aside. Bran knew for a fact those tanks were heavy as shit, but Mason—a.k.a. their resident Incredible Hulk—handled them like they were made of goose down. "He may've taken off that fuckin' uniform, but he still feels responsible for all of us. Still feels like he has to put us first. And since we've got all our eggs in his basket and are depending on him to come through with this big score..." He let the sentence dangle.

Wolf let out a deep, weary-sounding sigh before adding, "'Uneasy lies the head that wears the crown.'"

"Now *that* one I'm familiar with," Bran mumbled. For a few more minutes, they attended to their tasks in silence, the gentle bob and sway of the ship a constant reminder they were sailing toward uncertain waters.

And that was something Bran *hadn't* missed. That feeling that things would either come up dog shit or daisies, and there was nothing he could do to steer his destiny toward one or the other. Maybe it'd been growing up on the mean streets of Newark, New Jersey, after his son-of-a-bitching alcoholic father killed his mother and was sent to prison, leaving Bran all alone. Or, hell, perhaps it had to do with the number of times some armchair commander back at the Pentagon had sent them out on a mission without having firsthand knowledge of what was happening on the ground. But feeling like his immediate future was completely out of his hands... well...not to put too fine a point on it, but it made his ass twitch. Like, *seriously*.

"I wish Doc and Romeo were here," Mason said after

a bit, the change in subject a welcome distraction from
Bran's thoughts.

"Why?" Wolf asked. "Because seven of us against a
possible eight tangos would be better odds?"

"It feels wrong to be doing this without them."
Mason shrugged. "Plus, you know those fuckers will be
pissed when they get back to Wayfarer Island and find
out they've missed all the fun."

For a few minutes after Leo had been forced to take
Olivia up on her offer of a duffel full of Benjamins,
they'd discussed the efficacy of using their Marine VHF
radio to alert Doc and Romeo to their plans. But that
idea had quickly been axed when Olivia brought up the
possibility that the mole or moles could be monitoring
the high-frequency marine channels, waiting to hear if
there was any news coming in from the Coast Guard.

"Yeah, maybe they'll be pissed," Wolf mused. "Or
maybe they'll be happy as a room without a roof."

"You did *not* just Pharrell Williams us," Bran said
dubiously.

"I did," Wolf admitted. "Because, I mean, if you
had a choice between spending the day sailing the
catamaran back to Key West while taking turns going
belowdecks to get naked with a warm, willing woman
or having your brain squeezed in two hundred feet of
water in search of three capsules of deadly chemicals,
which would you choose?"

"Good point." Mason nodded, making a face. "Which
brings me back to LT and Olivia."

Both Bran and Wolf groaned. "I like it better when
he's playing the part of Mount McCarthy," Bran stage-
whispered to Wolf. "Big and *silent*."

"Agreed." Wolf nodded.

"Just hear me out, fuckheads," Mason said. "I was thinking maybe the reason LT hasn't called Olivia is because that thing they had in Syria was just some sort of foxhole *In Love and War* bullshit. Nothing real. Then again, that wouldn't explain the look on his face this morning."

"It was real," Bran gritted out.

"You say that like you're sure," Wolf said. "He said something to you?"

"Yeah, sure." Bran nodded, gifting Wolf with the facial equivalent of *Have you lost your ever-loving mind?* "He told me right after we exchanged manicure secrets, shared skin-care advice, and listed all our favorite Britney Spears songs."

Wolf simply sat there in that *Wolf* way of his. Totally still. Totally enigmatic. To date, Bran had yet to find what it took to ruffle Wolf's feathers. So, he was left with no recourse but to relent. "I mean seriously, dude. Can you imagine Leo 'the Lion' Anderson admitting he's in a state of serious forlorn yearning for a cute, raven-haired spook?" *Pigs will fly, hell will freeze over, and Sicily will elect an incorruptible government.* "No. He hasn't said a damn thing. And the truth is, at first I thought the reason he was walking around with a hangdog expression on his face like he'd been kicked in the apple bag was because of what happened back there."

Wolf shot him a look, one brow arched, one corner of his mouth quirked. "Like he'd been kicked in the apple bag?"

"What?" Bran grinned, spreading his arms wide. "You know me. The master of motherfucking tact."

"Unquestionably."

"But I've known the guy for over fifteen years now," he continued, unperturbed by Wolf's quick agreement. "I've known him to lose men and soldier on." Wolf opened his mouth to argue, but Bran raised a hand, cutting him off. "I know; I know. Rusty was different. One of *us*."

And by "us" he meant the original eight-man team they'd put together right out of SEAL training. The Crazy Eight. The Eight Amigos. The motherfriggin' Great Eight. One of whom was in the grave. One of whom, Michael "Mad Dog" Wainwright, had returned home to Atlantic City to build ships in his family's shipyard and make babies with the saucy redheaded diplomatic secretary they had saved from a bombed-out embassy in Pakistan during their final mission for the Navy. And six of whom—*them*—were living and working in the Keys, hoping like hell to find a better way of life than the one they'd left behind.

"But my point is that no matter what kinda shit-storm he's weathered, no matter how many good men he's loaded into flag-draped coffins for transport back home," he continued, "LT has never once sworn off the ladies. Not until Syria. Not until Olivia. So yeah, it's real. Now whether 'real' means unrequited *lust* or 'real' means unrequited *love* is anybody's guess."

He hoped to hell it was the first. Because there was no way Leo and Olivia could make it work in the long run. The huge list of divorced spec-ops guys and spies he knew assured him of that fact. Tradecraft and civilian life just didn't mix. And Bran sure as shit didn't want to have to stand by and watch while his best friend got his heart broken.

"So maybe we just need to make sure we give Olivia and LT some alone time," Wolf speculated. "Maybe after she's waxed his ax a few times, he'll realize one… um… What is it you Jersey boys call it?" he asked.

"Chucky." Bran smiled despite himself, remembering the conversation he'd had with Wolf their very first night on Wayfarer Island when he'd explained the origins of that particular piece of slang.

"Right." Wolf nodded. "Maybe then he'll stop pining and realize one *chucky* is as good as the next."

"That's possible," Bran mused. Though he had some doubts. He'd never seen Leo look at another woman the way he looked at Olivia, his eyes chockablock full of heat and hormones and…something else. It was the "something else" that made Bran twitchy. "And since we're on the subject of ax waxing and one chucky being as good as the next"—he turned his attention to Mason— "when will *you* get back on that horse and ride, eh?"

Mason shot him a look meant to shrivel his balls. "Who the fuck says I haven't?"

"Me," Bran declared.

"And me," Wolf added.

"It's complicated," Mason insisted, his expression about as friendly as a jar full of scorpions, which was pretty much SOP—standard operating procedure— whenever they dared bring up the subject of his philandering ex-wife. Bran had never hated a woman in his life. But he hated the former Mrs. Mason McCarthy with the fiery heat of a thousand suns. *No good* puttana.

"What it is, is *way* past time," Wolf was quick to insist. "Besides, it can't be healthy. How many years has it been now? Six?"

"I thought it was seven," Bran added helpfully.

"You can both immediately and rigorously go fuck yourselves; it's only been five. And I got your healthy right here." Mason flexed one arm, his massive bicep rolling into a hard sphere that looked about the size of a bowling ball.

"Have you ever noticed," Bran mused, grinning evilly, "that guys who work out and get super beefy are generally trying to overcompensate for embarrassingly tiny sex organs?"

"I *have* noticed that." Wolf played along, nodding sagely.

"Puh-lease," Mason snorted. "You could lay both your dicks end-to-end and they still wouldn't compare to the hog I have packed in my pants. And why did this get turned around on me, anyway? Weren't we talking about LT and Olivia?"

"Speak of the devil and she will appear," Wolf muttered softly. Then he raised his voice. "Come on in, Agent Mortier."

Bran spun in his seat to see Olivia standing in the doorway. And he could totally understand why Leo dug her. On the one hand, she was lean and mean, an honest-to-God government fighting machine. On the other hand, she was soft and pretty, a woman in her prime. And that combination was incredibly dynamic. And *very* hard to resist. Especially for guys like them who could appreciate more than most a woman with a backbone forged of white-hot alloyed steel.

"Am I interrupting?" she asked, her smoky voice rougher than usual. And from the shuttered look on her face Bran wasn't sure how much of the conversation she'd heard.

Hopefully none. Because Leo would skin them alive if he knew they were talking about his currently nonexistent sex life. But if he knew Olivia had overhead as well? *Good God*, a mere skinning would seem like child's play compared to what Leo would do to them. Bran imagined it would be something rather foul and undoubtedly painful involving their *coglioni*.

"Nah." Wolf motioned for her to come in. "We're just gearing up. So, what's up? Is there a problem with the receiver or something? Are the signals—"

"No, no." She shook her head. "Everything is fine. The signals are coming in loud and clear, and all indications are that the capsules haven't moved. I just got off the satphone with Morales. He says the contractors are about fifty minutes behind us, but headed our way to provide support should we get close and find the tangos are still on site. So we should be...uh...we should be good."

"Roger that," Bran said after she'd sort of stumbled to a stop. Standing there in the doorway, her expression appeared to be filled with... Was that doubt? Okay, now *that* wasn't very Olivia-like. "Was there something *else* you needed?"

"I..." She took a step into the room, then paused. For a split second, Bran thought she might turn tail and run. But then she squared her shoulders and marched toward them, stopping next to the table to spread her feet and balance herself against the gentle sway of the ship. "I was hoping Wolf would tell me about that promise he mentioned," she blurted.

For a couple of seconds, no one moved. Bran was pretty sure no one breathed. And not because their vow was a secret or anything—for shit's sake, they each carried the evidence of it right there on their bodies. But more because it wasn't something they talked about with anyone…*ever*. Why would they? No one but the seven of them, the remaining members of the Crazy Eight, could ever understand what it meant.

"Because it's been… Well, it's really been bothering me," she continued. "And I…I know I'm asking a lot of you guys and I know you all thought you were finished doing this kind of stuff but I figured a half a million would make it worth your while—*more* than worth your while—but if helping me means that you're going back on your word to someone, then maybe I should call Morales and tell him to find another dive team. I mean you guys *are* our best shot right now for retrieving the weapons *and* staying off the CIA's radar but it's not like we couldn't tap someone else if we had to and I just—"

"Whoa, whoa!" Wolf cut in. "Slow down. I don't know about these two"—he flicked a thumb at Mason and a finger at Bran—"but I could really use some punctuation here."

Olivia blinked, then grimaced, realizing she'd run through about ten sentences without pausing or taking a breath. As if to make up for it, she blew out a big, blustery one. "I just don't want you all to feel like I've backed you into a corner, that's all."

Wolf lifted an eyebrow, casually turning his wrist to glance at his big, black diver's watch. "And you thought to bring this up now? When we're an hour from our ETA?"

Olivia's lips flattened. "I figured better late than never." She stood her ground, hands on her hips, her eyes darting between the three of them for a good ten seconds before throwing her hands in the air. "Okay, so are you going to tell me about the promise or not? Because if not, then—"

"I'm thinking this is something you should take up with LT," Wolf said, his tone polite, though when Bran looked over at the guy, his eyes were flashing with suggestion. *Oh, ay! Well played*, Bran thought, suppressing a grin. "Probably in *private*," Wolf added, emphasizing the last word.

Olivia's narrowed gaze locked on Wolf for a couple long ticks of the clock. Then she swung her eyes over to Bran.

"Hey, don't look at me." He held up his hands. "Wolf's right. If you're having a crisis of conscience, you need to hash it out with the big guy upstairs." He pointed to the ceiling, and they all knew he wasn't referring to God.

"Fine." She shrugged. "Then will one of you come up and take over piloting for him?"

Bran exchanged a look with the two men sitting at the table with him and knew each of them was thinking the same thing. *Time for a little ax waxing?*

They seemed to come to a unanimous decision, because Mason nodded at the same time Wolf said, "I'll take over," and Bran simultaneously blurted, "Wolf's your man."

———

12:32 p.m....

"So what's with this whole 'We need to talk' song and dance?" Leo asked, his deep voice drifting back to Olivia as she followed him down the tight metal stairwell into the salvage ship's small galley. A large stove, half of which was a griddle, took up most of the space along the far bulkhead. The rest of the room was crammed with old floor-to-ceiling cabinetry and a little square table that was surrounded on three sides by a booth with faded orange cushions. "Is there somethin' about this mission you haven't told me? Will a Russian submarine be waitin' for us when we get there?"

She perched against the edge of the table, turning to find Leo sliding off his aviator sunglasses and hooking one earpiece over the collar of his T-shirt. Maybe it was the reflection of the azure waters coming in through the portholes, or maybe it was the dim yellow light shining down from the simple overhead fixture, but his usually hazel eyes looked intriguingly, almost mesmerizingly green.

Damn, he's a handsome bastard.

She'd noticed that about him before she ever met him, when she'd seen him walking across that airplane hangar on the outskirts of Aleppo. He'd been dressed head-to-toe in desert-drab fatigues and wearing a crap-ton of body armor. A combat helmet and those ever-present sunglasses had obscured much of his face, but there'd been no mistaking that impressively *male* mouth or the breadth of those fabulously wide shoulders.

And speaking of...

His sheer mass seemed to dwarf the already-tight quarters. She thought she could feel his body heat radiating out to her as he propped his lean hip against the countertop, crossing his arms and ankles. Or maybe she was just being fanciful, given she didn't have all that many clothes on and any subtle shift in the dense, humid air registered on her bare arms and legs.

Sidebar: She wasn't the *only* one without a lot of clothes on. There was a whole lot of Leo on display too.

And, okay, *yes*, so she'd caught herself staring at the crisp, brownish-blond hairs on his forearms more than a time or two since they pulled anchor and started making their way through the choppy seas toward the coordinates indicated on the handheld signal receiver Morales had supplied her with. It was hard *not* to stare, considering how deft he was at piloting the ship, and how every movement of his wide, capable hands on the controls caused his biceps to bunch and the tendons and veins in his forearms to stand out in harsh relief.

Of course, if her ogling had ended there, she wouldn't feel like a complete hussy. But you *know* it hadn't ended there. In fact, more times than she could count, she'd found herself watching his big jaw work over a piece of chewing gum, or she'd caught herself glancing down at the long, tan length of his legs, admiring the flex of his muscular calves as he adjusted his position in the captain's chair.

Then, as if all of that wasn't enough, she figured she'd spent a good ten to fifteen minutes lustfully gazing at the few whorling curls of burnished gold hair peeking from the center of the V in his T-shirt before she was able to pull her eyes away and concentrate on something other than—

"Olivia?"

She glanced up to find he'd paused in the middle of folding a stick of chewing gum into his mouth, one quirked eyebrow having nearly disappeared into his hairline.

Oh, for the love of God. There she'd gone again. What was it about Leo that made it impossible for her to keep her mind on task?

Oh yeah. Everything. From the way he looked—all golden and gorgeous. And the way he talked—all low and Southern. To the way he handled himself in every situation—with integrity and flat-out courage. In short, Leo Anderson was everything a man was supposed to be and then some. Which in turn made her insides go all soft and warm and malleable, making her feel like... well...like a *woman.*

Sweet baby Jesus. And now I'm channeling old Shania Twain songs. Sheesh, Mortier! Pull your head out of your ass. That thing isn't meant to be a hat!

And speaking of hats...she hastily donned her imaginary CIA cap. "Uh, sorry. Yeah, I, uh..." She swallowed and crossed her arms over her chest just in case, you know, all that gawking had caused her to nip out or something. *I mean, friggin'-A.* "No. No Russian sub. I was...I was just hoping maybe you'd tell me about that promise Wolf mentioned in the kitchen back on Wayfarer Island."

Leo cocked his head, narrowing his eyes. Green. They were definitely green in this light. "Why do you care about that?"

Okey dokey. That was a valid question. Why *did* she care about that? But, of course, she knew the answer.

She cared because of Syria. She cared because she owed them. She cared because she'd already cost them so much, and she'd be damned if she'd be able to live with herself if she ended up costing them even *more.*

"I just...I know how much you guys pride yourselves

on your honor, on your integrity. And I would hate it
if…if…" She stammered to a stop, trying to gather her
thoughts. "I would hate it if any of you felt forced to
renege on an…*oath* or something just because you all
can't say no when you think the lives of innocents are
on the line and because, well, on top of that you need the
money and here I am offering you some that is totally
skeevy and sort of makes you hookers…er…gigolos I
guess is the correct term since you're men, but that's
not as bad as me playing the part of a big slimy government pimp that has you by the short curlies and I-I-I—"
She realized she was talking without punctuation again.
Twisting her lips, she shrugged, hoping he'd been able
to make sense of that jumbled mess of run-on sentences.

"Who are you?"

"Huh?" She searched his face. Back when she first
met Leo, she'd thought he wore those damn sunglasses
to keep people from seeing his eyes, to keep them from
discovering whatever he was really thinking in that con-
sternating head of his. But it hadn't taken her long to
figure out that staring into the multihued pools of his
irises, like she was doing right now, told her no more
than staring into that old well in the woods out behind
the orphanage. In a word: nothing. *He would have made
an excellent spy.* "What do you mean, *who am I*?"

"I mean, the woman I met almost two years ago
wouldn't have thought twice about our honor or our
integrity. She would've used us and any means necessary to retrieve those capsules."

Each of his words felt like a knife slashing into her
gut. *Holy jeez.* Is *that* what he thought of her? *Ow!*
She resisted the urge to press a hand to her stomach.

"You don't know me as well as you think you do," she whispered, glancing away from him because, for a split second before that good ol' Langley training kicked in, she wasn't able to hide the hurt in her eyes.

Of course, she should have remembered that Leo was the most singularly *perceptive* man she'd ever met.

"Shit, Olivia." He pushed away from the counter to lay a warm hand on her shoulder. The calluses on his palm were scratchy, and up close like this he smelled of suntan lotion, sporty deodorant, and healthy sun-kissed skin. "I didn't mean it like that. I swear. My uncle says sometimes I come off as rough as a corncob." One corner of her mouth hitched at the analogy. "But I promise I wasn't criticizin' or disparagin' you. I *like* that you kick butt and take names—and make no apologies for doin' either."

No apologies? Well, that might be true. But that didn't mean she didn't harbor a boatload of regrets.

She lifted her chin. His eyes looked more blue than green now. Deep, grayish blue. Ocean-after-a-storm blue. But she couldn't let herself drown in them, even if she was really, *really* tempted to. "I don't want to *use* you. Not if it means—"

"Shh." He tapped her lips with his index finger, and the stupid things tingled like it'd been his tongue. "You're makin' too much of this. *Yes*, we need the money. And *yes*, we wish we didn't. But that's life, right? We make the best of bad situations."

And she couldn't help but notice *she* was the proverbial bad situation. *Hell.*

"And about that promise," he said, dropping his hand from her shoulder. The skin that had been beneath his palm felt cold and bereft, which was...*weird* and...*dumb*.

I mean, bereftness—if that's even a word—isn't really something skin can feel, is it?

"What about that promise?" she asked, her heart pounding.

"It's not like it's classified information or anything."

"You could've fooled me. The way the guys were acting"—she gestured toward the door to the galley—"you'd have thought I asked them to reveal a state secret. They said I needed to talk to you *in private*."

When she stressed the last two words, a strange look slid over his face. His eyes became even more shuttered, and his mouth tightened into a straight line. If she wasn't mistaken, a little muscle was ticking toward the back of his jaw. "No good, interferin' sonsofbitches," he muttered under his breath.

"What?"

"Nothin'."

"Doesn't *sound* like nothing."

He shrugged one big shoulder, and she took that to mean he wasn't going to expound on the subject. She was proved right when the next words out of his mouth were, "The promise Wolf was talking about has to do with Rusty."

And just like that, the air inside her lungs burst into flames and her stomach congealed into a ball of acid that was one part nausea and two parts heart-shredding guilt. Rusty Lawrence…the man she'd watched get leveled by five rounds of center-fire ammo. Rusty Lawrence… the man who had given his all, his last full measure of devotion to save her life and, ultimately, the lives of her assets inside the terrorist group that went by many names, one of which was the Islamic State.

Chapter Six

12:39 p.m....

LEO WATCHED OLIVIA'S THROAT WORK OVER A swallow and her big, blue eyes widen until they seemed to take up her whole face. "R-Rusty?" she asked, her voice breathless and weak. Neither condition struck him as particularly Olivia-like.

Then again, that awful day outside Aleppo had changed all of them, so...*right*.

"You see, we made this...um..." He trailed off, trying to find a way to explain the unexplainable. How did one describe what it was like to spend a decade and a half working and fighting beside a guy, being scared and cold and hungry on the battlefield, or sharing beers and bonfires and bar bunnies back stateside? How did one explain what it was to be part of a band of brothers and the incredible weight of a deathbed promise to live your life to the fullest because one of you wasn't going to live another sixty seconds?

"Look, Rusty had been talkin' about hangin' up his combat boots and camo for a while," he said, opting for the simplest of explanations. "He kept sayin' that none of us were gettin' any younger, that all of us had more than done our duty for our country, and that it was time to start makin' *real* lives for ourselves. When we found him alive inside that asshole general's compound—"

"I don't know how he lasted that long," she whispered, shaking her head, her voice catching. "When I left him, I would have *sworn* he was dead. If I'd known he was still alive, I would've—"

"He was the toughest sonofagun I ever knew," he cut her off. "And he *should* have been dead. Don't blame yourself, Olivia. There was nothin' you could've done for him. Except maybe get yourself killed too."

Something flickered in her eyes, something that had him cocking his head. Then it was gone. Just like that. And, yeah. He reckoned no matter what he said, nothing could make her stop second-guessing that day.

"Anyway," he went on, "he brought it up again. So, we made a pact"—though *covenant* was really closer to describing the promise they all made while huddled on the floor of that helicopter—"that we would do what he wanted. Quit the Navy as soon as our contracts were up and start making *real* lives for ourselves."

He lifted his arm, showing her the tattoo and leaving out the part where tears and snot had flooded from his face while he held his dying friend in his arms, his fingers and the fingers of his men plugging gunshot holes—so *many* goddamned gunshot holes—in a vain attempt to sustain a life that was quickly slipping away…

"Promise me," Rusty said, the gurgle of blood making his words nearly unintelligible above the loud whump-whump-whump *of the helicopter's rotors beating the hot air overhead. The big bird lurched forward, its landing skids scraping the ground for a couple of heartrending seconds before it finally hopped into the sky. The sound of rounds pinging off the chopper's metal skin grew fainter*

and fainter as they gained altitude and raced to get out of range. All the while Michael "Mad Dog" Wainwright maintained his position at the open door, raining death in the form of hot lead onto the rebels below.

Bwarrrrrrr! Bwarrrrrr! The big floor-mounted .50-caliber machine gun's mouth burned bright orange from the heat of the endless rounds it spat from its throat. Spent casings clinkety-clacked against the floor and walls all around them.

"P-promise," Rusty gurgled again, one side of his face covered in blood from the bullet that had grazed his skull and left his scalp torn.

"Don't talk, man!" Bran begged, yelling over the angry buzz of the weapon. Leo looked up to find his best friend's face shiny with far more than just sweat. Great streams of tears streaked down Bran's dusty cheeks and formed crystalline droplets in the bushy beard he'd grown to blend in with the local population. "Save your strength!"

"Pr-omise me, LT…" Rusty insisted, lifting his hands to curl his fingers around the straps of Leo's body armor. Considering most of Rusty's blood was coating the floor of the helicopter, the little jerk he gave Leo was surprisingly strong, "…that you're f-f—" He was racked by coughing then, blood filling his mouth to leak from the corners of his chapped lips in oozing rivulets.

"Turn him onto his side so he can breathe!" Doc bellowed, ripping open a package of QuikClot with his teeth.

"How is he?" Romeo yelled from his place in the copilot's seat. Leo didn't answer. He was too busy help-ing Bran, Mason, and Wolf keep pressure on Rusty's *myriad wounds while they carefully pushed him onto his side so the fluid filling his lungs and throat didn't choke him to death. Rusty grunted, hacking up a puddle of blood that coated Leo's knees. But that gruesome mess was nothing compared to the sight that met his eyes when Doc yanked up the side of Rusty's fatigues shirt, revealing a ragged wound on his flank that pumped deep red, nearly black blood.*

Oh shit. Oh, please God, no. *Leo was no doctor, but he'd been in the field long enough to know a punctured liver when he saw one.*

Doc glanced up at him, his expression a terrible perversion of its usual wholesome Midwestern self. And with that one look, he confirmed what Leo hadn't allowed himself to contemplate since the moment they dragged Rusty into the helicopter. Their friend and teammate, their brother in everything but blood, wasn't going to walk away from this one.

Leo let his head drop back on the column of his neck, gritting his jaw so hard it was a wonder his teeth didn't crumble. And for the first time in his life, he cursed God or Fate or whoever the hell else might be responsible for this unforgivable mistake. And it was *a mistake. Because Rusty was the* best *of them. The man they all counted on to keep them sane, keep them grounded when things went pear-shaped and the bottom dropped out from under their asses.*

This wasn't supposed to be happening. It couldn't be happening. It shouldn't *be happening!*

Fuck you! *he silently yelled to everyone and no one in particular.* Fuck you! Fuck you! Fuuuuuuck you!

If he'd been screaming the words aloud, he would

have shredded his vocal cords, flayed his throat raw. But he held them in until they exploded inside his chest like a handful of live grenades, burning and flaming until his heart and lungs were reduced to ashes.

And that's when he felt it...the warm liquid pouring down his face.

For a moment, he thought maybe he'd been grazed by a bullet. But, no. A second later he knew it wasn't blood that coursed unchecked over his cheeks. Like Bran, he could no more stop the tears spilling from his eyes than the mighty Mississippi could stop itself from spilling into the Gulf.

"LT! Madre de Dios!" Romeo called back again after Mad Dog finally laid off the trigger on the big sawgun. "How the hell is he?"

Leo lowered his head and turned to Romeo. He didn't need to speak the awful words aloud. His tears and the agony on his face said it all.

Romeo's mouth fell open, his nostrils flaring wide as his own eyes welled with wetness. And for a couple of seconds, the two of them shared the soul-shredding knowledge that these were Rusty's last minutes. The moment stretched and contracted, taking an eternity and simultaneously seeming over in the blink of an eye. Using his hands to wipe the moisture from his cheeks, Romeo jerked his chin in a quick downward motion of understanding, casting Rusty one last, lingering look before turning back to the helicopter's controls.

There was nothing Romeo could do for Rusty now. Nothing any of them could do except maybe try to make him comfortable.

It was as if Doc had read Leo's mind. When Leo swung

back around, he found the man reaching into his medical go-bag and pulling out two syringes of morphine.

"N-not yet, Doc," Rusty garbled when he saw what was in Doc's hands "Not until you all p-promise me t-to—"

Again, Rusty was unable to go on, coughing up life-sustaining blood that flecked the front of Leo's grubby fatigues. With each convulsion, Leo could feel warm, sticky fluid spurt against the hands he was still using to plug as many holes as he could, though doing so only prolonged the inevitable.

"Anything, man," he whispered to Rusty, his choked voice a parody of its usual timbre. Then he realized Rusty hadn't heard him above the rhythmic hum of the overhead rotors, so he tried again, this time yelling, "We'll promise you anything you want!"

"Don't re-up," Rusty pleaded, referring to the practice of signing another contract with the military after one's old contract expired. "Don't let them have one more…m-minute of your time," he managed to finish after dragging in a shallow, hacking breath.

And even though great gusts of wind were howling through the chopper's open door, Leo recognized that sound for exactly what it was. He'd read somewhere that it was referred to as a "rale." Which pretty accurately summed the sound up since it was a cross between a hair-raising wheeze and a bone-rattling clatter. But regardless of what name you gave it, the fact remained that terrible noise meant just one thing. Death…that bloody, fickle, heartless bastard was hovering somewhere nearby.

Chills erupted up the length of Leo's spine in opposition to the heat of the air around him. He sucked in a tortured breath that brought with it the smells of sweat, aviation fuel, and the iron-rich tanginess of vast amounts of congealing blood. Shuddering at the terrible clarity of it all, he knew this moment, right here, right now, would forever be etched into his brain, scored into his soul as if it'd been carved there with an oyster knife.

"Promise me," Rusty insisted, his voice steadier in these, his last few moments. It usually happened that way, the body filled with one final burst of energy, the mind brimming with a strange terminal lucidity. "Promise me you won't bleed anymore for the flag." As if to prove his point, he swiped a hand through the puddle of blood on the chopper's floor and lifted it up. Rivulets of the stuff ran down his wrist.

Christ almighty! *Leo understood for the first time in his life what it was to be heartbroken. And what surprised him most was that the condition came with actual physical pain. His chest hurt so bad he could barely draw a breath.*

"Promise me you'll all quit the Navy and live your l-lives. Live them for me b-because I—" Rusty couldn't go on then, tormented as he was with a spasm of coughing.

It was all so horrific. The most awful thing Leo had ever borne witness to. And that was saying something, considering the stinking shit-piles of things he'd seen.

"I promise, Rusty," he swore, no longer trying to hold back the sobs that shook his body. "I promise you!"

"I promise!" Wolf yelled a second later.

"I promise, too!" Mason and Bran chorused in unison.

Leo looked up to find Mad Dog towering above them, hands braced on an overhead rail. The big man's face was crumpled in on itself until it looked like a piece of wadded-up paper. "Mad Dog?" Leo pleaded, knowing there wasn't much time.

"I promise you, you big, beautiful sonofabitch!" Mad Dog yelled, his deep voice booming around the interior of the helicopter, drowning out the rhythmic hum of the massive engine.

Leo turned to find Romeo staring over his shoulder at them. And even through the haze of his tears he could see Romeo struggling to make the pledge. Of the eight of them, Romeo was the only one who claimed to be a lifer, a Navy man until the day he died.

Of course, Leo also understood that was Rusty's whole point. That death was going to find them all sooner rather than later if they stayed on their current path. Their luck wouldn't hold out forever. And Rusty was trying, here at the end, to save them from themselves, save them from the Rambo mentality—the belief in their own invincibility—that SEALs seemed to acquire when they'd grown too long in the tooth. Still, Leo couldn't command Romeo to make the promise if it wasn't something he wanted to do, and—

"I promise!" Romeo yelled back, surprising Leo. "I motherfucking swear it!"

A smile spread across Rusty's face, made horribly macabre by the blood staining his teeth. "Okay, D-Doc," he whispered, all the tension and fight leaving his body in an instant. He'd only held on this long to wring that vow from them. "I'm ready now."

Jesus H. Christ.

"LT?" Doc asked quietly, waiting for the go-ahead from his commanding officer. Leo was left with no

recourse but to nod his consent. It was the hardest order he'd ever given, and it felt like a little piece of his soul ripped away with each dip of his chin.

"Okay. All right," Doc said, tears pouring from his eyes. Despite his shaking hands, he gently inserted first one, then another syringe into Rusty's thigh. "I got what you need right here, buddy. You'll feel better in just a second." After pushing the plungers home, he softly removed the needles and tossed them out the open door.

"Thank you, Doc," Rusty whispered, already succored by the high-powered analgesic, his eyelids fluttering closed, his mouth going slack.

Then, the six of them—no, seven; Romeo had left his position in the copilot's seat to join them there on the floor—did what they always did. They worked as a team and gathered Rusty into their arms. Holding him close, each of them whispering words of love, friendship, and farewell, they gave what little comfort and support they could. And with one last rattling breath, Rusty's life whispered out of him, gone just that quickly. A second later, his bladder released, tainting the air with the sharp smell of urine.

Death wasn't just a bloody, fickle, heartless bastard—it was a demeaning, humiliating, contemptible one as well...

"And me coming here, luring you back into another mission, is making you break that promise to him," Olivia whispered, her lips curved down into a frown so deep it furrowed her brow.

Leo blinked at her, disoriented at having been yanked back into the present. The smell of blood and urine was replaced by hints of wild jasmine, the look of death on Rusty's face superseded by the vibrant life shining in Olivia's.

It took him a second to catch his breath, to squelch the tears gathered behind his eyes and calm the somersaulting of his stomach. *Damn*, that memory always kicked like a mule in heat. Eighteen months later, he was hard-pressed not to double over and puke his guts up from the impact of it. And he might have done just that had he not been completely distracted by the feel of Olivia's cool fingers running over his tattoo, tracing the five letters: *For RL.*

Blowing out a covert breath, he squeezed her fingers before quickly fisting his hands behind his back. They were quivering like the branches of a palm tree in a tropical storm, and he sure as shit didn't want her to see. Not if he had any hope of maintaining his guise as a hard-ass, hard-core fighting man.

"At first glance, sure, it might seem like we're goin' back on our word," he managed, his voice remarkably steady considering his insides felt like hammered shit. "At least that's how I was lookin' at it when you first made the offer and I turned you down. And hot damn, turnin' you down went against everything in me. You got to know that, right? It was a sort of a hip-shot reply at the time because I thought I'd be breakin' my promise."

She nodded.

"But I've since given it more thought. And if you view that half a million dollars you're payin' us as bein' just what we need to really get the search for the *Santa Cristina* under way, then your arrival on our doorstep falls under the title of Auspicious. In fact, I think it's exactly what Rusty would *want* us to do. This right here, what we're doin' right now, saving the world one chemical weapon at a time"—he sent her a look—"*is* grabbin' life by the balls and suckin' the marrow out of its bones. *This* is life in all of its messy, dangerous, astonishin' glory."

Her expression telegraphed her disbelief. And were those…*tears* standing in her eyes? She blinked and whatever wet sheen he thought he'd seen was gone. Clearly he'd been imagining things, because Agent Olivia Mortier didn't cry.

"I'm serious," he cajoled, feeling some of his strength return as the terrible memory faded back into his subconscious, a dark specter waiting to reappear some time when he least expected it. And with the return of his strength, an idea—a wonderful, amazing, *fantastic* idea—suddenly occurred to him. *Really, why didn't I think of this earlier?* "And then when you add in all that unfinished business between you and me, you could go so far as to say you comin' here is *exactly* what the doctor ordered." Or, in his case, exactly what *Rusty* ordered. Because what better way to really live than to act on all those unexplored feelings he had for Olivia?

Leo wasn't big on religion, didn't know exactly where he stood on the whole God issue. But if there were such things as guardian angels, he figured Rusty must be up there right now, looking down on him and wearing that patented shit-eating grin.

Thanks, man, Leo sent up a little prayer. You know, just in case.

"What unfinished business? What are you talking about?" Her adorable chin jutted up at him. Up close

like this, he could see lighter, turquoise striations flecking the deep sapphire of her irises.

And, yessir. As hard as it was for him to admit it,
Doc was right. He *had* been pining away for her, spending far too much time wondering what might have been
when he should have marched his ass up to Washington
to pursue the issue. I mean, for shit's sake! He'd been
eschewing willing bed partners for a whole eighteen
motherfrickin' months! And, yeah, yeah. At first he'd
been mourning Rusty's death. And then he'd been up
to his eyeballs in missions while working out the last of
his contract. Then there'd been retirement, fixing up the
salvage boat, and making Wayfarer Island livable, but
still…a whole eighteen motherfrickin' months!

Who does that? A crazy man?

And the answer to that was an unequivocal *yes*. He'd
been so crazy for Olivia since the day he met her that
he'd been unable to think of *anyone* else. She had con-
sumed him, haunted him, *possessed* him. And except for
that one all-too-brief kiss standing beside the weapons'
locker, what had he done about it? A big honking nothing. Zilch. Zippo.

Well, that stopped today, right now. Because the best
way he knew to keep his promise to Rusty to grab life
by the balls and suck the marrow from its bones was to
grab Olivia by the waist and suck that delicious bottom
lip of hers straight into his mouth.

He placed a hand on her hip. *Step number one complete.*

The pulse in her throat jump-started itself into a
rapid flutter at his touch, which delighted him in ways
he couldn't put into words. The skin beneath his hand
where the hem of her tank top pulled away from the

waistband of her shorts was soft and warm. And he wondered how much warmer, how much softer she'd be in that spot between—

"What unfinished business?" she asked again, her usually low, sexy voice having gone charmingly breathy.

"You *know* what unfinished business," he told her, his own heart beating a rapid tattoo against his ribs. Funny how the organ could remain rock-fucking-steady while he was in the thick of a gun battle or so deep beneath the ocean's surface that light ceased to exist, but put him within two feet of one dark-haired, big-eyed spy and the silly thing took off like a startled jackrabbit. "That kiss, Olivia."

As if uttering the word brought back the memory of his taste, her pink tongue darted out to moisten her bottom lip. Everything that was hot and *male* inside him watched that small move with something bordering on predatory interest. The urge to eat her alive, starting at her slender toes and working his way up, was remarkably strong.

"Leo..." She placed her hands on his chest. To push him away? He held his breath, waiting to see. But she exerted no pressure, simply allowing her palms to flatten over his pectoral muscles. Her breath hitched when she felt the rapid racing of his heart.

Yeah, darlin'. Feel that? That's what you do to me.

"Don't tell me you haven't thought about it," he cajoled. "Don't tell me you haven't wondered what would've happened had you not been called out to that rebel general's house right then." Not only had that call interrupted what was quickly getting out of hand between them, but it had been the genesis of the events that had ultimately changed all of their lives… Of course, he wasn't going to go there. Not unless he wanted that terrible memory to take over again. Which he most certainly did *not*.

Live your lives, Rusty had pleaded. *Live them for me…*

Goddamnit, Rusty! Leo sent the silent reply heavenward, you know, just in case. *I'm tryin', man!*

"I-I've thought about it," she admitted hesitantly. "How could I not? We danced around each other for three months. And then when we finally gave in to…"

"Lust," he finished after she trailed off.

She lifted a brow. "You don't mince words, do you, Lieutenant?"

"It's just plain ol' Leo now, Olivia." He inched a bit closer, close enough that the soft heat from her bare legs tickled the hairs on his.

"There's nothing plain about you." She caught her bottom lip between her teeth, and that was all she wrote. His heart double-timed it until the blood rushing between his ears was a dull roar.

"Should we try it again and see where it goes this time?" he asked, closing the distance between them. The thought of completing step number two had his dick twitching with interest.

"Where *can* it go?" she asked, her expression having gone from teasing to taken aback, her eyes searching his face. "How do two people in our positions make it work in the l—"

"Why, Agent Mortier," he interrupted, nudging his hips against hers. The bad thing about swim trunks—or the good thing, depending on your point of view—was that there was absolutely no way he could hide, no way she could *miss*, his burgeoning erection. "Are you askin' me to go steady?"

"Of *course* not," she was quick to answer. Maybe a little *too* quick, though Leo didn't allow himself to dwell on it. After all, *que será, será*. The future would be what the future would be. All that mattered right now was the present. And *presently* he still had step number two to complete.

On that note, he unhooked his sunglasses from the collar of his T-shirt, setting them behind her on the table. Then, with thumb and forefinger, he plucked his gum from between his teeth and tossed it into the nearby sink.

She watched all of this with a curious, breathless sort of scrutiny.

"So then what do you say to me puttin' my palm beneath your chin like this?" he asked. To illustrate his point, he cupped the side of her face, using his thumb to tilt her jaw.

When she swallowed, her graceful throat made a clicking sound. "I s-say okay," she managed. A bolt of hot passion shot through his body, replacing his earlier heartache with hunger, changing his grief into greed, and electrifying him from head to toe.

"And what do you say to me lowerin' *my* head until you can feel my breath on your lips?" When he did exactly that, she shuddered delicately. He felt that tremor from the top of his head to the tip of his d— um...*toes*.

"I say *yessss*." The last word ended with an eager hiss.

"And what do you say to—"

"Damnit, Leo! Just shut up and kiss me!"

12:51 p.m....

She'd gone from channeling old Shania Twain songs to channeling old Mary Chapin Carpenter songs—and she didn't even really *like* country music. *Sheesh*. She had Mr. Farmington, the old janitor at the orphanage, to thank for that, she supposed. He'd blasted the stuff from the portable radio he toted around with him while he mopped the halls. Of course, she immediately forgot about music, Mr. Farmington, and all other matters both big and small when Leo set his lady-killer smile on stun.

Holy shit!

She was instantly dazed, struck senseless. And that was before his lips claimed hers and all thought slid out of her head through her buzzing ears. Somewhere, back in the furthest recesses of her brain, something started scratching. Something that made her think maybe she shouldn't be doing this. Something that made her question whether or not Leo would want to come within ten feet of her, much less kiss her, if he really knew the truth about Syria.

But he would *never* know the truth about Syria. That mission file had been redacted, sealed, and locked away somewhere in the bowels of the Pentagon. And even if that wasn't the case, it wasn't like he was going down on one knee and asking her for forever here. Far from it. She got the distinct impression from his joking "Are you askin' me to go steady?" that forever was the dead-last thing on his mind. And when you added in that he'd been quick to fill in the blank with "lust" when she was searching for the right word to describe what had been between them a year and a half ago, she was convinced of it.

Did that last part prick her pride? Her heart? *Sh'yeaaah*. No woman liked to think all a guy wanted from her was a little bumping of the grumpies, especially not when that woman felt something decidedly *more* for the man in question. But since there *wasn't* any chance for something more to happen between them, she decided, *Oh, what the hell*, and gave herself permission to just go with it. Permission to let him have her any way he wanted. Permission to simply...*feel*...

The muscle-strapped hardness of Leo's chest cushioned her sensitive breasts.

The insistence of his thick erection throbbed against her lower belly.

The gentle sting of his teeth caught her lower lip.

"Bingo, bango, bongo," he murmured against her mouth. "Step number two complete."

"Huh?"

"Nothin'."

"Doesn't *sound* like nothing," she insisted, feeling a strange sense of déjà vu. But, then...oh! He was really kissing her, his thick tongue gliding into her mouth, and she forgot about everything but the taste of him.

Cinnamon. She remembered that flavor from the last time. Remembered how his tongue had been a wonderfully spicy reprieve from the hot dust of Syria. Recalled how kissing him had reminded her of candy canes at Christmas and the chewy Red Hots treats one of her foster families had kept in a glass dish by the door.

Rough. That was another thing that sparked a memory. How his beard had scraped against her cheeks, creating a delightful friction. His facial hair was close cropped now, the bristles tidily trimmed as opposed to the great fuzzy bush he and the rest of his men had sported overseas. But, still, there were enough whiskers left to tickle her lips as he kissed her so expertly, so brazenly—all languid stroking and deep, penetrating sucking—as only *he* seemed to know how to do.

"God, Olivia," he moaned, tilting her jaw to better align their lips. "Every time I get my mouth on you, I want to gobble you up."

She shivered at the unabashed longing in his tone. And for the life of her, she couldn't think of one good reason why he shouldn't do exactly that. Being eaten alive had never sounded so good.

"I like this plan of yours," she whispered, sliding her hands up over his shoulders and delighting in the feel of his muscles flexing beneath her questing fingers. His neck was warm against her palms in the second before she speared her hands into his hair.

Silky. She remembered that too. That his hair was softer, sleeker than any man's should be. Of course, she soon forgot all about his hair, because...

In and out. In and out. His knowledgeable tongue plunged and retreated, mimicking the sex act in a blatantly unapologetic way. Her body responded with a flood of liquid heat between her thighs, the center of her aching around its own emptiness. She wanted to be filled. She needed to be filled. With him. Only him.

"If you're going to gobble me up, do you want to add a topping?" she husked between deep, mind-numbing kisses. "Whipped cream? Or, oh!" He did something with his tongue that had her bare toes curling against her flip-flops. "Or maybe a cherry?" she finished with a throaty laugh.

"I don't need any toppings," he assured her, kissing the side of her mouth and rubbing his lips and whiskers along her cheek until he stopped at her ear. The feel of his hot, moist breath against the sensitive shell nearly had her eyes crossing. "You taste absolutely perfect all on your own."

Oh, this man! This man was...*everything*. Big and strong and tough and loyal. Charming enough to coax the fish out of the water. Smart enough to challenge her at every turn. And sexy enough to give Casanova, Don Juan, and Mr. Darcy all a run for their money.

She liked him *so* much. Liked him enough that she wondered if maybe what she was feeling was—

No. Don't go there. Nothing but disappointment and heartache down that path.

And she'd already had enough of those to last her a lifetime. Each Sunday when the orphanage would open up to childless parents that passed her over. Every foster family that eventually sent her back to the orphanage. Permanence, belonging, and love. They weren't for her. Never had been. Never would be.

So she'd take what she could from Leo, whatever he was willing to give. And in return, she'd give him whatever he wanted...

Chapter Seven

12:56 p.m....

Sixteen motherfrickin' years old.

Apparently that's the age one reverted to after having eschewed female companionship for a year and a half. Because if Leo's dick throbbed any harder, he was liable to go off right there in his swim trunks. *For shit's sake, man!*

Of course, Olivia wasn't helping matters, moving against him like she was. All sinuous and sexy, meeting him kiss for kiss, caress for caress.

He hadn't really meant for things to go this far this fast. Then again, he should have known from the last time that the minute their lips locked it was all gas, no brakes, Thelma and Louise holding hands and jettisoning off a cliff. Or in layman's terms…it was on, cowboy!

Well, giddyup!

He sucked her delicate earlobe into his mouth, delighted to discover her skin tasted exactly like it smelled: warm, exotic flowers kissed by the sun. Her flavor flooded into his bloodstream, intoxicating him and making his head spin.

"Leo," she moaned, pulling him closer, so close her breasts smashed flat against his chest. But still, he could tell by her busy, frustrated hands in his hair and on his shoulders that she didn't think they were nearly close enough.

By God, neither did he.

Releasing her earlobe and opening his mouth over her pounding pulse-point, he remedied the situation by running the hand that had been squeezing her hip around until he could cup one plump globe of her delightful ass. He sealed their bodies until not one inch of electrified air remained between them, imagining what it would be like to take a bite out of her scrumptious posterior.

Of course, *that* imagery caused his erection to throb so painfully he was pretty sure he felt a drop of moisture gather at the tip. And, *hello*. It was obvious he either needed to slow this way down or speed it way up. Since he was a guy, and since it *had* been a year and a half, he decided to go with option number two.

All right, and sure. There was undoubtedly a whole host of things he should be doing right now, like checking his tanks, filling some extra clips for his weapon, or searching for tears in his buoyancy compensator. But honestly, he couldn't seem to make himself care about anything other than Olivia.

Keeping one hand firmly on her butt to guide her in the bump-and-grind she had going, he used the other to grab the hem of her tank top, pushing it higher and higher. The pads of his fingers were met by rippling goose bumps. Despite that, her skin was remarkably soft. So *unbelievably* soft. And considering how tough she was in every other respect, that baby-fine skin was a delightful contradiction.

Soft, yet strong. Delicate, yet determined. Kissable one minute and kickass the next. She was all things paradoxical, and all things guaran-frickin'-teed to drive him wild.

"Kiss me, Leo," she demanded, grabbing his ears and offering her succulent, open mouth to him.

"Your wish is my command," he told her, reclaiming her lips, reclaiming that sweet, agile tongue. And for a few endless moments they danced to the age-old rhythm of foreplay. Mouths seeking, hands caressing, hips rubbing. His blood ran hot and thick through his veins, making every inch of his skin burn.

Bunching her tank top over the cups of her bra, he slowly pulled back, sucking her lower lip as he retreated and hearing her groan of disapproval. When he finally released her lip, he was charmed to see her catch the plump pad between her teeth, even more charmed to get a peek at that wonderfully sexy half-grin of hers.

"You have the best smile," he said, his gaze having latched onto her mouth like an antiaircraft missile locking in on its target. He imagined her mouth opening wide as he stroked her to orgasm with his fingers, or wrapped tight around the head of his cock, her eyes sparkling up at him teasingly. "It was the first thing I noticed about you."

She immediately rolled in her lips, shaking her head. "I should have had braces when I was a kid."

"Good God, no. Your teeth are perfect in their imperfection. They're part of what makes you *you*. And in case you can't tell"—he used the hand he still had planted on her ass to pull her closer, press her tighter against his raging hard-on—"I find *you* sexy as hell."

"You're crazy," she whispered, but he could tell by the tiny upward tilt of her lips that she was flattered.

"Maybe," he admitted. "Or maybe you just *make* me crazy." Not being able to stand it a moment longer, he dropped his eyes from her pretty face. He wanted to see her, let his eyes drink her in, become drunk on her beauty. He wasn't disappointed. The tender curves of her upper breasts swelled above the black lace cups of her bra, and all that soft, female flesh called to everything hard and male in him. He lifted a hand to weigh her, to mold her, to find she was a fabulously firm handful.

She gasped when his thumb passed over her distended nipple, when he used the blunt edge of his nail to add more friction to the lace covering it. "You're unbelievably responsive," he murmured. "I've barely begun to touch you and already you're…" What was she exactly?

Demanding? Her hips and hands were moving against him in the most urgent way. Aroused? There really was no mistaking the warm blush of passion that made her skin rosy.

"Wet." This time she finished a sentence for him. And boy howdy, what a finish it was! The top of his skull felt like it exploded, and at the same time, the head of his dick released another drop of moisture.

"Christ, Olivia," he groaned. "I need to look at you. I've fantasized so long about lookin' at you. Seein' you. Havin' nothing between us."

He didn't wait for her approval, simply yanked one cup of her bra down and marveled at the berry-colored nipple that sprang into view. Her breast was heavier at the bottom than the top, making the peak point upward, as if challenging him to resist it.

He couldn't.

He plucked at the tender bud with his thumb and forefinger, fascinated to see her areola tighten and crinkle until her entire nipple grew hard and engorged.

"Leo, please," she gasped. Her body bowed, becoming a graceful arc of feminine surrender. And that went to his head like a double shot of top-shelf whiskey, dazzling him, making him burn. Brave, strong, tough Olivia Mortier, spy extraordinaire, was surrendering to him. He was so overcome by the need to beat his chest Tarzan-style and lift his face to let loose with that famous yell that he figured he needed to find a better use for his mouth lest he scare her the hell away.

And three guesses what "better use" he came up with. *Of course, the first two guesses don't count.*

Dropping his chin, he sucked that sweet peak into his mouth. Her nails bit into his scalp, her ankle hooking behind his knee to better align their bodies, and then—

"Ahem!" A loud throat-clearing came from the stairwell outside the galley.

Olivia squeaked—a very un-CIA-agent-y sound—and pulled back. *Ow!* Leo was pretty sure her fingers took a hunk of his hair along with them. But that wasn't nearly as heartbreaking as having her delectable nipple pop free of his lips. In a flash, she yanked her bra cup up over her amazing breast and tugged her tank top back into place.

"Now *that's* a goddamn cryin' shame," he grumped, adding, "and I'm goin' to *kill* whoever that is."

"If there's any ax waxing going on down there"— Bran. Leo should have known. The guy had the *worst* timing—"I'm sorry to say, but it needs to be red-lighted right now!"

"Ax waxing?" Olivia lifted a brow, her voice low and breathless. Leo noticed with more than a little regret the passion-heightened color of the skin over her cheeks and

chest, and the glossy shine of her kiss-swollen lips. Yep.
Bran was a dead man. "What's he talking about?"

Leo rolled his eyes. "You don't want to know."

"Because Agent Mortier's boss is on the satphone!"
Bran added. "He says there's a problem with the contractors' boat."

"Oh, for the love of all that's holy," Olivia harrumphed, pushing past Leo and heading for the stairs.
"What else can go wrong?"

"Famous last words," he muttered. And without her
tender heat pressed against the length of him, he felt
unaccountably cold. Grabbing his sunglasses off the
table, he hooked the earpiece over the collar of his shirt
before glancing over his shoulder to stare at her retreating back. His eyes were no doubt broody as he watched
her disappear through the doorway. The last thing he
saw was the gun shoved into a holster at the small of her
waist above the round curve of her ass. Obviously, his
expression became even *more* malevolent when Bran
took her place in the opening.

"Don't gimme that look, you big *spostata*," Bran
warned. "I tried telling Morales she was otherwise
occupied, but he was having none of it. Besides"—
Bran glanced around the room—"the galley, bro? The
place where we clean fish? *This* is where you chose to
bump uglies with Olivia? I mean, you remember last
week Meat got seasick and upchucked his kibble along
with about five gallons of undigested water weeds in
here, right?"

"I didn't *choose* it," Leo grumbled. "It just...sort
of...*happened*." Like the last time. It was as if they were
a couple of tectonic plates, the tension that hummed

between them growing and growing until *snap!* The pressure erupted and they were helpless to do anything about it, caught up in its fury and power and swept along in its path.

Bran's face split into a wide grin, his lids flying at half-mast. "You're having all the smutty, sexy feels for her, aren't you?"

"I swear to Christ, man. Sometimes I think you're just a potato with four limbs."

"If you're gonna insult me"—Bran's grin remained in place—"at least get it right. I'm a really *well-hung* potato with four limbs."

"How about I go with something simpler and just call you an asshat?"

"That's Lord Asshat of Bigdicksburg to you, my friend."

Leo shook his head, sticking his tongue in his cheek because it was obvious Bran's internal switch was flipped back to its usual devil-may-care position. In which case, it was impossible to get one over on the guy, so he might as well quit trying.

"I sort of like that," Bran continued. "Maybe *that* should be the name of our company. Asshat Salvage or maybe Bigdicksburg Salvage. Has a certain ring, doesn't it?"

"You're worse than Romeo." Leo turned to follow Olivia up to the wheelhouse.

He'd gone no more than two steps when Bran squawked, "For crying out loud!" He held his hands up in front of his face. "I don't wanna see that! Warn a guy next time, will you?"

Leo looked down to discover his erection had turned the front of his swim trunks into a Boy Scout pup tent.

"Good God. If *this* is what happens to you when you haven't been laid in a year and a half, we need to get you some chucky *tout de suite*." Bran was still covering his eyes. "It's already too late for me. I've seen too much. I'll have nightmares for *weeks*. But at least we can spare the others."

"How the hell would you know whether I have or haven't been laid in a year and half? Are you markin' your calendar or somethin'?"

"These things just have a way of making themselves apparent." Bran peeked from between his fingers, then said, "Ah, goddamnit. Why is it still there? You think I'm pretty or something?"

"Or somethin'." Leo frowned down at his erection, which hadn't wilted one bit since Olivia's exit.

"Well, you better jump in the john and tug the pug before you come upstairs," Bran grumbled, heading up the stairwell. "Otherwise, you're liable to put someone's eye out."

Tug the pug? Wax his ax? Wobble his knob? "Did you guys hold a Who Can Come Up with the Worst Euphemism contest at some point and not invite me?" he called up to Bran's retreating back.

"Wouldn't you like to know? And, now, in the legendary words of Larry the Cable Guy"—Bran turned at the top of the stairwell—"'Git 'er done!'"

Christ.

Although…that *did* seem the best course of action, considering Leo couldn't head up to the pilothouse looking like *this*. But as opposed to resorting to middle-school tactics, he figured he should first give that old trick he'd learned when puberty hit and his damn dick grew a mind of its own, springing to attention at the most inopportune times. He pictured his gap-toothed, moley-foreheaded, muumuu-wearing third-grade music teacher, Ms. Meyer. He'd once heard his father remark to his uncle after parent-teacher conferences, "That woman's uglier than a mud fence and mean as a mama wasp." Two characteristics guaran-damn-teed to shrink up a pubescent boy's hard-on in no time flat.

Would it still work on a grown man's? He aimed to find out. But just as he was conjuring up the image of the three thick hairs that'd grown out of Ms. Meyer's biggest mole, the one above her lazy left eye, his mutinous mind snapped back to the memory of Olivia arched like an offering against him, her gorgeous nipple just begging for his kiss.

Sonofa—

Okay, there was nothing to be done for it. With a hobbling, shuffling walk—the fabric of his swim trunks chafed in the most unimaginable way—he made his way out of the galley, past the crew's quarters, and into one of the ship's two small bathrooms. Unrolling a wad of TP, he stood over the toilet, braced a hand above the tank to steady himself against the subtle dip and sway of the ship, and pulled down his swim trunks.

His erection sprang free, all red and angry and with so much enthusiasm he wouldn't have been surprised to hear a resounding *boing!*

"Sixteen motherfrickin' years old," he grumbled as he took hold of himself, letting his mind drift back to the galley, to Olivia's fingers kneading his shoulders, to her warm breath tickling his lips, and *definitely* to her plump ass filling his hand while the grip of her pistol rested against his wrist. Tough, yet tender. Hard as nails, yet soft as sin. That was Olivia.

It didn't take long. After eighteen months he'd gotten pretty good at this, at jacking himself off while imagining it was her hand on him, her mouth around him, her tongue laving over his heated head… And now that he actually *knew* the shape of her? The taste of her? Well, he might've just set some sort of world record. In a matter of seconds, his shaft pulsed in his fist, his balls going all tight and tingly. And then he was clenching his jaw against the deep groan rumbling at the back of his throat while he poured his unquenched desire for Olivia into the waiting clump of toilet paper.

Afterward, he stood there, his lungs working like bellows, his brain buzzing, the remnants of his orgasm making him shiver. When he managed to regain some control, he cleaned himself up and took a nice, long gander at his reflection in the mirror above the sink. "Christ, man. You're way too old to be doin' this."

As he pushed out of the head to make his way upstairs, he knew no truer words had ever been spoken. But Olivia made him feel young again. Like everything was new and exciting and fresh. Like the world was his oyster, and he was poised on the brink of discovering…something. Something precious and rare. Something…

Come on, now! he chided himself as he took the stairs two at a time. *Next thing you know, you'll be writing poetry about her!*

She walks in beauty like the night
Of terrorist-laden climes and mortar-filled
skies…

Yessir, Lord Byron had nothing on him.

―――⁂―――

1:21 p.m.…

Bran dropped the binoculars he'd been using to glass the seas in front of them when he heard Leo's heavy foot-steps pounding up the metal stairs. Turning, he had to suppress a grin when Leo joined them, his best friend's expression all *There! Are you happy now?*

Bran winked at his former commanding officer because he knew it would piss him off. And, sure as shit, right on cue, Leo flipped him the bird.

He rolled in his lips, turning back to listen to Olivia's end of the conversation. It seemed she and her super-visor were debating their options on what to do now that the contractors appeared to be delayed for God only knew how long.

Clusterfuck. That's what this was turning out to be. Although, without a doubt, it would all be worth it if Leo got the opportunity to finish what he started with Olivia down in that galley. Even though Bran wasn't totally in agreement with Wolf's assessment that all Leo needed in order to pull a Father Karras and exorcize Olivia from his system was a nice, long fuck-a-thon, he figured it was best if Leo at least gave it the ol' college try.

"Okay. I'll call you back after I talk to the guys, and let you know what we decide," Olivia said, signing off with her boss and turning her back on the bay of windows that made up three sides of the pilothouse. Bran knew the instant she realized Leo had joined them, because she flushed prettily and unconsciously caught her bottom lip between her teeth.

Huh. Would you look at that? If he hadn't seen it with his own eyes, he wouldn't have believed it, but Olivia Mortier looked…well…*coy*. And when he turned to see Leo *smoldering* at the woman—there was really no other word for it—he didn't even attempt to suppress the urge to roll his eyes.

The way those two were mooning over each other reminded him of when he was six years old and his mother took him to the rundown movie theater in the South Ward to watch a re-showing of the classic Disney film *Bambi*—one of the few times he could remember his father allowing her out of the house. Besides the fact that he had bawled his eyes out when Bambi's mother died, the only other thing Bran distinctly remembered from the film was when the old owl explained to Bambi, Thumper, and Flower why the animals acted so funny in the springtime. "Twitterpated," the condition was called. And he figured that summed up Leo and Olivia in one succinct word.

Thankfully, the way he understood it, being twitterpated was a passing phase. Once the mating instinct was satisfied, both parties were free to go their separate ways. *Let's hope…*

"So, what's up?" Leo asked Olivia, folding his arms over the back of the captain's chair Wolf was currently occupying.

"Apparently the A-Team…uh…" She shook her

head. "That's what Morales and I were calling the apprehension team."

"You guys sure go for the obvious when it comes to code names, don't you?" Wolf snorted, causing Olivia to pull a face.

"This isn't an *official*"—she made the quote marks with her fingers—"operation. So, we figured the simpler we kept things, the better." Wolf opened his mouth, but she was quick to cut him off. "And, yes. I know this has since turned into a shitstorm of complexity, but I swear to you it started out as nothing much more than a Sunday picnic."

Bran glanced at the faces around him, reading the varying levels of disbelief. Once again the word "clusterfuck" whispered through his head.

"Anyway," she continued, choosing to ignore their cynical expressions, "apparently they hit something in the water, and it bent the hell out of the propeller on one of their two outboard engines. They have an extra prop with them, but it'll take some time to switch out the old for the new."

"And in the meantime?" he asked. "Do we go dead in the water or do we carry on to…*the package*?" He couldn't help but stress the last two words, especially when doing so caused Olivia's whole face to flatten.

"That's up to you guys," she said after she'd tried to light his eyebrows on fire with her gaze alone.

"Pros and cons, men?" Leo asked, and the question was so familiar that Bran experienced a strong sense of nostalgia. That's how Leo had begun the planning for each and every op they'd ever run. And it was just one more reason why Leo had been perfect for the job of commanding officer. It took an incredibly intelligent and thoughtful man to be humble enough to know he didn't always have the right answer and to solicit as many opinions as he could before making any decision.

Of course, Bran would never tell Leo how much he admired him. *Where's the fun in that?*

"If those tangos are still on site," Wolf began, "it'd be better to wait for the…ah…*A-Team*." One corner of Wolf's mouth twitched and Bran slapped him a high five. Olivia rolled her eyes.

"True." Leo nodded, running a hand over his beard—if you considered the current trend to maintain what amounted to a slightly longer than a five-o'clock shadow an actual *beard*. "But if they're *not* on site, if they went down with their boat, we could be twiddlin' our dicks out here for hours for no good reason."

Bran opened his mouth to take a swing at the dick-twiddling softball Leo had lobbed his way. But Leo beat him to the punch by flicking him a look that promised untold misery should one word of what had happened belowdecks escape his lips. Bran wisely clamped his teeth together.

"Or we could always alter course and go pick up the contractors," Wolf suggested, adjusting the throttle when a larger-than-normal wave caused *Wayfarer-I* to list slightly. "But if they get that propeller repaired in the meantime, we'll have wasted a lot of time and fuel."

Fuel. The way Wolf spat out the word almost made it sound dirty. And, in a way, it was. Because even though that half a million dollars Olivia was paying them for this gig would go a long way in helping them search for the *Santa Cristina*, every dime—which translated into every drop of fuel—still counted.

"I vote we keep heading toward the package," Mason said. "We can always stop a few miles out and glass the area to see if there are any un-fuckin'-friendlies floating thereabouts. If there are, *then* we can pull back and wait for the contractors to arrive."

"Bran?" Leo asked. "Thoughts?"

"You know me, LT." He shrugged. "I like it best when we do things Han-style, so I say we keep on keeping on."

"Han-style?" Olivia asked.

"You know, Han Solo? So, solo?"

She lifted a brow.

"Oh, for shit's sake. You really need to get a subscription to HBO or Netflix. It loses its *oomph* when I have to explain it."

"Olivia?" Leo turned to her, or more like he'd never turned *away* from her. "Which side of the argument are you comin' in on?"

"Well, of course *I* want to go retrieve those chemicals as quickly as possible," she admitted. "So I vote for doing it"—she turned to smile at Bran—"Han-style."

He slow-winked at her.

"Something in your eye, Brando?" Leo asked. And even if his best friend hadn't used his full name, the warning in Leo's tone was clear. *She's mine*, it said. *So, ix-nay on the irting-flay.*

Bran sighed. *Twitterpated. Totally, completely, annoyingly twitterpated...*

Chapter Eight

1:43 p.m....

"NO GOOD DEED GOES UNPUNISHED."

Maddy glanced over at Captain Harry and frowned, her heart so heavy it was a wonder the thing hadn't sunk down to slide out of her ass. "I'm so sorry I got you into this mess," she told him, wishing with all her might she'd taken a minute, just one stinking *minute*, to consider the possible repercussions of approaching a boatful of strange men. There she'd gone again. Leaping before she looked.

That phrase should be tattooed across my forehead.

Although, in her defense, even if she *had* taken the time to consider the possible downsides to her decision, she never would have envisioned...well...*this*. Whatever the hell *this* was—she had yet to determine if it was a hijacking, a kidnapping, or just plain being in the wrong place at the wrong time. Regardless, she had to admit, "I should have listened to you and called in the Coast G—"

"You couldn't have known who they were," Captain Harry interrupted her, parroting her thoughts back to her. "Neither of us could have. And I'm the captain. Ultimately, all decisions concerning the *Black Gold* are mine. So *I* should be apologizing to *you*."

Sweet man. Sweet wrongheaded *man*.

"How 'bout we agree to disagree?" She gave him a friendly nudge with her shoulder. "Because you know damn well had I not been on board pleadin' the case of destitute Cubans riskin' life and limb in trying for the good old U.S. of A., you would have called in the authorities and none of this would be happenin'."

"Perhaps," he admitted, then added, "or perhaps not. How do you know *my* bleeding heart wouldn't have gotten the better of *me*?"

She shook her head at him. "Well, can we at least *share* the blame?"

"Deal," he told her with a sharp bounce of his head. "I'd shake your hand but…" He used his chin to gesture over his shoulder to his wrists, zip-tied behind his back.

"Yep. I feel your pain." She curled her lip. Her hands and feet hadn't turned blue yet, but an hour and a half was a long time to have plastic cutting into your skin. What had started out as a fairly painless manacling was growing more and more unpleasant by the minute.

As if Captain Harry were reading her mind, he adjusted himself on the love seat beside her. "Is it just me, or have the cushions of this settee turned themselves into bricks?"

"I wouldn't know. I can't feel a piddlee-O thing. My butt is completely numb."

"Wish I could say the same," he grumbled. "If I'm not mistaken, my posterior has made a permanent imprint on this cushion." He frowned at the cushion in question.

"It could be worse. We could be stuck outside with Bruce and Nigel."

Captain Harry grimaced. "Can you see them? Are they still on the front deck?"

She craned her head to try to get a peek out the bridge's forward window. But no amount of straining gave her the right angle. And the movement caused the zip tie around her ankles to dig painfully into the top of her bare feet. She settled back into the love seat, blowing out a frustrated, worried breath. "Nope. I can't see anything lower than the front rails."

"I'm sure they're fine," he said. She knew he was trying to soothe her, but there was no mistaking the concern in his voice.

Much to her dismay, Bruce and Nigel had *not* heard her screams and had subsequently been yanked from their cabins and trussed up on the front deck where not one sliver of shade protected their pale English skin from the harsh rays of the relentless subtropical sun. *Add one more thing to my list of regrets.* Then again, if the worst thing the men suffered from this ordeal was a sunburn, she'd count her lucky stars.

For a couple of minutes after Nigel and Bruce were properly tied, the dusky-skinned men had spoken in sharp tones while gesturing wildly toward her and the captain. Maddy got the impression they were trying to determine what was to be done with them, and she wondered why they were being treated differently than Nigel and Bruce.

But it all became clear after she and the captain were marched up to the bridge where they were quickly shackled and assigned permanent spots on the love seat. The man who had punched her in the throat said to Captain Harry in broken English, "If passing vessel call on phone, or…eh…" He shook his head and frowned like he was searching for the word. Then his expression cleared. "Or radio. If someone contact boat, you answer. My accent"—he pointed to his lips—"it bring questions, yes?"

When the captain just blinked at the man, his face took on the mien of a hurricane. Both Maddy and the captain shrank back, trying to dissolve into the love seat. "Answer me!" the man shouted, spittle flying from his lips to cling to his black beard, his obsidian eyes wild.

"Uh, c-certainly," Captain Harry stammered. "It's easy enough for someone to use a boat's name to check marine registries for the vessel's corresponding captain and crew. And I suppose if that someone heard your accent when they were expecting to hear mine, it would raise a few eyebrows."

"Yes." Their captor nodded matter-of-factly, smiling. Or…his face contorted into what Maddy suspected was *supposed* to be a smile. The corners of his eyes crinkled and his lips pulled back to reveal a string of discolored teeth. Then his smile turned to a sneer. "And no you yell for help. If do, my friend put bullet in woman."

He clapped a hand on the shoulder of the grubby guy standing beside him. In response, the scrawny A-hole raised his weapon, pointing the barrel directly between Maddy's eyes. Her lungs caved in on themselves at the same time her mind conjured up a series of satisfying mental images that involved her sticking forks into the necks of every one of her captors.

"Understand me?" the lead A-hole asked, glowering at the captain. Something seemed to move behind his eyes. Something dark and zealous. Something Maddy figured she could go her whole life without ever seeing again.

"I understand you perfectly," Captain Harry replied.

"Good." Lead A-hole dipped his bearded chin. "Then you sit. Stay. Like dogs." He threw his head back, laughing at his own joke, and disappeared through the bridge's door.

He hadn't been back since. Not once. Not when Skinny A-hole Number Two put the *Black Gold* in gear, sailing her to some mysterious spot in the Straits before cutting her engines. Not when the sound of the anchor motors buzzed, alerting Maddy and the captain that they'd reached their destination, which appeared to be exactly…*nowhere*. Not when a deep-sea fishing boat passed by a mile or so off their starboard side. And not when Skinny A-hole Number Two kicked back and fell flat asleep.

Not that she was complaining about Lead A-hole's absence, mind you. In fact, more than once she'd praised the Lord for small miracles. *Amen!* Because she could go the rest of her—

"*Zzzzz-hhhgwww-pppwww.*"

The resounding snore dragged Maddy's attention over to their lone…uh…she supposed the odorific man was now acting as their captain and guard. But given that he was sawing logs like a professional lumberjack, she wasn't exactly sure how much *guarding* he was actually doing.

She leaned over the love seat's armrest, craning her head until she could see around the sleeping man to the top of the console in front of him. *Right there.* The sat-phone was right there. If she could manage to hop over without waking—

"Don't try it," Captain Harry hissed. "The others

could come in at any moment. And if that English-speaking one catches you, I'm afraid..." He let the sentence dangle. After a bit he shook his head. "I was in the military long enough to recognize a man who has killed. And that man has most *certainly* killed. And liked it, if I'm not mistaken." Maybe *that* was that dark, zealous thing she'd seen in their captor's eyes. "Don't *you* be his next victim. We just need to stay calm, keep our heads about us, and do whatever they want."

"But what *do* they want?" she asked. "Are they some sort of...*pirates*? Are they lookin' for ransom? If so, why drag us out here? Why haven't they called—"

That's as far as she got, because the two-way radio on the console crackled to life, a deep voice suddenly filling the bridge. "Motor yacht, motor yacht...this is *Wayfarer-I* off your port-side, over?"

With a snort and cough, Skinny A-hole Number Two sprang awake. The dingy feet he'd propped on the console hit the floor with a *thud*, and he glanced around wildly, blinking as if he was afraid she and the captain may have disappeared on him. When he saw them sitting in the exact spot they'd been before he decided to catch some Z's, he relaxed. That is until that deep voice snapped over the airwaves again.

"I'm hailin' the yacht that is floatin' at the approximate coordinates..." The man on the radio rattled off some numbers, and their guard's bearded chin jerked back. "This is the salvage ship *Wayfarer-I* floatin' some distance off your port-side, do you copy?"

Maddy was equal parts delighted and dismayed by the words echoing through the bridge. A salvage ship could mean salvation! It could also spell doom for the people aboard if the pirates—or terrorists or whatever the hell these guys were—decided to lure them in and open fire.

Her heart started pounding in her chest like the stupid organ was a convict trying to break free of her rib cage. And when she glanced over, it was to find Captain Harry's eyes once again popping clean out of his head.

The skinny guy barked something unintelligible at the captain and pointed his weapon at Harry's chest. Then he did something truly strange. He stuck his thumb and forefinger into his mouth.

Gross. Maddy's top lip curled back. The guy's hands were filthy, caked with dirt. Then a high-pitched whistle blasted from between his teeth, startling her with its volume.

A second later, footsteps thundered up the interior stairs to the bridge and Lead A-hole threw open the door, entering the room with a snarl. He barked something to Skinny A-hole Number Two, who subsequently picked up the handset on the two-way radio.

When it came alive again with, "Motor yacht, motor yacht…this is *Wayfarer-I* off your port-side, hailin' on channel sixteen, do you copy?" Lead A-hole stomped over and snatched the radio from the skinny man's clutches. He turned in their direction, pulling a knife out of the waistband of his trousers.

Maddy's entire body broke out in a cold sweat. Her stomach went from attempting to slide out of her ass to turning a series of flips that made her want to hurl. "*No!*" she screamed when he brandished the weapon in Captain Harry's face. But he didn't stick the thing in the captain's gut as she feared. Instead, he reached around and sliced through Harry's restraints. Straightening, he thrust the handset at the captain. "Answer," he growled. "Send them away."

With shaking fingers, Captain Harry took the handset, pressing the button on the side. "*Wayfar*—" His voice cracked with tension. He had to clear his throat before trying again. "*Wayfarer-I, Wayfarer-I*...this is Captain Harry Tripplehorn on the *Black Gold*. Sorry for the delay in response. I just popped into the loo, over?"

Maddy lifted a brow at the captain—*Quick thinking, Harry, old boy!*—before sitting forward to crane her head to try to get a peek out the bridge's windows. Squinting her eyes, she searched the port-side horizon for the mysterious *Wayfarer-I*.

There! Far enough in the distance that only when the *Black Gold* bobbed to the top of a wave could she see the salvage ship's gray hull glinting dully in the afternoon sun.

"Ahoy, *Black Gold*," the voice crackled from the radio. The man's accent spoke of his Southern heritage. Louisiana or Alabama would be Maddy's guess. His slow drawl and the way he elongated his vowels was different from the Texas twang she was used to hearing. "It's a great day to be at sea, over?"

"A great day, indeed," the captain responded. "Which is why we decided to throw anchor and have a bit of a stay, over?"

Maddy settled stiffly back into the love seat, her mind racing with possibilities. Was the salvage ship far enough away to call in a Mayday without risking reprisal from the men aboard the *Black Gold*? *Yessiree, Bob*. She'd bet her best boots it was. Even though the *Black Gold* was one smooth-sailing vessel, under full steam that salvage ship surely had enough oomph to outpace her.

But how to let the crew on board *Wayfarer-I* know that things on the *Black Gold* were hell and gone from copacetic? How to *get* them to call in that Mayday?

And then she knew…

The next time Captain Harry depressed the button on the handset, she'd scream her lungs out for help. Oh, sure. She might get a bullet in her brain for the effort. But she might also save Harry, Nigel, and Bruce in the process. And since it was her fault they were in the mess to begin with…

Her blood sizzled with adrenaline, her muscles bunching in readiness. She could do this. She *could*. *Get ready, Maddy!*

"Good to hear," came the voice over the airwaves. "We'll be passing by on your starboard side."

She must have been vibrating or something, because Captain Harry dug a pointy elbow into her ribs. Hard. She glanced over at him, noting the nearly imperceptible shake of his chin. She widened her eyes slightly, the facial equivalent of *Now's our chance*. In response, his chin shake became a little more distinct.

Lead A-hole snatched the handset from Harry. Without the button pressed, the connection to the other ship was lost. "Enough," he snarled, leaning in so that some of his spittle landed on the captain's cheek. Knowing just how rank that stuff was, Maddy jerked back, out of the way of the flying dreck. "End it. Now!"

He shoved the handset back at Harry, and the captain took it while still managing to keep his elbow planted firmly in her ribs. "Roger that, *Wayfarer-I*, over and out."

He said the seven words so quickly that they sounded like one big word. *Damnit! There went our chance!*

"Over and out," came the reply as Lead A-hole snatched the handset from Harry and turned to replace it on the receiver.

Maddy narrowed her eyes at the captain.

"This is no time to play the heroine," he grumbled softly, barely moving his lips. But it wouldn't have mattered had he said the words flat out. Their captors were no longer paying them any attention.

Lead A-hole was pacing the length of the bridge, yelling and gesturing wildly. He seemed to be repeating one word a lot. *Banoo. Banoo. Banoo.* What the heck did "banoo" mean?

As for Skinny A-hole Number Two, he'd picked up the binoculars and was staring in the direction of the salvage ship. Occasionally, he answered his cohort with a shrug of his thin shoulders or a quick shake of his head.

Suddenly Lead A-hole, a.k.a. Mr. Rotten Mouth, stomped over to stand in front of the love seat. His face was contorted with rage. His hands clenched into fists. "CIA?" he yelled, flinging his arm out to point a finger toward the approaching vessel.

Maddy and Captain Harry exchanged a look. "Huh?" she asked at the same time the captain said, "I beg your pardon?"

"The ship! The ship!" Their captor was so worked up his voice screeched like a pubescent boy's. Maddy wondered if the big blood vessel pumping in the side of his neck was about to explode.

One can always hope!

"They CIA?" he screamed. "They CIA?"

If the guy thought repeating himself twice made his crazy ramblings any more coherent, he had another think coming.

"You mean the Central Intelligence Agency?" Captain Harry asked.

Maddy's eyes widened as her gaze flew up to Rotten Mouth. "Yes!" he bellowed, his extended arm vibrating with tension. His lips pulled back in a sneer made more revolting by those discolored teeth. And then there it was again. Something moved behind his eyes. Instinctively she shrank away from it.

"Why would they be the CIA?" she asked, her voice barely above a whisper. All that rage that had been fueling her since Lead A-hole hopped on board and punched her in the throat suddenly leaked out of her as if she'd turned into a human sieve. In its place was the fear she should have been feeling all along. *The CIA? For Pete's sake!* "Wh-who are you guys?"

Bam! The backhanded blow happened so fast Maddy didn't have time to duck. Which meant she caught the full force of it square on her cheekbone. Pain exploded. Her brain scrambled. And it took her a solid five seconds to realize she hadn't been run over by a bus or swept up by a hurricane.

Opening her jaw to try to relieve the acute throb in her cheek, it occurred to her that the cartoons got it all wrong. They always showed little birdies floating around the head of someone who was knocked silly, but they should have used bees instead. There was a definite buzzing in her ears.

"Stop it!" Captain Harry yelled, throwing up his hands in front of her. She looked through tear-moist eyes and realized their captor had lifted his arm for another blow.

Lead A-hole slowly lowered his hand, glancing back and forth between her and the captain. And for a heart-beat or two, Maddy got the distinct impression he was considering swinging the machine gun strapped to his back around to the front of his body so he could squeeze the trigger and fill their heads full of lead.

Her mouth went as dry as a West Texas well in a drought, and each of her nerve endings set itself ablaze until her whole body felt like it was covered in fire ants. They say when you're close to death, your life flashes before your eyes. But the only thing filling her vision was the hate-filled face of their captor. And just when she thought they were goners for sure, he turned toward Skinny A-hole Number Two and snarled, "Get rocket launchers."

Número Dos just blinked at him, and that's when Rotten Mouth realized he'd spoken in English. He repeated his order in whatever language they were speaking, and their skinny guard hopped into motion, quickly racing out the door.

"Did he just say rocket launchers?" Maddy husked, her breath wheezing out of her.

"I'm afraid so," Captain Harry answered, shaking his head in disbelief as Lead A-hole pulled a small satellite phone from the pocket of his trousers.

Her mind flashed back to those strange metal tubes she'd seen in the bottom of the dinghy. And she spoke aloud the words that had been circling around in her head for the last ninety minutes. "What did I get us into?"

1:48 p.m....

"See if you can understand what Nassar is saying." Banu angrily handed his satellite phone to Ahmed. "He's all worked up. And when he gets like that, what little English he speaks becomes completely incomprehensible."

Ahmed grabbed the phone, quickly asking a question in Arabic. Then he plugged his ear against the noise of the outboards and the waves splashing against the hull of the rented vessel.

I really should learn the language, Banu thought, leaning back in his seat in the wheelhouse. After his spectacular grand finale as CIA agent Jonathan Wilson, he'd most likely be seeking asylum in a country where Arabic was the mother tongue. And speaking of Jonathan Wilson...he wondered if his boss had noted his absence from work this morning.

Probably not, he figured. Even CIA agents were allowed to call in sick. Of course, his absenteeism would be noted eventually. Probably not today or tomorrow or even the day after. But soon. Fortunately, by then it would be too late. By then it—

"He says there is a salvage ship in the area," Ahmed shouted just as the fishing boat hit the bottom of a wave. It nearly had him dropping the phone. "He wants to know if you want him to sink it with the RPGs?"

"*What?*" Banu yelled, sitting forward. Between the whistle of the wind through the open windows of the wheelhouse and the roar of the engines, he wasn't sure he'd heard the man correctly.

"He wants to sink a salvage ship by using the rocket launchers!"

Okay, so he *had* heard him correctly. "For the love of—" He could feel his blood pressure rise so quickly that his face flushed hot. Nassar was a wonderful asset. Always quick to follow a lead, ever ready to forward the cause. But he was also a crazy sonofabitch. Fanatical to the point of psychosis. "*No!* He doesn't need to draw any unneeded attention to himself. Tell him to let the ship pass." And in case that wasn't clear enough, he added, "Tell him to stand the fuck down!"

Ahmed relayed his words, then his eyes rounded as he listened to Nassar's reply.

Banu's stomach tightened into an uneasy fist. "What?" he demanded. "What is he saying?"

"He says he thinks they are CIA!"

"Why the hell would he think that?" Banu yelled, getting the distinct feeling that Nassar's psychosis had slipped over the line into full-on paranoia. *No, no, no! He'll ruin everything!*

"He says the CIA knows everything, has eyes everywhere! He is determined to sink the ship!"

"Give me the phone," Banu growled, yanking the device from Ahmed's hand. "And cut the engines!" he yelled to one of the men Ahmed had brought with them.

Ahmed repeated his command, and the fishing boat's outboards choked off. For a couple of moments, their forward momentum carried them across the tops of the waves. Banu waited. Only when the boat finally glided to a stop, bobbing gently with the tide, did he lift the phone to his ear. Breathing deeply of the salty air and trying to ignore the overpowering aroma of marine fuel, he was careful to keep his tone modulated when he spoke.

"Nassar, I know you think the CIA knows everything. But the movies lie. This is a big world and the Central Intelligence Agency can't have eyes everywhere at all times. And I would know, right? I've been working for them for a very long time."

It took a brief moment to hear Nassar's reply, since the phones they were using routed their signals through fifteen different satellites to avoid detection and to thwart anyone from possibly trying to triangulate their position. Yeah, Banu knew all the tricks.

"They coming," Nassar hissed, then raised his voice until his tone bordered on berserk. In response, the hairs along the back of Banu's neck lifted. "The ship coming!"

"It's fine," he soothed. "I'm sure it's fine."

"No," Nassar insisted. "CIA know chemicals missing. They try trick us! They try—"

"Shut up and listen!" Banu yelled into the phone. Trying to calm the idiot wasn't working. So now he'd move on to tough love. "They are *not* the CIA! Yes"—he glanced down at his watch—"you're right. The Company probably knows the chemicals are missing by now. But with the security system malfunctioning in the warehouse, they won't have the first clue where to start looking."

"But—"

Banu continued speaking as if Nassar hadn't tried to interrupt. "It will take them hours, maybe days, to connect the dots to you and your men. And it will take longer than that for them to figure out you left Cuba by boat. But even if somehow they *have* already figured out it was you and that you left by boat, they'll be looking for that wreck of a boat you bought, not a big, shiny yacht."

And *that* had been a stroke of luck he hadn't counted

on. When Nassar called a bit ago to say he'd hijacked
the passing vessel, Banu began to suspect this mission—
despite the one little hiccup of the sinking trawler— was
indeed blessed by Allah. Too many pieces of the puzzle
were falling into place for it not to be. Of course, the four
people aboard the yacht would have to be killed once
they weren't needed as possible hostages, but that was
a minor inconvenience best left for later. For now, he
just had to make sure Nassar didn't do anything stupid.

"Do you hear me, Nassar?" he asked. "Do you
understand?" It was a rhetorical question. Even though
Nassar's spoken English was atrocious, the man com-
prehended every word of the language.

Banu waited a beat for the signal to bounce around
the globe and back. Finally, "Yes, Banu. I understand."

"Good." He breathed a sigh of relief. "That's good.
Now, hold steady until we get there. Can you do that
for me?"

"Yes. Good," Nassar said, and before Banu could add
anything more, the signal went dead. *Ah, well*. He blew
out a breath, soothing himself with the knowledge that
Nassar had sounded far less hysterical there at the end.

"All is as it should be?" Ahmed asked.

"I think so." He silently added, *I hope so*.

"Nassar is a passionate man. And sometimes he is too
quick to act. But he knows how important this is. He will
not disappoint you, brother."

This time Banu spoke the words aloud. "I hope so."
Then he waved a hand at the man behind the wheel.
"Okay, let's go."

The command didn't need a translation. As the motor-
boat's engines came to life with a coughing sputter,

Banu turned his mind away from the disturbing thoughts of Nassar and the possibility the man might indeed fuck everything up to more pleasant things. Things like the blow he'd deliver to the U.S. and its overfed, overconfident, overly entitled populace. Things like the scores of people who, after exposure to the cyclosarin, would foam at the mouth and scratch at their throats and eyes until they drew blood. Things like the news stories that would echo around the world.

He smiled with the knowledge that, as the mastermind of the whole thing, his name would go down in the annals of time, remembered by most, discussed by many, and revered by some. He would be like Timothy McVeigh or Osama bin Laden! The man to strike at the heart of an empire!

His dick twitched to life, swelling at the thought of what was to come. He had to covertly hook his heel over his knee and drop his hands into his lap. He sure as shit didn't want to give these guys the wrong idea...

Chapter Nine

1:58 p.m....

OLIVIA THUMBED OFF THE SECURE SATELLITE phone and turned toward the group still gathered in the pilothouse.

"Well?" Leo asked, unhooking the sunglasses from the collar of his T-shirt and sliding them onto his face when a beam of sunlight caught the crest of a wave and glinted in through the window. She couldn't help but recall how he'd casually tossed them onto the table in the galley right before he— "What did Morales have to say?"

"Morales? Oh yeah. Right." She shook her head. *What is your problem?* But she knew. It was Leo Anderson. Leo Anderson and his too-handsome face. Leo Anderson and his mind-numbing kisses. Leo Anderson and his—

"Y'okay there, Agent Mortier?" Bran asked. When she glanced over at him, there was a smug, knowing grin tilting his lips. Like Leo, Bran was nothing if not perceptive.

"I'm fine," she assured him, skewering him with her iciest expression, hoping to freeze that smile right off his face. To her utter annoyance, it didn't work. Bran's grin only became sunnier.

Jerk.

"Director Morales said the *Black Gold* is registered to some sort of Texas oil tycoon out of Houston." She turned her attention from Bran to Leo. *Nope.* That was no good. Not if she wanted to remember whatever the hell she was talking about. Because those lips…those fabulous male lips made her forget her own name, much less anything else. His ear, then. She would focus her gaze on his very innocuous earlobe…that she wanted to suck straight into her mouth. *Friggin'-A!* Okay, so that left…Wolf. There. Good. She would keep her gaze squarely on Wolf's fierce, uncompromising face.

"Its captain is listed as one Harold Tripplehorn, and its marine logs show it has docked in ports all over the Caribbean and some in Central and South America. Pretty standard for the yacht of a rich Texas businessman." She shrugged her shoulders. "Morales seems to think it's legit."

"And he doesn't think it's awfully coincidental that this yacht is anchored less than two hundred yards from the GPS coordinates those signals are sendin' us?" Leo asked.

Damnit. She was left with no recourse but to turn to him. To address Wolf when answering Leo's question would be…well…*weird.* Girding herself against that bearded jaw and that flyaway thatch of golden hair, she shook her head. "He checked the port registries. According to the marina in Nassau, the *Black Gold* checked out of customs and weighed anchor yesterday evening for a return trip to Houston. A slow sail would pretty much put her right about here."

"And a fast sail might have had her somewhere around Gitmo last night and out here this morning," Wolf said.

"That's a negative." She shook her head, thankful for a reason to turn her attention back to him. "According to Morales's calculations, even if the *Black Gold* was steaming at full speed, she couldn't have left Bermuda and made it to Gitmo in time to pick up the terrorists last night. Not by a long shot."

"And you trust Morales and his calculations?" Bran asked, his expression suddenly serious. It was beyond bizarre how the guy could do that. Go from frivolous to fierce in two seconds flat.

"He didn't get to his position by being an idiot," she assured him. Then she glanced around at the faces of the three remaining SEALs. Despite their retirement, they *were* still SEALs. She'd worked with the spec-ops community long enough to know there was no such thing as a "former" SEAL. Once a SEAL, always a SEAL.

"Thoughts, gentlemen?" Leo asked, not surprising her in the least with his question. He was the only commanding officer she'd ever met who never made a decision until he listened to the opinions of his men. Probably one of the reasons why the eight of them had lasted nearly fifteen years running the kind of operations that usually claimed one in five.

Then it hit her like it always hit her, a two-by-four right between the eyes. There were no longer eight of them. There were only seven. *Holy shit*, the memory of Rusty turning to her from where he had landed on the floor in that hall after armor-piercing rounds cut through his ceramic bulletproof vest flashed in front of her eyes. Blood had been on his lips, flecking his face. More had already begun to pool around his body...

"Run, Agent Mortier!" he bellowed, swinging around to return fire. The thump, thump *of his M4 discharging*

*rounds at a mind-boggling rate was interspersed with
the higher-pitched* tat-tat *of the rebels' AK-47s.*

I shouldn't have done that, *she thought, her mind
racing through the chain of events that had brought
her...brought* them...*here.* I shouldn't have shot the
general. *Though, given that he'd been dialing his phone,
she didn't see what other choice she'd had.* But surely
there was another way...

*Her pistol jumped in her hand as she fired from
around the relative safety of the corner, waiting for the
right moment, a lull in the shooting, when she could
drag Rusty down the hall with her. And it was strange,
but everything seemed to be moving in slow motion. The
plaster on the corner of the wall was crumbling under
the barrage of steady gunfire, but she could count
each chunk as it flew in front of her face. The* clack *of
her pistol cycling a fresh cartridge into the chamber
sounded particularly loud as her heart beat a steady*
lub-dub *like a bass drum.*

*Good God. She'd just killed a man. She'd pulled her
gun and placed a round right between his surprised
eyes, and—*

"Go!" *Rusty bellowed again. And with that one word,
time sped up. She couldn't count the plaster chunks.
There were hundreds of them. She couldn't hear her
pistol cycling rounds, not above the roar of the firefight.
And her heartbeat wasn't steady. It was thundering!*

*Turkey-peeking around the corner, she saw her
chance. Now!*

*She ran the three steps to Rusty, sliding on the tile
floor as she grabbed the strap on his body armor and
pulled with all she had. Gritting her teeth, her muscles*

straining, her combat-booted feet scrabbling on the slick tile, she inched his immense weight backward.

Thump! Thump! Thump! *His M4 spit forth a hail of cover fire.*

Bang! Bang! Bang! *In her free hand, her pistol pumped out hot lead. She was shooting blind at the corner the rebels were hiding behind. But she figured even if she didn't hit any of them, it was enough to keep them there. And that's all she needed. Just a little time. Just a couple of seconds…*

"Leave me!" *Rusty yelled again, even as he continued to lay on his trigger.* "I'm done!"

"No fucking way!" *she screamed just as…*click, click, click…*her clip ran dry. She shoved the Sig into the back of her cargo pants and grabbed the other shoulder strap on his body armor. With a mighty heave, she pulled him around the corner.*

The minute she did, the rebels opened fire and the wall once more began to disintegrate. The plaster exploded in powdery blocks, adding a chalky smell to air that was already rife with the scents of spent cordite and fresh blood.

Rusty rolled onto his stomach and angled his M4 around the corner to continue firing. He was racked by coughing, the sound wet and sickening. Chest wound. *She could hear it. Even now his lungs were filling with fluid.*

"I'm a dead man!" *he told her.*

"Not yet, you aren't!" *she yelled, retrieving an extra clip from her pocket. Grabbing her Sig, she ejected the old magazine and slammed in the new. And that's when a round crashed into Rusty's skull. Blood flew from*

*his head and he dropped to the floor, immobile in an
instant. Now he was dead...*

*"Rusty!" She screamed his name, the wall exploding
under renewed enemy fire. She ducked down, her heart
breaking into a million pieces, her stomach disgorging
her lunch so violently it hit the wall across from her.
And in those seconds when she was too busy puking her
guts up to fire, the rebels closed in. The sound of their
boots pounded down the hall in her direction. Getting
her mutinous stomach under control and realizing she
was left with no other choice, she spared Rusty one last
look before turning and running for the back door.*

"...like Morales seems to think," Bran was saying
when she suddenly found herself yanked from the past
back into the present. It happened so fast, she suffered
mental whiplash.

Holy hell. That memory always struck when she least
expected it, hitting her like a freight train and leaving
her emotionally broken and bloody. If she wasn't mistaken, that was her stomach crawling up into her throat,
ready and waiting to disgorge its contents all over the
pilothouse. She couldn't *believe* Rusty had survived
his wounds long enough for Leo and his men to find
him. She would have sworn on her mother's grave that
he'd died instantly with that last shot. And even though
Morales had assured her time and again there was nothing she could have done differently, nothing he said
could suppress her guilt at having left Rusty there. Still
alive. Still—

"I say we sail on by them and see what we see,"
Bran continued, and Olivia covertly sucked in a ragged

breath, forcing herself to exhale past the vise crushing her chest. After she managed that, she swallowed repeatedly until her stomach resumed its usual position. Then she pushed the terrible memory back into its safe, separate mental compartment and slammed the door shut. *And stay there!*

She couldn't change the past, no matter how much she wanted to. But at least she could concentrate on the present. And in the name of that…

"If everything is on the up-and-up, they won't bat a lash if we drop anchor and make a dive," Bran added. "We're a salvage ship. They'll just assume we found something worth salvaging."

"And if Morales is wrong and somehow they're not on the up-and-up?" Wolf asked.

"Well, I guess we'll need to be locked and loaded, won't we?" Leo said.

"Roger that." Bran nodded.

Mason muttered something, and Olivia looked over at him with a start. The man made being motionless an art. She'd forgotten he was in the pilothouse with them. Though how that could be, since he was the relative size and shape of a Mack truck, she'd never know.

"What did you say?" she asked.

"The contractors," he said, his Beantown pronunciation making the word sound more like "cahntractahs." "Did Morales say when the fuck they'd be joining us?"

"They're having trouble fixing their prop, and the current is pulling them in the opposite direction. Morales says the best-case scenario is an ETA of two, maybe three hours. Do you all want to wait for them? Or do you still want to do this Han-style?"

Leo looked around at his men, one brownish-blond brow lifted above the frames of his mirrored aviators.

"Let's just get this over with," Bran proposed. "I don't know about the rest of you guys, but I'm over this suck-ass gig. And those steaks I threw in the refrigerator back home won't eat themselves." He lifted his wrist to check the big, black diver's watch he wore. "I figure if we get the lead out, I can have them on the grill by nineteen hundred tonight."

"So in the legendary words of Larry the Cable Guy"—Leo smiled, that brow of his quirked even higher—"you're ready to git 'er done?"

Bran's mouth twitched, and for a couple of seconds the two men just stared at each other. Olivia frowned. *Apparently, I'm missing something here.* Then Bran winked and said, "Exactly."

"And the rest of you?" Leo asked.

"'Time and tide wait for no man,'" Wolf said, then added, "I could use a steak."

Mason simply grunted, which she'd come to understand was the same as a *yes*.

"Done." Leo smacked his hand on the back of the pilot's seat. "Wolf, put us in gear. Mason and Bran, you guys go downstairs and grab the weapons. You know, just in case."

And even though Leo was no longer their commanding officer, the men followed his orders without hesitation. After Bran and Mason disappeared belowdecks, Leo walked to the back of the pilothouse, motioning for Olivia to follow.

Her eyes automatically traveled down the length of his broad back to his trim waist. Then lower. To his ass.

Where they stopped so fast it was a wonder they didn't leave skid marks on the backs of her eye sockets.

She couldn't help herself. The man had an amazing ass. All high and tight and—

Oh, for the love of Peter, Paul, and Mary. There she went again. And this emotional roller coaster she was riding, filled with guilt and ready to blow chunks one minute and brimming with lust and eager to knock boots the next, was getting really old, really fast. Not to mention keeping her slightly disoriented and wound tighter than a suicide bomber.

"What?" she whispered after Leo stopped at the far wall, glancing surreptitiously over her shoulder at the back of Wolf's head.

The feel of Leo's big, callused hand gently gripping her upper arm had her head whipping back around. They were standing so close she had to tilt her chin way back to look up at him. She couldn't help but wonder which hue his hazel eyes had taken on behind those blasted sunglasses.

"I'm wonderin' what your plans are after we retrieve those chemicals," he said, his voice low and rumbling through her chest. Her stupid nipples perked up as if he'd specifically chosen the timbre to titillate them. And *wheeee! Here I go again, riding that damned roller coaster up another hill!*

"What do you mean?"

He stuck his tongue in his cheek. "I guess I was hopin' you'd be willin' to pass the capsules off to your A-Team and sail with me back to Wayfarer Island. I can have Wolf or Romeo fly you to Key West to catch a flight to DC tomorrow mornin'."

His words slid into her like a spoon into melting ice cream, and something warm and delicious unfurled low in her belly. "Leo Anderson, are you asking me to spend the night with you?" *Oh, please*, begged a part of her, the decidedly downstairs part. *Good God, should you be doing that?* asked a voice in her head. *I don't know if I'll be able to love him and leave him*, admitted her heart.

When he said, "You know I am," she studiously chose to ignore the latter two. Especially when he scooted closer so he was crowding her, letting her feel him against her. And the look he gave her, the arched brow, the twisting of his wonderful lips? Well, it ranked about a nine…no, ten…on the panty-melting scale. Her heart tripped over itself. Her breaths came so fast and shallow one would think she'd never been seduced by a man before. Although, in all honesty, she'd never been seduced by a man who could hold a candle to Leo.

"You don't beat around the bush, do you?"

"Not anymore," he whispered, leaning down until his mouth was a hairsbreadth from hers. "I want to finish what we started down there in that galley. *Hell*, what we started a year and a half ago in Syria. Don't you want to finish it too?"

"God, yes," she admitted, watching his lips curve into a smile that could only be described as triumphant and…*male*.

2:10 p.m.…

Leo stood on deck, binoculars raised to his eyes as the salvage ship sliced through the softly rolling seas. Waves shushed against her freshly painted hull, and the big engines hummed with newly tuned health. Beside him, Olivia mirrored his stance, one hand on the rail to steady herself against the gentle rocking of the vessel and the other holding a small pair of field glasses to her eyes.

And maybe he was just being fanciful, but he would swear he could smell her alluring scent drifting toward him on the breeze. Which, you know, might account for the semi he was sporting. Then again, perhaps that had more to do with the fact that she'd agreed to finally, *finally* be his.

For tonight, he was quick to remind himself. *Just for tonight*.

For some reason, that thought brought with it a vague sense of unhappiness. Not because he was against one-night stands. For shit's sake, one-and-dones were pretty standard for spec-ops guys. The covert nature of their jobs didn't lend itself to maintaining stable relationships, and it was a rare woman indeed who could send her man out the door time after time, not knowing where he was going, not knowing when he'd come back…*if* he'd come back. And then if he *did* come back, not being able to ask him anything about where he'd been or what he'd done. That's why most of the SEALs Leo knew, himself included, opted for the occasional trip to Pound Town with a woman who didn't want anything more than the use of his hard body for some sweaty, unbridled sex.

No, sir, that indefinite sense of…*discontentment* digging into the back of his brain like a damned chigger didn't have a motherfrickin' thing to do with him being against slam-bam, thank-you-ma'ams as a general rule. But more because he suspected he was against them when it specifically came to Olivia.

The truth of the matter was, he…well, he *liked* her. Like, really, really *liked* her. She was quick to crack wise and easy to laugh. She knew when to talk and when to shut up—like during those myriad sunsets they'd shared in Syria, sitting shoulder-to-shoulder on the hillside, not saying anything, just being near each other and taking comfort in that nearness, that small human connection.

He always knew where he stood with her; she didn't pull her punches with him. And yet he had a sense that she was keeping a part of herself separate, a part of herself…*secret*. She was a whip-smart open book wrapped in a riddle and tied up with a mystery. In a word: fascinating…or maybe captivating…or perhaps *intriguing* better described her.

Whatever she was, he remembered having an epiphany about two months into their assignment in Syria. *She's what I've been looking for…waiting for.* The thought had exploded inside his brain like an IED. Stunning him. Wrecking him.

Truth to tell, he hadn't been the same since. And despite having teased her with that whole *Are you askin' me to go steady?* business down there in the galley, the fact of the matter was he was scared shitless that once he finally got her in his arms, he wouldn't want to let her go.

"Holy jeez, Leo," she said, breaking into his thoughts. "You need to invest in some oil."

He lowered his binoculars to find her watching him. The wind and the sun had pinkened her cheeks, making her eyes seem that much bluer.

Arresting…

He snapped mental fingers. *That's the one!* She was

the most arresting woman he'd ever met. Of course, right now she was more like the most *confusing* woman he'd ever met. *Invest in oil? What the what?* He decided to go with his standard Einstein-esque rebuttal of, "Huh?"

"Those hamsters are running so fast up there"—she pointed to his head—"that their wheels are squeaking and I can hear them all the way over here."

See? What had he said? Quick to crack wise.

"Are you sayin' I'm thinkin' too loud?" He grinned down at her.

The wind caught the end of her ponytail, blowing some of the inky black strands across her cheek and lips. She brushed them away, and his gaze zeroed in on her hand. The memory of her fingers in his hair as she hungrily ate at his mouth had the semi he was sporting pulse into a full-fledged cockstand. Apparently the self-love belowdecks was no match for the power of that kiss. Or even just the *memory* of the power of that kiss.

"A penny for your thoughts?" she said.

He snorted so loudly it was a wonder he didn't swallow his tonsils.

"What?" She tilted her head.

"Nothin'," he told her.

"Doesn't sound like nothing."

He bit the inside of his cheek. "Do you ever get the feelin' we talk in circles?"

"Not me," she insisted. "It's you."

"Me?" he scoffed. "I'm not the one with somethin' to hide." He spread his arms wide. "I'm a civilian now. What you see is what you get."

"And what do you think *I* have to hide?" she asked,

her expression turning enigmatic. *Yessir, and* there's *the CIA agent I've come to know and…um…*know. Why did he keep getting hung up on that last part?

"If I knew that," he told her, "we wouldn't be havin' this conversation, would we?"

For a moment she studied his face, then frowned. "How did this get turned around to me, anyway? I thought we were talking about what's going on in *your* head." She lifted a hand to shade her eyes.

Without hesitation or conscious thought, he pulled off his sunglasses and slid them onto her face.

"Thanks," she told him. "That's very gentlemanly. Is it meant to be a distraction from my question?"

"I am nothin' if not gentlemanly, darlin'." He intentionally thickened his accent, smacking his gum cheekily.

"Mmm." She pursed her lips. The gesture could either be construed as annoyance or an invitation for a kiss. He decided to place his money on the latter and bent down to quickly—

"There's movement on deck!" Bran called from his position farther along the railing.

Smirking up at Leo, Olivia whispered in that smoky voice of hers, "To be continued?"

"You bet your ass." He was grinning when he straightened and lifted the binoculars to his face. Olivia did the same beside him. They were close enough to the *Black Gold* that minor details aboard the gleaming black yacht snapped into sharp focus. The bright glint of the stainless-steel fittings. The rich teakwood decking. And the line of four dudes standing at the railing. Leo narrowed his eyes. The men were thin, bearded, and wearing stained clothes—not at all the kind of crew one would expect on a multimillion-dollar yacht. But he cataloged all of that as an aside, because what immediately snagged his attention were the familiar diagonal belts fastened across their torsos.

Gun straps. Like the one he was wearing. The hair on his arms stood up at the same time Olivia whispered, "Sonofabitch!"

"LT!" Bran yelled, jogging toward them.

"Yeah." A quick spurt of adrenaline burned through Leo's blood as he quickly glassed the rest of the vessel, trying to count heads, trying to determine exactly what it was they were dealing with. "I see 'em."

"So much for Morales's calculations," Bran grumbled, stopping beside Leo and Olivia. The clanking sound his M4 made as he swung it around to the front of his body registered in the subconscious portion of Leo's brain. He'd hoped he was being overly cautious when he'd instructed his friends to lock and load. But he should have known better. Like most missions, this one was turning out to have more curves than a barrel full of snakes. *Son of a frickin'-frackin' bitch!*

"I don't understand it," Olivia said. "Morales isn't wrong about these things. Maybe the marina's records were tampered with or—"

"Oh, ay! Who cares how it happened," Bran interrupted her.

"I do," she hissed. "It doesn't make any sense. Even if the terrorists somehow had ties with the yacht or the captain or the Texas oil tycoon, why would they toss the chemicals overboard? Why would they—"

That's as much as Leo heard, because right then he noticed a man standing on the landing by the back door of the *Black Gold*'s bridge. The guy was looking through his own set of binoculars, and Leo knew the instant he saw the weapon in Bran's hand because the man lowered his field glasses and yelled something to the four guys on deck.

Leo quickly adjusted his sights to the yacht's lower level. And what he saw through the magnified lenses had his heart growing frog legs and jumping into his throat. Unlike most folks who froze in the face of danger or imminent death, spec-ops warriors were trained to use their adrenaline to sharpen their minds and enhance their reactions. Which was why, without a moment's hesitation, he dropped his field glasses overboard and grabbed Olivia's arm.

"Rocket launchers!" he bellowed, yanking her away from the rail. "Run!"

Chapter Ten

OLIVIA WASN'T SURE IF SHE WAS RUNNING ACROSS *Wayfarer-I*'s deck or being carried by Leo. She felt like her legs were spinning uselessly in the air, Scooby-Doo style. But one thing she *was* certain of was that the two words a person never wanted to hear back-to-back were "rocket" and "launchers." That *is* what he'd yelled, right?

Holy shit! What the hell is happening?

She didn't have time to think of an answer to that question because Leo grabbed the back waistband of her shorts and, with a mighty heave-ho, promptly tossed her overboard.

"Go with Olivia!" she thought she heard him yell. She couldn't be sure. Not with the humid air whipping by her ears and the bright turquoise water rushing up at her at an alarming rate.

Oh God! Oh God! Oh—

Sploosh!

She'd read somewhere that hitting the water from any sort of height was pretty much the same as hitting concrete. Sure as shit, she could vouch. The wind was punched out of her by the impact, her belly and chest on fire from the blow. She was immediately enveloped in the arms of the ocean, the warm water sucking her down, down, down...

Swim, Olivia! Kick your legs!

Yep. That's what she should be doing all right. And it's certainly what she *wanted* to be doing. But her body seemed to be experiencing some sort of disconnect from her brain. The shock of the collision with the water's surface had scrambled her synapses. Deeper and deeper she sank until the sea began to press in on her, squeezing her, lulling her with its liquid embrace even though her lungs burned.

A hard hand suddenly gripped her shoulder. And that physical human touch was all she needed to break the dark spell of the ocean, to jump-start her brain-body connection. *Hip-hip-hooray!* Her legs and arms were working again!

The first thing she did was let go of the binoculars that, strangely enough, she'd managed to hold on to during her free fall and subsequent brutal introduction to the sea. Then she kicked as hard as she could toward the surface, clawing against the water. She knew Bran was swimming beside her, a strong hand pulling her upward toward the light sparkling on the rippling waves overhead. Still, even with the two of them working…

Oh God! I'm not going to make it! She'd waited too long, allowed herself to sink too deep. The urge to suck in a breath was overwhelming. Her mouth opened of its own accord, filling with salty water. And just when she started to convulse against the need to breathe — "*Ahhhhh!*" — she broke the surface, sucking in a lungful of sweet, glorious air. Water too, from the wave that immediately slammed her square in the face.

She doubled in on herself, coughing and hacking.

"Are you okay?" Bran shouted, paddling beside her and helping her tread water as waves carelessly bobbed them up and down like so much living flotsam and jetsam.

"Y-yes," she managed, dragging in another gulp of oxygen only to dissolve into more retching coughs.

That seemed to be all the confirmation he needed because as soon as she was able to keep herself afloat, he released her to yell, "LT! What's doing up there, bro?"

There was no response.

Olivia brushed the water from her eyes, blinking as more dripped down from her sodden hair. They'd already drifted some distance from the salvage ship, the currents in the Straits being wickedly fast. She scanned the hull of *Wayfarer-I* for Leo, then the rail. Nothing. No shaggy blond hair. No broad, T-shirt-covered shoulders. Just a big, gray boat.

"D-did I hear him correctly?" she managed, coughing again and expelling the last of the moisture from her lungs. Her heart was pounding so hard her whole body throbbed in rhythm to it. "Did he say rocket launchers?"

"That's what I thought he—"

BOOM!

Wayfarer-I was rocked by a massive explosion. Olivia felt the percussive effects in her chest, like fireworks on New Year's Eve or mortar rounds in Syria. The displaced air blew her sodden hair back from her face.

He *had* said "rocket launchers." She couldn't *believe* it! Nor could she see exactly where the ship was hit. Somewhere low on the hull on the opposite side would be her guess, given the thin puff of smoke that drifted like a crooked, gray finger into the air. And although

Wayfarer-I still seemed to be mostly intact, her metal hull was squealing like a dying pig.

Where was Leo? Was he anywhere near where that rocket struck? Olivia became paralyzed by fear. Her heart stopped, her lungs froze, and her muscles went completely slack. Only her vocal cords continued to work as she screamed, her throat shredding with the effort, "Leo! Where are you?"

———————

2:15 p.m....

Leo cursed, his shoulder slamming into the bulkhead of the stairwell when *Wayfarer-I* took a direct hit to her hull. The ship groaned with the impact, shuddering and whimpering in the aftermath. The lights flickered on and off, on and off, then went out altogether. Somewhere up on the bridge an alarm sounded.

Shit on a shovel! This will be the end of her.

He knew it as surely as he knew his name was Leonardo David Anderson. And all that money, all that time and effort to clean up *Wayfarer-I* and make her into a vessel capable of hunting for the *Santa Cristina* had come to naught with one well-placed, likely Soviet-era rocket launcher.

And what are the odds?

He didn't know whether to laugh or cry. Reckoned he didn't have time for either.

"Wolf!" he yelled, sprinting up the stairs toward the pilothouse. "Mason!" He'd only climbed two treads when Wolf appeared in front of him, dark and quiet as a shadow. A well-armed shadow. Wolf's Colt was clutched in his right hand. In his left was Olivia's satellite phone. *Good thinkin', man.*

Before Leo could say the words aloud, Wolf growled, "Sonofabitching rocket launcher. Can you believe it? We need to abandon—"

"I know!" Leo cut him off. "Where's Mason?"

"He said he was moving the dive tanks from the computer room to the deck. I'll go find him."

"No." Leo shook his head. "Bran and Olivia are already overboard." Olivia… He hoped to hell he hadn't hurt her when he sent her flying—would never forgive himself if he had—but he'd seen no other way. The rocket could have hit the deck where they were standing, or it could have hit the fuel tanks and sent the whole ship up in flames, and he'd wanted…no, he'd *needed* to know she was overboard and safe. "You launch the dinghy. I'll grab Mason and meet you on deck."

"Copy that." Wolf followed him down the stairs, adding, "And damn it all to hell," which was as close as the guy ever came to expressing surprise or concern about anything.

"You said it," Leo concurred as they hit the landing. He turned toward the interior of the ship, but Wolf stopped him with a hand on his shoulder. "Hurry. They may not stop with one shot."

"Ten-four." Leo jerked his chin, their eyes meeting just as they had on countless missions and over myriad battlefields. The look they exchanged said it all. *Stay frosty, watch your six, and soldier the fuck up.*

Wolf disappeared through the exit. When the door slammed shut, Leo made his way farther into the ship. He was standing at the opening to the empty computer room when the second rocket hit the back of the vessel. *BOOOOMMM! Wayfarer-I* shimmied, her rivets popping, her seams bursting. He stumbled backward on impact, slamming into the hallway bulkhead. His weapon dug into his back, pinching skin and muscle, but his adrenaline levels were running at damn near full capacity, which meant he barely felt it. With effort, he steadied himself against the now-listing ship.

That one was *near the fuel tanks. Fuck. A. Duck!*

"Mason!" he yelled down the stairs leading to the galley and the crew's quarters. "Mason! You down there?" He couldn't see much; the only illumination belowdecks came from the few stray beams of sunlight drifting in through the portholes. He cocked an ear. Didn't hear a thing other that the death groans of his beloved *Wayfarer-I* and the high-pitched *bee-doo-bee-doo-bee-doo* of the alarm in the pilothouse. Acrid smoke drifted into the interior of the ship, scratching the inside of his throat like he'd swallowed chunks of coral. His eyes watered.

"Hold together just a couple minutes more, ol' girl," he begged as he raced back down the not-quite-horizontal hall toward the exit. He burst through the door like the Kool-Aid Pitcher Guy used to burst through the walls on those old commercials. But he decided to forgo the accompanying *Oh yeah*. The sun momentarily blinded him when he stumbled onto the deck, skidding to a halt to get his bearings and allow his eyes to adjust.

Once they did, he saw smoke curling from the ship's hull, a thin gray stream near the forward section, and a menacing black cloud puffing rhythmically from the aft. Wolf was by the railing, sawing away at the nylon

ropes attaching the dinghy to the hydraulic crane meant
to lower it into the water.

"Power's out!" Wolf yelled when he spotted Leo.

"I know!" Leo hollered back, frantically searching
the deck for Mason. Nothing. *Where are you?* Was it
possible the big guy had been down in the engine room
or generator room when that second rocket hit? *No.* Leo
refused to consider it. He would *not* lose a man on this
mission, by God!

"Have you seen Mason up here?" he yelled just
as the water rushing into the ship's hull reached a
tipping point.

The whole vessel lurched, groaning mightily. Leo
hopped out of his flip-flops to use his bare feet for better
traction on a deck that was now angled at about twenty
degrees from horizontal. For added security, he had a
white-knuckled grip on the corner of the bridge house.

Not much time now…

"Haven't seen him!" Wolf yelled. He'd managed to
cut the front of the dinghy free. The little boat dangled
precariously over the side of the vessel by a single rope
attached to one plastic cleat. Having already steadied
himself against *Wayfarer-I*'s new list, Wolf was hard
at work slicing at the remaining rope. "And she won't
stay afloat much longer!" he continued. "We need to—"

Snap! Whack! The nylon cord succumbed to the
razor-sharp edge of Wolf's blade, and the front of the
rubber boat hit the ship's railing. The whole thing somersaulted over itself before falling into the sea.

"I'm not leavin' until I find Mason!"

Wolf scanned the ocean, then the ship. "There!"
he pointed, and Leo raced, or more like *climbed*—the

deck was now at something approaching a thirty-degree angle—to the railing in time to see Mason emerge from the back of the vessel near the J-frame winch they were supposed to use to haul riches from the seabed. *So much for that!*

Mason held up an armful of orange life jackets—Leo's friends were nothing if not good in a pinch—then snapped Leo a saucy salute, climbed the railing, and chucked himself overboard. He hit the water like a bag of boulders and started stroking toward the dinghy that had landed upside down. Leo breathed a sigh of relief.

"After you," he told Wolf, gesturing toward the little boat below while adjusting the strap of his M4 more securely over his shoulder.

"Nah." Wolf shook his head. "After *you*."

"Don't make me kick your ass up between your shoulder blades, Wolf."

Wolf grinned, his face splitting around a mouthful of blinding white teeth. "Right on. Luck belongs to the brave and the…uh…stubborn, yeah?" Then he mirrored Mason's salute before leaping from the ship, an ululating Cherokee war cry piercing the air on his way down.

Only after all his men…his *friends*…were in the water did Leo jump.

———

2:20 p.m….

Olivia's muscles burned with the effort of fighting the waves and the current, but she didn't register any pain. The relief and elation she felt watching Leo haul himself into the dinghy after the three men managed to flip it over eclipsed everything else.

Thank God!

If she thought she'd been paralyzed by fear when that first rocket slammed into *Wayfarer-I*, it was nothing compared to the soul-shredding terror she experienced when that second rocket hit, accompanied by a huge fireball that had risen some thirty feet into the air. She'd frantically searched the railing, looking, looking, *hoping* he hadn't been anywhere near the point of impact. Then ash fell like great, gray snowflakes into the sea. She'd caught herself watching them detachedly, her mind struggling to grasp the reality of just how badly this entire mission had gone off the rails.

Like a locomotive driven by the devil and shooting straight to hell...

Weird how that phrase had come back to her after all these years. It'd been Timmy's favorite expression during that summer he spent with her in the orphanage while his mother did a stint in the county jail. He'd been her friend. The only friend she'd ever made there, actually. But then his mother got out, picked him up, and the letters he promised to write never came. Olivia had been heartbroken at the time, and maybe that sense of heartbreak was what had brought the memory back.

Next thing she'd known, Mason was flying off *Wayfarer-I*, an armful of life jackets trailing their straps behind him. Then Wolf took the plunge, his banshee scream enough to raise goose bumps on the dead. And then, finally, *finally*...Leo appeared. He climbed the rail, turned to give his beloved ship one last glance—even from a distance, the look on his face had completely gutted her—and jumped.

She noticed he was the last to abandon the vessel. No doubt waiting until all of his men were safe before saving his own neck, the big, brave, *foolish* sonofabitch.

Now she heard the choking cough of the dinghy's small outboard engine trying to come to life. Wolf was yanking on the pull cord with all he had, his deeply tanned skin shiny with water. But the sound of the unresponsive engine was soon drowned out by the shriek of the salvage ship as her hull buckled with the heat of the fire burning somewhere deep in her belly. *Wayfarer-I* was listing severely now, tipped almost completely on her side.

Come on, come on, Olivia silently begged the dinghy's engine. *Start. START!*

"I can't see the yacht. Can you?" Bran asked, spitting out a mouthful of briny water when a wave momentarily washed over his face.

She craned her neck, kicking her bare feet harder in an effort to lift herself higher out of the water. Lord knew where her flip-flops were. Somewhere on the bottom of the Straits, along with her binoculars and Leo's sunglasses, no doubt.

"No dice," she told him. "The salvage ship's hull is in the way."

"So we have no idea if they're satisfied with sinking the *Wayfarer*," he said, unconsciously reaching behind his head to finger the butt of the weapon protruding over his left shoulder, "or if they plan to come and finish us off."

"I can't even think about what happens next," she

said before she considered her words, her eyes glued to Leo's broad shoulders. "He needs to get the hell away from the ship in case she blows. For right now, that's all that matters."

She felt Bran's intense gaze land on her face and realized exactly what she'd said, exactly what she'd *revealed*.

"You care about him, don't you?" he asked, his voice so low she could have pretended she didn't hear him over the shushing of the warm waves around them. But she was no coward.

Or at least that's what she told herself when she admitted, "Of course I do." Then she hedged her bets and proved she was just a wee bit chickenhearted when she added, "I care about all of you. And I'm so sorry I dragged you guys into this m—"

"Forget that," he cut her off. "I wanna know your intentions toward LT."

She turned to him, lifting a dubious brow as she continued to kick and paddle like mad. "Are you kidding me?" she asked. His soaking hair curled against his forehead, his brown eyes were sullen, and his expression? Well, it appeared for all the world as if he was being completely, one hundred percent, deadeye serious.

"Okay, first of all, this isn't the antebellum South, Leo's not a debutante, and you're not his shotgun-toting father. So I don't see how my intentions are any of your business. Secondly"—she panted with the effort to remain afloat—"you really want to do this *now*?"

"First of all, I'm his best friend, and that means it *is* my business. Secondly," he said, mimicking her and maybe mocking her a little too, "I can't think of a better time to do this, can you?"

"*Sh'yeaaah*." Ugh. She shouldn't have let her jaw hang open on that last word. A wave took advantage of the opportunity, filling her mouth with salt water. "How about when we aren't floating in the middle of an ocean full of sharks? Or maybe we wait until terrorists aren't launching rockets at us. Or perhaps this conversation is better left until after Leo and the others are safe from—"

"But that's what makes this perfect," he interrupted. *Good God*, he made treading water look easy. His arms barely seemed to move below the surface.

"How do you figure?"

"Because we might not make it outta this thing alive." And the unvarnished truth of that hit her like a wrecking ball, filling her with grief and a sense of dread so heavy it took everything she had not to let it drag her beneath the surface of the sea. Luckily, the sound of the motor on the dinghy finally catching and coming to roaring life distracted her.

When she looked toward Leo and the little boat, it was to see both headed in her direction, plumes of water jetting out behind the small outboard engine and catching the sunlight to create tiny rainbows. *Hallelujah!*

"And since that's the case," Bran continued, seemingly unmoved by the fact that the others were headed their way, "there's no reason for you to lie to me. I mean, who needs that on their conscience so close meeting their maker?"

"You don't really believe—"

"So what's the deal?" He spoke over her as if she hadn't said a word. "Are you two just hot and heavy for one another, or is it something more?"

And damn him, she felt herself answering with the truth. Not because she was scared she would be standing at the Pearly Gates and explaining herself to St. Peter anytime soon, but more because…well…it seemed disrespectful to Leo—to his bravery and honor and…and… everything he stood for—to lie.

"I don't know about him," she admitted. "But for me it's…more. I *like* him, Bran. I really do."

Okay, and she could not *believe* she'd just said that. Out loud. To another person. She'd never been very good at being vulnerable. Didn't know why she'd decided to give it a try now.

He stared at her for a moment, then two. Finally he muttered, "I wish you didn't."

Her chin jerked back. "Why?"

"Because there's no future for the two of you."

"Why do you say that?" I mean, *she* knew why. It was because she could never tell Leo the truth about Syria. And even though she didn't know a lot about personal relationships, having never had many of her own, she knew enough to know that a stable one couldn't be built on a foundation of lies, but—

"You're a spy and he's a civilian," Bran said simply. "Anyone with an ounce of brains knows those two things are oil and water."

"I'm not banking on forever here," she admitted, as much to herself as to him.

He bobbed his head. "Well, that's good to hear. Now let's—"

He didn't have time to say more because the dinghy slid to a stop beside them. The next thing she knew, strong hands gripped her armpits and she was being hauled over the side of the rubber boat and straight into Leo's warm, muscular arms.

And it didn't matter that there was no future for them. It didn't matter that their luck could very well take a turn for the worse—*I mean, given its current trajectory*— because she'd learned early in life to appreciate the little things, to luxuriate in the moment since by its very definition, it was fleeing. And for this second, for this one crystalline heartbeat of time, he was safe and whole. And he was hugging her to him as if he never wanted to let her go, as if he *cared*. And she'd take it. What little there was, she'd take it.

She squeezed him back with all she had before searching his face. "You okay?" she asked, wiping a smudge of soot from his furrowed brow with her thumb. She had to catch her bottom lip between her teeth. For some mortifying reason, tears were pricking behind her eyes.

What the hell? She wasn't a crier.

Luckily, Leo didn't see the mutinous wetness. His wonderful multihued eyes ran over her from head to toe, checking for injury. "Fine. You? Did I hurt you when I tossed you overboard?"

"No," she assured him. "No, I—" She adjusted herself into a more comfortable position on his lap. Something was poking her. Then she realized that something was Leo. He was so hard a cat couldn't scratch him. And *that* was just what she needed to keep herself from becoming a watering pot. "Really, Leo," she tsked, shaking her head, "now isn't the time to—"

Despite the gravity of their situation, he grinned. "Normally," he told her, "that would all be for you. But right now I suspect it has more to do with the adrenaline.

We call 'em battlefield boners. And why the good Lord
saw fit to hamper a man with a hard-on during life-or-
death situations, I'll never know." He turned to Wolf
before she could come up with a witty reply. "Get us the
hell out of here."

The nose of the dinghy plowed over the top of a wave
when Wolf laid on the throttle. Then Leo pulled her
close again and stuck his nose in the crook of her shoulder. He inhaled deeply, like maybe he was trying to suck
her scent all the way down to his toes. And then, right
there in front of his men, with his ship sinking behind
them, he kissed her.

—⁓—

2:24 p.m....

Leo didn't care that his friends were watching. He didn't
care that now was not the time or the place. All that mattered was that Olivia was safe and unharmed. Dripping
wet and shivering despite the hot sun beating down on
them, but safe and unharmed. And kissing him back as
openly and passionately as any man could wish for…

"Leo," she breathed against his mouth. His own name
had never sounded so good.

Salt clung to her lips, and she might be a pickled form
of Olivia, but that didn't mean he didn't still want to eat
her up. In fact, he wanted to go on kissing her forever.
And he might have given it his best shot had not the
fire burning in *Wayfarer-I*'s big belly hit her fuel tanks.
KABOOM! A ball of flames exploded from her aft section to belch into the sky like dragon's breath.

"Jeez!" Olivia hissed as Wolf cut the throttle. The

rubber dinghy glided to a slow stop as the heat of the blast rolled over them. It wicked the water from their skin, leaving nothing but salty residue behind and filling the air with the scents of melting metal and burning paint.

"Son. Of. A. *Bitch*," Bran breathed.

Four sets of eyes quickly turned to Leo. And it was no wonder. His father's legacy, his birthright was burning and sinking. But, more importantly, it was all of their futures.

What are we goin' to do now? His friends had invested everything in this venture, put their trust in him. *And just look what it got 'em.*

"God, Leo," Olivia whispered. "I don't even know what to say. 'Sorry' doesn't *begin* to cover—"

"It's not your fault," he told her, unable to take his eyes away from the ship during her death throes. She was going fast, the ocean swallowing her and the flames that covered her in one long gulp.

"Of *course* it's my fault," Olivia insisted. "If I hadn't—"

"Save your apologies and recriminations," Wolf growled, pulling back the charging bolt on his Colt and flipping off the safety. Both sounds seemed particularly loud on the open water despite the fact they were competing with the dinghy's softly purring outboard engine. "Company's coming."

Leo glanced away from the charred carcass of *Wayfarer-I*—now nose down in the drink, only her mostly destroyed aft section and a portion of her rudder remained visible—to look in the direction of Wolf's extended finger. And sure as shit, beyond the wall of smoke he could just make out a skiff detaching itself from the yacht. Five...no...*six* men were aboard. All armed. All, no doubt, with death in their hearts.

Well, they weren't the only ones. His ol' ticker pumped a toxic blend of rage and revenge.

Olivia scrambled off his lap, going down on her knees in the bottom of the dinghy and leaning over the side so she could squint toward the yacht. He instantly missed her warmth, the feel of her pressed against him. But he registered that with half a mind. The other half was busy running through possible scenarios, trying to find one that allowed them to live.

Apparently Bran was doing much the same thing. "Should we try to outrun them?" he wondered aloud.

Leo nodded. "Olivia can call Morales and have him give our coordinates to the contractors. Even if they have to run on one engine, if they bust ass in our direction, they might have a shot at reachin' us before we run out of fuel or before the tangos catch up."

"I'd say that's a negative," Wolf said, grabbing the satellite phone from the small, webbed pouch attached to the inside of the dinghy. When he lifted it, water poured from the phone's plastic case. "I stuck it in there thinking it'd be safe. I wasn't banking on the skiff ending up facedown in the drink." He punched a button on the satphone, then another, before shaking his head. "No go."

"Doesn't matter anyway," Mason grumbled, the butt of his M4 raised to his shoulder so he could use his scope to get a better view of their targets.

"Why's that?" Leo demanded.

"Those cocksuckers have a six-HP engine on that fuckin' thing. They'd catch us before we banged out two miles."

"So we make a stand," Wolf said.

Usually *making a stand* didn't fill Leo with dread. He'd made plenty of them during his Naval career, been outnumbered and outgunned too many times to count. But he'd never had Olivia by his side while doing any of that. And, by God, he'd be damned if he'd have her by his side now.

"Get into a life jacket, Olivia," he told her, grabbing one of the bright-orange preservers and thrusting it at her. "Then get out of the boat."

"What?" Her face showed equal parts confusion and alarm.

"We're about to have ourselves a real-life gun battle here. And I can't have you in the middle of it."

"No." She shook her head, letting the life jacket drop to the bottom of the dinghy. "No, I can help you."

He flicked a glance at the skiff and the terrorists now whizzing toward them. The heat of rage burning through his blood froze solid at the thought of her taking part in what was coming next.

Over my dead body.

But it was the thought of *her* dead body that had him picking up the life jacket and pushing it toward her again. "Put it on," he told her in his best commanding-officer voice.

"I've got my…" Her eyes widened when she reached behind her back to feel for her pistol. It was gone. No doubt sitting on the sandy bottom some two hundred feet below them. He was pretty sure he'd inadvertently unclipped the top strap on her holster when he sent her flying overboard. But there'd be time for explanations later. For now, he needed her to Get. The. Hell. *Out!*

"Exactly," he told her. "You'll just be a distraction. One we don't need."

"But I—"

The gentle *whir* of an outboard engine reached his ears. *Time's up.* Hating himself for what he had to do, but seeing no other choice, he stood and grabbed Olivia around the waist. Before she registered his intent, he tossed her overboard.

She hit the water a couple of yards from the dinghy, arms and legs akimbo, and came up sputtering. "Goddamnit, Leo! Stop doing that!"

He flung the life jacket after her. "Grab it before it floats away! And then stay put!" he bellowed. When he saw her reach for the bright-orange life preserver, he turned to his men. *Yessir.* In this situation they were certainly his *men.* "Okay, gentlemen," he said. "It's time to Jason Bourne some things. I know it's been a while, but I suspect it's like ridin' a bike. So let's give it to 'em with both smokin' barrels and a punch to the throat, hooyah?"

"Hooyah!" three voices rang out right before Wolf laid on the throttle and they took off on an intercept course with the terrorists.

Chapter Eleven

2:29 p.m....

I'M GOING TO KILL HIM! OLIVIA THOUGHT AS SHE struggled to thrust her arms into the life jacket. *If we live through this, I'm going to—*

But that's as far as she got before the bullets started flying and all thoughts of murder instantly turned to prayers for his safety. For the safety of *all* the men. Her heart became a black hole, sucking away everything but her fear as she watched helplessly—utterly, infuriatingly helplessly—as the two dinghies raced toward each other.

The *rat-a-tat-tats* of the tangos' AKs were constant, but the distance between the little boats was too great for their rounds to hit their marks with any accuracy. In contrast, Leo and his men had yet to take a shot. Wolf was piloting the zooming skiff with one hand, his weapon raised to his opposite shoulder. Mason was in the middle of the boat, his M4 resting against the side, ready and willing. And both Bran and Leo had positioned themselves on the front of the dinghy, lying lengthwise along each side, one leg in, one leg out, their weapons poised for action like a couple of snipers, waiting until it was time to lay on their triggers and make their rounds count. She held her breath.

Suddenly—*Thump! Thump!*—Bran's machine gun jerked once, twice. He was the best shot of the bunch, his reputation as a crackerjack gunman known far and wide within the spec-ops community. That point was proved a split second later when blood exploded from one of the terrorists' skulls in a pink cloud. The tango toppled overboard, arms flying wide and AK-47 falling from his lifeless fingers before he hit the water and rolled in the wake of the boat.

Olivia had only seen two other men killed in her entire career—well, one, really; she'd only *thought* Rusty was dead—and those memories still haunted her, made her sick to her stomach anytime she replayed the gruesome scenes in her mind. This time wasn't any different. Her gut contracted, spewing burning bile into her throat until she gagged. Being shot at with RPGs *should* have been a mitigating factor for squeamishness and a motivating factor for vengeance, but apparently she'd been absent the day they handed out steel stomachs in field-agent training.

She managed to blow out a breath, beat back the urge to spew, and whispered, "One down. Five to go."

Her words drifted out over the waves, which is when she realized she'd basically been turned into a cheerleader, rooting from the safety of the sidelines. And that thought was a shot centered directly in the bull's-eye of her pride. Missing steel stomach aside, she was a trained agent for the Central Intelligence Agency, for shit's sake! Even weaponless, she was an *asset*, not a liability. She was just about to swing back around to thoughts of wrapping her hands around Leo's stupid, gallant neck when she got distracted by the terrorists' dinghy quickly changing course, pulling a U-ey and racing back toward the yacht.

And just like that, the game changed. Leo and his

men were now the pursuers. Wolf altered course as well, steering their boat in a wide parallel line, no doubt trying to give Bran and Leo an opportunity to see past the great, white plumes of water jettisoning from the terrorists' outboard so they could get a clear bead on their targets. But the tangos had more horsepower. And they were pulling away fast.

Still, that didn't stop Leo from taking a shot. His weapon barked, the sound echoing over the water. Once. But that was enough. One shot. One kill. Olivia couldn't see where he'd hit the terrorist, but the tango toppled overboard, smashing into the water and tumbling in the wake of the whirring engine before his body sank beneath the surface. The absence of gore allowed her to keep her stomach acid where it should be. Inside her stomach.

"And then there were four," she murmured to herself, paddling against the current that was trying to pull her away from the action. The adrenaline surging through her body heightened all her senses. Her sight—it was like she was watching it all on a movie screen in HD. Her sense of smell—along with the pungent aroma of marine fuel, she would swear she could detect the iron richness of blood. And definitely her *terror*—Leo and his men were a far cry from being out of danger. And if one of them was killed or injured because of her, because she'd dragged them on this mission, she'd never forgive herself.

With gritted teeth and ragged breaths, she watched the two boats slice and weave. She thought she heard one of the terrorists scream an order in Arabic above the whir of the engines. It sounded like *Turn!* But she couldn't be sure. Of course, when their dinghy spun around in a tight circle a half second later, she knew she'd heard right. The tangos barreled toward Leo and his men like they were playing a watery game of chicken, or else they were friggin' kamikaze-ing it.

The move caught the SEALs off guard, evidenced by the fact that Wolf didn't adjust their course quickly enough, and Leo and Bran were forced to dive for cover in the bottom of the dinghy when the front of their rubber boat lit up with enemy fire. A second later, their engine took a round and sputtered and died.

"No!" she yelled, the skin over her entire body tightening until it was a wonder her bones didn't poke through to the surface. Leo and his men couldn't lose the boat. They'd be sitting ducks! Cannon fodder for the terrorists who—

What's he doing? What's he doing?

She couldn't believe her eyes. Or maybe she didn't *want* to believe them. Leo was standing up in the middle of the dinghy, roaring like the lion from which he'd taken his nom de guerre and squeezing his trigger until the barrel of his M4 was a nothing but a black blur, orange fire blinking from the end of the muzzle.

The terrorists returned fire, and a hail of rounds bit into the ocean around Leo's little boat. Then one found its mark in Leo. An ugly spray of red burst from his shoulder.

"No!" she screamed again, just as a wave... a god-damn, mothersucking *wave* obliterated her view for a few interminable seconds. When she floated to the crest, it was to find the terrorists' dinghy dead in the water, its engine smoking ominously. From the corner of her eye, she saw *Wayfarer-I*'s rudder finally slip beneath

the surface, the big ship slowly sinking, leaving nothing
but a swirling eddy of water and floating debris to mark
its passing. She spared it barely a thought, because Leo
and his men... They were nowhere to be seen, their boat
completely empty and bobbing gently, silently, *eerily*
with the current.

She didn't think. She just started swimming.

———

2:35 p.m....

"You okay, LT?"

Leo glanced down at the rip in his T-shirt sleeve and
the deep, bloody furrow cutting through the skin on his
right shoulder above his tattoo of the Navy SEAL tri-
dent. "Just a scratch," he told Bran. Though that didn't
mean the thing didn't still bite like a bag full of alliga-
tors. Getting shot was never fun. Getting shot and then
immediately dousing the wound in seawater was even
less of a party.

"We still need to stop the fuckin' bleeding," Mason
muttered, reaching beneath the surface of the water to
dig in the pocket of his cargo shorts. He came up with a
sodden red bandana. Grabbing two corners, he twirled
the fabric around on itself, then grunted and jerked his
chin, which Leo knew to be the nonverbal equivalent of
Lift your arm. He did as instructed and watched Mason
give him a slapdash field dressing.

"Please tell me that thing's clean," Leo said, gritting
his teeth when Mason tightened the bandana over his
wound. "I think I'm due for a tetanus shot."

"For the most part," the big Bostonian said, one

corner of his mouth curling. "But maybe you should have Doc dose you once we get home. Worst-case scenario and all."

"Perfect," Leo grumbled. Of course, right about now thoughts of home were so sweet he would have allowed Doc to make a pin cushion out of him if he could somehow transport them all there. Unfortunately, he wasn't Captain Kirk and Scotty wasn't going to beam them anywhere. Which meant they were stuck. Here. Using the only part of the skiff that was still afloat—the back section and the motor—as cover. But that wouldn't last for long.

The dinghy had a one-way ticket to Davy Jones's locker, and there was nothing they could do to stop it. Luckily, he had managed to take the terrorists' boat out of action before he and his men were forced to dive overboard. So even if those suckwads weren't in the drink right now, they would be soon. And that was a good thing. In the water, Leo and his SEALs had all the advantages.

"So what's the plan?" Bran asked, floating easily beside him.

"We wait until their boat goes under. Then we swim over and take 'em out." He glanced at his men. "Unless you guys can think of a better idea?"

"Negative."

"Mmph."

"Sounds like a plan to me."

"One tiny little caveat though," Leo said, pulling the strap of his M4 over his head and twisting the weapon around until it lay flat against his back.

"You mean the fact that our rounds will only travel

four feet underwater, and even then they won't have enough kinetic energy left to do the tangos any real damage?" Wolf lifted a brow.

"That's exactly what I mean."

"So we swim up from underneath them, drag them down, and slit their throats."

"Uh…problem." Bran lifted a finger out of the water.

"Wolf's the only one with a fuckin' knife," Mason grumbled.

"Bingo," Leo said.

"We could try to surface close to them," Bran mused. "Take aim and fire before they get a bead on us. But that's taking one pisser of a risk. Considering the rat bastards will probably be waiting with fingers on triggers for us to do exactly that."

"'The cruel and evil are feared, especially by the wise,'" Wolf muttered.

"Buddha again?" Bran rolled his eyes. "I don't think now is the time to spout your woo-woo religious mumbo-jumbo bullsh—"

"For the record," Wolf said, "that was a *Hindu* proverb. But it doesn't matter. Because translated into layman's terms, it means we'd be smart to come up with a better plan."

"So Wolf pulls his guy under and slits his fuckin' throat. The rest of us pull our guys under and do it the dirty way," Mason said, shrugging one massive shoulder. "We snap their fuckin' necks."

Leo glanced at Wolf and Bran. It meant getting close. Real close. Hand-to-hand combat without a useful weapon was always tricky. Still, it was their best option. "Anyone opposed to Mason's plan?"

"Negative," Bran said.

"I'm in." Wolf nodded.

"And just in time too," Leo muttered as the dinghy made a wheezing sound followed by a portentous bubbling. "We've only got a few seconds of cover left. And on that note…" He peeked around the edge of what was left of the watercraft and made a quick scan of their surroundings before ducking back. "Okay. Their skiff is under. They're huddled in a pack about sixty yards away. We'll have to surface three times between here and there. The last time will be close."

"'The only easy day was yesterday,'" Bran said, quoting the Navy SEAL motto, his face like stone. He was in full warrior mode now.

Mason was his usual silent self, simply jerking his chin in a quick downward motion.

Wolf replied with, "*Wakan takan nici un*," which was his standard comeback when they were about to rush headlong into battle. He'd told them it was Cherokee for "May the Great Spirit walk with you." From Hindu proverbs to Cherokee incantations. Only Wolf…

"Okay, men." Leo nodded. "Let's do this!"

He desperately wanted to peek around the other side of the craft to see if he could snatch a quick look at Olivia in her orange life jacket. But there wasn't time. The dinghy was slipping beneath the surface of the water. He had to trust that she was holding her own—and if anyone could, it was her—as he spit out his gum and then inhaled deeply, expanding his diaphragm and increasing the capacity of his lungs. He quickly blew out all his air until he could exhale no more. Lowering his head as close to the surface as he could without going under, he sucked in oxygen until his lungs couldn't hold another drop.

Go time!

He quickly dove down three feet, far enough that he wouldn't have to fight the wave action at the top. Within seconds, all his men were beside him. He could see them, blurry though they were since he wasn't wearing goggles. Each gave him a thumbs-up. And that was the signal to start swimming.

Then it was all about the muscle memory… All those endless days and weeks spent in hell, otherwise known as the pool at the Naval Amphibious Base in Coronado, California, all those long hours practicing the right stroke for the right conditions, all those training exercises geared toward crushing their fear of the ocean meant their motions were smooth and sure. Instinctual. Their heartbeats a steady tempo to match their pace.

It was quiet underwater, the only noise a gentle crackling that was the feeding of nearby fish and shrimp and the occasional burble of bubbles that trickled from between their lips. They swam ten yards in a flash. Fifteen came and went as Leo counted his strokes in his head, operating on autopilot. Little by little, he released the air in his lungs until a subtle *buzzing* sounded between his ears. A harbinger of low blood-oxygen saturation.

A tap on his ankle had him glancing back. Mason had fallen a bit behind the group. The guy's muscle mass meant he had to work harder than the rest of them to stay afloat, using up oxygen faster. That ankle tap said his gas tank was running on empty. The rest of them could have continued for a few more yards, but they'd

been trained to rise as a team. Reaching over, Leo poked
Bran's shoulder and Bran immediately grabbed Wolf.
Slowly, the four of them broke the surface, just their
noses and mouths breaching the sanctity of the water.

Inhale. Exhale. Inhale. *Dive!*

Back below the waves, they continued their journey,
pouring on the speed, cutting the distance to their targets
as the warm water sluiced through their hair and over
their skin like the gentle fingers of a lover welcoming
them home. Little air bubbles tickled and teased. Eddies
created by their cupped hands rushed sensuously down
their bodies. Some might think it odd that free diving
soothed him, calmed him.

But even as a kid, well before SEAL training had
enamored him of the sanctuary found in bosom of the
ocean, Leo had liked being underwater. He glanced to
his right, watching Bran easily swim, then to his left,
seeing Mason's big shoulders part the drink like he was
fucking Moses and this was the Red Sea, and he knew
his friends felt the same.

Tap, tap.

Again, Mason was the first to run out of O_2. When
they bobbed to the surface this time, Leo lifted his head
to peek above the swells, blinking the water from his eyes
and getting a bead on their enemies. Diving down again,
he indicated with exaggerated hand signals—exaggerated
because it was difficult to see in salt water—the direction
and approximate distance to their targets.

The four of them took off again. Five more yards.
Ten. Twenty. And when the blurry outline of legs kicking in a tangled clump came into sight, like a flock
of birds in flight Leo and his men moved in unison,

swimming to the surface, careful to ride the rise and fall of the waves as they refilled their lungs for the last time. Sinking deeper, they swam until they were directly below the terrorists, far enough down that their shadows in the water wouldn't alert their enemies to their presence. There they hung, paddling at depth. He indicated which of them would grab which pair of churning feet. And after receiving a thumbs-up from each of his men, he gave one last hand signal. *Go!*

Like honest-to-God seals, they shot through the water, grabbing the ankles of the man they'd been assigned, unmercifully yanking their adversaries beneath the waves.

Rough hands clawed at Leo's shoulders, his head, as he pulled his foe deeper, deeper, deeper still. The butt of his enemy's AK grazed his temple, but he was able to twist the weapon out of the man's hand, letting it go and absently noting its lazy descent toward the bottom. A knee landed in his groin. *Oomph!* Another blow connected with his midriff, forcing a bubble of air to burst from his lungs. But he was too pumped, too full of purpose and stone-cold determination to feel much of anything.

He realized his foe wasn't actually trying to fight him. The man was simply frantic to return to the surface, struggling upward with everything he had, his limbs jerking wildly this way and that. And *that* was his first mistake.

With deadly resolve, Leo locked his legs around his opponent's thighs, effectively thwarting the man's bid for the surface. *Now* the terrorist clued in to the real danger. He landed blows on Leo's face and head. But the water leached all the power from his punches.

This close, the man's face was clear, the absolute horror in his dark eyes visible even beneath the sea.

Leo hardened his heart just as he'd done many times during his career and grabbed the back of the tango's head with one hand, his bearded chin with the other. It was the work of an instant to twist. And in the silence of the ocean, the snapping of his enemy's vertebrae was as sharp as a cracking whip.

The man was dead before he knew what hit him—a merciful death, really—going slack in Leo's grip. Leo allowed the body to slip from his hold, barely sparing the sinking corpse a glance.

He'd heard it said somewhere that guys often entered the services because they had high ideals. But when push came to shove and the bullets started to fly, they didn't end up fighting for a cause; they didn't end up fighting for their country. They ended up fighting for the guys in the trenches beside them. And, in his experience, he'd found that to be true. Which was why he was immediately searching the sea around him, looking for his friends.

Above him, a red cloud blossomed in the water like a macabre flower and the body of a terrorist sank past him, drifting down into the deep, leaving a lingering trail of blood in its wake. Wolf had obviously made quick work of his opponent. Leo glanced to his left, but Bran was nowhere in sight. To his right, he could just make out a mass of writhing shadows, one so big it could only be Mason.

Without hesitation, and ignoring the whirring between his ears that told him it was time to surface, he kicked with all his might in that direction. He was barely four feet away when a familiar snapping sound echoed dully through the water and Mason pushed away from the dead tango to kick and claw at the water like all get-out. It was obvious the fight had taken too long. Mason was desperately low on air.

He ain't the only one, Leo thought as he pulled up beside him, abbreviating his strokes to match the shorter man's just as black began to edge into his vision. The buzz in his ears was now a roar. His muscles burned as they struggled to work without the benefit of oxygen. It occurred to him things might get pretty dicey when suddenly Wolf and Bran were beside them. They must have surfaced to refill their lungs because their strokes looked damn near spritely.

Wolf hooked a hand beneath Leo's armpit, and Bran grabbed on to Mason's gun strap. Then it was a matter of teamwork. The sun glinting on the waves gave them a bright, golden goal to shoot for. But it was going to be a very close thing. *Too close.* The need to breathe was overwhelming, speaking to the lizard part of Leo's brain, trying to overrule all his reasoning and higher functions. Up, up. Higher, higher. *Come on, come on!* They kicked like mad, but…

Aw, hell. I think I—

Just as he felt his lungs begin to spasm against the desire to rake in the air that wasn't there, Bran gave him a mighty push toward the surface and, "*Uhhhh!*" bright, delicious oxygen rushed into his lungs. Beside him, Mason's loud indrawn breath was followed by the harsh sound of a deep, wet cough. The latter told Leo that Mason had choked down a mouthful of ocean water. Somehow, though, Mason had managed to keep from sucking the stuff into his lungs. And that was a damn good thing. Trying to perform CPR in the middle of the drink was a bitch and a half.

"What the hell was that, Mason?" Bran demanded, breathing heavily. Leo opened his eyes to see stars dancing in front of them. His head felt like it might blow off his neck at any moment. It was a strange phenomenon, how the body could become drunk on oxygen after it'd been deprived of the stuff for too long. "You nearly got yourself killed! You shoulda surfaced when he pulled that knife on you. You *knew* it was gonna take too long to disarm him a second time and do the deed. You big *asshole*!"

"What?" Leo managed, the waves bobbing him up and down, the warm wind caressing his face and trying its best to sober him up. It was working. Sort of. His head was no longer threatening to float up into the clear, robin's-egg-blue of the sky. "What knife?"

"A monster goddamned knife, that's what knife," Bran said. "After Mason wrestled his target's AK away, and *before* he could get the guy in the right hold to snap his neck, I saw the tango pull a hunting knife the size of my dick from the back of his pants."

Leo ignored Bran's ridiculous allusion to his johnson and wondered how Mason managed that laconic shrug while treading water and still trying to clear the moisture from his windpipe. "Not a lot of"—*cough, cough*—"options. If I let go, there was a chance the fucker could've stuck you in the kidney on his way up. Your hands were full at the time."

"So then *after* you wrestled the blade away?" Bran asked, eyes wide despite the seawater dripping off his eyelashes. "Why the hell didn't you surface then?"

"Just seemed easier to"—*cough*—"finish it."

"And nearly drown yourself in the process, you stubborn sonofabitch."

One corner of Mason's mouth curled. "Stubborn *and* well-endowed."

Apparently Bran only enjoyed big dick references when he was the one making them. "Seriously, Mason"—he squinted and lifted a hand to shade his eyes—"your stupidity and misplaced self-sacrificing heroics are blinding me. Would you mind turning them off?"

"Is this your way of saying you fuckin' *love* me and you were worried I'd—"

"Uh, guys," Leo interrupted when the engines on the *Black Gold* thrummed to life with a deep purr. The sleek yacht was still anchored forty yards away. But by the sound of those engines, it wouldn't be there for long. *Shit.* And just like that, he was stone-cold sober. "You mind if we file this argument under To Be Continued? Because if we don't catch that yacht before it takes off—"

"We're fucked," Mason finished unnecessarily.

"In a word."

"You go get Olivia," Wolf suggested. Olivia… *Holy Christ. Where the hell is she?* Leo glanced over his shoulder but couldn't see her anywhere. "Me, Tweedle Dumb, and Tweedle Dumber will go appropriate ourselves a yacht."

"Be careful," Leo advised. Suddenly, the thought of catching the yacht seemed inconsequential when compared to making sure Olivia was okay. Which, all right, was completely asinine. But there you have it. When it came to her, he had a tendency toward myopia. Complete and total tunnel vision. "There could still be two tangos aboard, not to mention the crew or whoever else was in on this little scheme."

"I don't know about you three," Bran said as he took off toward the gently bobbing vessel, "but I like those odds. Race you!" *Flip!* And, just like that, the guy was back to his jovial self.

Watching his friends cut across the waves, Leo treaded water and kept a close eye on the deck of the yacht through the scope of his rifle to make sure no one came out of the bridge or popped up from below to start taking potshots at his friends. But as the seconds passed...nothing. No one. Hopefully that meant there weren't many people left on board, making it easy for the guys to mop things up.

And that wasn't ego talking. It was the plain ol' truth. When it came to three *armed* Navy SEALs who collectively had nearly forty-five years of experience and training under their belts, pretty much nothing short of an exploding volcano or hurricane—i.e., a force of mother-frickin' nature—could stand in their way. *Hooyah!*

When Leo saw they were approaching the back of the vessel and the swim deck, he allowed himself to finally, *finally*—it had felt like an eternity—turn away. Swinging the strap of his M4 over his shoulder, he yelled, "Olivia!" His eyes searched the vastness of the ocean, looking for that spot of orange that was her life jacket. It was difficult to see. The sea was speckled with debris from the *Wayfarer*'s sinking. A bright-white life ring here. A dark blue corner of plastic he thought belonged to the cooler he and the guys had kept on deck there. There were buoys and a few chunks of Styrofoam. A whole sleeve of red Solo cups and a couple of cushions from the deck chairs.

He hadn't witnessed the ship's final seconds and was glad of it. It would have been like watching a friend draw a last breath. And he knew from experience that was one sight better left unseen. Once again, he wondered what would become of him and the others now that their futures were officially sitting on the sandy bottom of the Straits. But before the self-condemnation and remorse could set in, he saw two dots of orange on the far horizon bobbing on the waves.

Olivia? He squinted his eyes. No, not Olivia. They were the empty preservers Mason had stowed in the bottom of their dinghy before the thing made its journey into the deep.

"Olivia!" he hollered again, fear beginning to sink its razor-sharp teeth into his heart and squirming in his belly like a venomous snake. His mind raced through all the possibilities...

Drowned. *No. I saw her grab the life jacket.*

Sharks. *Hell no. That's too awful to contemplate.*

Caught in a current and carried out of sight. *But she's strong. She wouldn't let herself—*

It didn't matter that none of the scenarios seemed likely; ice-cold terror still froze his brain and iced over his lungs. Chills raced up his spine. Goose bumps erupted over his skin. *Jesus Christ on the cross!* He was having a panic attack. An honest-to-God panic attack. *After all the shit I've seen and done, now is when I—*

And then he understood. In a flash of clarity he realized. If she'd met some horrible fate, if he never saw that crooked smile or those beautiful blue eyes again... well, he'd be tempted to give up and meet her in the watery depths. And it was that acute realization, that his life ceased to have the same importance in the absence of hers, that made it suddenly, starkly clear. He didn't just *like* Olivia. He *loved* her. Heart and soul. Body and brain. With every step and every breath.

But somehow he'd missed it. And all those months he'd missed *her*, all those times he'd turned down some buxom broad at the bar, all those days he'd spent wondering where she was, what she was doing suddenly made sense. He wasn't crazy. He was just in love. Head over heels. Ass over teakettle. All in. Nothing held back.

And it was beautiful. So goddamned beautiful.

And so utterly terrifying…

"Olivia!" His voice broke because his heart was busy striking hammer blows against his ribs. "Olivia! Damnit! Where are you?"

"Here!"

The relief that poured through him at the sound of her husky voice was so intense it made him dizzy. He sank a couple of inches into the water, closing his eyes and sending up a quick prayer of thanks to anyone who might be listening. *You know, just in case*.

When he blinked open his eyes and spun around in the water, there she was. The woman of his heart. No more than ten yards away and splashing in his direction. Which meant she hadn't heeded his advice to stay put. In fact, she must've started swimming toward the action as soon as they took off, the brave, reckless, *lovable* creature. Her ponytail had come undone, so her sodden hair lay plastered against her skull. Her cheeks were flushed scarlet from exertion. And her mascara was smudged in huge, black swaths beneath her wide eyes, making her look like a startled raccoon.

He'd never seen a more gorgeous sight in his whole sorry-assed life…

Chapter Twelve

2:46 p.m....

"Leo!" Olivia yelled, lifting her arm out of the water to signal him. He didn't hear or see her. He'd already dived beneath the waves, headed her way.

She choked on a sob that should have mortified her with its strength. But she was so damned happy he was *alive* that she couldn't make herself care that her tough outer shell had developed a series of huge, gaping cracks. When she hadn't seen him or his men emerge from behind the dinghy after it sank, she'd contemplated the worst, that they'd all somehow been killed in the seconds her vision was obscured by that stupid, idiotic wave.

But as she'd swum and swum and swum, her muscles on fire from the exertion, she'd refused to let herself *really* believe it. Repeating the same mantra over and over as she fought the wind and the tide: *He's not dead. He can't be dead. He's not dead. He can't be dead...*

Then, just as one of the terrorists noticed her and took aim in her direction—yeah, that would be one second she relived in her nightmares—the bearded men were all yanked beneath the surface of the sea as if they'd been set upon by a school of sharks. But she'd known it wasn't sharks that dragged them down. It was frogs. As in frogmen. As in Navy motherfriggin' SEALs!

The relief had overwhelmed her, filling her chest

with choking cries. She'd thought maybe she was about to turn into the spokeswoman for Kleenex and Visine, and have a good ol' fashioned breakdown of hysterical, tear-filled happiness, but ten seconds stretched into twenty and then thirty…and no Leo, just waves upon waves lapping over the surface of the sea. She'd held her breath when she saw two dark heads briefly breach the surface, her eyes searching, her whole heart hoping… but no blond head bobbed up next to them. Then the two dark heads disappeared again.

She'd renewed her efforts, paddling against the current, buffeted by the surf, spitting out the occasional mouthful of salt water when a wave hit her full in the face, or pushing aside a piece of the floating debris left behind because the *Wayfarer* had given up the ghost. Just when she began to think there was no way—no way *anyone* could hold their breath for that long—all four men blasted out of the sea like human torpedoes. And she hadn't stopped swimming in their direction until now when she simply floated, waiting for him to come to her, her heart so full of joy it was a wonder the organ didn't burst from trying to contain it.

Then…he was there, surfacing next to her, water sheeting over his head and down his wonderful face. He pulled her into his arms and she was instantly enveloped by his wet warmth, his impossible strength, his…*everything*.

"You okay?" he asked, his deep voice purring in her ear.

"Leo," she breathed, burying her nose in his neck while their legs briefly tangled as they kicked to keep themselves afloat. "I'm so sorry."

"Stop apologizin', Olivia," he told her, cupping the

back of her head in his wide palm and hugging her tight despite the blasted life preserver that kept distance between them. "There isn't a damn thing you could've done differently."

"But if I hadn't involved you—"

"Shhh." He pulled away, pressing a finger to her lips. His hazel eyes reflected the ocean, appearing almost turquoise. Then his bearded, scarred chin popped back, and he cocked his head. "Are you…are you *cryin'*?"

She thought about admitting to him that it'd been a very close thing. But, instead, she went with, "Nope. I think the salt water is just testing the limits of my waterproof mascara."

He gave her a sidelong glance. "Well, I think it's found those limits, darlin'."

She flattened her lips, but silently blessed him for making a joke and lightening the mood. Then she remembered he'd been shot. *Goddamnit!* How the hell could she have forgotten that? Her gaze darted to his right shoulder and the red bandana tied around it. Given the color of the fabric, it was hard to tell how bad the wound was.

"How bad are you hurt?" she demanded.

"It's nothin'," he assured her, and now *she* was the one to give him a sidelong glance. "The bullet just grazed me. I've had much worse."

And she knew he had. After all, she'd seen some of his scars. Still, she was tempted to undo that bandana and assess the damage herself. But a quick flash of movement over his shoulder caught her attention. She narrowed her eyes.

"What's up?" he asked, craning his head around.

There was nothing back there except waves upon waves, a few floating pieces of white Styrofoam, and the sleek, black body of the yacht.

"I guess it was nothing." She shook her head, wondering if the wind and sun and tide and...*exhaustion*—both physical and emotional—had finally gotten the better of her. "It's entirely possible I'm hallucinating at this point."

"The sunlight on the waves can play tricks on you." He winked. And how the man could act so blasé after watching his ship get blown to smithereens, after being shot, and after fighting an underwater duel with a terrorist was beyond her. She was a wreck. *I hope it doesn't show.*

"Are you okay to swim to the yacht?" he asked. Okay, so obviously *some* of it showed. *Damnit!* "I'm itchin' to go see how the others are farin'."

Oh yeah. The others. The men she'd dragged into this mess who were probably, right at this very moment, fighting off who-knew-how-many more tangos. "Hell yeah," she told him, glad her tone was filled with far more determination than she actually felt.

He bobbed his head once, but before he could turn, a big, black weapon appeared behind him. And behind *that* were the murderous eyes of a radical. It felt like a bolt of lightning had buzzed across the top of her skull. She opened her mouth to scream a warning, but Leo's spec-ops soldier ESP beat her to the punch. Before the tango could squeeze the trigger, Leo whirled in the water, grabbing the end of the barrel in one hand and the stock of the AK-47 in the other. As he twisted the weapon out of the radical's grip, a spine-tingling *crack* echoed through the air. It could only be one thing: the terrorist's finger bones against the trigger guard.

And, sure as shit, the man screamed in agony. His piercing cry cut off a half second later when Leo propped the confiscated AK against his shoulder and—*Bam!*—fired. A red hole bloomed in the middle of their enemy's cheek, the back of his neck—

She looked away, fighting the urge to puke.

"Come on," Leo said, slinging the strap of the AK over his shoulder before grabbing the front harness on her life jacket. He dragged her through the water toward the yacht and away, *thank God*, from the corpse of the radical.

For a couple of seconds, she was too nauseous to help him. Then she gave herself a mental kick in the ass for being a big, ol' ninny and began paddling. "I got it," she said, swallowing the bile burning at the back of her throat and forcing it back down into her roiling stomach. Eyebrow raised, he gave her a look so stoic that one would never think he'd been a split second away from taking a bullet to the brainpan. "Really. I *got* it."

With a quick nod, he released her to make her own way. "Sorry you had to see—"

"You're not really going to apologize for saving my life, are you?" she huffed.

"Nope." A muscle near his mouth trembled. "Wouldn't think of it."

"Good," she grumbled. "Because that would be ridiculous."

"Like a trapdoor in a canoe or a back pocket on a shirt," he said, intentionally thickening his accent.

Huh? Oh, she got it. Things that were ridiculous. "Like a screen door on a submarine," she added.

"Like an ejection seat in a helicopter."

"Like a white crayon."

"Hey, now!" he said. "I used white crayons on black construction paper the time I made Casper the Friendly Ghost Halloween cards for my second-grade class."

"My bad," she relented, trying to imagine big, bad Leo "the Lion" Anderson as a second grader. She'd bet money he'd been adorable and smart and brave, the kind of kid to stand up to the playground bully. "So you win that round."

"As it ever was and ever shall be, darlin'."

"Ugh. And *there's* that oversized ego all SEALs come equipped with. Somehow I was under the impression the Navy factory inadvertently forgot to install yours."

"That ain't the only thing that's oversized on me." He wiggled his eyebrows.

She rolled her eyes, fighting a smile. This was the kind of flirtatious banter they'd bandied about for three long months. Banter that made her hoot with laughter one minute and want to jump his bones the next. And now, like then, he always seemed to know when she needed him to throw in a little levity. Or, more specifically, in their jobs it was known as "gallows humor."

When life served you a nice slice of shit pie, or when you were forced to do something awful—like put a ball of lead into someone's face—the only way to keep from curling into the fetal position in a corner was to force yourself to remember there were still things to smile about, to laugh about. To remember the world wasn't all bad.

See? Perceptive.

For a couple of seconds, they swam in silence. Leo easily sliced through the water beside her, the two weapons strapped to his back gently clacking against one another. She could tell he was tempering his momentum to match hers. And hers was pretty damn slow. She glanced up. Twenty yards... Just twenty more yards and they would be at the yacht.

Come on, Mortier. Power through.

"Where did that guy *come* from?" she asked.

"He was the one I shot off the dinghy," Leo said. "I must've only winged him."

"Ah." She nodded, gulping when the image of the terrorist's ruined neck flashed before her eyes and the bile threatened again. And that's when it occurred to her. Four... She'd seen four men die violently in her life. And each time she'd been overwhelmed by nausea. To the point that it impeded her ability to function.

And that doesn't bode well for the rest of my career. A CIA field agent who couldn't do what was necessary when push came to shove was of no use to anybody, certainly not the government, and definitely not the other agents she sometimes ran missions with.

If I can't do my job, what am I left with?

Before she allowed herself to contemplate the answer, the groan of the anchor motor on the yacht and the *clank-clank-clank* of the heavy chain rolling into its hull sounded over the water. The *Black Gold* was making her move.

Leo held out the AK by its strap. "You know how to shoot this?"

"Oh, *now* you're ready to let me help?" She took the

weapon at the same time she grabbed on to the stainless-steel ladder attached to the *Black Gold*'s swim deck. If the muscles in her legs and arms had voices, their combined cry at finally getting a break would've sounded like a hundred gospel choirs.

"Actually, I was sort of hopin' you'd be willin' to hang back here while I went up to see what's what," he admitted.

Okay, and given her recent epiphany regarding her inability to stomach the killing, maybe he was right to ask her to stay behind. Still, had he kept her aboard the dinghy, she could have warned him that the terrorists were about to turn and head right for them. She *was* an asset, by God. Just as long as she could make herself sac up and do her friggin' job.

"Not on your life," she told him.

"I reckoned as much," he said with a wry grin, though there was something…*more* in his expression.

And then before he hauled himself out of the sea and onto the swim deck, he kissed her. Just a quick peck on the lips, but it was enough to make her heart take flight.

———

2:52 p.m….

Bran ripped the tape from the mouth of one of the men he found trussed up on the main deck. The dude's face was lobster red, his eyes bloodshot, but he appeared to be otherwise unharmed. "Who are you?" Bran demanded in a harsh whisper, keeping his weapon trained on the guy. Mason and Wolf were watching his six in case some shit-for-brains tried to sneak up behind him. They'd already systematically checked the back of the main deck and the topside portion of the living quarters, but they'd yet to search the crew's cabins belowdecks or the bridge. "What the hell is going on here?"

"N-Nigel Moore. First mate," the man managed, his scratchy voice a testament to his dehydration. His English accent reminded Bran of the old Monty Python movies. In a different situation, he'd have asked the guy to say, *Your mother was a hamster, and your father smelt of elderberries!* "We-we were hijacked by a group of armed men after lunch. They sailed us here and dropped anchor." He shook his head, his expression wild as his eyes darted to the black hole at the end of Bran's M4. "I d-don't know why."

Bran did.

And it looked like Olivia was right. Morales *hadn't* screwed up in his calculations. The *Black Gold* had simply been sailing by the wrong place at the wrong time. The guy hog-tied beside Nigel grunted, and Mason yanked the duct tape from his mouth. "And you are?"

Unlike Nigel, this guy wasn't all that eager to open up. "Who am I? Better question is who the bloody hell are *you?*" he spat. "And what the bloody fuck just happened? We heard explos—"

Bran slapped the tape back over the dude's mouth because he didn't have time for explanations. Someone up on the bridge had just pushed the button for the anchor. The automatic windlass—the cylinder made for raising and lowering the forward mainstay—began spinning, and the steady *clank* of the heavy chain collecting in the hull below them was the audio equivalent of a semaphore flag waving around and telling him to get his ass in gear.

They needed to gain control of the yacht now. Before whoever was operating the controls motored them so far away from Leo and Olivia that Bran and the boys would have a tough time relocating them. Two people floating in the middle of the ocean were the proverbial needles in a haystack.

"How many others are on board?" He turned to Nigel, the more accommodating of the two.

Nigel swallowed, glancing over at his compatriot.

"Don't look at him," Bran growled, making sure his expression broadcast his impatience. "Look at me. I'm the one asking the questions. How many more are on board?"

"I'm not sure," Nigel admitted, shrinking back from the mouth of Bran's weapon as if it were a viper poised to strike. "There were s-seven hijackers, I think. And the captain and Maddy Powers."

Bran could only assume Maddy Powers was the Texas oil tycoon Olivia had mentioned. *As in Powers Petroleum?* It made sense. And *seven* hijackers? One short of the eight assets Olivia seemed convinced took the chemicals. Which meant either one of the dickheads had drowned, or ol' Nigel boy had miscounted. Still, Bran liked his chances.

"Where are they? Belowdecks or on the bridge?"

"I saw them take Maddy and the captain to the bridge," Nigel said. "But that was a while ago." When he swallowed, his Adam's apple appeared to stick in the column of his long, skinny neck. "Please, sir. I need w-water."

"Later." Bran waved him off. "After we check your story."

He slapped the tape back over Nigel's mouth despite

the man's sputtered objections. But he wasn't as heartless a bastard as he was making himself out to be. He
turned to his friends. "Help me drag them into the shade
next to the living quarters."

He grabbed Nigel's collar while Mason, the sorry
sonofabitch—Bran still hadn't *quite* forgiven him for
that stunt he'd pulled earlier—took hold of the other
dude. Together they scooted the men along the deck
until they were flush with the main cabin and in the
soothing cool of the shadow it cast.

Mission of mercy complete, Bran said, "Let's double-
time it up to the bridge."

The three of them opened the forward door to the
living quarters. Crouched low, their fingers on their
triggers, they advanced while checking left, right, and
center. As they crossed the big, central room with its
plush furniture, gargantuan-screen TV, and expensive-
looking art, Bran resisted the urge to whistle.

So this *is how the other half lives?*

He couldn't imagine it. Although ever since he'd come
down with the treasure-hunting bug, he'd been trying his
best to do just that. *All* of them had big plans for their
share of the loot. *Important* plans. *But sayonara and see
you later to that little dream.* Because without a salvage
ship, it would be impossible to locate the remains of
the *Santa Cristina.* And even if they pooled the limited
funds they had left and combined them with the half-mil
Olivia was paying them, they still wouldn't have one-
fifth of what it would take to replace *Wayfarer-I.*

*Clusterfuck...a motherfriggin' clusterfuck if ever
there was one.*

But he'd have to worry later about what he now

planned to do for the rest of his life. Because the three
of them were at the stairs leading up to the bridge. And
this is where it got tricky. Hallways and alleys weren't
called fatal funnels for nothing. If whoever was at the top
of those stairs decided to throw open the door and start
spraying lead, there wasn't much they could do to protect
themselves. The usual duck-and-cover wasn't an option.
Well…the ducking part could still be accomplished,
but the only cover available was each other. And *that*
thought sucked so hard he decided to name it Hoover.

"Stay frosty, boys," he whispered softly, his senses
on high alert. Taking the lead, he saw the muzzle of
Mason's rifle appear in his peripheral vision. Once again,
Wolf was bringing up the rear, watching their backs so
they didn't have to keep their heads on a swivel. As a
group they advanced, slowly, steadily. Then the sound
of a thickly accented voice shouting, "*Move boat or I
shoot!*" necessitated they pick up the pace.

"Go, go, go!" Bran commanded, and the three of
them raced up the stairs. Throwing open the door and
looking down the sight on his rifle, he took in the scene
in an instant. A gray-haired man wearing a captain's
uniform—Tripplehorn, no doubt—stood at the controls,
his ankles shackled together by a neon-green zip tie.

A blond-haired boy in a navy-blue bathrobe was on
his knees near the captain's feet, hands and feet cuffed
by more zip ties, the yawning black mouth of the terrorist's AK-47 leveled at his temple. *Maddy Powers? Must
be the* son *of the oil tycoon*. As for the terrorist himself?
He looked like a cannoli full of crazy when his dark
gaze shot up upon their entry, his mouth morphing into
a ghoulish sneer.

Bran had seen that expression a hundred times on the faces of fanatics. It was devoid of reason, devoid of humanity, and completely devoid of mercy. This guy was outnumbered and outgunned. But instead of throwing down his weapon and giving up, he was itching to take the captain and the kid with him while he chose suicide by SEAL. *Goddamnit all to hell.*

The world around Bran disappeared, his entire focus squeezing down to a two-foot-by-two-foot area that was the tango's head and torso. His finger tightened on his trigger as he automatically ran through the five *S*'s: slow, smooth, straight, steady, squeeze. But the boy must've come to the same conclusion about the terrorist's intent, because with a banshee cry, he rammed his head into the terrorist's crotch. It gave Bran just the opening he needed. As soon as the barrel of the Kalashnikov was no longer pointing at the kid's face, he squeezed off a round that echoed around the well-appointed bridge like a cannon shot, rattling the windows and making his ears pop. It hit the rat bastard just above his left eye-socket.

Even though the movies got most things wrong in portraying gunshot victims—for instance, a body very rarely flew backward upon impact—one thing they got *right* was what happened to a human skull when it was introduced to a 5.56mm NATO round. Blood and gray matter splattered onto the bridge's port-side window in a macabre mess, and the tango crumpled to the floor like a rag doll, his knees simply folding beneath his lifeless body and his arms falling wide. The AK-47 clattered on the polished hardwood floor and slid to a stop against the bulkhead.

It all happened in under three seconds.

Bran lowered his weapon, the world snapping back

into focus as he drew in a deep breath, clocked his heart rate and breathing, and advanced into the room. Mason and Wolf continued to draw down on the scene, ever ready, ever steady.

He'd made it two steps in when he realized the boy wasn't a boy at all, but a diminutive woman. His first clue was the hot-pink panties—after head-butting the terrorist, and with her wrists tied behind her back, her forward momentum meant she'd ended up face-first on the floor, her bottom thrust into the air, the hem of her robe pooling around her waist. His second clue was the *shape* of her plump ass. Seriously, it was the type of heart-shaped butt worthy of worship by native peoples.

The third clue was her voice, all cute and girly. Of course, her words were anything but. "Jesus Christ and all his followers! Quit starin' at my ass and help me up, would you?" She rolled onto her side. "This guy stunk like buzzard bait *before* he was dead. Lord help me if I get a snoot full of what he smells like now. We'll have more than blood and brains to clean up, if you catch my drift."

Huh. He would have expected crying, not cursing. Pleading, not pluckiness. Clearly the woman was—

He stopped dead in his tracks when she lifted her chin to look at him. She was a mix between Miley Cyrus and Carey Mulligan, with one hundred percent Julia Roberts lips—the top being slightly plumper than the bottom. Most people would call her "cute as a button." Bran would call her the yellow mist to his Green Lantern, the kryptonite to his Superman, the water to his Human Torch. Because one look at her and he was powerless, speechless, and…strangely, inexplicably…*captivated*.

Chapter Thirteen

2:55 p.m....

IN ANY OTHER SITUATION, ONE WHERE SHE HADN'T been beaten, hog-tied, held hostage, and forced to watch a man get shot right in front of her, Maddy might have considered the tall, granite-shouldered man standing in the middle of the bridge house swoon-worthy. *I mean, there's all that tan skin, that wide chest, and that shock of wavy brown hair.* As it was, she *had* been beaten, hog-tied, held hostage, and witnessed a violent death, so his mute, slack-jawed stare left her feeling decidedly... er...unsettled. *Pissed* even. Anger *was* her go-to emotion today, it seemed.

"Hello?" she huffed. "Mr. CIA Agent?"

That seemed to jog him out of whatever stupor he'd fallen into. He shook his head, sending water droplets raining onto the floor at his feet. His *bare* feet. *Hmm. Nice toes.* And *that* was a weird thought to have at a time like this, wasn't it?

Shock. She was clearly in shock.

"Why did you just call me that?" he demanded as the two men who'd stormed into the room with him started forward. One looked like he belonged as an extra in the movie *Dances with Wolves*. And the other should be sporting a leotard and slamming chairs over other men's backs. She'd swear on a stack of bibles his thighs were the size of the trunks on the camphor trees growing in her backyard. Or, as her daddy would say, he was *big enough to hunt a bear with a switch*.

"I—" she began, but stopped and gulped when the *Dances with Wolves* extra came at her with a knife. Thankfully, he only attacked the zip ties at her ankles and wrists before moving on to Harry—who had collapsed into the captain's chair, his eyes glued to the body of the man whose brains were now outside his skull and all over the bridge's window.

Don't look, Maddy, she told herself as she pushed into a seated position, her fingers and toes coming alive in a rush of pins and needles. She didn't keep her gaze averted because she thought Lead A-hole didn't deserve what he'd gotten. She'd seen that...*thing*...move behind his eyes when the door burst open, and she'd known he was going to kill her if she didn't do something quick; hence the head-butting. But she'd gone nearly thirty years without suffering night terrors that starred near-headless corpses, and she'd like to keep it that way, *thank you very much*.

Suddenly, Mr. Swoon-Worthy-on-Any-Other-Day was stalking toward her, the machine gun he'd used to bring down Lead A-hole now strapped to his back. And when she pictured CIA agents, they were smooth-talking, martini-drinking, 007 types. Definitely nothing like the three scruffy, tattooed men who surrounded her.

"*Why* do you think I'm CIA?" he demanded again, wrapping a hand around her upper arm and pulling her to her feet, not *un*-gently. Still, there was no mistaking the strength of his grip. She sucked in a breath and was pleased to discover he smelled like salt water and good, healthy American male. A welcome reprieve from Lead A-hole and the stank-ass of his odor-whelming cohorts.

"I say," Captain Harry blustered, "unhand her." He tried to push up from the chair, but Mr. Swoon-Worthy-on-Any-Other-Day's friends each slapped a hand on his shoulder, keeping him firmly seated.

"I'm all right," she assured the captain.

"Yeah," the guy manhandling her said. "She's fine. As long as she tells me why she thinks I'm CIA."

He was like a dog with a bone. "Oh, for the love of— Because *he* thought y'all were CIA," she said, waving in the general direction of Lead A-hole's body. Was his hand twitching? No. No, it most certainly was not. That would be too awful and…*gulp*. "And then when he sank your ship with rocket launchers and I watched you come after his men in a dinghy with guns a-blazin' Yosemite Sam-style, that pretty much sealed the deal for me."

She addressed her answer to the hollow of his throat, where his strong, steady pulse beat heavily. But she was fairly sure his gaze was drilling a hole into the top of her head, so she chanced a glance into his eyes. Instantly, she forgot about the body and twitching hand. Because this guy's eyes were…well…*pretty*. With very girly-looking lashes. Promptly she decided to shorten his name. *Mr. Swoon-Worthy, it is*.

"Why?" she demanded. "Are you *not* CIA?"

"Not by a long shot," he told her just as the back door to the bridge banged open, admitting a wild-eyed woman holding yet *another* machine gun. *Sweet blue blazes! Did I stumble into World War III?* And if these folks weren't with the Central Intelligence Agency, then just who the heckfire *were* they? DEA? NSA? Definitely not Coast Guard…

"Damnit, Olivia!" the big, golden god who shoul-
dered his way into the bridge behind the woman bellowed. "I told you to let me go first!"

The lady, Olivia apparently, quickly took in the scene
and lowered her weapon once she realized Mr. Swoon-
Worthy had already neutralized the threat.

"And I told *you* I'm not one of your men to go following your orders," she replied with a huff. "I'm an
asset. Which you'd *know* if you pulled your head out
of your ass and stopped with the high-and-mighty
this-is-men's-work-so-why-don't-you-go-paint-your-
fingernails-darlin' bullshit."

Golden God rolled in his lips as if fighting a smile.
And even though Maddy hadn't a clue what was going
on, and even though her heart was still racing a million
miles a minute, she found herself feeling an instant kin-
ship with this Olivia woman. She considered any chick
who wasn't afraid to stand up to men twice her size to
be a sister from another mister.

"Gentlemen"—Olivia turned away from the dripping-
wet Golden God to address the others on the bridge—"I
take it the yacht has been secured?"

"We haven't checked belowdecks yet," Mr. Swoon-
Worthy said. "But one of the two dudes trussed up on
the main deck said he counted—"

"You spoke to Nigel and Bruce?" Maddy interrupted,
her galloping heart tripping over itself. *Lord*, she'd been
worried sick about them. "Are they all right?"

Swoon-Worthy glanced down at her. Once again, she
was struck by those eyes. Brown. So heavily lashed it
looked like he was wearing eyeliner and mascara. *Warm*.
The light in them certainly didn't say coldhearted killer,

but there was a body on the floor to prove that wrong. A body she continued to studiously ignore because that *wasn't* liquid and solid matter she heard dripping off the window and onto the floor. Nope. Nah. It surely wasn't.

"If you call being sunburned and dehydrated all right," he said, "then, roger that, they're fine. Although, come to think of it, I can't really vouch for the one with the foul mouth. He strikes me as a guy suffering from asshole-itis."

Foul mouth? He had to be talking about Bruce. Maddy had noticed the engineer used "bloody" every other word. But if he was strong enough to curse, that meant he was okay. She blew out a relieved breath. No one had died or been seriously injured by her decision to approach that dinghy full of strangers—well…except for the strangers themselves—and for that she sent up a silent prayer of thanks.

"As I was saying," Swoon-Worthy continued, "Nigel said he counted seven tangos. Given the six in the dinghy we took out, and this one here, we may've got them all, and—"

"Tangos?" Maddy interrupted again. "That's what the military calls terrorists, isn't it?" So she'd been right all along. She really *had* been hijacked by a group of radicals. *Good God almighty!* It was one thing to *suspect*, another thing entirely to *know*. Her knees threatened to give out on her. Good thing Swoon-Worthy still held her in a firm grip. She could feel the heat of his wide palm all the way through the terrycloth of her robe.

"What do you know about what the military calls things?" He scowled heavily. A lesser woman might have shrunk away from that look. But growing up in a house filled with males meant she was immune to testosterone-laden facial threats.

"I watched *Captain Phillips*. The Navy SEALs in the movie called the bad guys 'tangos' and…" It suddenly hit her. These rough-and-tumble men looked *a lot* like the ones portrayed in the film. "Are y'all SEALs?" she asked, glancing over her shoulder at Dances with Wolves and Sir Lifts-Weights-a-Lot. Both of their eyes rounded, and she turned back to tilt her chin back, *way* back—being five feet tall had its disadvantages—to search Swoon-Worthy's face.

"We're not—" he began, then shook his head. Once again little drops of water showered from the thick strands of his hair. A few landed on her face. For some odd reason, she didn't brush them away. They grounded her. Gave her something to concentrate on besides her somersaulting insides and spinning head, not to mention they distracted her from that hand that *wasn't* twitching and those sounds that *weren't* biological matter splatting onto the floor.

"It's not—" She lifted a brow when he stopped again. "*We're* the ones asking the questions here!"

"Well, there's no need to get your boxers in a twist about it," she scolded him.

He blinked down at her, his expression one she'd seen plenty of times on the faces of the men in her life. It was a mixture of exasperation and bewilderment. "Can you believe the balls on this one?" He posed the question to the people in the room while pointing a finger at her.

"Maddy," Captain Harry said, "perhaps it's best if you—"

"First things first," the woman cut off the captain. She

walked in Maddy's direction, water sluicing down her bare legs and leaving wet footprints on the floor. Maddy noticed she didn't spare the body sprawled in front of the console a single glance. Maddy couldn't blame her. No one wanted to see *that*. She considered asking someone to run downstairs and grab a sheet to cover it, but the raven-haired gal preempted her with, "We need to make sure the boat is secure. Are there any more tangos on board?"

"No," Maddy assured her. "There were just the seven."

"Good." Olivia nodded, smiling. Maddy was surprised to discover the woman was much younger than she initially assumed. The way she handled the weapon and the confident fashion with which she carried herself—not to mention she sort of seemed to be in charge here—spoke of years of experience. But her unlined skin and bright, twinkling eyes said she was either *really* well-preserved or not a lot older than Maddy herself. Late twenties, *maybe* early thirties.

"Your Intel and the footage from the warehouse said there were eight," Golden God said, and now that he wasn't shouting, she recognized his voice and his Deep South accent from the radio.

Intel. As in intelligence? And they claimed they weren't CIA or SEALs? *Who else talks like that?* She'd seen enough Jason Bourne and Mission Impossible movies to know government-speak when she heard it. Not that movies always got it right, but still…

"It did," the woman agreed, letting her eyes drift back to Maddy. "You won't care if I send two men belowdecks to check your story, will you?"

"Be my guest."

She watched Olivia glance toward Dances with

Wolves and Sir Lifts-Weights-a-Lot. She didn't utter a word. None were needed apparently because the men re-shouldered their weapons and disappeared through the bridge's interior door.

"Now," the woman said, her voice dark and throaty, reminding Maddy of an NPR host. "You want to tell us what happened?"

"I do." Maddy nodded. "Just as soon y'all tell me who the hell you are."

"My name is Olivia," the woman answered easily.

"Well, duh." She frowned. "These things on the side of my head are called ears." When Olivia lifted a brow, Maddy tilted her head toward the blond behemoth. "I heard the golden god over there call you that when you came bargin' in."

"Oh, ay!" Swoon-Worthy interjected. She'd bet her bottom dollar he grew up somewhere in east Jersey, close to New York City. "A set of balls *and* a smart mouth. Anyone ever told you neither of those things is very attractive on a lady?"

"Yep. All the time," she assured him. "Anyone ever tell *you* that when you find a group of folks who just got shanghaied by terrorists they *thought* were Cuban refugees, and then after that same group of folks watched you *kill* all those not-really-Cuban refugees, you should skip the personal introductions because, Lucy, you got some serious 'splainin' to do? When I—"

"Maddy," Captain Harry tried to interrupt again, but she kept talking right over him.

"—asked who the hell you were, I meant who the hell are you workin' for and what the hell is goin' on here? And just what the hell did we stumble…er…*sail* into?"

And, sure enough. She was probably pushing her luck. But between the shock of everything that'd happened, the dead body on the ground at her feet, and the weirdly distracting warmth caused by Swoon-Worthy's nearness, she feared she was edging her way toward a full-on emotional or psychological breakdown, or both. And since she abhorred appearing weak, she tended to go in the complete *opposite* direction, putting on a brazen, in-your-face, won't-back-down front.

Thankfully, it seemed to work. "You're right," Olivia said. "You deserve to know what's happening." Maddy blew out a covert breath. "But first, go back. You thought those men were Cuban refugees? Why?"

"Well..." Maddy lifted her hands, relieved to discover they were no longer tingling from lack of circulation. But they were shaking. Definitely shaking. *I'll just keep them clasped behind my back, how about that?* Yessiree, Bob, that sounded like a good plan. "Because they were floatin' in a broken-down dinghy out in the middle of the Straits of Florida. And they *looked* the part."

"Fits yours and Morales's theory about their boat sinkin'," Golden God said.

"Yeah." Olivia nodded at him before returning her attention to Maddy. "And you...what? Tried to bring them on board so you could take them to the authorities?"

Not knowing just *which* government authority these folks reported to, and wanting to avoid any time in an eight-by-ten—she looked *ghastly* in orange—she decided it was probably best to keep her answer vague. "Somethin' like that."

Swoon-Worthy grunted, a deep sound that reverberated low in her belly. When she looked up, it was to

discover his pretty eyes were narrowed into slits that
caused his thick lashes to cast crescent-shaped shadows
on his cheeks. He wasn't buying her story. No real surprise there. She'd never been very good at lying. Her
mama always told her she had an honest face and any
fibs flashed across her expression like neon signs on Las
Vegas Boulevard.

"I, uh, I see," Olivia said, and Maddy suspected she
just might. But, thankfully, she didn't pursue the subject further. Instead she said, "Okay, so here's what you
need to know. Those *were* terrorists. They were floating
out here because they—"

"You really think you should be tellin' her all this?"
Golden God interjected.

"Come on, Leo," Olivia said. Leo? *Hmm. Fits.*
"After everything they've witnessed here today"—she
hooked her thumb over her shoulder at Lead A-hole's
corpse—"they'll have to be debriefed and made to sign
nondisclosure contracts, and the yacht will have to be
impounded for evidence collection. Given all that, I
don't see the harm in letting them in on the basics."

The basics. Not too hard to read between the lines of
that one. Of course, the fact no one was going to give
her the whole truth and nothing but the truth was playing
second fiddle in her mind to the word "debriefed." She
imagined herself sitting in a soundproof room, hooked
up to a lie detector while a bare overhead bulb shone
down on a bunch of men in suits who would pummel her
with questions while recording every single word out of
her mouth. *This day is crazier than a three-dollar bill.*

"You're the boss." Leo threw up his hands, but it was
obvious from his expression that he didn't *really* believe

that. *Also* what was obvious from his expression was
that he had a thing for Olivia. It was the way he looked
at her, his eyes following her every move, his gaze cov-
etous and molten. Lava hot. Some other time, Maddy
might have taken a moment to wonder what the dealio
was with those two. But today she had bigger things to
wonder about. Starting with…

"*Why* were they floatin' out there?" she prompted
Olivia, itching, as Paul Harvey used to say, to hear the
rest of the story.

"Because they stole something from us and were
making a run for it."

And it didn't take a Rhodes Scholar to figure out that
Olivia wasn't going to elaborate on exactly what had
been stolen. "And by 'us' you mean…?"

"Let's just say we're working for the government.
And that's all you need to know."

Maddy tilted her head toward Lead A-hole's body.
"He thought you were CIA." She jerked her chin at
Swoon-Worthy. "But he says you're not."

Olivia shrugged, but there was a definite gleam in
her eye.

"Okay." Maddy puffed out a breath. "So, let's say
I'm buyin' what you're sellin' and willin' to go along
with it because, hey, what choice do I have? Y'all have
the weapons, right? I only have one question left."

"What's that?" Swoon-Worthy asked.

"Did you come out here to kill those men? Or did you
come out here lookin' to recover what they stole?"

"The latter," Olivia admitted. "We didn't even know
for sure if they'd survived the sinking of their boat."
Which would make sense, seeing as how Olivia and

the boys obviously hadn't been prepared to face those dadgummed rocket launchers. "And, quite frankly, their deaths cause us more problems than they provide solutions. There are questions they could have answered. Very important questions."

Very *secret* questions, apparently. But that was fine by Maddy. She figured the less she knew about the nitty-gritty of it all, the better. Government agents were known to fit pesky, inquisitive civilians with cement galoshes, right? Or, again, was that just in the movies?

Something caught Olivia's attention. It was the satellite phone that Lead A-hole had smashed in a fit of rage when he realized his men weren't going to emerge from beneath the undulating surface of the sea. She bent down to grab it, and the golden god…er…*Leo* basically smacked her ass with his eyes. Maddy thought just maybe she could hear a tiny thwacking sound echo through the bridge.

"What's this?" Olivia asked, holding up the decimated clump of plastic and wires.

"Lead A-hole's…er…that's what I was callin' the guy…satellite phone," Maddy said. "Or what's left of it anyway."

"Did he make any calls?" That gleam was back in Olivia's eyes.

"Yeah. He made one right after y'all hailed us on the radio. But I couldn't tell you what he said other than he wanted to sink your boat with his rocket launchers. He was speakin' in another language most of the time. I think maybe it was Arabic." Of course, it could have been Farsi or Tajiki. An expert in Middle Eastern dialects she was not.

"He didn't make another call after firing the rocket launchers? After the guys here killed his men?"

"No."

Olivia's eyes swung back and forth, the way a chess player's did when contemplating the next series of moves. Finally, she glanced up, pinning Maddy in place with a hard, searching stare. *If this gal isn't a spy, she missed her calling.* That look reminded Maddy of Angelina Jolie when she played Salt. "And there was nothing he said that you understood? No phrase or word that he repeated?"

"There was something," Captain Harry piped up. When she glanced over, Maddy saw he had some color back in his face. That was good. For a while there, after Lead A-Hole demanded they weigh anchor—and after he forced her to her knees execution-style—she was worried Harry might suffer a coronary. "But now I can't remember what it sounded like."

"Oh, yeah." She nodded, frowning. "He kept sayin' 'Banoo, banoo, banoo.'"

"Mean anything to you?" Leo asked Olivia.

She shook her head. "Not a thing. Could be a person's name."

Feet pounded up the stairs outside and Leo, Olivia, and Swoon-Worthy—*I wonder what his name is?*—all armed themselves, their big, black machine guns up in firing position in a split second. The destroyed satellite phone fell out of Olivia's hand and slid toward the bulkhead, butting up against Lead A-hole's weapon. Maddy prepared herself for another blast of gunfire, lifting her hands to her ears and grimacing. But it was just the hugely muscle-bound guy who threw open the door.

"Find anything, Mason?" Leo asked. Mason, Mason, Mason... Maddy committed the name to memory as she lowered her hands. She certainly couldn't call him Sir Lifts-Weights-a-Lot to his face.

"Nothing. Yacht's clean."

"And Wolf?" Leo asked. "Where's he?" Maddy blinked. What were the odds she'd been calling him "Dances with Wolves" when his real name was Wolf?

"Down uncuffing the rest of the crew and getting them some water. What's the plan now?"

A strange silence descended over the room, and then Leo glanced at Olivia. "With the *Wayfarer* and all our gear gone, there's no way we can dive down and retrieve..." He let his sentence dangle, flicking Maddy and the captain a look. "The jig is up. We have to mark this one in the *L* column."

"Uh...we have dive equipment," Maddy offered, ignoring the little voice in her head that was screaming, What *the hell are you doin'? Just stay calm, stay quiet, and get yourself out of this as quickly as you can!* Calm she figured she could handle. The *quiet* part was never something she'd been good at. "Wet suits and tanks, buoyancy compensators and—"

"We need special deep-dive gear," Leo cut in. "The bottom is two hundred feet down."

"Right. So you'd want tanks with oxygen, helium, and nitrogen. Trimix, yeah? And a special high-performance regulator?" *What the blue blazes do you think you're doin'?* She felt all eyes in the room land on her. "What? My oldest brother is a diver. And he wanted to go down on a wreck that was past the 130-foot mark, so he got certified. All his gear is on board and—"

"Maddy," Mr. Swoon-Worthy said, and she glanced up to see him smiling at her. She nearly ass-planted at the sight. Because if he was swoon-worthy before, now he was panty-melting. She'd never seen a man quite so handsome. *It should be outlawed*.

"What?" she asked, unconsciously licking her lips.

"Anybody ever tell you that big brass balls and a loud mouth are sexy as hell when they're combined with deep-dive equipment?"

She snorted, the sound not at all ladylike. "Nope," she told him, a wry smirk kicking up the corners of her mouth. What the heckfire was wrong with her? Nothing about this situation should make her smile. But here she was, grinning like a loon. "You'd be the first."

Chapter Fourteen

3:37 p.m.…

"HAVE THEY FOUND IT YET?" LEO ASKED, CLOSING THE refrigerator door and leaning against it.

Olivia propped her hip on the counter in the yacht's galley. Unlike the one on *Wayfarer-I*, this floating kitchen had all the bells and whistles. Stainless-steel countertops, rich teakwood cabinets, and a wine refrigerator stocked to the gills with expensive vintages. *Fancy*. But she preferred the salvage boat's galley. Probably because it reminded her of Leo. No frills, no frippery, a little rough around the edges, but completely, one hundred percent dependable. Practical. Unfortunately, thanks to her, *that* galley was now sitting at the bottom of the Straits.

Guilt and regret had pretty much become her constant companions since Syria. And when you added in the steaming pile of shit that this day had become? Yeah, she might need to come up with some pet names for the twin emotions soon.

"No." She shook her head. "But it's not for lack of trying. Everyone except the engineer and the deckhand, who I suspect are in their cabins slathering themselves in aloe, is on the bridge with eyes on the depth reader and the fish-finder sonar."

"That can't be fun," Leo said, twisting off the cap on a bottle of Fiji water.

"Well, it's not nearly as high-tech as the equipment on *your* ship, but since we know approximately where to search, the gear on board should be enough to do the job."

"I meant bein' up on the bridge. You know, what with the near-headless terrorist and all."

"Oh. Yeah." There was *that*. "Maddy put a sheet over him and another over most of the mess." The woman was like a shaken soda can, fizzing with energy and vitality. "So it's not as bad as it was. But, still…" She shuddered.

"You're not very good around dead bodies, are you?" He took a swig of water, his tan throat working over the liquid. She wanted to stop talking about corpses and walk over there to run her tongue over his pulse point, feel the life in him thrumming hot and heavy against her lips. He would welcome it, she knew. *More* than welcome it. He'd probably make that low, growly noise in the back of his throat, the one that was both a supplication and a warning. But to do that would be the coward's way out.

She crossed her arms, not sure if the gesture was one of self-defense or more because the interior of the yacht was air-conditioned and the cool air against her damp clothes raised goose bumps. "Is *anyone* good around dead bodies?" she asked.

He shrugged one huge, bare shoulder. *He* didn't seem to notice the chill. Probably because he'd already changed out of his soaking clothes and donned a wet suit. Or *partially* donned a wet suit. He was only really wearing the lower half. The upper half was unzipped and rolled down around his trim waist, the neoprene arms dangling beside his thickly muscled thighs. That meant his mile-wide chest with its smattering of burnished blond hair was on display. Maddy had called him a golden god. Olivia couldn't refute her. All that tan skin, all those gleaming muscles, all that health and breadth and height *did* make him seem almost ethereal. Too perfect to be mortal.

But then there were his scars…

Add one more to the list. He'd hurriedly pulled the edges of the torn flesh on his right shoulder together with a half-dozen butterfly bandages. But no amount of suturing would keep it from leaving one whopper of a mark above his big, colorful Navy SEAL Budweiser tattoo. And besides revealing that he was, indeed, corporeal, all the evidence on his body of past injuries spoke rather loudly of the life he'd led. A life of fighting and violence. A life of *killing*.

"Do you ever think maybe the things we do in the name of the flag make us bad people?" she asked, fiddling with the long black thread that had come unraveled from the hem of her tank top. Not meeting his eyes.

"Nope," he said, his lips making the *P*-sound really pop. "I *know* I'm a bad person." And *that* had her gaze snapping up to search his face. "I think you have to have a bit of bad in you to do what we do. But we're bad people workin' on the good side. And that makes it okay. Because the bad people workin' on the good side are the only things standin' between the good people and the bad people who are workin' on the *bad* side. Every lie I've ever told, every life I've ever taken was in the name of keepin' innocents safe. And *that's* what lets me sleep at night."

Which made sense. *Perfect* sense. Still...

"I just feel like—" She blew out a breath and glanced over her shoulder toward the line of oblong portholes and the rays of golden light shining through them. Dust motes danced on the beams like tiny sparkling fairies. So pretty. So simple.

Why can't everything be that simple? A dance of dust in the sun?

But that was a ridiculous question, wasn't it? Considering she'd spent her entire life dreaming of being a spy, which was about as far from *simple* as a person could get. Of course, there was that saying about being careful what you wish for. And its bosom buddy: "Nothing is ever what it seems."

Maybe she'd just *convinced* herself that's the kind of life she wanted because it was easier. If she *chose* a solitary existence, a life that kept her from ever getting too close to anyone, no one could ever reject her or pass her over again. Remaining aloof and unloved would be *her* decision and—

Whoa there, Nelly. Don't go getting all maudlin. Next thing you know, you'll be sporting sweats, eating frozen dinners, and drinking boxed wine. Olivia Mortier: cover girl of Woe Is Me *magazine.*

Okay, so, armchair psychoanalysis aside, the fact remained that she still had physical symptoms to worry about. "I get sick to my stomach when I see mortal violence," she admitted to him. "Literally sick. That's why I had to leave the bridge. It was either that or introduce everyone up there to the breakfast I had on this morning's flight to Key West."

"You say that like it's a bad thing."

She turned to find him walking toward her. His loose-hipped strut emphasized his coordination, his extreme agility. And she could have gone on simply watching him move, watching his muscles ripple, his skin catch the light and gleam, for the rest of her life. But he finished off the bottle of water in one long gulp—hydrating before the dive because hydrated blood meant thin blood which, in turn, meant more easily oxygenated blood—and set the empty container on the counter behind her. He kept his hands planted on the cabinet top on either side of her waist, boxing her in. She was instantly awash in the waves of heat coming off him. It was delicious, *comforting*. She wanted to snuggle into him like a cat curling up in a patch of sunshine.

"Do you *think* it's a bad thing, darlin'?" His tone was hot and dark, his accent as syrupy as burned sugar.

"Considering my line of work," she said, not surprised to hear her voice had gone hoarse. His nearness always had that effect on her, "tossing my cookies at the first sight of violence could be a bit of a hindrance. To me. To whoever my partner might be at the time."

"Listen." He placed a warm hand on her shoulder. She was instantly reminded of the feel of his callused palm on her breast, how the roughness had abraded and stimulated her nipple. "If the loss of life, whether that life be one of good or evil, didn't make you sick, *that's* when I'd start to worry about you."

She pursed her lips.

"I've seen it happen," he continued. "Men who've grown so hard over the years that death and violence no longer affect them. *Those* are the guys who wind up on the news because they ran into a village and murdered a bunch of women and children. Killin' *shouldn't* be an easy thing to see *or* to do, Olivia. When it *becomes* easy, that's when you can go from bein' a bad guy workin' on the good side to bein' a bad guy workin' on the bad side."

"*You* make it look easy," she whispered, remembering the quick, efficient way he'd dispatched the tango who drew down on them in the water.

"There's a world of difference between proficiency and ease," he said. "I'm *proficient* at it. But don't think for an instant it's ever easy. I *live* with the lives I've taken. Every day. And even though I feel each kill was necessary, even righteous in some cases, even though I have no trouble sleepin' at night, that doesn't mean I'm not changed by each one of them. Just a little. Made less somehow. And made more somehow too."

Again, everything he was saying made sense, but... "I'm afraid I won't be able to do my job," she admitted. "I'm afraid someone will be depending on me to cover their backs, and I'll be too busy horking my guts up to do it."

He pulled her close and she went willingly, wrapping her arms around his waist and flattening her hands against his warm back. His skin was impossibly smooth, and the hard muscles made a deep groove of his spine. When she pressed her cheek against his chest, next to the old silver coin he wore around his neck, he smelled like sea and sand, like sunshine and Leo. He smelled like everything she'd never known was missing in her life.

"That won't happen," he assured her. "You won't *let* that happen."

Oh, she wished she felt as sure as he sounded...

—∞—

3:41 p.m....

"And the truth of the matter is, I don't want to be a bad guy. Even if I *am* working on the good side," she admitted, her soft lips moving against the skin of his chest, her hot breath tickling the hairs there. "I want to be a *good* guy."

Had Leo not heard it with his own ears, he wouldn't have believed Olivia's tone could ever be described as plaintive. And because he loved her, those three pitiful sentences curled themselves around his heart and squeezed. He wanted to roll her in bubble wrap, lock her in a closet, and stand guard outside with an Uzi. Just to keep her safe from the world, from ever feeling like she wasn't good enough or worthy enough, from ever having to witness death or dying again. For all her bravery and bravado, Olivia Mortier had a tender, sweet heart.

He hoped one day, maybe someday soon, to win that heart for himself.

Pulling her closer, he planted a kiss atop her damp head, loving the way her hair felt against his lips. "Did somethin' happen in the last eighteen months?"

She pushed back to blink up at him. Were her eyes overly bright? He cocked his head. *Nah.* She might be letting him see her softer side, but that stopped well short of tears. He wondered absently what it would take to bring Special Agent Olivia Mortier to tears. Then immediately hoped he'd never get the opportunity to find out. The sight would likely bring him to his knees.

"What do you mean?" she asked.

"I just mean...and don't take this the wrong way, but I can't help but notice you seem different."

"How's that?"

"Gentler, maybe? More circumspect?"

She caught her bottom lip between her teeth. He tried not to let the fact that he got a peek at that front tooth register with the moron in his wet suit. Unfortunately, the moron was nothing if not observant, ready to spring to life at the drop of a hat. *For chrissakes*.

"You mean nervous, right? Less sure of myself?" Her tone definitely wasn't plaintive now. It was...*shaken*. And that gutted him like a fish.

"No," he assured her, but her eyes slid away from him. A sure sign she didn't believe him. He grabbed her chin, forcing her to meet his gaze. "*No*, Olivia. That's not what I meant at all. I mean you seem more careful, more cautious. And I can't help but wonder if somethin' happened that caused you to—"

"Oh, other than my life happening?" she blurted, her blue eyes wild. "Other than I spend every day trying to stay two steps ahead of people who would like nothing better than to see our country burned to ashes, and the whole awful truth is that it's terrifying and exhausting? Other than I'm thirty years old and I don't even...don't even..." She stumbled to a stop, shaking her head. "Forget it." She sliced a hand through the air karate-chop style. "I'm just having a crisis of confidence, I think. Given the way this whole mission has gone, can you really blame me?"

He clocked her change of subject with a raised brow but decided not to push it. "You couldn't have known any of this would happen, and besides—"

She shoved a finger against his lips, and it took every ounce of restraint he possessed not to suck it into his mouth.

"Don't," she warned him, her husky voice like a wet tongue swirling around inside his ear. Her hair was starting to dry, and the salt water made it wave around her face and shoulders. He liked it. It made her look unkempt, a wilder, freer version of Olivia.

"Don't make any more excuses for me. This has been a shit show since minute one. And I swear…I *swear* I'll make it up to you, Leo. I'll have the CIA buy you another ship, a *better* ship. I'll have Morales increase the fee we're paying you. I'll—"

"Don't make promises your boss won't let you keep," he told her kindly. He'd been in the biz long enough to realize Uncle Sam expected guts but rarely gave any glory. "And speakin' of your boss, what did he say when you called him?"

She'd been forced to break protocol and contact Morales via the yacht's unsecured satellite phone. But Leo suspected she'd kept things short and sweet, speaking in the kind of Company code-talk that sounded like nothing but said everything. Even if the mole or moles had somehow been listening in, Leo suspected they would be hard-pressed to make heads or tails of what had been discussed.

"He's unhappy we couldn't manage to keep even *one* of the radicals alive to interrogate, but the fact that you'll be going down to retrieve the capsules makes up for it a bit."

"Can't fault the guy for wantin' it all, I reckon," he mused with a half-grin. He'd met Morales once. The man was impatient and rude, but utterly brilliant. A mind like a steel trap. Leo took comfort in knowing Morales had his finger on the pulse of international intrigue.

"I don't want you to do it."

"What?" His chin jerked back so hard it was a wonder his head didn't go tumbling off the column of his neck.

"It was one thing when I thought you'd have your team by your side, but it's another thing entirely to send you down there all by yourself. Leo"—she placed her hands on either side of his face—"it's dangerous. If something goes wrong with your regulator or your tanks, there'll be no one to help you."

"I've checked Maddy's brother's equipment," he assured her. "It's good to go. And Wolf will suit up in the regular scuba gear and hang out at the halfway point. We'll attach a rope between us. If things go wrong, he can reel me up and—"

"Don't bullshit me, Leonardo David Anderson," she spat, giving his head a little shake. His mouth curled at her use of his full name, and he was keenly aware of the cool pads of her fingertips against his cheeks. He wanted to feel them skimming over every inch of his body. Over his shoulders, his belly. Rubbing over his nipples, the head of his—

"If something goes wrong, there's nothing that can be done for you at that depth. You'll either drown, or you'll have to rise too quickly and get DCS."

That she knew the divers' abbreviation for decompression sickness surprised him. Though, it probably shouldn't. Olivia prided herself on being at the top of her game, keeping herself apprised of every little detail of her missions.

"And if I *don't* go down and get those capsules, then what?" he asked.

"Morales can call in an active SEAL Team to retrieve them, go the whole nine yards and—"

"Obliterate your chances to keep flyin' under the radar," he finished for her. "Christ, Olivia, the point of all of this was so that you and your boss could try to make sure this snafu stays under wraps so you will have another shot at catchin' the traitor or traitors inside the CIA. Now you want to throw that all away? It'll make the sinkin' of *Wayfarer-I* completely meaningless. Everything will have been for nothin'."

"But Maddy said that terrorist made a phone call after we hailed them from the *Wayfarer*. He thought we were CIA, which means it's likely he passed his supposition along. The mole or moles, whoever they are, are probably already busy covering their tracks."

She was reaching, and that wasn't like her. "First of all, Bran said one look in the guy's eyes told him the dude was crazy on a cracker. And crazy on a cracker usually goes hand-in-hand with paranoia. He was probably seeing government spooks lurkin' in every corner. So the question becomes, even if he *did* pass along his supposition, would the traitors really believe him? And do you really want to risk everything you've worked for on the off chance they did? And second of all, you can't be one hundred percent certain it was even *them* on the other end of the line. That phone call could have been to anyone."

"But—"

"Darlin'…" He placed his hands on her hips, loving the subtle roundness of them. They fit perfectly into the curve of his palms. "I've done this dozens of times before. I'll be all right. Let me do this for you." *Because I love you.* "Let me finish it." *Could you love me, too?*

She blinked and, after a bit, hesitantly nodded. Her expression remained troubled.

He knew just how to take her mind off her worries. "How about you give me a little kiss for luck, though. You know, just in case."

She bit the inside of her cheek, her eyes taking on a definite sparkle. *Bingo, bango, bongo.* "That'll never work," she said, squeaking when he pulled her close so they were pelvis-to-pelvis, so she could feel what she did to him, *know* what she did to him. She gasped at the contact, her succulent mouth falling open the tiniest bit. An invitation to put something in there, perhaps?

Most certainly. But that would come later. For now… "Why won't it work?" he asked, bending to run his nose over her temple, closing his eyes and breathing her in. Salt water and jasmine and…Olivia. *His* Olivia.

"Because we're incapable of *little* kisses," she told him, her voice going all through him, lighting him up, burning him down. He wanted her to go on talking forever. Just so he could listen. And enjoy. "Our little kisses turn into *big* kisses. And then our big kisses end up with one of my nipples in your mouth."

He groaned at the memory. "Exactly," he murmured, framing her beloved face with his hands and hungrily claiming her lips.

She met him openmouthed, eagerly, her agile tongue darting out to greet his. And then there were no more words. No *need* for words. They spoke with their bodies, with their hands. With their sighs and their moans of pleasure and encouragement. And just as she'd said, the little kiss turned into a big kiss. Into a *long* kiss. It went on and on, lips and teeth and tongues mating over and over. It was delicious. Decadent. But he wanted more. So, *so* much more.

Thankfully, he knew the way to more now, had mapped this part of the journey before, back on the *Wayfarer*. So he reached around to palm her sweet ass and simultaneously pulled the hem of her tank top over the tops of her breasts. This time he flicked open the back closure of her bra before yanking both cups down. He broke the sanctity of the kiss because he just had to look.

And the sight that met his eyes had his blood roaring through his veins like lit kerosene. Black tank top above. Black bra cups below. And in the middle were two lovely, creamy mounds of feminine flesh with quarter-sized, berry-colored nipples. She was perfect. Perfectly edible. From the plump of her cheeks when she smiled to the subtle arch of her back where her waist met her ass. Curves. She was endless, delicate curves. And he was going to feast on all of them.

Starting now.

"Leo…" She breathed his name when he released her amazing derriere to cup a luscious breast in each hand. He pushed them up and together, so he barely had to turn his head to lave first one pouting nipple, then the other. "Oh God," she moaned when her areolas contracted, forcing the tips of her breasts to rise high and tight against the rasp of his tongue.

He flicked gently at first, then more forcefully. He was rewarded by the motion of her hips, rubbing, rubbing. She lifted her leg to hook her heel behind his knee,

opening herself wider, giving herself room to get the
friction just where she needed it. He could feel her sultry
heat even through the layers of her cotton shorts and his
neoprene wet suit. He wanted to touch. *Now!*

Keeping one hand on her breast, his lips suctioned
tight around her sweet nipple, he slid his other hand
down her warm, quivering belly until he reached the snap
on her shorts. It came free with a flick of his fingers. The
zipper seemed to melt away, and then… *Sweet Christ!*

He palmed her over the top of her black lace panties
and discovered just how wet, just how hot she really
was. Pressing the heel of his palm into the top of her sex
where he suspected she was swollen and begging for
stimulation, he moaned when her fingers speared into
his hair, her nails biting into his scalp. A little pinch
of pain to go along with the pleasure of the woman he
loved panting and shaking in his arms.

"Please, Leo. I want you to—Oh, God, *yes!*"

He slid his fingers into the waistband of her panties, past the patch of neatly trimmed hair and into the
wet, hot channel between her swollen lips. She instantly
bathed him in her passion, coating the tips of his fingers as he rubbed back and forth, back and forth over
the distended nub of nerves. *Just as I thought. Beggin'
for stimulation.*

Her head fell back. Her hips undulated up and down,
showing him without words how she liked to be stroked,
how she liked to be loved. He committed every subtle
move, every slight shift to memory.

Her hands left his hair to run over his shoulders and
chest, her nails skimming lightly over his nipples, both
satisfaction and threat until he was forced to suck in a

ragged breath. It was almost as if she'd run those cool fingers over the head of his dick. And then... *Jesus Christ on the cross!* She was doing exactly that, shoving her hand beneath the material of the wet suit to palm him. His cock jumped at the contact of her fingertips. A tiny drop of passion oozed from his tip. She used her thumb to spread it around his aching, swollen head. And that's when he knew it was time to taste her.

———

3:51 p.m....

He was just the sexiest man alive...

That's all there was to it. The way he kissed, all soft, languid thrusts of his tongue, was a dream. The way he moved, every action both natural and at the same time calculated, was heaven. The way he felt, hot skin over hard muscles, was bliss. And when he fell to his knees in front of her, dragging her shorts and panties down to her ankles along the way, she thought she might faint. Her head was spinning. Her blood racing. The room around her was swaying back and forth.

Or was that just the rocking of the yacht? *Doesn't matter. The effect is the same.* She was on a carnival ride of sensation, her stomach rising and falling in anticipation and delight.

His nostrils flared, as if he was scenting her. And perhaps that should have been disconcerting. Maybe it *would* have been disconcerting had those flaring nostrils not been accompanied by the low groan in the back of his throat, the one that went to her head like a straight shot of tequila. He licked his lips like a starving man presented with a buffet. His tongue flashed deep pink against the brown stubble of his beard. "Step out of your shorts, Olivia," he instructed, his voice having gone guttural, the low purr of a big cat.

She wanted to. Oh, how she wanted to, but... "Jesus, Leo. *Here?*"

"My men will know to steer clear," he assured her.

Despite her protests, she found herself toeing out of her shorts and panties. "And the others?"

"A risk I'm willin' to take if you are."

Some people got off on the idea of allowing strangers a little voyeuristic pleasure. *She* usually preferred to do the deed in private, so all of her attention could be focused on her own responses and the responses of her lover. But a stroll to the nearest cabin would take precious few minutes she didn't have. She was so achy, so empty. She needed him now.

"Yes," she breathed. "Please, Leo."

A victorious growl rumbled through his chest and, inexplicably, through her sex. It was almost as if he'd put a vibrator inside her. Her bare toes curled against the polished hardwood floor. She expected him to rise, to pull down his wet suit and impale her on his thick, pulsing length.

She was preparing herself for it, girding her loins, quite literally, to receive all that hot, heaving flesh. Which is why she squeaked when, instead, he hooked her leg over his shoulder and buried his face in her. His lips found the swollen bud at the top of her sex unerringly. And he sucked it into his mouth, boldly laving it with the pad of his raspy tongue.

Now, in her experience, very few men were experts

at pleasuring a woman with their mouths. Most were too frenzied, trying to turn their tongues into windup toys. Others were too gentle, like they thought the vagina was a delicate flower needing the softest of touches lest its petals fall off. In fact, in her whole life she'd never met a guy who knew the exact amount of friction to use, the appropriate amount of pressure to apply. That is, until she met Leo. He was the Goldilocks of cunnilingus. He did everything *just right*.

As a result, her body was instantly humming. The passion running through her veins, the liquid heat tightening her womb, telling her she wouldn't last long under his oral assault. And, *oh,* the sweet, welcome agony of it!

"Yesssss," she hissed, burying her fingers in the coolness of his shaggy hair and looking down to see his lips on her, see her leg over his shoulder obscuring part of the tattooed lettering that ran in an arc across his back from shoulder to shoulder. *Not All Treasure Is Silver and Gold.*

And ain't that the truth. Right now, her treasure was the man loving her so well, with so much dedication and passion.

"You taste amazin'," he growled. Then he proved he wasn't lying by vigorously feasting on her like a condemned man devouring his last meal. Her breasts felt heavy, hot. Their tips ached with arousal and thrummed with the pleasure his mouth and teeth and tongue had forced on them. Her clitoris began to buzz, sending tendrils of sensation radiating outward toward her extremities. She would swear she could feel the pleasure throbbing in her toes, her fingertips. The hot coil

of delectation wound tighter and tighter. *Almost there.*
Almost there. In fact, if he would just—

It was like he was reading her mind, because he
inserted one long finger inside her. It was nearly enough.
She clenched her inner muscles around him and his
groan of approval resonated through her. "Leo…" She
moaned his name again when he inserted a second digit.
He pumped into her once. Twice. Seating himself to the
last knuckle each time. His fingers curled slightly in a
come-hither motion, and the rough pads of his fingertips
caressed her in just. The. Right. Spot.

She fisted her fingers in his hair, anchoring herself
to him as she rode his hand and mouth, as she was
flung over the edge and into the dark chasm of physical
release. A kaleidoscope of colors exploded behind her
lids. Waves upon waves of pleasure rushed over her,
through her, until she was reduced to nothing but a mass
of pulsing delight.

She whispered something—his name, maybe?—
over and over again, her head limp on her neck, her
hands falling listlessly to her sides. He kissed the inside
of her quivering thigh before gently lowering her leg
and standing. It was a good thing the cabinet was at her
back, supporting her, because she was completely boneless. Nothing but a soft, gooey thing in the aftermath of
his lovemaking.

He kissed her exposed throat, sucking on her ham-
mering pulse-point, growling at the feel of her racing
heart against his tongue. She didn't open her eyes. She
was pretty sure she wouldn't be able to see anything
even if she did. Cloudbursts of colors were still painting
themselves on the backs of her lids.

She licked her lips, smiling. Languid with release, yet yearning for more. "Your turn," she promised, panting. "Just as soon as I catch my breath."

His deep chuckle rumbled through her chest, knocking against her heart. "You are," he told her, sucking her earlobe into the wet, hot wonder of his mouth and keeping her blood running wild, "hands down, the *sexiest* woman on the planet. And I intend to—"

Whatever he intended to do or say was cut off when a series of pounding steps echoed from the stairs leading down from the living quarters. "Sorry to interrupt! Again!" Bran's deep voice rolled into the galley.

Leo growled. A sound of murderous frustration if ever there was one. "I'm seriously goin' to kill him this time."

Olivia opened her eyes to find color riding high on his cheekbones. His eyes were dark with unfulfilled passion. *Oh*, how she wanted to fulfill that passion, feel him pulse deep inside her, see his jaw clench and his eyes sparkle as he found his own release. "I'll help," she groused as she pulled up her bra, yanked down her tank top, and bent to retrieve her panties and shorts.

Holy shit, I'm dizzy. All the blood in her body was still circulating around her happy bits. She had to blink and shake her head, trying to jog her brain and body out of let's-get-it-on mode and back into business mode. *Easier said than done.* Especially with Leo standing so close. The length of his hard-on was a massive wedge beneath his wet suit.

"Give us a second, will you?" Leo called, turning to make sure she was decent. When her fingers fumbled on the button of her shorts, he gently brushed them away, doing up the fastening himself. A small smile played around the edges of his mouth. That brilliant, *brilliant* mouth.

"You're pretty pleased with yourself, aren't you?" she asked.

He lifted a brow. "Shouldn't I be?"

"*Sh'yeaaah.*"

Now he was grinning in earnest. *Men. They give a woman an orgasm, and it's like they think they split the atom.*

"Admit the thundering herd," he called toward the door after she'd smoothed her hair as best she could. There was no hope for the beard burn she knew pinkened her cheeks, or the flush of the skin over her chest that was the telltale sign of her recent orgasm. She'd been caught getting busy with Leo. *Yet again.* His men must think her the easiest woman on the planet. And the truth? When it came to Leo, she absolutely was.

"We found it," Bran said from the doorway, taking in the scene with a leering smirk. "The tangos' sunken vessel. We've dropped anchor and a location buoy."

Leo sighed heavily and turned toward her. She wasn't prepared for the hand he wrapped around the back of her neck. Neither was she prepared for the deep, wet kiss he pressed on her mouth. Instantly her knees were weak…uh…weak*er*, her womb humming, her head spinning. Then he broke the seal of their lips and leaned his forehead against hers. "To be continued?" he asked, his words as slow and sweet as molasses.

"You bet your ass," she told him, smiling.

"We *do* seem to have the same conversations over and over again, don't we?" The question was purely rhetorical, because he released her to turn back to the two men standing by the door. And talk about a couple of voyeurs.

"Am I the only one who needs a cigarette after that?" Bran mock-whispered to Wolf.

"It's almost better than late-night Cinemax." Wolf chuckled.

Because she was a firm believer in the *If you can't beat them, join them* philosophy, and also because she couldn't allow them to know she was even the teensiest bit flustered, she called to Bran, "You have the *worst* timing, you know that? I mean, jeez, cliterference much?"

"Huh?" Bran asked. "What the heck is cliterference?"

Olivia grinned and winked at the men in the room. "It's the female version of cock-blocking. You know, cliterference? Damnit, Bran. It loses its *oomph* when I have to explain it."

Leo threw back his head and laughed. It was a good laugh. Deep and rolling. The kind that made you smile when you heard it. The kind that boomed around the room and inside her heart.

Chapter Fifteen

4:31 p.m....

THE INSTANT LEO'S FINS TOUCHED THE SANDY BOTTOM of the Florida Straits, he checked his diver's watch, then the dive computer beside it. The glowing readout said he was at a depth of 198 feet. *Deep*. But he'd been deeper. Numerous times. Of course, he'd always had a team of well-trained men swimming beside him.

He noticed the comfort he usually experienced when wrapped in the arms of Mother Ocean was strangely absent, the sense of solace oddly missing. In fact, as he switched on his headlamp, illuminating the dim water around him, he realized all he felt was...*alone*. Not scared or panicky, simply...*separate*.

Or maybe that's the gases messin' with my head. Was he a little dizzy? He checked his mixture, adjusted it a bit, tapped the gauges on his tanks to make sure they were reading correctly, and concentrated on his breathing. The gentle *sssskkkk, sssskkkk* of his regulator joined the chorus of bubbles that burbled happily as they traveled toward the surface. The water here wasn't cold...more like cool. A pool on the first day of summer. Still, he was glad for the protection of Maddy's brother's wet suit. The exposed skin on his hands and face grew chilled.

After a bit, he felt more clear-headed, though a

twinge of loneliness remained. He supposed that was natural. He *was* alone. No other human being anywhere around. In fact, he might as well be on another planet.

Havin' yourself a bit of a "Ground control to Major Tom" moment, are you?

He shook his head at his own whimsy, then lifted his chin, his gaze following the beam of his headlamp as it traveled up the line of the nylon rope that attached him to Wolf and Wolf to the positional buoy they'd launched. He couldn't see his friend hanging out at the halfway point. The water was too murky at this depth. The minimal sunlight that managed to filter in from above was barely enough for him to see five yards in either direction.

He jerked on the rope twice. The signal he'd arrived safely on the bottom. Waiting, he counted off the seconds. *One. Two. Three. F—* A double bump on the loop of rope attached to his weight belt told him Wolf had received his message and was standing by. *Good.* Even though Wolf was thirty feet above the cutoff point where it was safe to breathe regular oxygen, it was still possible to suffer nitrogen narcosis—what divers referred to as "rapture of the deep." It made you feel stoned, impairing your reactions and decision-making abilities. But Wolf's quick response told him the man was A-okay, good to go.

Leo puffed out a breath of relief, bubbles emerging from his regulator to trickle over his cheeks and into his hair. He detached the handheld flashlight from his gear belt and flipped on the switch. A thick beam of light blazed through the water, cutting through the gloom like a shooting star through the night sky.

There. Ten yards away. The rusting hull of the tangos' sunken boat—it looked like an old recreational trawler—rose like a phantom from the ocean floor. An intruder in this alien world. He swam in its direction, managing his breathing and carefully reeling out the loop of rope attaching him to Wolf as he went.

The trawler had landed right-side up. A blessing. Because Olivia suspected the only reason the tangos hadn't been able to get to the capsules before the vessel had sunk was because they'd stored them in the cabin or the engine compartment. And he hadn't welcomed the thought of having to wiggle his way between the boat and the sand in an effort to access the entrance to either room.

Olivia… He would swear he could still taste her on his tongue, that salty mix of woman and passion. And the way she smelled…musky and sweet, all health and life and sexual heat. She'd been so wet for him, so swollen for him, so unbelievably soft… And yet, *not*. The strength of her inner muscles clamping down on his fingers when she'd climaxed had surprised him, left him breathless, anxious to feel those same muscles squeezing the head of his dick when he—

Oh great. Now I'm hard. In a wet suit. Nearly two hundred feet beneath the surface. In search of three capsules of deadly chemical weapons.

He blew out a breath of self-disgust and adjusted his goggles. It occurred to him as he hovered above the trawler's deck that being in love with a spy came with more than its fair share of complications. She was going to disappear on him for weeks, sometimes months, on end. She would keep secrets, tell lies by omission. Not because she wanted to, but because she *had* to. It was going to be hard. He *knew* it would be hard. But if there was any man on the planet who would understand, who wouldn't push for answers, Lord knew it was him. He'd been there. Done that. And he had a Navy SEAL Budweiser pin to prove it.

Of course, now he just had to convince her to give him, give *them* a shot. Her body was already his for the taking. There was no mistaking the way she responded to him, with such unabashed longing and desire. The question was how to make her head and heart follow suit. But he suspected he knew where to start.

He was grinning around his regulator when he pushed open the warped wooden door to the trawler's main cabin. A plastic cup floated slowly past him, followed by a bright-orange life ring, trailed by a few other pieces of buoyant whatnot. He waited until the debris cleared and then ducked through the door, careful to keep his tanks and hoses from hitting the frame.

Panning his flashlight around the interior, he looked for the stainless-steel case Olivia had described. *About the size of two briefcases stacked atop one another*. But there was nothing on the console. Nothing sitting on the floor. Letting out more rope, he swam farther into the cabin. His grin disappeared when he saw the body.

In the far left corner, beneath a table surrounded on three sides by a cushion-less booth, protruded a pair of hairy legs. The skin over the limbs looked gray and waterlogged. Crabs had already begun to feast on the corpse, and they scuttled away from the beams of his headlamp and flashlight.

Where there be drowned tangos, there be chemical weapons, he thought in his best pirate's voice.

And sure enough, when he swam over, he saw what he was looking for. The case was wedged beneath the table. He tried to pull the tango's body out so he could get to it, but the corpse seemed to be stuck. He swept his flashlight over the drowned man, trying to figure out what was holding him there. *Ah*. The dead man's belt loop was hooked on a rusty screw sticking out from one of the table legs.

Quickly unhooking the material, Leo grabbed the tango's waistband and yanked. The body floated from beneath the table, slowly drifting by him. He studiously ignored the gaping black holes that used to be the man's eyes—the bottom-feeders always went after the most tender parts first—and gently hauled the steel container from its hiding place. He set it atop the table.

And just to make sure… Because Olivia had insisted he do so.

He flipped up the latches and lifted the lid. Inside, three canisters about the size of two-liter soda bottles were nestled in a bed of foam, all neatly in a row, all looking completely innocuous. Yet they were anything but…

The hairs on his arms lifted, and since they were flattened inside his wet suit, the resulting sensation was that of a mass of millipedes crawling over his limbs. The *sssskkkk, sssskkkk* sound of his breathing increased, and pockets of bubbles gathered in a strange living glob against the ceiling of the cabin. He shuddered at the thought of what could have happened had the terrorists actually found a way to combine and aerosolize the stuff.

Carefully closing the lid and securing the latches, he hauled the case from the cabin. He avoided the floating corpse and reeled up the rope attaching him to Wolf. Once he was clear of the boat, with his fins sunk deep into the silt and sand at the bottom of the Straits, he detached a set of bungee cords and carabiners from his gear belt.

Tying the bungee cords around the case like the ribbons on a Christmas present, he secured the container to the rope with the carabiners. Then he attached two lift-bags to the bungee cords. It took less than ten seconds to inflate them using the compressed CO_2 canister he pulled from his belt. And then the case with the chemicals was drifting up the rope, climbing toward Wolf and ultimately the buoy at the surface.

Leo watched until it was out of sight. Then he dropped his weights, checked his dive computer, and inflated his high-capacity BC—buoyancy controller. The sound of the tube filling with air was a loud *hissssss* in the water around him. With a subtle kick of his fins, he was headed upward toward the light, toward the woman who turned him inside out and upside down. *And around and around!*

All right, so he'd run the gamut from David Bowie to Diana Ross. The pressure and the isolation were obviously getting to him. Or maybe he was just going a little crazy because he'd been *seconds* away from sinking into Olivia's wet heat when Bran had interrupted them. *Again*. The man was just itching for an ass-kicking, no doubt about it.

However… Leo smiled around his regulator again when he realized there'd be no more interruptions. The radicals were dead. The chemicals were safe. There was nothing left to do but…*Olivia*.

Anticipation burned through him as he made his first safety stop, allowing the gases in his tissues and blood to adjust to the lessening pressure. He pictured Olivia laid out on his queen-sized bed back on Wayfarer Island. Her black hair fanned over his pillow. Berry nipples pointing toward the ceiling. Smooth, tan thighs spread wide so that he could see her wet, pink center and—

Oh, perfect. Now I'm hard again…

———

4:43 p.m.…

"She's goin' to wear a hole through the deck."

Bran pulled his gaze away from the deep-sea fishing boat passing about a mile and a half off their starboard side to glance over at Olivia. She was pacing back and forth across the yacht's teakwood swim deck, chewing on her lip and wringing her hands. He'd never seen someone actually do that…wring their hands. Had sort of thought it was just a figure of speech. But Olivia looked close to snapping off a finger.

He wasn't in much better shape. His stomach was in knots while he waited for his friends to emerge from the drink, to pop up beside the bright-white positional buoy they'd launched next to the wreck. And, yo, Leo was the most experienced, most intuitive diver Bran had ever seen. Still…accidents happened in the deep. The pressure played havoc on equipment—breaking hoses, causing regulators to wig out, keeping buoyancy compensators from inflating. The list was endless. Not to mention what the inert gases inside a guy's body could do to him if worse came to worst and proper safety stops couldn't be observed during an ascent.

"She's worried about him," he told Maddy Powers,

who was leaning on the rail next to him. *Worried and probably riddled with guilt too*. And wasn't that just peachy? There were too many goddamn recriminations floating around for his tastes, what with Olivia being beside herself because of the catastrophe that had become this pisser of a mission and Leo blaming himself for what the sinking of the *Wayfarer* meant to their futures. *Shit*. Bran really wanted a do-over. Where was good ol' H. G. Wells's time machine when he needed it?

"And she should be," he spat, his bad mood evident in his tone. "A deep dive isn't a walk in the park, you know?"

"I *do* know." Maddy curled her lip, properly chastised.

It wasn't fair for him to vent his spleen on her. After all, she was just an innocent bystander who'd found herself caught up in a bad situation. Considering that, she was holding up remarkably well. No tears or theatrics, no demands to be told what was happening or threats to get a high-priced lawyer involved—though he figured her walls would probably come crumbling down later, after everything she'd experienced finally had a chance to sink in. But fair or not, he *was* in a bad mood. And some of that was due to her nearness. It made him itchy. Twitchy. Like his skin was too tight.

He didn't like it. Not a bit.

It didn't help matters that she'd changed out of her robe and into a set of loose, gray yoga pants and a soft, pink V-necked T-shirt. The latter accentuated the bright glow of her platinum-blond hair, setting off her dewy cheeks and rosy lips. Dude, the woman was a real-life cherub. A *sexy* cherub. And standing next to her made him aware of himself like he'd never been before. Here he was, this big oaf, all hairy and hard and menacing.

The polar opposite to her tiny delicacy. Like a grizzly bear next to a crystal vase or some such shit.

And it was that tiny delicacy that made him want to march up the stairs to the bridge and kill that asshole terrorist all over again. Because when he'd asked about the tender-looking bruise on her cheek and the bigger one on her neck, she'd admitted the rat bastard had hit her. *Three times!* And for that the man should've had to suffer. He should've had to—

"Waitin' on them to come up with whatever it is y'all are lookin' for sort of makes me feel like Brad Pitt in the movie *Seven*," she mused.

He may not like her nearness, but he *did* like the sound of her voice. It was high and sweet, filled with elongated, twanging vowels. And it was a good thing he liked it, because in the nearly two hours he'd known her, she hadn't shut up. In case she wasn't aware, he felt it was his place to inform her of the fact.

"So, is your mouth just naturally attached to a motor? Or is talking nonstop the way you deal with stress?"

The look she gave him was the same one she might have given a hair stuck in her dessert. Ballsy. "The former," she informed him. "My mama says I could talk the legs off a chair. But it's been my experience that when it comes to motormouths, it takes one to appreciate one."

His chin pulled back. The woman was so goddamned *ballsy*. For all she knew, he could be the kind of guy to chuck her overboard for saying something like that. Lucky for her, he wasn't. Unlucky for *him*, she was right. He *had* been accused by his teammates, more than a time or two, of never knowing when to zip it.

"Touché," he allowed. "And sure, I'll play." He fig-ured there were worse ways to spend the time waiting for Leo and Wolf. "*Why* do you feel like Brad Pitt in the movie *Seven*?"

"You know…" She made a face, waving her hands. "What's in the box? *What's in the boooxxx?*"

Despite himself, he felt one corner of his mouth twitch. "Are you a Brad Pitt fan?"

Please say no. 'Cause I look nothing like the dude… Whoa! Where the shit did that *come from?*

"Nah." She twisted her lips. Because the upper was fuller than the lower, it made her look like she was pout-ing. He'd always had a thing for upside-down mouths. "I'm more of a cinema-in-general fan. You name it," she boasted, "I've seen it and can tell you the leads, the director, and usually the writer too."

Now *that* was interesting. He considered himself a bit of a movie connoisseur. Or, more truthfully, a film geek. When he was a teenager, he would sneak into the theater just about every night of the week. Initially he'd done it because it was a warm place to sleep in the wintertime and a cool place to sleep in the summertime. But then he'd started to actually *watch* the movies, and he'd fallen in love with the idea of spending two hours getting whisked away on an adventure or running from a serial killer or watching two people fall head-over-ass in love. Yes, he liked romantic comedies, so there.

He turned to face her fully. "That sounds sort of like a challenge," he said, crossing his arms over his chest.

She looked up, her steel-gray eyes sparkling in the sun rays glinting off the waves. He had to suppress the urge to kiss her cute, uptilted nose. *Weird*. He'd just gotten laid last night by a bodacious redheaded tourist he'd picked up in the Green Parrot Bar on Key West. She'd ridden him like a rodeo cowgirl for a good forty-five minutes before finishing him off with a sloppy, though intensely exuberant blow job. Which meant it was too soon for him to be suffering from too-much-backed-up-testosterone-itis. Then again, he'd always been a sucker for blonds. Especially ones with upside-down mouths and tight little bodies.

"A challenge?" She shook her head. It caused the long swoop of her bangs to fall across one delicately arched brow. "Nah. It's just a fact."

"Care to prove it?" he taunted.

"Hit me with your best shot, big boy," she taunted right back, scooting a bit closer. She smelled fruity, like pears or something equally feminine and delicious. One sniff and all his internal gadgets went haywire.

Somehow he managed to ignore the upheaval in his body and came back with, "I thought we were playing Name That Movie not *Name That Tune*, Pat Benatar."

"Stalling?" Now she was smirking. And she looked sort of…*devilish*. He *liked* it.

Racking his brain for a good one, he was eager to put her to the test. *Aha!* "Okay, so James Dean plays Cal Trask who's unhappy with just about everything in his life, including his relationship with—"

"*East of Eden*," she interrupted, shaking her head. "I expected so much more from you. I mean, it's James Dean, for the love of two-steppin'. The man's a legend among women. Show me someone with ovaries who *hasn't* seen everything he's ever played in."

He stuck his tongue in his cheek, narrowing his eyes. Obviously, he'd underestimated her. Now he was attempting to take her measure.

She waited a beat. Then two, before impatiently asking, "So that's it? One piddle-O volley and suddenly you're—"

He didn't let her finish. "Naomi Watts plays an amnesiac who searches for clues to—"

"*Mulholland Drive*." She shook her head as if he were pitiful. Just pitiful. "And, really, that one is *not* director David Lynch's best."

"What?" he blurted, getting into it and, astonishingly, enjoying himself. His bad mood vanished like mist hit by the heat of her wit. "And I suppose you think *Lost Highway* was?"

"Sure enough."

"Ha! I'm sorry. But there's no comparison between Bill Pullman's performance and Naomi Watts's performance. She blew the roof off that role."

"Says you." She shrugged a shoulder. "But maybe that's because you're a *guy*, and Naomi Watts is a hot blond. Oh, and also because it's now clear you're an idiot."

The twinkle in her eyes and the way she was fighting a smile told him she was having as much fun as he was.

"In case you weren't aware," he informed her haughtily, "idiots are a barrel of laughs and super cool to hang around. That's why they're the rage in all the villages."

She couldn't hold it in any longer. She barked out a laugh. And then they stood grinning openly at each other, caught up in the game and the banter.

"I've got one for you," she said after a bit, the tilt of her head decidedly feline, like that of a cat watching a mouse's nose protrude from a hole. "But fair warnin', this one's a doozy. If you get it, I'll..." She trailed off.

He was suddenly breathless. "You'll what?"

"I don't know." She shook her head, laughing. "I have no idea what kind of boon to give a guy who's basically a big question mark."

How about a kiss? Okay, this was getting out of control. He was pretty much a hornball 24/7, but...wow. Just wow. "How about..." He tapped his chin. "If I win, then you hafta tell me the most embarrassing thing that's ever happened to you." For some odd reason, he wanted to know more about her.

"And if *I* win?" she asked, reaching toward her hair as if to push it behind her ear. Her fingers faltered when she discovered there was nothing to tuck back. *New haircut, apparently.* A pretty daring one at that. And, *damnit,* he liked *that* too.

"I tell you the most embarrassing thing that's ever happened to *me.*"

"Deal." She stuck out her hand. He hesitated to take it. And when he finally did, he realized *why.* Her palm was baby soft, her hand tiny compared to his, and his dirty mind immediately conjured up an image of what her fingers would look like wrapped around his dick. Said dick twitched to life. *Oh great. That's just great.*

"So, Alan Ladd stars as a Naval gunnery officer durin' World War II," she began. "But here's the thing. He's a pacifist. And he refuses to fire on an unidentified plane. Of course, when this gets out to the others in his unit, they label him yellow-bellied, a guy they can't depend on. Turns out the plane was one of their own, but that doesn't really change anything. The whole movie is about the conflict between conscience and duty. Name that film."

Oh, *fangul*. It was right there. On the tip of his tongue and the edge of his brain. "Who directed it?" he asked.

"Are we allowed to give clues?" She was smirking, sure she'd won.

"Since we never officially stated the rules, then yeah."

"Hmm." She narrowed her eyes. "I don't think that's…"

"Aha!" He pointed at her face. "It's because you don't *know* who directed it. And you said you could name every film, the leads, the director, and usually the—"

"Rudolph Maté," she said. He grinned gleefully. "Hey! You tricked me!"

"Maybe," he admitted with an exaggerated shrug. "But regardless, I now know what the movie is. Drumroll, please."

She rolled her eyes. When he looked at her expectantly, as if he was prepared to wait all day, she huffed and started rolling her tongue. "*Ddddddddddddd*."

"*The Deep Six!*" he crowed triumphantly. She blinked up at him, her mouth hanging open. Yeah, because he'd pulled that one straight out of his ass. Talk about an old, totally esoteric film. He was impressed with her choice. Of course, he wasn't going to tell her as much. Because where was the fun in that? "What?" He grinned. "No applause?"

The sound of clapping—slow clapping—echoed from behind him. He looked over his shoulder to see Mason standing there. "Hey, bro. What's up?"

"I think you just named our salvage company," Mason said, head cocked contemplatively.

Bran blinked at him, trying to comprehend. He

couldn't, so he asked the only question available to him. "What the huh?"

"Deep Six Salvage." Mason rolled the words around on his tongue like he was tasting them. "It's fuckin' perfect. There are six of us. We make our living in the deep."

"And in case you're forgetting," Bran said, "our salvage ship was *deep-sixed* a couple of hours ago. Without it, we don't *have* a company, nameless or otherwise."

"That's not true," Olivia chimed in from the swim deck below. "I told Leo I'd make sure you guys—"

"Hang on just a cotton-pickin' minute here," Maddy interrupted. Bran looked over to find her hands fisted on her hips. Her very *curvy* hips. Some people might say they were *too* curvy for her small frame. *Yo, and some people are morons.* "Y'all are really salvors?" Her light-brown brows were drawn together. "I thought she said you worked for the government." She hooked a thumb over her shoulder at Olivia.

"It's…uh…" Bran rubbed a hand across the back of his neck. He thought he'd left the days of keeping secrets behind him. And quite honestly he'd *preferred* it that way. "It's complicated," he finally admitted, watching her cute button-nose wrinkle. The freckles across the bridge melded together, like brown sugar atop a scoop of vanilla ice cream. "We're salvors working for the government on this gig, and—"

That's all he managed because a subtle splashing had all eyes swinging toward the location buoy. Bobbing beside the white marker was a shiny metal box kept afloat by two neon-yellow lift bags.

Maddy turned back to him, her expression wry. "What's in the box? *What's in the boooxxx?*"

Chapter Sixteen

5:15 p.m....

BANU PUNCHED THE END BUTTON ON THE SIDE OF HIS satellite phone and narrowed his eyes. Through the tinted windows of the wheelhouse, the sea was a pristine, endless undulation of low waves as far as the eye could see. But that had not been the case five minutes ago...

"Nassar is not answering?" Ahmed asked, frowning.

"No," Banu growled, his jaw sawing back and forth, his mind conjuring up all the unique and exciting ways he could slowly kill Nassar if the asshole had fucked things up for them. For *him*.

"It's possible the debris we just passed had nothing to do with us or Nassar or that salvage ship he spoke of," Ahmed assured him. "Styrofoam breaks off docks and floats out to sea all the time. Cushions that are not tied down fly off boats every day. There was nothing out of the ordinary, if you think about it."

"You're right." Banu nodded. Inwardly he couldn't help but wonder, though. Because the currents in the Straits were viciously strong. And if Nassar had sunk the salvage ship, it was possible some of the wreckage could have floated out this far. He checked his watch. *Three and a half hours since the last time we spoke*, said the hour and minute hands. *And the man's a fucking lunatic*, added a voice in his head. "So why isn't he answering?"

Ahmed made a rude noise. "Nassar probably forgot to put a new battery in the phone. And since their ship sank, there is no way for him to charge the one he has or get a new one. I am sure it is nothing, brother. Wait and see. You will triumph still. And your name will be immortalized in songs of jihad for centuries to come."

Now *that* turned Banu's frown upside-down. Immortalized in song, huh? Like Davy Crockett or Rasputin. *Like fucking Beethoven or Henry VIII!* Okay, okay. Maybe he *was* overreacting. Seeing problems where there weren't any. But could you blame him? This was his chance. This was The One! And it *had* to work. He'd come too far to go back now. Too many arrows were now pointing in his direction for him ever to return to Jonathan Wilson's life…

5:42 p.m.…

Hallelujah! And thank you, sweet baby Jesus!

From the corner of her eyes, Olivia saw Wolf toss his fins and goggles onto the swim deck before climbing the ladder. It was from the *corner* of her eyes, because her gaze was laser-locked on Leo, bobbing in the water at the back of the yacht, waiting his turn to climb aboard.

The hour between the capsules rising to the surface and *his* emergence had felt like an eternity. *Two* eternities. Mason and Bran had assured her it was *good* it was taking him so long to make the ascent. It meant things were solid gold, hunky-dory. He was hitting all of his safety stops, and so on and so forth, yada yada.

In her gut, she'd known they were right. And her

head couldn't refute their logic, not after everything she'd read about deep dives on her flight from DC. *Was that just this morning?* But her heart? Yeah, her heart was another matter entirely. She would swear the thing had refused to beat the whole time he was down there, only stuttering to life when his blond head poked above the waves.

"Are you experiencing any joint pain or dizziness? Any shortness of breath?" she called to him, frantic to hear his voice. She'd never forgive herself if—

"Nope," he told her, whipping off his goggles and shaking the seawater from his shaggy hair. The burnished-gold locks glinted in the light sparkling off the water and she squinted, not able to look directly at him. He was like the sun himself, all bright and beautiful. *So damn beautiful.* He grabbed the ladder and tossed his fins and goggles onto the deck. "And my dive computer says there were no decompression violations. I should be good to go."

"It's too soon to tell," she insisted. Mason and Bran grabbed his arms and hauled him aboard. Water sheeted off him and his equipment, creating an immense puddle at his feet that gathered in the grooves of the deck before racing back to rejoin the sea. "But nearly half of the cases of DCS present symptoms within the first hour, so if you don't show any signs of—"

He leaned over and smacked a kiss on her lips, effectively shutting her up. "Relax, darlin'. I'm fine."

Darlin'. The endearment went all through her, and it sounded delicious in his Deep South accent—*dawlin.* No one had ever given her a pet name before. Well, there was that French asset she'd slept with a time or two who'd called her "*ma belle*." But he'd only done it when he was in the middle of an orgasm, so she figured that didn't really count.

"Did you get the package?" he asked, shrugging out of his tanks and handing them to Bruce, who was waiting nearby. The crew of the *Black Gold* had been extremely helpful, thanks in no small part, Olivia presumed, to the former positions she'd learned they held in Britain's Royal Navy. They had probably taken part in their fair share of operations just like this one where the name of the game was Don't Ask, Don't Tell. As for Maddy? Well…as far as Olivia could ascertain, the woman was just flat-out imperturbable.

"Yes," she assured him. "Mason swam out to retrieve it as soon as it surfaced. Captain Tripplehorn agreed to lock it in the *Black Gold*'s safe until the A-Team arrives."

Having shed his gear belt and dive computer, Leo reached behind his back and hooked a finger in the loop of the cord attached to the wet suit's zipper. Pulling it down to his waist, he peeled the neoprene off his arms and chest. Miles upon miles of tough, tan skin glowed with health. And when he lifted one arm to glance at his diver's watch, the muscles in his arms and shoulders bulged.

"Speakin' of," he said. "Shouldn't they be here by now?"

She shook her head. "I called…uh…my *boss*." She was careful not to name names since it was common knowledge that Morales was the director of the CIA. And until he told her otherwise, she was keeping as much information as she could about who they were and who they worked for from Maddy and her crew. "I told him the package was safe. He said to thank you, and—"

"I didn't do it for *him*," Leo rumbled, giving her a "look." One that was full of heat and promises of dirty deeds done between cool, cotton sheets. *Oh God*.

"I...I know you didn't," she whispered. He'd done it for *her*. Because he had a thing for her, a carnal, *complicated* thing—though she suspected the "carnal" part was something they shared while the "complicated" part was hers alone. That two-eternity hour had given her a lot of time to think, to delve into the depths of her feelings for him.

And what had she found down there, do you suppose? Well, none other than...*love*. An ocean of the stuff, deep and warm and endless. How she could have missed it all these months was beyond her. But it probably had something to do with the fact that she hadn't felt the emotion for anyone since her mother died, and had never felt romantic love at all, so it'd been hard to recognize. Also, if she was being completely honest, for a year and a half she'd studiously kept herself from looking too hard at her feelings regarding Leo. Scared shitless of what she'd find.

But now that she *had* looked? Well, there was no *un*-looking. So, yeah. She loved him. Like a magnet loves metal. Like a flower loves the sun. Like fish love the sea, and any and all other applicable comparisons. Intrinsically. Unquestionably.

Who wouldn't? There wasn't a man alive who was as brave or loyal or *sexy* as Leo. As funny or as kind. In short, the guy was lovable. That's all there was to it.

Fat lot of good it does me.

Because, just like Bran said, there was no future for them. There might have been a chance once. Before Syria. Before she lied to him about...well...*everything*.

And before her deception forced her to make a decision that ultimately got his friend killed. But not now.

"Anyway," she went on, disguising the lump in her throat by blowing out an exaggerated breath, "he said the A-Team wasn't able to fix their propeller, and they're having to limp our way on one engine. They should be here pretty soon, though."

"Uncle John would say they're like a blister," Leo said, and she cocked her head. "They don't show up until the work's all done."

"Oh yeah. Right." She glanced out at the softly rolling sea. He'd made a joke, but she couldn't even fake a laugh. She was going to disappoint him. Maybe even piss him off. But there was no way around it. At least none that she could see.

"You okay?" he asked.

"Of course," she lied. Again. "My boss, he, uh, he hopes they can fix the issue once they're here and have the proper tools to work with. Then he wants us to give the package to them. With two engines at full speed, they can make it back to Key West in a few hours. He's itching to get the package secured as quickly as possible."

"Makes sense," Leo agreed, eyes narrowing. He could tell, either by her tone or her expression, that there was more to the story. She tucked a strand of hair behind her ear. His gaze narrowed further, as if he knew it was sign of nervousness.

She quickly dropped her hand. "He wants me to follow the A-Team back to Key West with the crew of the *Black Gold*. Once we dock, he and I will debrief them, gather the evidence, do the cleanup, and send them on their way to Houston."

Leo was no dummy, easily catching her use of the singular pronouns. "And me and the guys? What are *we* supposed to do?"

"He put in a call to Romeo and Doc," she told him. "After they load up on fuel, they'll fly the Otter out to pick you up and take you back home."

For a second he said nothing, just stood there blinking at her. She would swear the air around her dropped ten degrees. Goose bumps peppered her skin. "Just like that, huh?" he finally said. "Thanks, but our services are no longer needed?"

She swallowed, unable to meet the molten heat in his gaze. "It's not my call, Leo," she whispered.

"I know that," he said, then blurted, "I could come with you to Key West. After you finish with everything, we could—"

"I'm needed back in DC," she interrupted, trying not to wince when yet *another* lie sliced into her tongue like an old, rusty cutlass. It was one thing to contemplate spending the night wrapped in his strong arms when mutual lust with a nice side of mutual *like* were the only two things on the menu. But add in a heaping helping of love? Yeah, buddy. That changed everything.

She *couldn't* sleep with him now. Give herself to him mind and body, *heart and soul*. If she did, she'd have to spend the rest of her life knowing what that was like, the glory of it, the absolute wonder of being with the man she loved. Which would make all the long, lonely nights that stretched out in front of her that much more impossible to bear. *No. It's better not to know.*

"We still have to find..." She trailed off because

there were civilian ears listening in. "There are things
we still have to deal with. As you know."

"And how about after you deal with those things?"
he demanded. The man was relentless. Was he going to
make her spell it out for him?

"I'm sorry, Leo." She shook her head, her eyes pleading for him to understand, though she knew he wouldn't.
How could he? He had no idea she'd been bowled over
by a grand epiphany. And she sure as shit wasn't going
to *tell* him. Though, maybe she should. Dropping the
L-bomb might guarantee he ran screaming in the opposite direction.

"Yeah," he sighed, nodding. "I'm sorry too, Olivia."
The frustration and confusion in his voice were palpable.

―※―

5:59 p.m....

She liked him.

He knew she liked him.

And, more than that, she was *hot* for him. There was
no mistaking the way her skin flushed when he got close
to her, the way her mouth opened eagerly to the press
of his tongue, or the way her sweet center went soft and
wet when he touched her, licked her. The memories of
her smell, her taste, her unabashed release had his blood
running hot, heavy. He was hard. Again. Or maybe he'd
never *stopped* being hard.

So why the hell is she willin' to leave it at that?

He contemplated the answer as the *Black Gold*'s
hot water tank disgorged its contents over the top of
his head. When Maddy had suggested he hop in the

shower to warm up because "it had to be colder than a witch's tit down there"—she was cute as a button, a fact Bran seemed to be well aware of—Leo hadn't wasted a minute taking her up on her offer. He'd needed some time alone. To think. To try to solve the jigsaw puzzle that was Olivia Mortier.

Unfortunately, after washing the expensive, fruity-smelling shampoo from his hair—at least he *hoped* it was shampoo; the words on the bottle were printed in French so he couldn't be sure—he was no closer to figuring out the riddle than he'd been before. He wiped a hand across the steam on the shower door, peeking into the well-appointed bathroom with its gray slate tiles and deep mahogany cabinetry. Nope. The clues to what was lurking in Olivia's head weren't out there.

Then, as if his unhappy thoughts had conjured her up, her husky voice drifted through the bathroom door. "Leo?" The sound was muffled by the water hitting the tiles at his feet.

"What?" he barked. Then chastised himself for his harsh tone. The woman had a *job* to do. He couldn't fault her for that. But he could fault her for not at least *trying* to make some time for him. And, okay, right, so he'd made it sound like all he wanted from her was a one-night stand, and why would she be willing to put her career on hold for *that*, no matter how amazing it would undoubtedly be? But, surely, *surely* she knew there was more to it. Surely she could see it in his eyes every time he looked at her.

"I…uh…I just wanted to check on you," she called. "Make sure you're still feeling okay."

He opened his mouth to tell her he was fine. Hot.

Horny. *Frustrated*—and maybe a little heartbroken. But otherwise fine. Then a thought occurred. A devilish, devious thought. It made him grin. "No!" he yelled, his voice dramatically hoarse. "I-I'm feelin' a little dizzy! I can't...can't..." He wheezed like a two-pack-a-day smoker.

The door to the bathroom burst open, and Olivia blew in like a hurricane. Hair flying, long legs churning. She *more* than liked him. She cared for him. It was written all over her face when she whisked open the shower door.

Satisfaction and...*happiness*...washed through him. He promptly yanked her inside.

"Wha—?" She blinked up at him, the ceiling-mounted rain showerhead soaking her and turning her khaki shorts brown. Her long hair plastered itself to her cheeks and forehead.

He didn't give her time to say more before slamming his mouth over the top of hers, ravaging her and punishing her for thinking to leave things undone between them. *Again*. She softened, her tongue eagerly meeting his. Then she stiffened and pulled back.

"I thought you said you were dizzy." Her eyes searched his face, sleek brows drawn together. She pressed two fingers to the pulse in his neck. Lifted his wrist so she could keep time using his diver's watch.

She was adorable when she was in drenched mamabear mode. Her teeth worrying her bottom lip and silvery drops of water clinging to her long, thick eyelashes.

"I lied," he admitted, smiling lecherously when her delightful, biteable chin jerked back. He gently brushed her fingers away from his carotid, shuffling her backward until her shoulders hit the tile wall. The water continued to fall behind them, a constant *shhhhhh* of sound that, combined with the steam, cocooned them inside a private, hazy oasis.

"You. Giant. *Ass*hole!" she spat, blue flame shooting from her eyes as she pushed her sopping hair away from her face. *Christ, she's fierce*. And hot. She made his head spin. His whole frickin' *world* spin. "You nearly gave me a heart attack!"

"Mmm," he hummed, not apologizing, simply bending to kiss the frown from her lips. "It was the only way I knew to get you in the shower with me."

She turned her cheek with a huff. No matter. He'd satisfy himself with nibbling on her delectable ear. She sighed when he sucked the soft lobe into his mouth, then caught herself and cut it off so it ended on a little squeak. "Leo." Her tone was scolding, breathlessly scolding; he fought a grin. "The c-contractors arrived and—Oh God, that feels good."

"Mmm-hmm," he growled, swirling his tongue into the delicate shell. "And so what? Can you help 'em fix their boat?"

"N-no," she conceded, squirming under his assault. Not trying to get away necessarily, just trying to ignore the heat sizzling between them. *Right*. Like he was going to let *that* happen. "But I need to give them the case with the capsules in it."

"They may look about as smart as a box of rocks, but I assure you my guys can handle that without too much trouble." He moved his lips to the pulse point of her throat. She liked it when he sucked on that spot. It always made her whimper. *Bingo*. A throaty mewling sounded in his ear. His dick throbbed against the fabric of her shorts where he'd pressed himself against her.

"But—"

"Don't you want this?" he asked, interrupting her protest. "If we can't have tonight, then at least we can have this. These couple of hours before Doc and Romeo arrive." *And all the ones after that when you come runnin' back to me for more*.

He intended to love her so well that she'd have no choice but to return to him time and again, pulled inexplicably like the moon tugs the tides. And once she returned to him enough times, he'd tell her he wanted her to *keep* returning to him because, you know, he *loved* her. He would have confessed as much now if he thought it would do him any good. But something in her demeanor, something in her eyes, said she wasn't ready to hear it. And he'd learned long ago to trust his instincts.

"I don't think—"

"Good," he rumbled, peppering the corner of her mouth with quick, darting kisses. "I don't want you to think, Olivia. I just want you to feel. *This*." He palmed her face, sealing their lips. The immediate suction of her mouth—as if, despite all her protests, she'd been waiting for him to kiss her—sent a thrum of sensation all the way through him, swirling in his stomach, tugging at his balls. His shaft pulsed and ached until it was nothing but a rod of hot, hungry flesh.

She stabbed her tongue into his mouth, a delightful intrusion of wet, silken heat. He caught it between his teeth and sucked, just like he'd sucked on her sweet, pulsing center. She must have recognized the technique. She moaned into his mouth and went boneless in his arms, the skin on her cheeks flushing bonfire hot against his palms.

Shoving his bare thigh between her legs, he kept her where he wanted her, reveling in her sultry heat. She was steamier than the shower. Hot enough to singe his fingers, burn his tongue.

God, I want to taste her again. And again and again and again. Just feast on her like a glutton. And he would. For the rest of his life, he vowed he would. But first he had to show her what she would be missing if she tried to hightail it back to DC.

"And *this*," he growled, grabbing her hip bones and forcing her to ride him, rubbing her back and forth over the hard muscle of his thigh until the friction made her gasp.

He could feel the struggle in her. The need to give in to the electricity and power that sizzled between them as if they were connected by live wires competing with… whatever it was that was making her hold herself back. Luckily, he'd been through enough battles to know how to maneuver things so she'd end up on the winning side. *His* side.

"And *this*." He grabbed her hand, guiding it to his raging shaft, hissing when her fingers wrapped around him. His hips bucked of their own accord, the muscles of his ass clenching. His sac drew up tight when her cool palm hit the heated skin over his head.

"And *this*." He undid the buttons on her shorts and slowly peeled down the zipper. Placing his palm on her belly, he was delighted to feel her stomach muscles quiver at his touch. Her skin was fiery satin. And the small patch of pubic hair that met his thumb when he

slid his hand between their bodies and inside her panties
was soft as goose down.

"Leo, please, I—Oh *Jesus!*" He pressed his thumb
between her dewy, swollen lips, finding the nub of
her distended clitoris. The motion of her hips hump-
ing over his thigh grew more frenzied. Her hand on his
cock squeezed. Hard. Until a large drop of pre-ejaculate
oozed from his tip. It trickled over his head, coating his
shaft and her fingers. Then she began to stroke him.

Up and down. Up and down. Her palm, with its tiny
calluses, was deliciously smooth and at the same time
wonderfully abrasive. His dick grew to prodigious proportions under her ministrations. And he could so easily
let her rub him to completion. It'd been so long since a
woman had touched him like this. And Olivia's touch?
It was the sweetest he'd ever known.

*All right, I really am goin' to come if she doesn't
stop that.* And he didn't want that. He wanted *her*. All
of her. Surrendering herself to him. Abandoning herself
to his every want. Every need.

He stepped back, and she growled her displeasure. "I
know, darlin'. I know," he soothed, kissing her lips, her
cheek, her ear, her neck. "I just have to—" He didn't
finish, as eager as she was to get back to business as
he pushed her shorts and panties down her long, slender legs. *More* eager probably, which is why he almost
ripped her underwear when he bent to pull them off
and they got hooked on her left heel. He was up like
a shot once they were free, whipping her tank top over
her head and tossing it over his shoulder. It landed with
a *splat* somewhere behind him. The clasp on her bra
sprang open with a flick of his fingers. And then…

There she was. Olivia Mortier. The woman of his dreams. The woman he loved. And she was…naked.

No, *nude*. Because when skin was that flawless, breasts that perfect, hips both lean and curvy, naked just didn't cover it. She was nude in the way great masterpieces were nude. A work of art that was femininity incarnate. Her little oval belly button beckoned. Her tightly furled, upthrust nipples tempted. Her tiny patch of neatly trimmed, ink-black pubic hair charmed.

She was…woman. And when she reached for him, he'd never felt more like a man.

———∿∿∿———

6:17 p.m.…

What am I doing? What am I doing?

Exactly what she'd promised herself she wouldn't. She was making love to Leo. No, scratch that. She was having *sex* with Leo. No, scratch *that*. She was having sexual *relations* with Leo. And if Bill Clinton taught the world anything, it was that sex and sexual relations were two different things.

She could do this. She could give him pleasure with her hands, with her mouth. It was his turn, after all, and she was nothing if not a fair-minded woman. As long as she stopped things before actual intercourse, before the intimacy of joining her body with his, before they shared pleasure so intense that she lost track of where he began and she ended, she'd be okay. She. Would. Be. Okay.

You're rationalizing, Mortier. And *shit*. Maybe she was. But that was her story and she was sticking to it. Because she *wanted* to give him pleasure. *I mean, just* look *at him*. All golden and glorious, broad-shouldered and heavy-chested. His stomach was a washboard of muscles bisected by a line of light-brown hair. His thighs were huge and corded, the kind of legs that would keep him standing tall for decades to come. And between his thighs, jutting hungrily, unabashedly, was the most inspiring erection she'd ever seen.

He was long, thicker than her wrist, and heavily veined. His shaft was wider than his head, the perfect male instrument to part a woman's delicate folds and prepare her to receive the bounty of his girth. In a word: impressive. In two words: Mama want. And in three words? *Holy friggin' shit!*

Liquid heat pulsed from her core, wetting her thighs and making them quiver. Her nipples were so hard they hurt. So sensitive the subtlest shift in the air, the faintest wisp of steam curling around them felt as decadent as a wet tongue. She licked her lips, panting as she reached for his shoulders, careful of the butterfly bandages when she pulled him against her. He groaned—a sound of both surrender and warning, like her touch was the source of all pleasure and pain—when they were hip to hip, breast to chest, flaming hot skin against flaming hot skin.

"God, Olivia." The shower pounded behind him. A gentle hiss of noise that, instead of diffusing other sounds, only seemed to magnify them. Each breath. Each moan. Each flick of a tongue against skin. "You're beautiful."

She smiled. She couldn't help herself. "I was going to say the same thing about you." She lifted her face for his kiss, reveling in the molten press of his tongue into her mouth, the eye-crossing pleasure of his hands on her breasts, plumping, callused thumbs circling,

circling, until she couldn't hold back a gasp of pure, aching pleasure.

He smelled fruity and clean, but still amazingly like Leo, all sun-drenched sand and coconut oil. And maybe she was being whimsical. But in Syria, anytime he got near, she was reminded of tropical islands and frosty boat drinks. Maybe it was because he'd spent his whole life rubbing on sunscreen that his skin just naturally smelled like good times and lazy days at the beach. A golden god from a golden land.

Catching her top lip, he flicked his tongue over her teeth. "I love…" He let the sentence dangle for a bit, and her breath hitched, the hair on her scalp lifting. He loved…*what? What?* "Your crooked front tooth," he finally finished. And she wasn't sure if she was relieved or disappointed. *The first* she assured herself, concentrating on the delightful feel of his beard stubble rasping against her lips and cheeks. His roughness against her softness. His maleness contrasting with her femaleness.

She shook her head, pulling back to look into his eyes. This close she could see each striation of color meld into the next. The deep brown near his pupils turned into gold. The gold gave way to turquoise, then green, then deep sapphire blue at the very edge of his iris. They were gorgeous, mesmerizing, the most beautiful eyes she'd ever had the pleasure of staring into.

"You love my crooked front tooth? Well, that makes one of us," she admitted. But she could see by the tick of his jaw, feel by the insistent throb of his cock, that he really believed what he was saying.

"I wanted to run my tongue over it the first time I saw it," he whispered reverently, his voice a low rumble inside her chest and lower, in her belly. "When the station captain introduced us and you smiled at me."

"Oh yeah?" The thought enchanted her, charmed her. "Then what took you so long?" She grabbed his ears, pulled his mouth back to hers. She needed to taste him again. Taste him a million times more before she left him for good.

"Hell if I know," he admitted with a chuckle, kissing her to within an inch of her life. All the while, he kept up that constant assault on the tips of her breasts, plucking and caressing her nipples until she was so hot she thought she might die of heat stroke.

Her womb was a persistent pulse of longing in her center, a deep, yearning void that needed to be filled. And Leo, ever perceptive, gave her what she wanted. He played briefly at her entrance, circling with two fingers, spreading her juices around, teasing her, tempting her, *preparing* her. And then he sank two fingers deep, making her gasp, making her head fall back against the tile wall. He pumped expertly, knowing just where to touch, just where to rub. When his thumb landed atop the bundle of swollen nerves to press and circle, she knew she better get her hands on him right now or she was going to climb that steep hill to orgasm all by herself. Again.

Yeah. No way in hell. This time we both go.

Wrapping her fingers around him as far as they would go, she marveled when they didn't quite touch. Now it was her turn to pump, to stroke. To try to elicit from him another drop of silken passion. He didn't disappoint. His erection pulsed and jerked in her fist, a hard, hot, living column of greedy flesh. And soon a satiny drop rolled over his head. She rubbed it along his thick shaft, coating him before fisting him again.

"Christ, Olivia," he growled, gnashing his teeth as he pulled back from the kiss. "You keep that up and you're goin' to make me come."

"Let's come together," she coaxed, licking the tiny tip of his flat, brown nipple into her mouth. And *she'd* wanted to do *that* since the first time she saw it, when he'd peeled out of his combat gear after a particularly hot afternoon of training with the Syrian rebels.

"Ah, hell," he growled, using the hand that wasn't busy pleasuring her to cup the back of her head, to hold her to him while she suckled and played, flicked and licked. The little bud was hard as a rock and sweet as sin. The hair on his chest tickling her lips and cheeks.

He was so unbelievably hot. So unbelievably *good* at…everything. Absolutely everything. As if to prove that point, her channel pulsed around his fingers, clamped down on his knuckles. She needed more. Just a little…

He let go of her head to place his hand low on her belly, pushing gently while pumping harder, faster. *Oh, holy SHIT!* Her womb contracted into a hard ball. The walls of her vagina spasmed as if they'd received an electrical shock. Her whole sex lit up with sensation, with pleasure. She'd never felt anything like it. Never knew her body could—

"Leo!" His name was a hoarse cry torn from her throat as waves of intense, mind-numbing bliss rolled through her, rolled over her, radiating out from her womb in bright golden swells. She'd never come so hard, so fast. Never experienced rapture so intense that she lost track of time. Of place. She was floating in an endless ocean of sensation that bore her up, holding her aloft. She was blind. Deaf to everything but the buzz of her own blood rushing through her veins like raging, flood-swollen rivers.

She didn't know how long she stayed there in that alternate universe of liquid ecstasy. But she knew when the cosmic blip was over, when the rip in the space-time continuum repaired itself, because her ears started working again. She could hear Leo breathing hoarse encouragement in her ear, "That's it, darlin'. That's it. Ride it out."

An aftershock of rapture raced through her, making her shudder, making her moan. She realized at some point she must have released his cock, because her hands were gripping his shoulders. As if she'd had to anchor herself to him. And maybe she had. Maybe her death grip on him was the only thing that had kept her from getting lost in that other plane.

He slowly, reverently removed his fingers. Her body instantly missed his presence, her walls closing tight around the void he left behind. She opened her eyes to find the world just as it was before she'd left it. Warm, steamy, filled with Leo's overwhelming sexual hunger. She was dizzy, panting. She got even dizzier when he lifted his hand and licked his fingers, closing his eyes so he could savor the taste of her.

Just the sexiest man alive. And still violently, hugely aroused. *Damnit, Mortier!*

She blew out a breath, dragged in another. And when she was steady enough, grounded once more in this universe, on this plane, she sunk to her knees. Determined to give him as much ecstasy as he'd just given her...

Chapter Seventeen

6:31 p.m....

"AH, HELL," LEO GROWLED, HIS STOMACH MUSCLES clenching, his dick jumping up and down like it was doing some sort of happy dance. Which it *was*. The *happiest* of dances. Because Olivia, beautiful, beloved Olivia was on her knees in front of him, licking her lips like she was preparing to taste.

He held his breath when she grabbed him by his base, curling her fingers around him and pulling him down because he was standing damn near vertical. He looked huge in her small hand. A rod of angry male flesh stretching the capacity of her feminine grip. She must have thought so too, because she hesitated, catching her bottom lip between her teeth.

Lack of oxygen made him feel faint. The room was tilting on its axis, his heart was racing, and he was hotter, hornier than he'd ever been in his entire sorry life. Her orgasm...it'd been immense, unabashed, completely explosive. Her silky channels had become a molten vise around his fingers as she pulsed again and again, whispering his name, eyes squeezed shut, completely abandoned to the pleasure he gave her.

He'd almost gone off right along with her. Even after she'd released his cock to grab his shoulders and ride out her orgasm, it'd taken everything he had not to lose it.

Just watching her, head thrown back, gorgeous nipples tightly furled and pointing toward the ceiling, breasts jiggling as she shook from rapture had been enough to have his balls buzzing for release. She was an amazingly erotic woman.

And now she was kneeling like a supplicant before him. The posture spoke to his basest instincts, to the animal in him. He *wanted* her to surrender to him, to service him. To submit her sweet feminine desire to his hot male dominance. Because he might be in love with her but, by God, he was no saint. Still a man with a man's wicked, uncompromising needs.

She licked her lips again, her pink tongue an instrument of torture. *Oh yes. Oh yes. Oh yes.* If his cock had a voice, it would have been howling for joy and begging for mercy. *Oh please. Oh please. Oh please.*

"Where to begin?" she said after a beat, grinning up at him, her blue eyes sparkling through the haze of steam.

He blew out the breath he'd been holding and realized his knees felt weak. It was a rhetorical question, but he answered it anyway. "I've…um…I've always heard it's best to start at the top and work your way down."

She chuckled, the sound deep and throaty, making the hair over his body stand stick-straight. Then she sobered as she glanced at his raging length, tilting her head this way and that as if she was truly wondering how she would manage. Her wet hair fell over her shoulders, one strand getting caught on her tight nipple and curling lovingly around it. "You realize this thing is completely intimidating, right?"

He wanted to feel her mouth on him so badly, but… "You don't have to do it if you—*Fuck me.*" She swallowed his head in one gulp. "Olivia…" Her name was a hoarse moan, her mouth a hot, wet haven as he clenched his jaw and screwed his eyes closed. He panted, fisting a hand in her wet hair to hold her steady, to give himself time because that's all it took, her mouth on him and he was close to losing it all over again.

She accommodated him for one second, two, keeping her lips and mouth motionless while he burned, while he ached, while his blood turned to lava and he fought for control. Then, as if *she* couldn't stand it any longer, she flicked her tongue over his swollen head, bathed him, traced the weeping, tender slit, and he couldn't have stopped her had he wanted to. For the record? He *didn't* want to.

With a groan, he gently flexed his hips, careful to push in only a little further, mindful not to go too far, too fast. She hummed, the sound one makes when they've tasted something delicious, and he was able to unscrew his eyes long enough to glance down. *Oh shit.* The sight of her pink lips stretched tight around him was the sexiest thing he'd ever seen, made sexier by the fact that their eyes clashed. She was looking up him, watching his reaction as she applied suction, her cheeks hollowing out.

A jolt of electricity shot up his spine until he shuddered, growled. And then she was working him over, sliding her fist along his shaft, bobbing her head, alternating sucking and laving.

"I won't last long like this darlin'," he warned, the muscles in his ass and thighs spasming with his fight to hold off.

With a strong suck that made a popping sound, he

came free of her mouth. He thought he might die, just expire on the spot. And the urge to grab his glistening dick and shove it back between her wet, succulent lips was overwhelming.

"I don't want you to last," she said, eyes like sapphire lasers shooting up at him. And then *she* was the one to grab him and shove him back into her mouth. *Sweet. Christ!*

He gritted his teeth, tried to find a reason to stop her. And there was something…a little voice whispering at the back of his brain that said something to the effect of *but this wasn't the plan*. Unfortunately, most of his brain cells and *all* of his blood had migrated south, which made thinking impossible.

He hissed when she cupped his testicles, massaging gently as she made love to him with her mouth, reverently, expertly. Too soon a telltale burn flamed to life near the base of his spine. His dick jumped in reaction, and that was all she wrote. He was done for.

"I'm goin' to c—" He didn't manage more than that before his orgasm burst from him, sending fingers of decadent fire along his shaft. "*Olivia!*" It was a roar of sound.

―――

6:32 p.m.…

His name was Bran. And Maddy couldn't make heads or tails of him.

On the one hand, he seemed warm and affable. He'd listened to her jabber about anything and nothing most of the afternoon—her usual MO, just as she'd admitted—and he'd withstood it all stoically. Never tell-ing her to can it. Even joining in with that whole movie trivia contest, smiling and laughing and teasing her until his chocolaty brown eyes glinted with laughter. On the other hand, he epitomized the phrase "cold as ice." Not only had he taken out Lead A-hole with one pragmatic shot, but she was pretty sure he hadn't given the matter a passing thought since.

A man of contradictions.

And she didn't know if that turned her on or scared her out of her gourd. She was beginning to lean more toward the latter. Of course, that could be due to the fact that the sun was setting, and the adrenaline that had fueled her overconfidence all day long was now sliding out of her ass as surely as the glowing orange ball was sliding into the ocean in the west, leaving a cold, eerie void in its place.

It had begun to sink in. All the things she'd seen. All the things she'd done. A chill whispered up her spine like the frosty breath of a wraith. She rubbed her hands over the goose bumps on her arms and tried to maintain her brazen front.

"I feel like I should be cryin'. Or screamin'. Or pukin' my guts out," she admitted, almost to herself.

"I wish you were," he muttered.

She turned to stare at him, frowning. "Now why in the world would you wish for *that*?"

"Because then you wouldn't be alone when it finally happens. I'd be here to help you through it."

"Oh." This time she didn't attempt to hide the shiver that shook her from head to toe. Even so, Bran missed it. He was too busy handing over the metal suitcase to one of the six mysterious, mean-looking men who'd suddenly appeared in a fifty-foot ocean cruiser. The new arrivals had been short on time and even shorter on words, apparently, because no introductions had been made.

They'd simply thrown a couple of bumpers over the side of their boat before tying up to the *Black Gold* and asking Bruce for some tools. After fixing one of their motors, they'd demanded to be given "the package," and now they were on their way, untying, pushing back, the two giant motors on their cruiser coughing to growling life.

She couldn't be happier What's-in-the-Box was off her father's yacht. She hadn't the first clue what was actually *in* the box—*glory be and praise Jesus!*—but given that it seemed to be the source of today's hullabaloo, she knew she wanted absolutely no part of it. *My mama and daddy didn't raise no fool.*

"So what can I expect?" she asked him when he turned back to her.

"What do you mean? When everything that's happened today finally hits you?" The sky played jazz behind him. It was a cacophony of colors shooting this way and that, and the low light turned the tops of the waves silver, the tips of his dark-brown hair golden.

"No." She quickly shook her head, not wanting to go there. Not yet. Even though, according to him, it would be better if she did. "From the interrogation… er…debriefin' on Key West? What can *they* expect?" She motioned over her shoulder to where the crew of the *Black Gold* stood at the railing, watching the cruiser get up on plane, twin jets of water rooster-tailing out behind the boat as it roared away from them.

"You'll have to answer a lot of questions and probably sign a bunch of forms promising, upon pain of death, that you'll keep your traps shut about what happened here today. But then I figure you'll all be on your happy way to Houston with nothing more than a *grazie* for your trouble."

"And that'll be the end of it?" she asked. "No tapped phone lines? No mysterious visitors showing up and telling me the snow this year is better in Innsbrook?"

He smiled. And it gleamed over his features like a full moon on a cloudless night. All big and bright and beautiful, reaching up into his eyes, warming them, chasing away some of her burgeoning fear and doubt. "James Bond. *For Your Eyes Only*, right?"

She nodded.

He squeezed her arm. "It'll be like it was a dream, Maddy. I promise." When he released her, his touch left behind a ghostly imprint. A phantom tingling sensation in the exact shape of his hand.

"Nightmare," she corrected, covertly covering the spot with her hand, as if to hold in the sensation. *Okay, young lady, you've done gone off the deep end*.

"Probably more accurate," he conceded.

She searched his face, and something there had her blurting, "And will I ever see you again?" She realized how that sounded—exactly like she'd meant it—and quickly corrected herself. "*Any* of you again?"

He got very still, his expression turning enigmatic. "Probably not," he admitted after a couple of interminable seconds.

She blew out a breath. "I reckon I should be grateful for that, huh?"

"You're not?"

She curled her upper lip, feeling…something. Traumatized, maybe? Exhausted, certainly. *With a big-O side helpin' of stupefaction and a bizarre-O attraction to a stranger for dessert.* "I don't know." She shrugged. "I guess so."

And then for a long time they just stood there, staring at each other. She had the weirdest urge to reach up and brush back the whorl of Superman-esque hair that had fallen over his brow. Just to test its texture. Just to see if it was as soft as it looked.

"Maddy…" he finally whispered, his tone dark, beckoning. She took a step toward him before making the conscious decision to do so. "Would you…"

"Yeah?" She held her breath, leaning forward.

"Happen to have a pen and some paper?"

She was so cantilevered over the centerline of her body that his words had her stumbling. She didn't know what she'd expected him to ask, but it wasn't *that*. "I… uh…yeah." She brushed an imaginary piece of lint from her yoga pants. "Sure. No problem."

Except it kind of *was* a problem, because she'd wanted…*something*.

"Thanks. I need to slip a note under the door of the bathroom to LT and Olivia." She'd noticed that no one but Olivia called the golden god "Leo." The men all called him "LT." *Initials, perhaps?* "Let them know the…um…the guys"—he hooked a thumb over his shoulder toward the quickly disappearing cruiser—"have the case and are headed back to Key West. I'd knock, but"—he grinned—"I don't want to disturb them."

Uh-huh. It'd become obvious to just about everyone

on board that more than showering was going on in the bathroom of one of the guest cabins. So to recap. Hijacked by terrorists: check. Watched a guy get his head blown off: check, check. Helped government agents retrieve a mysterious metal case from the ocean floor: triple check. And now trying to ignore the fact that said agents were busy doing the deed in one of her father's yacht's showers: quadruple check.

Holy shitfire. Can this day get *any weirder?*

She immediately called back the question. Because even though she wasn't superstitious by nature, she knew better than to tempt fate.

"A note. Gotcha." She winked at Bran, pressing her finger to the side of her nose.

Motioning for him to follow her into the living quarters, she tried to figure out exactly what that odd feeling was. And then she recognized it. Disappointment. She was disappointed because for a minute there she'd thought he wanted to kiss her.

When he'd said *Maddy, would you*…she'd had the crazy notion that he was going to finish with…*let me kiss you.* So clearly she *was* turned on by this man of contradictions. This man she knew nothing about except that he was handsome as homemade sin, was kinda, sorta, maybe a real-life salvor who worked for the government, and was cold and dangerous enough not to bat a lash before putting a bullet in the skull of a terrorist.

Yep, sister. It's official. You are crazier than a bag of wildcats.

-----⁓-----

6:41 p.m....

Banu dropped the binoculars and cursed. They were anchored far to the east of the *Black Gold*, far enough away that the rays of the setting sun didn't reach them, though they continued to highlight the activity on and around the yacht—activity that had the hair atop Banu's scalp standing on end.

"What?" Ahmed asked. "What is it? Did you see Nassar?"

"No." Banu shook his head, his voice reduced to a hoarse whisper. *What the hell? How the fuck?* His eyes darted about, searching the rented fishing boat as if it might hold the answers. But of course he saw nothing, *nothing* to explain how, *why*—

"Brother." Ahmed grabbed his shoulder. Banu blinked wildly at the man. "What has happened?"

"I—" Banu shook his head. "I don't know."

"Nassar—"

"Isn't on the yacht. At least not that I could see. And it's crawling with men. None of them ours." He swallowed and glanced about again. Although he didn't know why. He was blind to the holy fighters gathered around him, to the fishing rods and the life jackets, to everything but what he'd seen through the magnified lenses of his field glasses. "I just saw one of the men moving a set of dive tanks and fins. Someone has been diving. And the only thing down there to dive for are our chemicals."

"Are you sure?"

He wished he wasn't. "Maybe Nassar was right. Maybe the people on the salvage ship really *were* CIA." And either the descending twilight had caused the temperature to drop, or an icy fist of failure was squeezing Banu's heart. Didn't matter which. The result was the same. Goose bumps erupted over every inch of his body. He shivered, dragging in a ragged breath. The sour smell of defeat rose from the drops of cold sweat beading on his upper lip.

Ahmed frowned. "But it does not make any sense."

"I *know!*" Banu bellowed. All his dreams, all his aspirations were circling the drain, and he couldn't figure out how the hell it had happened. Unless... Could it be that someone *else* knew about the chemicals? Was there a third party at play here that had somehow tracked the case and was now claiming the capsules for themselves?

Or *had* the CIA discovered the theft early on, early enough to find Nassar and torture him into giving up the coordinates of the wreck so they could go down and retrieve the sunken chemicals? But then, where was this salvage ship Nassar had spoken of? Had he sunk it? Was that the debris they saw? If so, how the hell had Nassar allowed the yacht to be overtaken? Unless...had he simply been outgunned?

All of it was possible, Banu supposed. None of it made any real sense.

His heart raced, his lungs ached, his thoughts whirled in a series of tight circles that made him dizzy. And then, suddenly...calm. It poured over him, welcome as a rain shower on a hot summer day, cooling his frenzied heart, soothing his burning lungs, focusing his mind on a single point.

This was his chance. This was The One. And it didn't matter who those men were or what had happened. He had to get those chemicals back. And he might know just how to do it.

There weren't many rules when it came to the high seas—a powered vessel always gives way to a sailing vessel; two powered vessels always pass each other port-side to port-side—but one standing, inviolable principle was that you never ignore a Mayday or call for assistance.

It was gutsy, this plan of his. And maybe a little crazy too. But nothing ventured, nothing gained. And if he *did* somehow manage to pull it off, just *think* of what that would mean to his story. He could see the headlines now: MASTERMIND BEHIND TERROR ATTACK PULLED OFF AMAZING HEIST TO RE-SECURE CHEMICALS AFTER INITIAL LOSS. And perhaps this had been Allah's plan for him all along. A road map to even greater glory.

He turned to Ahmed who lifted a brow at the smile splitting his face. His tone was gleeful when he said, "I have an idea."

—◦◦◦—

6:42 p.m....

"Hey, now," Leo said. "Where are you goin'? We're not finished here."

Olivia stepped out of the shower and grabbed one of the navy-blue towels hanging over a rod, wrapping it around her body. Warm. It was so soft and warm. *A heated towel rod. Some people really know how to live.*

Looking down at his semi-flaccid cock—even wilted it was still impressive—she lifted a brow, donning a saucy smile so he wouldn't see what she was truly feeling: heartbreak.

She'd been an idiot to think she'd be fine as long as she stopped things short of full-on sex. Or maybe Bill Clinton was the idiot. Because when two people shared intimacy like that, giving pleasure and taking pleasure, it forged a bond between them. A bond that, when welded together with the love she felt, became unassailable. *Unbreakable*. She was going to remember what they'd done for the rest of her life. Remember the way he'd loved her with hands and mouth. So tenderly. So precisely. Remember the way he'd given himself over to her. So unhesitatingly. So unquestioningly.

In that moment, she'd known what it was to be trusted, to be cherished, to…belong. To him. She'd *belonged* to him. And him to her. And now she was doomed to mourn the loss of that belonging for the rest of her life.

But she couldn't let him know. *Keep it casual. Keep it fun. Don't let him see you're hurting. Keep that CIA-agent cap screwed on tight, Mortier.*

"Not finished?" She winked at him, gesturing with her chin toward his manhood. "I'd say we are. At least for a while." Her voice was rough with unshed tears, but she hoped he mistook her tone for that of spent passion.

When he wiggled his eyebrows, she breathed a sigh of relief. He turned off the shower, and the resulting silence pressed in on her, seeping into the hollowness in her chest until she wanted to scream. She needed to get out of there. Get some air. Get some perspective. Get—

"Never underestimate the regenerative powers of a man who has finally gotten his hands on the woman he's been fantasizin' about for almost two years," he told her, grabbing a towel and rubbing it over his wet hair.

He gave himself a few good scrubs, then held out the terrycloth, one sandy-brown eyebrow raised. "This thing's hotter than burnt toast."

"I know, right?" His hair was standing out every which way, making him look…*adorable*. Still big and tough, but a little bit boyish too. And, *ow*. Her heart hurt. Like, seriously *hurt*. It took everything she had to maintain her smile. When she couldn't quite manage it, she swiped another towel off the rack and bent at the waist. Flipping her hair upside down, she twisted the towel around it turban-style. *Breathe, Olivia. Just breathe. Keep it casual. Keep it fun. Keep that CIA-agent cap screwed on tight.* And that had become her new mantra, apparently. "What wonders will we discover next, do you think? I'm half expecting Jeeves to come in and offer to help us don our dinner attire."

She straightened to find him applying the towel to his chest and shoulders, then down his legs. The way he moved was poetry. Each flex of his muscles in rhythm and rhyme with the whole of him. "If he does, I'll be forced to punch him in the face."

"Huh?" She frowned.

"I'm feelin' pretty territorial right about now," he admitted, grinning unabashedly. "And I'd like to keep the number of eyes who get to see *this*"—before she knew what he was about, he hooked a finger in her towel and whipped it off—"to a bare minimum."

"Leo!" she squeaked. "Good grief." Without thinking, she covered her breasts with one hand and cupped her privates with the other.

He bit the inside of his cheek, eyeing her protective

stance. "I hate to say it, darlin', but the cat's out of the bag. There's no need to hide what I've already seen, touched, and *tasted*."

She dropped her hands with a huff. It caused her breasts to bounce, and he tilted his head, groaning like a dying man. Movement in her peripheral vision had her glancing down. And sure enough, he hadn't been lying about those regenerative powers. His penis was twitching and swelling, the skin growing turgid, the heavy veins standing out in harsh relief. An answering rush of liquid heat gathered at her core.

She should have been satisfied after the shower. *He* should have been satisfied. Her orgasm had been explosive, transcendent. And all evidence suggested his had been the same. But obviously, neither of them was completely appeased. She bit her lip, wondering if they would *ever* be completely—

A shushing sounded behind her, interrupting her thoughts. When she turned toward the door, she saw a white piece of paper lying on the gray slate tiles. Lifting a brow at Leo, she wondered aloud, "What the heck is that about?"

"Only one way to find out." He tilted his head toward the paper. Shrugging, she bent to grab the missive only to hear him growl, low and guttural, like a wild animal warning its prey of its presence. "That might just be the most beautiful sight I've ever seen."

When she realized he was staring at her bare ass poking up into the air, she straightened so quickly she felt dizzy and the towel fell off her head, landing in a navy-blue heap on the floor. "You meant for that to happen," she accused, turning to find him clutching his heart.

"Meant for it to happen? Hey!" He held his hands up. "I'm not the one who slipped a letter under the door." She narrowed her eyes. He chuckled, shrugging those massive shoulders of his. He needed new butterfly bandages, she noted absently. The old ones were starting to curl loose around the edges. "All right, so maybe I took advantage of the situation when it presented itself. Can you blame me?"

"Hmph." She pursed her lips, easily falling into their familiar banter. The truth of the matter was, when she was with Leo like this, teasing and tormenting, she was the happiest she'd ever been. *And, Jesus, that just makes it hurt worse!* "No, I suppose I can't. Once a pervert, always a pervert, right?"

"As it ever was and ever shall be, darlin'." He winked. Then, "What's it say?"

She unfolded the note and read aloud, "'Congratulations on the ax waxing.'" She looked up at him and he shook his head, making a face that said, *You don't want to know*. "'I gave the package to the contractors and they're well on their way to Key West. Romeo is still a ways out, so take your time.'" When she read further, her cheeks ignited. "It's signed 'Jeeves.'"

Leo's face took on the mien of an Abrams tank, bristling with menace. When he stomped past her, there was no ignoring the erection that bobbed heavily between his big thighs. She was staring unabashedly when the side of his heavy fist landed against the door. The resultant sound was that of a cannon shot. She jumped at the same time a yelp sounded in the cabin outside.

"Get lost, suckwad!" Leo bellowed through the wood.

Bran's chuckle drifted into the bathroom. "Can't blame a guy for wanting a little vicarious thrill!"

"Pervert!" Leo yelled back.

"From what I hear, it takes one to know one!" Bran's voice was growing fainter.

Leo opened the door and stuck his head out. "Sorry about that," he said after he'd slammed it shut again. "In case you didn't know it, Bran is an asshat and a board-certified idiot."

And despite being *completely* abashed at having gotten caught waxing Leo's ax—yeah, she finally light-bulbed that one—she heard the undeniable affection in his voice. "But you love him in spite of it."

He rolled his eyes, crossing his arms over his chest. And, yes, he was still one hundred percent, holy-shit-would-you-get-a-load-of-that-thing aroused. But if he could ignore the giant cock in the room, so could she. Maybe. *Okay, probably not.*

"Right," he said. "Like I love flat beer and tofu burgers."

She slid him a sidelong glance. "Why do men have such a hard time admitting affection for one another?"

"It's not so much admittin' it as talkin' about it," he told her.

"Isn't that the same thing?"

"Nah." He shook his head. "We admit it when we slap each other's asses, talk shit about each other's mamas, and give each other colorfully repulsive nicknames. But we're not *talkin'* about it."

She made a rude noise that caused him to grin and start moving in her direction. Her heart took off like a startled rabbit. Instinctively, she took a step back. Instinctively because, even though he was smiling that Leo smile of his—the one that crinkled the corners of his gorgeous eyes and made his teeth flash white against his tanned face and beard—there was something decidedly predatory about his advance. In fact, she probably would have retreated another step had her butt not bumped up against the bathroom vanity. The cool stone countertop was almost as much of an assault on her senses as Leo's looming nearness.

"What are you doing?" she squeaked. Yes, *squeaked*. She seemed to do that a lot around him, and she was *not* the squeaking kind.

"I'm goin' to kiss you," he declared. "What happens after that is anyone's guess."

"Oh, I suspect I know what happens after that," she informed him with a wry twist of her lips. "Which leads me to believe you're trying to change the subject."

"Am I that obvious?" He placed a hand on the bathroom counter on either side of her hips, caging her in. His body heat reached out to her, soothing her and at the same time igniting all her nerve endings like she'd doused them in gasoline and his nearness was the match. Then he leaned forward, ever so slowly, until his mouth was a hairsbreadth from hers.

You will not *squeak again!*

"More like completely predictable," she said breathlessly. He seemed to be taking up not only all the space in the bathroom, but all the air too. "All guys try to find a way to change the subject when *feelings* are the topic of discussion."

"Well, far be it for me to be predictable," he said and grabbed her waist, hoisting her up on the bathroom countertop. Her ass hit the cold stone at the same time he latched on to her pulse point like he was friggin' Bill Compton from *True Blood*. See, she wasn't a complete moron. She got *some* pop-culture references. Though, she'd sooner eat her own combat boots than ever admit to *anyone* that she'd been a huge—we're talking *major—True Blood* fan.

She tried to wiggle away, but he sank his teeth into her throat, a caress and a threat in one. She squeaked. *Damnit!* "Leo! What if Bran's outside again?"

"He won't be," he assured her, soothing the bite with the flat rasp of his tongue. It made her eyes cross. "He and the rest of the guys have been tryin' to get the two of us together like this for too long for him to distract us now."

"Trying to get us together?" she asked, running her hands up his strong arms to grip his shoulders. *Holy hell*, he really knew how to use his mouth. "Why?"

He kissed his way across her throat to nip at her chin. "Because they know I've been pining for you ever since Syria."

Pining for her. She'd never been pined for before. A thrill of delight radiated from her center out to her limbs. If he'd told her he thought she hung the moon and stars and set the world spinning on its axis, she wouldn't have been more charmed.

"So *that's* what all of those innuendos and all of those veiled looks have been about today," she said, gasping when he nibbled on her earlobe. There was a part of her—the smart, rational part—that wondered if maybe she should stop things here to save herself from even more heartache, from even more *knowing* what she'd be missing once he hopped on that floatplane and flew out of her life for good. But the stupid, *horny* part of her was doing a fairly decent job of convincing her there was no

way to re-break a heart that was already broken, so…
yeah. Get your groove on, Mortier!

"Sorry about that. They're not very subtle. But they
love me, so…you know." He shrugged.

"Wow!" She pulled back, blinking up at him. His
eyes were half-lidded and full of heat.

"What?"

"You just *talked* about your friends loving you."

He grinned, leaning in to kiss the corner of her mouth.
"Told you I wasn't predictable."

"You're lucky to have them." She sighed when his
lips dallied with hers, nipping, tasting, retreating, and
nipping again. The sound of their play filled the bathroom. "They're your family. In all the ways that matter."

To her utter dismay, he was suddenly gone, having
pulled away from her.

Chapter Eighteen

6:49 p.m....

THERE WAS NO MISTAKING THE NOTE OF MELANCHOLY in Olivia's voice when she spoke of family. And it punched Leo in the gut like a heavyweight fighter, forcing all the air from his lungs. He knew she was an orphan. She'd said something to that effect once. And even though he'd wanted to question her then, one look at her narrowed, guarded eyes had told him the topic was off-limits. Like *way* the hell off-limits. The Siberia of subjects. But now...

Had she opened the door to him? Just a crack? He stood in front of her, searching her face, looking for permission to step through, *wanting* permission to step through because...he *loved* her. And he longed to know everything about her. All her fears and hopes and dreams. Her past and her present, because maybe that would give him the key to her future.

He tucked a strand of wet hair behind her ear and chose his words carefully. "I *am* lucky, even if they're a pain in my ass most days."

She smiled, and it looked almost...*wistful*. He nearly moaned at the sight. Managed to hold it back at the last minute. "I'm told most families *are* a pain in the ass. That's what makes them great."

He couldn't stand it a second longer. He barreled

through the door she'd cracked open. "What happened to your parents?" he whispered. This was a test of sorts. If she had enough faith in him to share her story, then maybe, just maybe she thought there was a chance for them.

Her face blanked, her eyes taking on that glassy, near-doll-like sheen that said all her inner walls had sprung up. His stomach somersaulted over his disappointment and self-reproach. He'd gone too far. Pushed too fast. She didn't trust him enough to—

"I…uh…" Her gaze slid from his face to his throat, where his pulse was pounding. "I never knew who my father was."

He swallowed, his Adam's apple sticking. He was afraid to move, afraid to breathe lest he scare her away.

"I don't think my *mother* knew who my father was." She made a face, her eyes taking on a faraway look, as if she were thumbing through the Rolodex of old memories in her mind. "I can remember a lot of men going in and out of our house…um…trailer. We lived in a broken-down trailer park on the outskirts of Cincinnati. And I remember her telling me when I asked where my father was that it didn't matter because she loved me enough for a mommy *and* a daddy."

He began to form a picture in his mind of Olivia as a child. Wild black hair and blue eyes that took up her whole face. She had probably been a serious kid, *too* serious. "And your mother? What happened to her?"

Even though she was still staring at the hollow of his throat, he could see her eyes cloud over. The pain flashing in them was as bright as lightning bolts. "Drug overdose when I was five." His lungs became lead ballast stones in his chest, his heart an anchor. He wanted to travel back in time and tell her everything would be okay. That she'd grow up to be this strong, brave, amazing woman.

"She usually met the school bus at the end of the road to the trailer park. But that day after kindergarten she didn't. I walked home by myself and found her lying at the end of the drive. I thought she was sleeping. She slept a lot because of her *medicine*—that's what she called it. But when I couldn't wake her up, I started screaming. The neighbors heard me and called the police. I was placed with social services that night and stuck in an orphanage by the end of the week."

"No grandparents? No aunts and uncles?"

She managed to meet his eyes. "My mother was an only child. And *her* parents died in a flash flood when she was seventeen. Weird, I know. To die in a flash flood. But it's true. She dropped out of high school, got a job as a gas station attendant, and had me a couple of years later."

And then died soon after, leaving a five-year-old girl all alone in the world, adrift, parentless, friendless, and afraid. He tried to imagine it and couldn't. When he was five, he was chasing fireflies, playing in the sandbox at the park, and pretty much getting into everything his dad told him not to. "And foster parents?"

She shrugged, her expression droll. "The first couple who took me in *wanted* to keep me, I think. But I was too young to understand death. I thought my old mommy would come back for me if I acted like I didn't want my new mommy. I was a royal terror, wetting the bed, drawing on the walls with permanent markers, throwing tantrums one minute and withdrawing into sullen

silences the next. They were a young couple. They
didn't know how to cope. I was back at the orphanage
after six months. And then my *second* foster family
only took me in as a placeholder. They really wanted an
infant, and the minute their adoption petition for a baby
was approved, they sent me back."

Sent back. Like a pair of pants that didn't quite fit. It
took every ounce of self-discipline he had not to wrap
his arms around her, bury his nose in her damp hair, and
tell her over and over again how sorry he was she'd had
to go through that. But she wouldn't welcome his pity.
She was a proud woman…as well she should be. *Just
look how high she's risen from such meager beginnings*.
"And that was it?"

"No." She shook her head. The overhead light glinted
against the auburn highlights in her hair. "There were
other foster families in between stints in the orphanage.
But by that point, I'd been in the system a while, had
been passed over for kids who were younger than me,
cuter than me, more outgoing than me. So when I *was*
placed with a new foster family, I was so afraid they'd
reject me in the end that I always rejected *them* from the
beginning. Isolating myself, never showing any affection. Never *accepting* any affection. You know, basically being a stupid, insufferable little shit."

Some of what he was feeling must have shown on his
face, because she wrinkled her nose and attempted a smile.
"I know, right? I'm a modern-day Oliver Twist. Just without the pickpocketing and the all-around misadventures."

"Olivia…" Her name was four hoarse syllables on
his tongue.

She held up a hand, the look on her face going steely.

"Don't feel sorry for me, Leo. It could've been worse. I was never abused. Which, from what I hear, is a miracle for a kid in my position. I got my GED when I was seventeen, went to community college, then university, then filled out an application for the CIA. And the rest, as they say, is history."

"You're amazin'," he breathed.

"No." She shook her head adamantly. "I'm not. Not at all. I just happened to survive a rough start. A *lot* of kids do that." He opened his mouth to say many survived it only to turn down a dark path of drug abuse, crime, and overall self-destruction. But she continued before he could utter a single word. "In fact, didn't *you* lose your mother when you were young?"

And once again he clocked her change in subject—the dear woman wasn't very subtle about such things—and decided to let it slide. She'd told him what he wanted to know. And while the story broke his fucking heart, her faith in him, in letting him hear the awful truth of where she came from and what she'd endured, gathered up the sharp pieces and made it gloriously whole again.

"I was three when she died of ovarian cancer. The only memories I have of her are from the stories my father told me."

"And your father died a couple of years ago, right?"

"Four months before our stint in Syria." Looking back on it, that had been one *hell* of a year. He'd lost his father and one of his best friends, but he'd met the woman of his dreams.

"So now we're both orphans."

He sucked in a startled breath when the truth of it sank in. He'd never thought of himself as an orphan before.

He always associated that word with a child. But, in the strictest definition, he *was* an orphan, parentless—but, unlike Olivia, far from alone in the world. And, oh, how he wanted to tell her what was in his heart. Pledge himself to her. Promise to be her family, to help her *make* a family if that's what she wanted. But he held it all in and stuck with the plan…

———

6:57 p.m.…

"What are you…" she squeaked—*damnit!*—when Leo scooted her closer to the edge of the counter, stepped between her legs, and proceeded to kiss her cross-eyed. He came up for air—Two minutes later? Ten?—and her entire body was soft as butter, hot as Hades, and trembling like a leaf in the wind. Apparently, her brain was mush too, because talk about Simile City…

"You really know how to change the subject," she purred, running her hands over the smooth skin of his shoulders where a soft sheen of sweat, caused by the steamy bathroom and their even steamier kiss, made his skin glisten.

Not that she was complaining about the right turn in topics. She was *glad* of it. He already had her heart and her body. Now he had her story too. Which felt *intimate* on a whole different level. And that sense of belonging she'd experienced earlier? It had grown to the relative size of the sun. Was just as warm and welcome. Which meant the cold she'd feel in an hour or so when they waved their farewells would sting all the more.

Keep it casual. Keep it fun.

Sh'yeaaah. I think we blew past that a long *time ago.*

"We can keep talkin' if you want," he murmured against her throat, licking his way beneath her jaw.

"Nope." She palmed the back of his head, threading her fingers through his damp, shaggy hair. "I'm all talked out."

"So what do you reckon we should do instead?" And just in case she thought to answer with *How about a nice game of Parcheesi?* he scooted her forward another couple of inches until his manhood pressed against her belly. He was hard as stone, hot enough to singe her flesh, and throbbing so insistently that an answering pulse of pleasure resonated through her. She was instantly achy. Instantly wet. She would say she was instantly *wanton*, but that was pretty much a foregone conclusion when Leo was in the same room with her.

"I'm open to suggestions," she murmured when he nipped the edge of her jaw and lifted a big, warm hand to plump her breast. And even though a tiny part of her still thought it best to hold back—to keep from, in the middle-school vernacular, *going all the way*—the rest of her figured, *What the hell?* She was already sunk, lost, completely deep-sixed where he was concerned. So why shouldn't she take everything he had to give, experience everything he wanted to share with her? Didn't someone once say you regret the things you *don't* do more than the things you do?

Or maybe I'm just rationalizing. Again. *But holy shit!* It was so hard to think when Leo was plucking at her breast, making her womb twang as if her nipple and her womanhood were somehow connected.

"I want to make love to you, Olivia," he said,

searching her eyes. Make love. Not fuck or screw. Because even if all he was after was a quick lay so they could finally, *finally* bank the fire that burned between them, he respected her enough, *liked* her enough, to make it sound as though it was special.

Oh, this man… This wonderful, sexy, sweet man…

"I want that too," she whispered and saw triumph blaze in his eyes the second before he reclaimed her lips. And then it was nothing but teeth and tongues, hungry lips and ragged breaths. They made love with their mouths. Their hands followed suit. He lovingly attended to her nipples, plucking and rubbing until she was mewling and achy. She ran her fingertips over his chest and belly, lower, so she could wrap her hand around him and pump.

"Olivia," he gasped, ripping his lips away. "I need to—"

"Yes." She nodded, her skin on fire, her blood running hot. Her center was a pulsing emptiness. She wanted him inside her, filling her up, stretching her to the limit. "Yes, Leo." She angled him toward her entrance, watched as his swollen head parted her folds. He was so red he was nearly purple, his veins throbbing angrily. She was pink and swollen and so, *so* wet.

They both held their breath when he pushed inside her, just the tiniest bit, just so the flaring ring around his head remained visible. His shaft looked huge between her legs, and she was as hesitant to accommodate him as she was eager to feel him pushing inside her. She bit her lip, prepared herself for his first thrust. It never came.

Looking up, she discovered his eyes on her face. "What?"

"Condom," he rasped, then wrenched open the drawer beside her, pulling out a box of Trojans.

"How did you—" she began, but he cut her off.

"I was lookin' for bar soap. That frou-frou shower gel was slimy and smelled like"—he ripped a packet of foil open with his teeth, his cock still kissing her entrance—"black licorice. I *hate* black licorice."

They both moaned when he stepped back, breaking their delicate connection. Then he placed the ring of rubber over his head, handling his dick unabashedly.

"Will that thing fit?" she asked, her delicate folds missing the branding heat of his flesh, pulsing, grasping as if to draw him back to her.

He grinned, rolling on the condom and hissing like his skin was super sensitive. She suspected it was. He was so swollen he was tight and shiny. "No need to stroke my ego, darlin'. I'm all set in that department."

"I wasn't—"

But that's as far as she got because he stepped back to her, using his thumb to angle his shaft toward her entrance and push the tip of his head back inside her. Only, instead of stroking, he placed his thumb over her clit, rubbing, caressing, making the bundle of nerves thrum. Making her groan.

"Leo," she breathed, wriggling. Her womanhood sucked at him with greedy pulls, trying to drag him inside. But he remained frustratingly still.

"I want to make sure you're ready," he said, licking the fingers of the hand not busy between her legs. He rubbed them over her right nipple. The aching tip furled into a bud so tight she thought she might die from the exquisite torture.

"I'm ready," she assured him, hooking her heels behind his knees, grabbing his ass in both hands and forcing his hips forward. "*Ohhhhhhhh!*" she groaned at the same time he sucked in a startled breath.

"Slow, Olivia," he instructed, and she knew not to disobey him. He was a big man. She was *not* a big woman.

She bit her lip, watching his shaft part her, stretch her, fill her inch by slow, delicious inch. Her rapacious nerve endings sizzled to life under the friction, her hungry walls slipping over his iron hardness. It was pleasure unlike anything she'd ever experienced, because it was tinged by the slightest bit of pain. She was at capacity. She couldn't take any more. Luckily, she didn't have to. His tip bumped into the entrance to her womb at the same time his testicles pressed against the lower curves of her ass.

They were joined, utterly, completely. Her trimmed patch of inky-black pubic hair in sharp contrast to the golden brown of his. He claimed her lips then. His kiss hot and eager, his tongue stroking into her mouth over and over again. But his cock…his cock remained completely still, buried inside her, throbbing so forcefully she felt each pulse stretch her further, but he didn't move.

"Leo," she husked against his lips, squirming. "Please, Leo. I need you. I want— Yessssss." Her head fell back on her shoulders as he pulled out of her, just a bit, just an inch or two, before pressing home where he remained still. Again. She growled her impatience.

"I want t-to…" he stuttered, kissing the side of her mouth, her neck, "make it last."

She grabbed his ears, stared him straight in the eye, and let him know exactly what *she* wanted. "I want you to *move* that fine ass. *Now*."

——◆——

7:01 p.m....

Never one to ignore a direct order from a lady, Leo stroked into Olivia's heat, gritting his teeth against the mind-numbing pleasure. He wanted to make it last, but she was so tight. So wet. And every withdrawal was friction-filled heaven. Every stroke forward a wonder of gripping, pulsing sensation. It was too good. Too much.

And then there was Olivia. Her head thrown back. Her gorgeous breasts pointing upward, her legs wrapped tight around his hips as if she never wanted to let him go. And by God, if he had his way, she never would.

Bending to suck one tightly furled nipple into his mouth, he pistoned into her. Over and over again. Slowly. Then more quickly. Joining their bodies in that age-old dance of love, of devotion and passion and communion.

His entire world became the two of them. Moving together. His hands on her hips as he rocked against her, listening to every indrawn breath, cataloging every subtle shift that made her moan and tighten around him. Her fingers in his hair as she held him tight, as she met him thrust for thrust, as she pushed him higher, faster, harder. Seconds became little eternities of divine pleasure. Minutes turned into centuries of bliss.

Then his name rose from the back of her throat, and she exploded around him. Her fingers digging into his scalp. Her silken walls clamping down, squeezing and pulsing, milking and sucking. He clenched his jaw, screwing his eyes shut, wanting to hold on, to continue making love to her forever, until she came down from this high and he pushed her up toward the pinnacle again. And again.

But he couldn't.

He'd waited too long for this. For her. And her violent climax triggered his own. His balls pulled up tight, tingling, buzzing, and then he was coming. In her. With her. The ecstasy shooting along his shaft and rippling out into his limbs, until every inch of him was alive with throbbing, incandescent pleasure. With happiness. With love. It was better than anything he'd ever known. Sweeter than anything he'd ever dreamed.

And then, sated, languid, they collapsed against each other, his head on her shoulder, her ankles crossed above his ass. Their chests rose and fell with shared breaths, and he didn't know why it happened, but a deep chuckle sounded low in his throat.

"What's so funny?" she panted, kissing his ear. A delicate caress. A little love peck that he felt all the way down to his thundering, happy heart.

"Just that I reckon *that's* what Rusty was talkin' about when he said we needed to start really livin'. What we just did, you and me, darlin', that's what it's all about."

She stilled for just a second, and he wondered if he should have kept his mouth shut about Rusty. But then she hummed her agreement, nibbling on his earlobe, and he relaxed, smiling. He was softening inside her now. He needed to pull out. Because he wanted her returning to him for this, because this connection they shared wasn't something to ignore, to toss aside, not because the condom leaked and they had to make a decision about an accidental pregnancy.

Olivia...round with my baby. The thought of getting

a woman pregnant had always terrified the holy frickin' hell out of him. But imagining Olivia carrying his child filled him with a sense of…*rightness*. A sense of completion that he didn't know had been missing in his life until now, when she—

No sir. He shook his head. *Don't get ahead of yourself. You've yet to convince her to*—

A tentative knock sounded on the door.

He growled his displeasure at the same time Olivia groaned. "That better not be you out there, Bran!" he barked, hissing as he pulled out of her wet heat. He watched his retreat with avid interest, noting how pink and swollen she was. How wet. And just like the motherfrickin' sixteen-year-old he'd regressed to today, the sight was enough to have his blood warming again, pooling low in his groin. He couldn't get enough of her. Figured even if he had her a thousand times, the sight of her, naked, sated, biting her lip, would have him wanting to have her, *needing* to have her a thousand times more.

"Sorry to interrupt," Bran said through the door.

"Again!" both Leo and Olivia called in unison.

"I needed to let you guys know we're about to have some company," Bran said. "A deep-sea fishing boat was sailing by us on its way back to Miami. They hailed on the radio to say they've sprung an oil leak. They're gonna tie up to us in a couple minutes and borrow a few quarts in the hopes it'll be enough to get them where they're going without having to call in a tow from the Coast Guard."

"A fishing vessel?" Leo called, pulling off the condom, wadding it in toilet paper, and tossing it in the trash before reaching for the swim trunks and T-shirt he'd laid over the opposite end of the bathroom vanity when he changed into Maddy's brother's wet suit.

"Yeah, we must be close to a good fishing hole or channel or something," Bran said. "I've seen three or four deep-sea fishing boats pass by our starboard side since we've been anchored. And get this, the name of the boat with the oil leak? It's *Breaking Wind*, for crying out loud. You gotta love those crusty, beer-loving fishing boat captains and their warped senses of humor." He chuckled.

"I'll be on deck in a sec," Leo assured Bran.

"No need. We'll handle it. I just figured I better let you guys know—"

"I'll *be* on deck in a sec," he said again.

"Yeah. Roger that."

He heard Bran's muffled steps move toward the door of the cabin as he stepped into his swim trunks. Olivia hopped down from the countertop. It caused her breasts to jiggle in the most amazing way. He groaned. "Stop bein' so damn sexy, woman. You tryin' to kill me, or what?"

"You're one to talk," she said with a saucy grin, leering at his package before he pulled his swim trunks over his hips. Then she stepped into the shower, bending to retrieve her soggy clothes. He not only got a peek at her pert bum shoved in the air, but the plump pink lips of her womanhood as well. The blood rushed from his head so quickly that he had to grab the counter to steady himself against the sudden onset of dizziness.

"You're doin' that on purpose," he accused.

"Just taking advantage of an opportunity when it presented itself," she said, parroting his earlier words back to him. And *this* was why he loved her. Yes, she was beautiful. Yes, the sex was amazing. But it was her wit, her spark, her…intangible *something* that made him grin, that made his heart warm, that made him want to listen to her tease him for hours before he grabbed her up and hugged her, kissed her, screwed her blind.

He was grinning like an idiot as he pulled on his T-shirt, watching Olivia wring the water from her clothes. "I could ask Maddy if there's a clothes dryer on board," he offered.

"I'll finish wringing the water out, slip on the robe"—she pointed to the navy-blue terrycloth garment hanging on a hook on the back of the door. The precise way the belt was folded and tied told him the robe was freshly cleaned—"and then meet you upstairs and ask her myself."

"I suspect everything with the approachin' fishin' boat is on the up and up. But the way this day has gone, I'm not takin' anything for granted. So just in case things *aren't* on the up and up, I was sort of hopin' you'd be willin' to hang down here for a bit," he said, his grin widening because he already knew what her answer would be. The same as it was the last time. And right on cue…

"Not on your life," she harrumphed.

He chuckled, shaking his head as he turned the knob and opened the door. The love inside him was so huge he thought it a wonder his skin was able to contain it without bursting open to spew forth heart-shaped confetti. "I reckoned as much."

Chapter Nineteen

7:22 p.m....

OLIVIA BLEW OUT A BREATH THE MINUTE LEO CLOSED the door and simply stood there, trembling. He had no idea how much his words had both touched her and brutalized her—*That's what Rusty was talkin' about when he said we needed to start really livin'. What we just did, you and me, darlin', that's what it's all about.*

Touched her because he was right. What they'd shared was beautiful. Glorious. The reason poets composed sonnets, musicians wrote songs, and writers penned stories of love and triumph.

Brutalized her because...Rusty. That one name, spoken aloud, reminded her why the beautiful, glorious thing they'd shared could never last. Because she'd lied to Leo from the first minute she knew him, betrayed him each moment after that by withholding the truth, and killed a man he loved like a brother with one split-second decision...

"I received an interesting bit of information yesterday," General Al-Ambhi said in his thick accent, leaning back in his desk chair and spinning a letter opener in his right hand. *Its sharp edges caught the overhead light, glinting ominously with each twirl.*

"What was that?" Olivia asked from her seat across

from him, careful to keep her expression only mildly curious though all her internal green lights had flicked to a foreboding yellow. Ever since she'd received the call from the rebel general to come to an impromptu meeting at his house, she'd been uneasy.

On the surface, the two of them had a friendly relationship. She was the CIA attaché to the SEAL Team charged with training his men in battle tactics for the ongoing fight in Syria. And he was the rebel leader who was sympathetic to Western ideals and the promise of what would hopefully one day be a democratic society.

But that was just what was on the surface…

Because underneath all that charm and ideology, General Al-Ambhi was a traitor to the rebel cause he claimed so fiercely to fight for. He was secretly in league with the Islamic State—ISIS or ISIL or IS or whatever else you wanted to call them. She preferred the title Evil Incarnate. And little did he know that she was playing both sides of the board too. The CIA had grown wise to his double dealings and had sent her in to feed him disinformation. The wide world of international intrigue coming full circle.

"I heard you were to meet five of your assets within IS last night in a coffee shop," he said slowly. "So I followed you to determine their identities."

Okay, now her internal green lights weren't yellow, they were flashing red and blaring out warnings. Only those within The Company knew she'd planned the clandestine meeting. How the hell had Al-Ambhi found out? It didn't make any sense. *Unless…* Is it possible there's a leak?

The thought sent a cold chill slicing up her spine until she fancied it was the tip of that letter opener he was holding.

"Why would you want to know their identities?" she asked carefully, remaining perfectly still though her thoughts were spinning.

Al-Ambhi tsked. "Come now, Agent Mortier. Let us stop playing these games. You know I am not really fighting for the rebels. And I know that you know. I have known that you know for a while now."

Her breath wheezed out of her, dry as the wind whipping around the concrete wall surrounding the perimeter of the general's compound. The cold metal of her Sig P228 was an acute ache against the small of her back, and the smell of her own fear was sharp in her nose. "How?" she asked, surprised to hear her tone was steady, considering her heart was racing a mile a minute.

"Really?" He cocked his head, dropping the letter opener on his desk. The resulting thunk sounded particularly loud. Her insides winced, but her outside remained rock steady. "You find the how more interesting than the why?"

Play along, Mortier. Just play along.

"Okay." She shrugged unconcernedly, so he wouldn't know she was sweating bullets and close to pissing her pants. There were a million ways for this to go horribly wrong and not one way she could fathom for it to go right. "Why? Why wait so long to let me know you're on to me?"

"Because I needed leverage." He smiled, his tanned face splitting around a mouthful of white teeth. Al-Ambhi was a handsome man. With curly black hair and flashing dark eyes. But that beauty was only skin deep. On the inside, he was hideous. What else could explain his affiliation with a group that slaughtered, raped, and beheaded on a whim?

"Leverage for what?" It was hard not to spit out the words like rancid meat.

"For blackmail, of course." His smile widened. He sat forward, running one long, knobby-knuckled finger over the cellular phone lying faceup beside the letter opener. "You see, I am sick of this whole mess. The fighting. The sneaking around. The endless battle for this beastly country. I left my position in the Al-Assad regime because I thought, like in Libya and Egypt, the rebels would quickly see victory. Take over governing. And I wanted to make sure to position myself at the very top of that new government."

And suddenly it was perfectly clear. He had no morality. No conscience or cause. He was simply an opportunist, a man out for no one but himself. And that was what accounted for his inner ugliness. "And when that proved to take too long, you threw in your lot with IS," she snarled, no longer able to maintain her emotionless facade.

"Exactly." He continued to stroke the phone. A shiver of repulsion rippled through her. "But I have come to realize there is no hope for them. They are too violent, too unstable. They have too many enemies in the region now. They will never be allowed a caliphate. At most, they may be able to rule a small plot of sand somewhere no one wants or cares about. It is not the future I pictured for myself."

"Which is where I come in." She curled her hands into fists when he nodded. "What do you want?"

"Fifty million dollars in a Swiss bank account and assurances from your government that I will not be hunted."

Jesus, fifty million? He's got a giant set of brass clackers!

"*And if I don't give you these things, you'll call your buddies in the IS and out my assets,*" *she said, gritting her teeth until they creaked.*

"*Precisely.*"

Her mind raced through the possibilities. She knew Morales wouldn't go for fifty thousand, much less fifty million. The lives of the five locals she'd groomed and trained to infiltrate IS weren't worth all that much to the CIA, worth even less to Uncle Sam. But they were worth something to her. Because those five men had families and homes. They had loved ones who were counting on them to come back to them. They had everything she'd never had. So very *much to lose and yet they'd still agreed to lay it all on the line. They were brave, good, valiant men, and she couldn't just sit back and let them die.*

"*My boss will never agree,*" *she told the general.*

"*Then I am left with no other choice.*" *He grabbed the cell phone.*

Olivia's Sig was in her hands before she even realized she'd reached for it, pointing it straight at Al-Ambhi's face. "*Don't.*" *Just the one word.*

"*Ah.*" *He smiled again. That oily smile. That wretched smile.* "*But you see, I must. If I cannot have the Americans and their money protecting me, then I will have the IS and their gratitude protecting me.*"

"*I'll kill you before you ever make the call,*" *she warned.*

"*No you won't,*" *he scoffed.* "*If you kill me, my men will kill you. You* and *the soldier you have waiting outside.*"

The soldier she had waiting outside...Rusty Lawrence. The SEAL who'd been assigned her bodyguard for this meeting because, even though they were all supposed to be friends here, an unaccompanied female was always a target. Al-Ambhi was right. She and Rusty wouldn't make it out alive if she pulled her trigger. But when she weighed two lives against five, she just couldn't see how the ledger added up in their favor. Except, maybe…

"Not if I tell your men you're really working for IS." She was breathing hard now. She couldn't help it. And her Sig was trembling in her grip.

"Pfft." He waved a hand through the hot, arid air. "They will never believe you. You are an American, after all. A great infidel. A great liar." He waited a beat, and when she didn't lower her weapon, he rolled his eyes and punched in a number, holding the phone to his ear.

He would do it. She could see it in his eyes.

And he must have seen that she would do it too. Because his face slackened and his mouth fell open right before she squeezed her trigger.

Olivia gripped the handle on the door of the shower, anchoring herself in the here and now. Trying to forget the way the general's skull had exploded, the horror of the blood and the gore. Trying to forget the way Rusty had burst into the room, taking one glance around before yelling at her to run. Trying to forget the sound of the rebel gunfire that had cut him down when they were racing through the hall toward the back of the general's house.

A million times she'd gone over that day and tried to figure out what she could have done differently to keep everyone alive. And a million times she'd come up with nothing.

She blew out a ragged breath and stepped from the shower, draping her wet clothes over a towel rod. She was just slipping on the robe and cinching the belt when she heard raised voices out on deck. The hair along the back of her neck lifted in warning, and her heart took off like it was in a race and someone had fired the starting pistol. She was slipping out the door, running across the guest cabin, and dropping to her belly in the main living area two seconds later.

She could see through the big windows and in the glow of the *Black Gold*'s exterior lights that a fishing boat had indeed tied up to the back of the yacht. But that's not what had her kissing carpet. Hell no. What had her kissing carpet was the five dark-skinned men who were standing at the fishing boat's railing pointing weapons straight at Leo and his guys. For their part, the SEALs were locked and loaded, aiming their M4s right back in a good ol' fashioned high-seas standoff.

She lifted her chin, trying to see where everyone else was, and got a glimpse of Maddy and the crew of the *Black Gold* standing stock-still and slightly off to the side. Their hands were raised in the air. And the deck-hand, Nigel, appeared to be holding two quarts of oil.

What the ever-loving fuckety fuck? How? Why? Who?

She hadn't a clue. Figured whatever the hell was going on, whoever the hell these new guys were, it was simply the olive atop the shit sandwich that was this day.

She glanced at the occasional table where she'd laid the AK-47 and crawled over to it, the carpet beneath her smelling so strongly of deodorizer that her eyes watered. Carefully slipping the weapon onto the floor, she checked the clip, found it half full, and gently reinserted it, wincing when it clicked into place with a loud *snick*. Then she was belly crawling toward the door that led out onto the main deck.

Fear was a hot fist squeezing her heart. Guilt was a rough stone sitting in the pit of her stomach. Leo was out there. Brave, beautiful Leo. The man she loved. And there was a rifle aimed at his head. It was unthinkable. Untenable. She would never forgive herself if—

She cut off her own thoughts as she slowly, cautiously slid open the door. A night breeze blew into the main cabin. It ruffled her damp hair and slipped under the lapels of the robe, bringing with it the smell of fish and sea. And the sound of a man's voice…

"Give us the case with the chemicals," he said, his accent so slight it was hard to tell exactly where he was from. Certainly not Miami, though the brief glimpse she'd gotten of his attire would say otherwise.

"No!" Leo yelled in return. She held her breath and scooted over the threshold, standing slowly, careful to keep herself concealed behind the wall of the living quarters. Night had fallen over the Straits of Florida. Only a dim line of sunshine kissed the sea along the western horizon, limning the sky in an eerie orangey-red. Silver stars were beginning to punch through the darkness overhead. And since the waves had died down, the glassy water reflected the pinpoints of light until it looked like there were two skies. She noted all of this in passing as she skirted around the side of the main cabin and carefully took the port-side stairs down to the lower deck. She crept forward slowly, turkey-peeking around the edge of the living quarters twice to get her bearings.

"Give us the chemicals!" the stranger shouted again, his voice carrying out over the dark water.

"Fuck you!" Leo barked.

"I believe you are the one who is fucked!" The stranger snorted a laugh. "We have you outgunned."

And that's when Olivia made her move. She stepped from around the corner, the AK-47 raised to her shoulder, a head wearing a floppy hat smack-dab in the crosshairs of her sights. "Count again!" she yelled.

7:26 p.m....

At the sound of Olivia's voice, Leo briefly closed his eyes and managed, just barely, to stifle a pained groan.

Brave, fearless, idiotic *woman! Why can't she just stay put?* Oh, right. Because she's brave and fearless. *Shit on a shovel.*

The group of men glanced at her from the corners of their eyes, but they didn't stop aiming at Leo and his friends in order to center her in their sights. He took comfort in that. *That's right, assholes. Just keep pointin' those sawguns right here.*

"We don't want to hurt anyone," the asshole in the ridiculous T-shirt and floppy hat called. It had been clear from the get-go he was the ringleader. He'd been the one to convey orders the whole time the fishing boat was throwing over bumpers and tying up to the *Black Gold*. Leo and the SEALs had remained leaning against the bulkhead of the main living quarters, their M4s carefully concealed behind their backs—you know, just in case—as the yacht's crew helped tie off ropes and started handing over quarts of oil.

And *that's* when things went to hell in a handbasket. Because just as Nigel the Deckhand was poised to toss over a couple more plastic bottles of Pennzoil Marine Motor Oil, Floppy Hat drew down on him. And then it was a case of *who can arm themselves the quickest*? For the record, it was a draw. Which is why they were now in the middle of a *Wild Wild West*-style showdown.

"Did you hear me?" Floppy Hat called. "I said we don't want to hurt anyone."

Yeah, right. Leo barely refrained from snorting. Over the years, he'd looked into the eyes of enough radicals to recognize a killing gleam when he saw one. And these boys? Well, they wore those familiar gleams in spades. Chemicals or no chemicals, they planned to kill everyone on board the *Black Gold* the first chance they got.

"We just want the case," Floppy Hat insisted.

"You're too late," Leo growled, biding his time and channeling the adrenaline coursing through his veins until all his senses were heightened. Floppy Hat's face was crystal clear. The sound of the boats rocking against each other with a gentle *thunk, thunk* was amplified, and the smell of outboard engine fuel and silver polish hung heavy in the air. "The chems are already gone."

Floppy Hat's eyes narrowed. "You lie."

Leo lifted one shoulder, sensing Olivia behind him as if there were an invisible cord attaching him to her, tugging at his heart. He *wished* she'd just stayed inside. This situation was a powder keg waiting to go *kaboom*, and he wanted her hell and gone when it did.

"I don't make a habit of it," he said.

From the corner of his eye, he saw Bran adjusting his stance, slowly slipping one foot back, twisting his body just slightly. It was a posture Leo knew all too well. The one his best friend assumed when he needed to take out multiple targets in quick order.

Right. So that's the plan.

He, Wolf, and Mason would each pop off one guy—the one who was directly across from them. And Bran, Mr. Crack Shot, would pop off the two who were directly across from him. Now, they just had to time their shots at precisely the same moment, taking the whole group by surprise.

Good thing they'd trained for exactly this type of situation.

"You say they are no longer here. So then, where do you propose they have gone?" Floppy Hat demanded, his tone telegraphing his belief that they hadn't gone anywhere.

"Doesn't matter," Leo said, tightening his finger on the trigger, breathing out slowly to steady his heart and solidify his hold. He could feel his friends' tension vibrating through the night air like a storm about to break. They were ready. And waiting on his signal. His world squeezed down to Floppy Hat and the spot in the center of his forehead. "You'll never see hide nor hair of 'em." And before Floppy Hat could reply to that, he bellowed, "*Now!*"

The roar of three simultaneous shots and another a split second later boomed over the deck, making his eardrums pop. Even still, he heard his own trigger *click* ominously. Jammed. *Fuuuuuccckkk!* Down the length of his sights, he saw red holes erupt in the heads of Floppy Hat's men just as the muscles in Floppy Hat's forearm bunched when he tightened his finger around his trigger.

Bang! The sound of a fifth shot blasted by Leo's

head. The whiz of the bullet slicing through the air by his ear told him Olivia had been the one to take aim.

Floppy Hat's neck burst open at the same time his eyes flew wide. He dropped his weapon to claw at the wound that was spurting thick sprays of blood in rhythmic, steady streams. He made an awful gurgling noise, then collapsed onto the deck of the fishing boat next to two of his men, his legs scrabbling dreadfully in his death throes. The remaining two men had fallen over the railing, their arms dangling down, their heads dripping blood into the sea between the boats. Five dead in less than two seconds. It was as gruesome as it was impressive.

So much needless horror today. So much dying. He wished there could have been another way and sent a prayer of thanks up to Rusty once more for making them all promise to stop living in a world that required this of them on a daily basis.

Blowing out a breath, he turned to see Olivia lower her weapon to the deck. She was trembling, her face completely drained of blood like she'd been exsanguinated, and her blue eyes taking up her whole face.

"See," he said, realizing he was trembling too. "I told you that you didn't have anything to worry about. You had my back, stepped up, and did what you had to do and—"

He stopped right there because she bolted upright and raced for the railing, the back of her robe billowing out behind her in a navy-blue ripple of terrycloth. Leaning over the side, she gasped again and again like she was trying to keep from retching. He shook his head at the brave, fearless, *softhearted* woman he loved. He felt a lump in his throat as he swung his M4 over his shoulder and started in her direction.

He'd gone no more than two steps when he saw the barrel of a machine gun edging from around the corner, pointing straight at Olivia's slender back. He didn't think, he didn't hesitate, he simply roared her name and ran. Three leaping steps brought him to the corner of the living quarters. His right hand connected with the barrel of the weapon, pushing it off target just as the motherfucker operating it squeezed the trigger.

Boom! The shot flew wide. *Thank Christ!* From the corner of his eye, Leo saw Olivia spin around, hands raised to her mouth. Then he was ripping the weapon away from some guy in a wet suit, snarling as he tossed it overboard. He started pummeling the sack of shit in the face with both fists. The rage was on him now. He was seeing red. This man, whoever he was, had been a split second away from shooting Olivia in the back. And that meant Leo would kill him, beat him to a bloody pulp and then stomp on his remains.

Wet-Suit Guy's nose exploded under Leo's fist, blood streaming over his mouth and chin. He staggered back against the bulkhead as Leo aimed body blows to his midriff over and over again, growling, howling, loving the ache in his arms and the skin that split over his knuckles. He was a beast. An animal bent on protecting its mate. Savage and unyielding. Mindless. Berserk.

He didn't know how long he stood there slugging away at the guy, hearing the crunch of bone meeting bone, watching as skin flayed open and bled. But at some point, he realized Olivia had laid a hand on his shoulder and was whispering his name in that smoky, beloved voice.

"Leo. Shhh. Stop now." The red slowly eased from his vision. The rage roaring through his veins like molten steel cooled. He dropped his hands, flexing his fingers. And without his fists keeping Wet Suit upright, he crumbled to the ground at Leo's feet, curling in on himself.

"It's okay." Olivia brushed his hair back from his face. "Leo, look at me." He glanced over at her, breaths sawing from his lungs. She smiled and stood on tiptoe to press a soft kiss to his lips. It anchored him, grounded him, settled him in a way nothing else could have. "I'm fine," she whispered. "See? I'm alive. You got him."

To his utter dismay, what sounded like a sob burst from somewhere deep in his chest. And then he was grabbing her up, holding her close as his friends and the crew of the *Black Gold* gathered around them. For a few glorious moments, he breathed her in and felt her strong heartbeat against the lips he pressed to her neck. Then the guy lying in a heap at his feet groaned, and Olivia turned her head, gasping.

"What?" Leo asked, reluctantly releasing her. If he had his way, she'd be permanently attached to him. *Conjoined twins, connected at the genitals.* Okay. All right. He was making jokes, which meant he hadn't gone off the deep end for good. He covertly released a pent-up breath. For the first time in his life, he understood how it was possible for a man to lose it, to slip over the edge of sanity. And it was a chilling glimpse into the dark void. Goose bumps lifted the hairs on his arms.

"I think I…" Olivia bent down, looking at the stranger. "You're Agent Jonathan Wilson, aren't you?"

Chapter Twenty

7:48 p.m....

"SO TELL ME, AGENT WILSON, ARE YOU WORKING WITH someone inside or are you working alone?"

Maddy sat on the plush sofa in the yacht's main living quarters, watching Olivia question the bleeding, trussed-up sole survivor of the shootout. And she must be in shock or something...or...maybe *more* shock was what she was in. *Is it possible for shock to compound on itself?* Because her hands weren't shaking. Her heart wasn't racing. And she wasn't ten seconds away from passing out. As far as she could figure, after witnessing what she had secretly titled "Yosemite Sam-style Dustup *Número Dos*," she should be experiencing *all* those things.

Or maybe Bran was right when he'd told her the repercussions of what she'd seen would likely hit her hours later, when she least expected it and was all alone. *Shitfire. That's probably it.* She'd probably be a blubbering mess in about... She checked her watch but got distracted when the Bleeding Dude snarled, "Stop calling me Agent Wilson! My name is Banu az-Harb!"

So *that's* what Lead A-hole had been saying over and over again. *Banoo. Banoo.* Clearly, he'd been talking to this guy.

"Your *name* is Jonathan Wilson," Olivia insisted,

standing beside the man who was tied to a chair at the
big mahogany table. Even wearing nothing more than
one of the yacht's terrycloth robes, she still managed to
look cool and in charge. Completely kickass. *Get down
with your bad self, my sister from another mister!*

"I know that's your name because we've been in a
dozen meetings together. We've sat across the table
from one another and given situation reports. And things
will go better for you if you cooperate with me now.
I'll make sure the higher-ups know you were helpful,
and my testimony to that fact will go a long way when
it comes to sentencing. So, now, who are you working
with inside? Who else has been leaking—"

"Ha!" Banu or Jonathan or whatever his name
was—Maddy was going to go with Jonathan simply
because the balding blond man didn't look anything
like a Banu—barked out a laugh. It was overly loud and
sort of insane-sounding. It caused the three men seated
around the table to frown. Leo shifted unconsciously
closer to Olivia.

"You think I needed *help*, Agent Mortier?" Jonathan
thundered. "You think I couldn't have done everything
alone? *I* am it." Maddy fancied that if his hands weren't
tied, he would have punched a thumb into his puffed-up
chest. "*I* am The Company's worst nightmare!"

The company? Was that capitalized? Also, *Agent
Mortier*? So Olivia actually *was* CIA. Maddy knew that
much from the movies. And speaking of the movies,
right about now she could really go for a bag of popcorn.
She had a real-life, honest-to-God drama unfolding in
front of her eyes.

And goshdarnit! Where the heckfire was Bran when

she needed him? She had a great quote from *A Few Good Men* she would love to share. Unfortunately, he was outside with the captain, Bruce, and Nigel, making sure no more wet-suited men climbed aboard to cause mischief. Also, they were securing the fishing boat to the back of the *Black Gold* so they could tow it with them back to Key West—and that was *one* job she was happy to leave to the men, thank you very much. Then again, she couldn't help but wonder if that pit planted firmly in the center of her stomach was there because she was missing Bran's presence, his ready smile, and his even-readier wit. But that was so completely nutso, she didn't allow herself to really contemplate it.

I mean, seriously, Stockholm syndrome much, Maddy? Although was it still Stockholm syndrome if she wasn't technically a captive and he wasn't technically a captor? Was there a name for a swift, irrational attraction to the person who saved your life?

She'd have to look it up once she got home. For now, her attention was glued to Olivia, who tilted her head and let her gaze drift over Jonathan. Her upper lip curled with disdain. "Well, you don't look very nightmarish right now, Agent Wilson."

Olivia was trying to rile the guy. From what Maddy had seen so far, it wouldn't take much. Johnny Boy seemed to have a pretty exaggerated opinion of himself. In fact, if he had green hair and a perpetual smile painted on his face, he would have made an awesomely good nemesis for Batman. *This place deserves a better class of criminal, and* I'm *gonna give it to them! Bwahahaha!*

For Pete's sake! Bran really needed to get in here. All her good material was going to waste!

"In fact," Olivia continued, "you look like the idiot who acted on a planted piece of Intel in a Company memo and then got caught sneaking onto a boat full of SEALs." SEALs? *But I thought Bran said they were salvors working for the government, so what the heckfire is—* "You look like a guy whose grand master plan got blown to shit."

Jonathan muttered something under his breath.

"What's that?" Olivia asked.

"I didn't know they were SEALs!" he shouted, spittle flying from the corner of his mouth. Maddy was happy she was seated on the sofa and not at the table. *Bleck.* "I thought they were either CIA or some other government agency! In which case, they would have negotiated and haggled for a lot longer than two fucking minutes before opening fire!"

"Allowing you the time to sneak up behind them," Olivia mused, "lay on your trigger, and catch everyone in the crossfire. Then, once we were all dead, you could take your time scouring the yacht for the case of chemicals. Which, by the way, actually *are* already on their way back to the mainland."

Jonathan glared at her, and Olivia lifted a brow, laughing, the sound low and husky, *taunting*. "Come on, you have to admit it was a ridiculously risky move. And that, combined with the fact that you fell for the trap Morales and I laid for you, proves you're an idiot."

Johnny Boy called her a filthy name, and Leo slammed his hand down on the table. It sounded like a rifle shot. "Watch your mouth," he warned, his tone the audio version of a hazard sign. *Proceed at your own risk.*

"Fuck you!" Jonathon roared.

Leo didn't flinch. He simply allowed his mouth to curve into a grin. "Not on your best day, buddy."

"Don't worry, Leo," Olivia said. "Nothing this asshole says can hurt me." She turned to the asshole in question. "So why do it?" she prodded now that Johnny Boy was literally foaming at the mouth. The blood crusting around his ruined nose bubbled with each of his ragged breaths. And his one good eye glared feverishly. The bad one was swollen completely shut. Leo had sure enough done a number on the man. Maddy shivered at the memory of his huge fists connecting with the guy over and over again. For a while there, she'd thought Leo would beat him to death. SEALs? Yep, she could totally buy that. "For money? Is someone paying you to—"

Olivia didn't get any further than that because Jonathan launched into a tirade about the "great evil that was the United States of America" and the "sacrilege of American combat boots setting foot on holy Muslim soil." Then he went on to spout something about being "born to bring down the infidels" and "seeing his name burned into the annals of time."

It was at that point in his rant that Wolf cut in. "You're not a Muslim," he said, a heavy dose of disgust lacing his deep voice. "At best, you're a megalomaniac who wants a place in history. At worst, you're a psychopath who glommed on to an ideology you thought would explain your need to wreak havoc on the world and justify your thirst for mass murder."

"What would you know of Islam?" Jonathan hissed. "Allah commands us to slay the infidels wherever we catch them. To cut off their heads and their fingers!"

Wolf shook his head. "You're mangling the scripture and quoting it out of context. Have you forgotten the Quran also teaches that Allah delivered Prophet Mohammed to humanity to make us more merciful to one another? And that Allah commanded you to take not a life because it will be as if you have slain all of humanity, and if you save a life it will be as if you saved all of humanity?"

Wow. Maddy wouldn't have thought it to look at him, but the man knew his stuff. Jonathan obviously came to the same conclusion because he turned beet red under all the dried blood on his face and started spewing even crazier crap about murdering nonbelievers and cleansing the world through holy jihad.

Instead of rising to the bait, Wolf simply crossed his arms over his chest. "You can't pick apart pieces of a religion to make it fit your narrative. You either take it in context, as a whole, and with the knowledge that its historical significance has changed over the years, or you don't take it at all. You're worse than the radicals who are raised in the religion. At least they have the excuse of having been brainwashed by crooked imams. People like you—"

"Forget it," Olivia cut in. "There's no reasoning with a crazy man."

"I'm not crazy," Jonathan spit. "Just because I believe in something—"

"You *are* crazy," Olivia interrupted, provoking a growl of rage from him. "*And* you're a traitor. You do realize the penalty for treason is death, right?"

A vicious smile curved Jonathan's busted lips. "And just *think* of the headlines. It will be the trial of the century! A CIA agent who managed for years to devolve top secret information and wreck countless missions. I will make you all look like fools. They will write stories about me, make movies about me. And my death as a martyr will—"

"See?" Wolf flicked a finger toward him, interrupting. "What did I tell you? Nothing more than a megalomaniac with a psychotic streak."

Olivia sighed, shaking her head. "You're right, Wolf. I just wish—"

"Wait," Jonathan cut in. He'd been vibrating with fervor in his seat since they brought him in, but now he was eerily still. Maddy sensed something portentous was about to happen and sat forward. "Leo and Wolf?" He sent a one-eyed glance around the table. "Oh, this is rich. This is good. You're working with the guys who were your cover in Syria? Did you tell them you made the decision that got their teammate killed?"

—∾∾∾—

7:55 p.m....

Olivia hadn't realized she was tempting fate when she said there was nothing Agent Wilson could say that would hurt her. And she always thought the phrase "my heart sank" was metaphorical. But since hers was lying on the floor at her feet, broken and bloody, she realized it was an actual physical condition.

"What's he talkin' about?" Leo asked, one brow lifted.

"Leo, I—"

"You *didn't* tell them, did you?" Agent Wilson crowed gleefully.

"Shut the fuck up!" she barked at him before turning back to Leo. There was confusion on his face. And something more. A spark, just an inkling of suspicion, and maybe...*hurt*? Oh, sweet Jesus. This was her worst nightmare come true. She wanted to wrap her hands around Agent Wilson's throat and squeeze the life right out of him. *To hell with my aversion to killing! I'd put him six feet under in a second!*

"Al-Ambhi, that rebel general in Syria," she began, noting absently the gentle, unmistakable *whir* of a propeller-driven engine in the distance. The cavalry was arriving to take Leo home. Too bad they were too late to keep her from having to spill her guts and admit the whole, awful, unforgivable truth. "He wasn't really working for the rebels. He was aligned with the Islamic State."

"I know that." Leo frowned. "And you found out. That's why he drew on you at that meeting at his house, forcing you to kill him."

Agent Wilson threw his head back, laughing maniacally like some sort of vaudevillian villain. And she supposed that's pretty much what he was. Almost cartoonish in his psychosis and narcissism. She did her best to ignore him.

"That's not exactly true," she admitted, biting her lip when Leo's second eyebrow winged up his forehead to join his first. Now there was *definitely* suspicion flashing in his hazel eyes. Each glimmer was an ice pick to her gut. "The CIA knew months before that Al-Ambhi was double-dealing so they sent me in under the auspices of being an attaché to your team, but the real reason I was in Syria was to watch him and keep him nosing in the wrong direction about actual rebel advancements and...

and…and…" She realized she was suffering another episode of verbal diarrhea, talking without punctuation, and stumbled to a stop.

A hard muscle was ticking in Leo's jaw, a sure sign he was upset. Now she not only wanted to wrap her hands around Agent Wilson's throat, but after she was finished with that, she wanted the floor to open up and swallow her whole, just drag her down into nothingness so she wouldn't have to see the pain in Leo's face. Since neither of those things was likely to happen, she sucked in a steadying breath and continued.

"The day of that meeting he tried to blackmail me. He'd discovered the identities of five of my assets inside IS, and he threatened to out them unless the U.S. agreed to pay him fifty million dollars. When I told him that was a nonstarter, he picked up his phone." She screwed her eyes closed, not able to look at Leo when she admitted this next part. "I shot him before he could make the call."

"Al-Ambhi was an idiot," Agent Wilson snarled, and she opened her eyes to blink at him. "The whole reason I told him you were on to him was so that he could use you to forward the cause, not so he could try to extort money—"

"*How could you?*" she screamed, slamming her hands on the table and leaning down until they were nose to nose. The fury burning inside her was hotter than an H-bomb. How could he so blithely, so callously admit he'd been the one behind that awful day? "You traitorous motherfucker! I swear to God I'll—"

"Our ride is here!" Bran called after throwing open the door, his eyes narrowed as he took in the scene.

"And Romeo says we have to bust ass. There's barely enough fuel left in the floatplane to get us home, and he's burning more with every second he's sitting out there idling."

7:59 p.m....

Bran glanced over at LT and Olivia on the far side of the lower deck. They were deep in conversation, and clearly he was missing something. Whatever it was, it had been wallpapered all over Mason's and Wolf's faces when they shuffled out of the main cabin. But when he'd asked, "What's doing?" Mason had done what Mason did best, which was grunt. And Wolf simply replied, "Later."

But since he'd never been accused of having an overabundance of patience, and since he didn't really enjoy mysteries, Bran took a step in LT and Olivia's direction, ready to demand a goddamned explanation. He stumbled to a stop, however, when Maddy laid a hand on his arm.

Her palm was small and soft, the tips of her fingers cooled by the whisper of sea breeze blowing across the back of the yacht. He thought maybe he trembled under her touch and was surprised to discover he had an overwhelming urge to drag her against him and warm them both with a kiss.

"I reckon this is good-bye," she said, wrinkling her cute button nose. "Mr. Navy SEAL."

He lifted a brow, his lungs seizing.

"Olivia let the cat out of the bag when she was questionin' Jonathan Wilson," she explained.

He blew out the breath he was holding and ran a hand over the back of his neck. "We're retired from the Navy," he said, happy to be able to finally admit the truth to her. Why that should be, he didn't know. *But there you go.* "We really *are* salvors now. Swear to God."

She cocked her head, eyeing him. "Well, then I reckon this is good-bye, Mr. Salvor."

"That's…that's usually the way these things work," he told her, missing the feel of her hand when she lowered it to her side.

"I, um, I just wanted to thank you for today. For savin' my life…twice." Her twang turned the words "life" and "twice" into "lahf" and "twahss."

"It was nothing," he assured her. "Just doing my job. Uh…my *old* job I guess, huh?"

Her slate-gray eyes searched his face, and she pursed her lips. The upper one, the pouty one, did one hell of a number on him. He was no longer chilled. In fact, he felt a sheen of sweat break out all over his body. "I didn't peg you for an overly modest man."

He couldn't stop the grin that split his face any more than he could stop the clock from ticking. The constant *whir* of the floatplane's engine was a not-so-gentle reminder that he needed to wrap things up. Mason and Wolf had already hopped overboard, swimming out to the aircraft. They were in the process of pulling themselves onto one of the pontoons.

It's now or never, shit-for-brains.

Reaching into the pocket of his shorts, he took out the piece of paper he'd scribbled on earlier. Then hesitated. Would she even *want* to hear from him after this?

I mean, she'll probably want to forget any of it ever happened. But just in case…

"I, uh, I figured I'd give you my email address. I'm sure you'll be sworn to secrecy about everything you've seen today. So…" He rubbed a hand over the back of his neck again. *Come on, you cowardly* spostata, *soldier the fuck up and take a chance*. "If you need someone to talk to, maybe…" He barked out a laugh, shaking his head. This shouldn't be so hard. "Maybe you'd consider talking to me?"

The smile that split her face was brighter than the big half-moon rising into the night sky. She took the slip of paper from him, their fingers brushing. And even that small contact sent tremors of delight and awareness dancing up his arm. Then she did something truly amazing. She went up on tiptoe, wrapping a hand around his neck and dragging his head down.

He held his breath. Everything inside him, every cell, every synapse waiting, wondering if she would—

She placed a soft, chaste kiss on his cheek, her lips smooth and warm and plump. And when she whispered, "Thank you," the words were hot against his skin.

He sucked in a pained breath. It filled his nose with the smell of her. That fruity aroma of pears and berries. Everything sweet and delicious and edible. Later, he would question the wisdom of his next move. But right then, he didn't think. He simply acted on the lust, the *longing* burning through his body and brain like a five-alarm fire.

Yanking her against him, he claimed her adorable upside-down mouth in a hard kiss. Her lips fell open in a shocked little *O* of surprise, and he took advantage.

Tasting her. Plunging deep, stroking home. His head
spinning because she was intoxicating. Sugary and
warm. Like honey mixed with good Southern whiskey.

Her tongue timidly stroked into his mouth, causing
him to groan, causing her to make a cute, little humming noise at the back of her throat. And that's when
he realized…twitterpated. He was completely, utterly
twitterpated. *And that won't do*. For *many* reasons. Too
many goddamned reasons… *Fangul!*

He set her away from him as quickly as he'd pulled
her close. She seemed slightly off balance. Hell, *he*
was off balance too. The whole world was spinning. Or
maybe that was just his head. One thing he knew for
sure, they were both panting. And the air between them
was positively buzzing with sweet, sexual tension.

"I hafta go," he said. *Great. Spoken like a true gentleman and scholar*.

"O-okay," she whispered, lifting a hand to her lips as
if she wanted to hold the sensation of their kiss in place.

That one unconscious move fired him up like a fire-
cracker with a lit fuse. He needed to cool off. A dunk in
the ocean might just work. "LT!" he called. "Let's get
the lead out, bro!" And then, sparing one last look at her
face—which was adorable even despite the dark bruises
that marred her complexion—and mop of pixie-cut hair,
he chucked her softly on the chin and then chucked *himself* into the ocean.

~~~

8:03 p.m.…

"You need to go," Olivia said, worrying her bottom lip

with her teeth as the cool night breeze played with the
ends of her hair.

Yessir, he did. But he didn't want to. "Since you
caught the mole and don't have to race back to DC, I
reckon I could come with you to Key West," he blurted,
feeling antsy, feeling uneasy, feeling like everything
was about to fall apart.

But maybe that was because he was still reeling from the
revelations he'd heard inside the main cabin. All that time,
all those months, she'd managed to fool him. He couldn't
quite believe it. Had always prided himself on being able to
read people. Clearly, he hadn't been able to read her. Then
again, he'd known from the get-go that along with being
the most fascinating, intriguing, *arresting* woman he'd
ever known, she was hiding something, keeping something
secret. He guessed he just hadn't been expecting *this*.

"Why?" She searched his face, her blue eyes
unspeakably…something. Sad, maybe? Resigned? *Who
the hell knows?* It was obvious he could no longer trust
his instincts when it came to her. "Now that you know
what really happened in Syria—"

"Don't." He shoved a finger against her lips, trying to
ignore the sweet warmth of her breath against his skin.
He couldn't stand it. He had to drop his hand away. It
was either that or grab her up and kiss her senseless.
And then nothing would ever get hashed out because
they'd be too busy tearing each other's clothes off. *And
that's a bad idea because…?* Well, because they had
some shit to hash out, damnit! "I don't blame you for
what you did," he assured her. "You were in an untenable situation, havin' to weigh the risks to yourself and
Rusty against the lives of five people."

"I never expected to live," she whispered.

And that confession, those five little words, were like rockets launched at his heart. Brave, fearless, tender-hearted, *selfless* woman. "But you *did* live. And now the two of us have a chance at—"

"What?" she cut him off. "What do we possibly have a chance at?"

His mouth opened, but nothing came out. The truth was, he didn't know how to tell her he thought they had a chance at it all. The whole kit and kaboodle. Fucking happily-ever-after. Because he loved her. And the way she looked at him sometimes, the way she cried out his name when she unraveled in his arms, made him think maybe, just *maybe* she might love him too.

"Look…" She sliced her hand through the air, step-ping away from him. And that one small move opened up more than space between them. It opened up a tiny crack inside his chest. Doubt and insecurity flooded into the void. *Is it possible I misread her again? Is this thing I'm feelin' all one-sided?* Her next words seemed to answer his questions. "We've scratched our itch. And it was wonderful. Absolutely phenomenal sex. I'll cherish the memory, Leo. But let's leave at that, okay?"

Leave it at that? How could she possibly think that he—

"Yo, LT!" Bran called from the floatplane. He was standing on one of the pontoons, the wash from the front propeller making his wet hair dance wildly around his face. "Romeo says it's now or never, *capisce*?"

"Just give me a frickin' second here!" Leo yelled over his shoulder.

When he turned back to Olivia, she'd taken another

step away from him. And that gulf in the center of his chest widened. The self-doubt and uncertainty were now brimming over the sides of the chasm.

"You'd better go," she said. "And I know this doesn't count for much, but *thank you* for everything you did today. It means the world to me. And I can never repay you for…for…*everything*."

Thanks? He didn't want fucking *thanks*. He wanted *her*.

"Miss Olivia!" Captain Tripplehorn was standing on the landing outside the back door of the bridge, waving a satphone in his hand. *No, no, no!* Everything was happening too fast. Spinning out of control. He needed a minute to— "A gentleman who says he is your boss is on the line! He's asking to speak with you!"

Olivia nodded at the captain. "I'll be up in a bit!" Then she turned back to Leo and smiled. But the expression was completely cheerless. "I *will* get you a new salvage ship," she declared vehemently. "Count on it."

And then she was walking away from him. Climbing the steps to the bridge and taking the pieces of his shocked and shattered heart with her.

Chapter Twenty-one

Three weeks later…

HAH-AH-HAH-AH-HAH-AH—

"Hey, mouthbreather!" Leo scowled down at Meat, who was sitting beside the creaky old wooden chair that went with the creaky old wooden writing desk pushed into the corner of the living room in the creaky old Wayfarer Island house. The fugly mutt was panting up at him, waiting for him to throw the tennis ball lying beside his left foot. "Why don't you go bug Mason, huh?"

Meat cocked his head and licked his ridiculous underbite. *Woof!*

Cock-a-doodle-doo! Li'l Bastard answered from somewhere outside.

"Oh, for chrissakes." Leo bent to retrieve the ball. Meat spun in happy circles, stopping suddenly and staring toward the hall leading to the kitchen when Leo faked a toss. Meat looked up to find the fuzzy, yellow ball still in Leo's hand and growled. "Not as dumb as you look, are you?"

He threw the ball, watching it bounce down the hallway. Meat raced after it, slipping and sliding on the polished wood floor. When both bulldog and ball disappeared, Leo turned back to the laptop and the email he was finishing. This was the sixth such missive he'd typed to Olivia since that momentous day—which his friends had since termed Whackass Wednesday. This email pretty much said the same thing the others had. *I don't feel like things are finished between us. I'd really like to see you. Please call me as soon as you can.* But unlike the previous emails, he ended this one with *If I don't hear from you by next week, I'm coming to Washington.*

Not that he really thought that last part would persuade her to answer, but he was grasping at straws here. He hadn't been able to call her since she didn't have a landline, and there was no way to find her secured encrypted cellular number. All the calls he'd made to Langley had resulted in the same message: "Special Agent Mortier can't take your call. We'll relay your message." *Click.*

He kicked himself in the ass for waiting four whole days before trying to contact her after she turned tail and walked away from him, wondering for the zillionth time if she was simply ignoring his emails, or if during those days when he'd been incommunicado she'd been assigned a mission to parts unknown.

And speaking of those four days… They'd been complete and utter hell. He'd been a wreck. A *brokenhearted* wreck. Spending the evenings drinking Budweiser and staring sullenly into the ocean or the beach bonfire. Devoting every minute of every day to going back over everything she'd ever said to him. Every look she'd ever given him. Every second of their time together. Wondering how the frickin' shit he could have misread her so completely.

But at the end of those four days, he came to the mindblowing conclusion he *hadn't* misread her. He may've missed the mark in Syria, but he hadn't missed the mark in the *Black Gold*'s bathroom, by God! The woman *cared* about him. A lot. He reckoned she might even love him.

And either she thought he could never feel the same way about her after all that had happened, or she was just so used to being rejected by the people in her life that she was falling back on old habits and rejecting him first. Either way, she was deadeye wrong. And he aimed to prove it to her.

If she would just answer my goddamned emails!

That is if she *could* answer his emails. If she wasn't in some desert hut somewhere, surrounded by unfriend-lies and—

Shit. Now his stomach was in knots.

Fuck it. He hit Send.

"Writing another email, eh, *paisano*?"

Leo turned to find Bran leaning against the propped-open front door. The gentle sea breeze played at his back and teased the ragged hems of his swim trunks. "Me?" Leo snorted. And because he was a guy and didn't want to *talk* about it, and also because he was a guy and couldn't resist turning the tables on his best friend, he said, "You're one to talk. How many times a day do you email Miss Maddy Powers, huh?"

Bran acknowledged Leo's quick conversational reversal with a flattened expression, but didn't call him on it. Instead, admitting, "Too many damn times." He rubbed a hand over the back of his neck and offered Leo a sheepish grin. "I can't help myself. The woman is *funny* and…and…challenging, I guess. Trying to outwit her has sorta become an addiction."

Leo lifted a brow, chewing thoughtfully on a wad of Big Red. "That sounds serious," he mused.

"Hell no," Bran scoffed. "It's fun is what it is. There's nothing physical. No strings. No pesky feelings or emotions to deal with. Just...*friends*."

Leo stopped chewing to narrow his eyes. "Since when have you *ever* been friends with a woman, Brando?"

Bran shrugged. "Since Maddy Powers, I guess. First time for everything."

"Hmm." Leo didn't buy it. Especially since he and Olivia had started out as *just friends*, teasing and taunting and one-upping each other. And look where *that* had landed them...

With her ignoring my emails. Because even if she *was* on assignment, surely she would've had the chance at some point to check her account, right? Although, maybe it was possible—

"But, yo..." Bran interrupted his thoughts. "I've got something that'll take *both* our minds off the fairer sex."

Leo pushed up from his lazy sprawl, suddenly alert. "It's here?"

Bran grinned, nodding. "Just dropped anchor. The others have already taken the dinghy to check it out. Mad Dog and Harper are piloting the skiff back to pick us up."

"How does it look?"

"Like a fucking dream." Bran wiggled his eyebrows, motioning over his shoulder with his chin. "Come on."

Leo was up and out the door in under a second, taking the porch steps two at a time and sliding on his sunglasses. The sun was sinking low in the western sky, painting the clouds in pinks and purples. The fluffy confections were being pushed eastward by the same breeze that rattled the leaves of the palm trees.

When he stepped onto the beach, the warm sand sifted between his bare toes. But he didn't feel it. His eyes were glued to the big salvage ship anchored just past the reef.

Her hull gleamed a shiny gray on the upper two-thirds and a deep red on the lower one-third. There was a J-frame crane on the aft section and a HIAB hydraulic loader on the bow. She had what looked to be a pilothouse, a laboratory, and a computer room, and that's just what he could see above deck. What was below was probably just as impressive. She was a beauty. No doubt about it.

But honestly, he wouldn't have expected anything less from Michael "Mad Dog" Wainwright. When Morales called the morning after Whackass Wednesday, asking Leo if there was any place he preferred to purchase a new salvage ship—Olivia hadn't been shitting him; she'd come through like a champ, which was just one more reason on top of the ten billion reasons why he loved her—he hadn't hesitated to point the man toward the other remaining member of the original Great Eight. Mad Dog's family had been building ships in Atlantic City since before there was a boardwalk.

Leo supposed he could have gone on ogling the gorgeous vessel for a good solid six hours, watching his friends and his uncle crawling around the deck inspecting things, if not for the fact that there was an extra person in the dinghy with Mad Dog and his wife, Harper. His former teammate had contacted him last week to say they'd be the ones delivering the ship—a second honeymoon and a chance to see Leo and the boys again. And that extra person was…survey says? Special Agent Olivia Mortier.

Hot damn! Leo was so happy to see her black hair blowing in the breeze as the little skiff zoomed across the lagoon and up to the beach that he felt dizzy. Would have planted ass right there if not for Bran slinging an arm over his shoulder and keeping him steady.

"I used to think civilians and operators could never make it work in the long run," Bran said, watching Mad Dog cut the engine, hop out of the little rubber boat, and pull it onto the sand. "But I gotta say, I think you two have a fighting chance."

Leo was able to rip his eyeballs away from Olivia long enough to slide his best friend a glance. "I never said—"

"You didn't have to." Bran chuckled. "It's written all over your face when you look at her. And all over hers when she looks at you."

Leo closed his eyes and blew out a breath. Even though he'd convinced himself he hadn't misread her, it was still good to hear he wasn't the only one who thought she felt more for him than could be satisfied by a quick slap-and-tickle in the belly of some billionaire's yacht.

"Steady as she goes, bro," Bran said, giving him a squeeze before jogging toward the trio walking up the beach.

Leo was able, just barely, to unstick his feet from the sand and follow. He'd gone no more than ten steps when Mad Dog wrapped him in a bear hug pretty similar to the one he'd just given Bran, pounding him on the back until he feared the man might jostle a lung loose.

"Aren't you a sight for sore eyes, LT, you big piece of shit!" Mad Dog boomed.

Leo chuckled, hugging him back. "Takes one to

know one." And as soon as Mad Dog set him down, Leo glanced over at his redheaded wife. "Harper," he said, dipping his chin at her. "It's good to see you again. Was the sail down from Atlantic City all right?"

She made a face. "It would've been if I wasn't already green with mornin' sickness. I think I threw up over the side of her"—she hooked a thumb toward where the new salvage ship was bobbing with the tide—"about fifty times. Consider her good and christened."

Leo widened his eyes at Mad Dog. "Pregnant?" *Now that's how you grab life by the balls and really live it. Good for you, man.*

Mad Dog's face split into the kind of satisfied smile only men who've planted a baby in the belly of the woman they adore can pull off. "Ten weeks."

"Mazel tov!" Bran crowed at the same time Leo offered the happy couple his congratulations. Then Bran threw his arm around Harper, hugging her until Mad Dog was forced to growl, "Get your dirty mitts off my wife, or find both of them cut off and shoved up your ass."

Bran chuckled, bending to kiss Harper's cheek before dancing out of reach when Mad Dog took a swing at his head.

Leo couldn't put it off any longer. He had to look at her. Olivia. *His* Olivia—if she'd just pull her head out of her ass and admit it. And when he did look at her, he felt like he'd taken a haymaker to his diaphragm. He couldn't breathe because she was so beautiful. Her inky hair wild around her face. Her soft cheeks pink from the sun. She caught her lower lip between her teeth, giving him a glimpse at her sexy front tooth.

"Hello, Leo," she murmured in that smoky voice he'd

been hearing in his dreams for three long weeks now. Her subtle perfume drifted on the evening breeze, causing his nostrils to flare.

"Olivia." He nodded, giving himself major points for playing it cool when cool was the dead last thing he was feeling.

"You ever get the feeling we've done this before?" she asked, tilting her head and referring to their initial salvos, which were basically the exact same greetings they'd given each other when she first arrived on Wayfarer Island the morning of Whackass Wednesday.

"I'm beginnin' to think that when it comes to you and me, it's a case of as it ever was and—"

"Ever shall be, darlin'," she finished for him. "I think we need to get some new material."

"You won't hear any complaints about that from me," he said, his tone full of innuendo. His point being that simply "leaving it at that," as she'd said that night before walking away from him, wasn't going to cut the mustard.

"Uh." Bran glanced back and forth between them, no doubt feeling the tension radiating in the air. Quick to change the subject, he turned to Mad Dog. "Did you guys build that beauty in record time or what?"

"As luck would have it," Mad Dog said, flicking a look at Leo, then at Olivia, his expression turning contemplative, "we were already ninety percent done with her when the original buyer backed out a little over a month ago. Which is why I could tell Morales it'd only take us a week and a half to build her when he called asking how fast I could get a salvage ship done. And then it took us four more days to add the bells and whistles *this* one"—he shot a finger gun at Olivia—"insisted on. She was there every step of the way. Making sure we got it just right. Even down to the font we used on her name."

Leo glanced out at the ship, at the stark red lettering just visible from that distance. It read *Deep Six*. And it was perfect. The perfect name for the salvage company the six of them had finally gotten around to incorporating. Any other time he would have appreciated that fact. But right now he had something else on his mind.

"So *that's* where you've been all this time?" he demanded, feeling his blood pressure rise. "Atlantic City?"

"Annnnddd that's our cue," Bran said to Mad Dog and Harper, motioning for them to head up the beach. "How about you two come up to the house with me? Let's get something fun to drink. Uh…"—he stopped herding them and shook his head woefully at Harper—"sorry. Mad Dog and I will get something fun to drink and *you*, Mrs. Wainwright, will get something decidedly *un*fun to drink."

Leo watched them go, silently seething. She'd been in Atlantic City the whole time, and she hadn't taken two minutes to let him know that she—

"I got your emails," she said, breaking into his heated thoughts.

"Right." He jerked his chin. "And you didn't respond because?" He made a rolling motion with his hand.

"Because I d-don't…" She shook her head and swallowed. "I don't understand. After everything that's happened, how could you possibly want to keep seeing me?" And he'd been right about the first reason she'd been so willing to walk away from him. He figured he was right about the second reason too. "I mean, I get that the sex was—"

"Stop right there," he warned her, fisting his hands lest he reach out and shake her. Shake some *sense* into her. "This doesn't have a cotton-pickin' thing to do with the sex, and you know it."

She searched his face, her expression so damned sad and unsure it nearly had him grabbing his chest and falling to his knees. "Then what *does* it have to do with, Leo?"

And having never been a coward, he gave her the straight, unvarnished truth. "It has to do with me lovin' you and wantin' to spend the rest of my life with your crazy, *stubborn* ass."

As soon as he got the words out, something awful happened. Her lower lip trembled. Her adorable chin quivered. Her blue eyes got *huge*. And then she collapsed in the sand, sitting cross-legged as if her knees had given out on her, wrenching sobs shaking her chest.

He knew then what it took to make brave, fearless, tenderhearted Special Agent Olivia Mortier cry. It was something as simple and as monumental as having someone tell her they wanted her, that they *loved* her...

"Shh, darlin'," Leo crooned, sitting next to her in the sand, an arm around her shaking shoulders. "It's okay. I've got you."

And he *did* have her. But not only that, he loved her and he *wanted* her. For now. Forever. *Oh God!* She dissolved into another round of hiccuping sobs that shook her from head to toe. She was a hot mess. There were just no other words for it.

What the heck is wrong with you, Mortier? When a

man says he loves you, you're supposed to tell him you love him too. Not sit in the sand and turn into a soggy heap of snot and tears.

"Come here." He dragged her into his lap so he could tuck her head under his chin and rock her gently, running his big hand over her hair. He was so warm and solid against her. And he smelled like Leo. Another round of blubbering gripped her in a hard fist, shaking her like a rag doll. He groaned. "You're killin' me, Olivia. You've got to stop that."

Yes, she did. She most certainly did. Because besides being inappropriate, it was completely mortifying. But no matter how hard she tried, she just couldn't. "I-I'm s-sorry," she sobbed. "B-but nobody has l-loved me, nobody has wanted me since my m-mother, and…and…"

"Okay. All right." He continued to rock her, to pet her, to place warm kisses atop her head, on her brow. "Just let it on out then. Just let it *all* out. I've got you. And I'm not goin' anywhere."

And true to his word, he didn't. He stayed with her for who knows how long as wave after wave of emotional upheaval crashed through her, over her. It felt like she'd been holding back rivers of tears for years, and his love had broken the dams that contained them. Now, there was no stopping the flood.

But eventually, it did stop. And after she settled to sniffles and the occasional shudder, he whispered against her hair, "Now, in case part of why you're so shaken up is because you think everyone's right when they say there's no way for this thing we got to work in the long run, I want to assure you I've thought all about that. And I figure I'm better suited than most at dealin'

with the repercussions of your job. It's goin' to kill me
to send you off to—"

"I'm not shaken up about that," she interrupted,
her heart so full of love and joy and hope that she was
amazed it didn't explode inside her chest and blow apart
her rib cage.

"Good." He squeezed her tight.

"Because I quit."

"What do you mean? Did somethin' happen with
Jonathan Wilson? I haven't seen anything in the
news about—"

"No," she was quick to assure him. "It doesn't have
anything to do with that. Agent Wilson is still being held
and questioned. At first, he insisted he wasn't going to
say anything until his trial, wanting to martyr himself so
that he would make big, splashy headlines." She twisted
her lips in disgust. "But that only lasted a couple of days.
When the reality of lethal injection set in, he caved. He
made a deal to give up his assets and divulge all the
information he ever gave our enemies in exchange for a
commuted sentence of life in prison. And you probably
won't see much in the headlines. The Company and all
involved are doing their best to keep everything about
him and his perfidy on the down-low."

"So then…I don't understand. Why did you quit?
When did you quit?"

"I turned in my resignation to Morales the day I got
back to DC." And that had been one of the scariest and
most freeing decisions she'd ever made.

She could feel him hesitate, sense him holding back, not
knowing if he should congratulate her or give her his con-
dolences. "Why would you do that?" he asked cautiously.

"Because I...well, I didn't like it anymore." She frowned, shaking her head. "I think maybe I never liked it. Not really. And I *hated* the violence," she admitted with a shudder. Every night since it happened, she'd had nightmares about killing that terrorist, about the AK-47 jumping in her grip, about his neck flaying open. "I realized I wanted something more from my life than assets and assignments. I wanted..." She trailed off. *A home. A family. People to love me. People I could love.*

"What?" he prodded.

And it was then she realized all those things she wanted were bundled up in just *one* thing. One person. One man. "You," she admitted. "I wanted *you*. I love you so damn much, Leo."

He sucked in a breath and got very still. She could hear his heart beating steadily beneath her ear, its rhythm matching the advance and retreat of the waves shushing against the beach.

"Say it again," he demanded, his low, syrupy accent sliding into her, traveling down to swirl delightfully her belly.

"I love you."

He kissed her then. All deep, slow glides of his tongue and cinnamon-flavored deliciousness filling her mouth. His scratchy beard stubble abrading her cheeks and lips. She gave herself over to the moment, reveling in the feel of his strong arms around her, holding her tight. Imagining what it would be like to have those arms wrapped around her every day of her life. Her happiness was so complete she wondered if she was glowing, lit up like a roman candle. And just when the kiss changed, when it went from one of tenderness and warmth to one of passion and heat, a low buzz sounded in the sky to the south.

They broke apart, and she was breathless. She glanced up in time to see a floatplane coming in for a landing in the lagoon. "Are you expecting company?" The aircraft's pontoons hit the water with a *sploosh* and a *hiss*.

"Christ on the cross," he grumbled. "I forgot all about that."

"What?"

"That historian I hired to translate the documents from the Spanish Archives emailed yesterday to say he'd be headed our way. He thinks he's found somethin' that might interest me."

Olivia could feel the sudden excitement in Leo, a buzz that radiated through him. It was clearly catching. Because she was unexpectedly anxious, itching to hear what the historian had found. Scooting off his lap, she stood and wiped the remaining tears from her cheeks as the plane nosed onto the beach. It was a Seaplane Charters aircraft, and the minute the propeller clicked off, the captain propped open the door and hopped out. He was barefoot, wearing a wifebeater and sporting a scraggly beard that hung down to his beer belly. He looked more beach bum than pilot.

Only in the Keys, Olivia thought with a snort.

"Larry!" Leo called, pushing to a stand and dusting the sand from his shorts. She was appalled to discover the front of his white T-shirt was soaked with her tears. "How's the wife?"

"Got a pot roast waiting on me back home," Larry called, opening the door to the fuselage. A giant duffel bag was handed out to him. Following that were the shapely legs of a woman. She hopped from the aircraft and took the bag from the pilot, saying a few words to him before heading up the beach toward them. If she was one inch over five feet, Olivia would eat her flip-flops for breakfast. And the woman looked about twelve years old.

No one else exited the plane. And then Larry lifted himself back inside, cranking the engine.

Oh, this should be good. Olivia quirked a brow at Leo. "I thought you said this historian you hired was a *him* not a *her*."

"Uhhh," was all he managed before the flame-haired woman was standing in front of them, dropping the duffel and extending her hand.

"Hi!" She grinned, her green eyes bright with enthusiasm. "I'm Alex."

"As in…Alexandra?" Leo asked, shaking her hand.

The new arrival cocked her head. "Yup. Why?"

"Just…" Leo stuck his tongue in his cheek. "A bit of a mix-up on my end. I was expectin' a man."

"Oh." Alex wrinkled her nose. "I guess those are the perils of online correspondence, huh?"

"I reckon so," Leo said, introducing himself and then Olivia.

"Good to meet you." Alex pumped her hand enthusiastically. The *whir* of the floatplane's engine grew louder as it reversed out into the lagoon.

Leo lifted a brow at the departing aircraft, then glanced down at the duffel at Alex's feet. "I take it you'll be stayin' with us for a spell?"

Alex nodded vigorously. It caused her wild mass of

hair to bounce around her face. "I've got a proposition for you in regards to that," she said. "But before we go there, I want to show you this."

She bent to unzip the duffel bag. It appeared to be stuffed haphazardly with all manner of unfolded clothes. Shoes were tossed here and there. Olivia and Leo exchanged a covert glance. This Alex woman might not *look* like much of an absentminded historian, but her packing skills certainly fit the bill.

"Aha!" she crowed when she located a giant binder. She pulled it out and thrust it at Leo with a flourish just at the floatplane caught air and sailed out over the whitewater frothing up around the underwater reef. Leo took the binder, holding it in front of him like it might be a bomb. Olivia had to bite her tongue to keep from laughing.

"Well, don't just stand there," Alex huffed. "Open it! To the page marked with the blue sticky note."

Leo did as instructed, and Olivia craned her head to see what was inside. *Huh.* It appeared to be a photocopy of an old text. The writing was tiny, smashed together, and didn't really look like any language she recognized.

"Read that first paragraph," Alex insisted, nearly vibrating with glee.

Leo slid another covert glance over at Olivia, and she could read his mind. *Is this chick nuts, or what?* But what he said aloud was, "Um. I wouldn't have the first clue how to transl—"

"Oh!" Alex hopped, shaking her head. "Sorry. Turn the page. That's where I've typed up my translation." Leo flipped the page in the binder, and sure enough, on the back was a neatly typed, single-spaced translation. "Go on," Alex encouraged.

Leo slid his sunglasses onto his head, cleared his throat, and read, "'This is the account of Captain Quintana…' That's the captain of the *Santa Cristina*'s sister ship, *Nuestra Señora de Cádiz*," he said for Olivia's benefit before going back to reading. "'Who swears on the holy bible that the followin' words are true. He and Captain Vargas of the *Santa Cristina* made the decision to split the armada one hour after sunrise on May twenty-six, the year of our Lord sixteen hundred and twenty-four. He would shelter the *Nuestra Señora de Cádiz* on the leeward side of Bone Key…' That's what they used to call Key West," he explained, again for Olivia's benefit, before returning to reading. "'And Captain Vargas would attempt to sail home to Havana. It was Captain Vargas's intention that if he could not make his home port, he would take shelter behind the ringed island along the way.'"

Leo stopped, looking expectantly at Alex. "Right. Marquesas Keys. Those are the only islands in the Keys that form a ring. We *know* that's where—"

"No." Alex shook her head, taking the binder from him and tucking it under her arm. It was about as big as she was. "The timing doesn't make any sense. If the captains decided to split the armada one hour after sunrise and Captain Vargas turned the *Santa Cristina* for home directly after that, he should have made it much farther than the Marquesas Keys by the time the hurricane hit in late afternoon."

"But my father found cannons and pieces of eight around Marquesas Keys." He lifted the coin around his neck as proof.

"Yeah"—Alex frowned, narrowing her eyes—"that's

the part that doesn't make sense to me. Unless the cannons fell overboard somehow. A rogue wave, maybe?
Or else it's possible the crew of the *Santa Cristina*
tossed them to try to lighten their load in heavy seas."

Olivia glanced back and forth between the two of
them. Feeling the excitement radiating off Alex. Seeing
the confusion in Leo's eyes. *Her* Leo's eyes. Holy hell!
It felt so good to say that, even if the words were only in
her head. *Her* Leo. *Her* Leo. *Her*—

"I don't get it." He shook his head, running a hand
over his beard stubble and the scar that cut through the
dense hair. "Are you sayin' there's more than one ringed
island in the Keys?"

And now Alex was positively sparkling. She pointed
out past the lagoon where waves piled up and swirled
atop the underwater reef. "Four hundred years ago, sea
levels were lower. Low enough to have that reef line
sticking above the water. To anyone looking at Wayfarer
Island circa 1624, it would've looked like a ring instead
of a crescent moon."

Leo became perfectly still, his hazel eyes zeroed in on
the ocean beyond the reef. When he swallowed, Olivia
heard his throat stick. Her heart was pounding, the hair all
over her body standing straight as she laced her fingers
through his. He squeezed her hand and said, his voice
hoarse, "A-are you sayin' you think the *Santa Cristina*
is out there?" He pointed his chin in the direction of the
salvage ship and the gently undulating waves beyond.

"That's exactly what I think," Alex squealed, biting
her lip and clapping. "And I have more to show you as
proof if—"

Neither one of them heard what she said after that

because they only had eyes for each other. Leo was breathing heavily. So was Olivia. The excitement of the hunt for sunken treasure, combined with the thrill of new love, was almost too much to bear. "I don't know what you had in mind to do with your time now that you've quit the—"

"I hadn't gotten that far," she admitted.

"So then what do you say to helping me search for the holy grail of ghost galleons?" he asked her, his deep voice full of awe, full of hope, full of happiness.

And she knew he was asking her more than the question implied. He was asking her to stay. Here. With him. He was asking her to build a life with him and share his dreams. He was asking her for forever. She said the only four words she could. "I say hell yeah!"

He pulled her into his arms, lifting her off her feet, laughing and spinning her around the beach. She laughed with him, sharing in his joy, his delight. And as she hugged him tight, her chin over his shoulder, she glimpsed the edges of his tattoo peeking from the neck of his T-shirt. *Not All Treasure Is Silver and Gold.* She'd never known truer words. Because she'd found *her* treasure in a brave, loyal, wonderful man. And the orphan in her had finally, *finally* found a home...

Epilogue

May 26, 1624…

HE WAS DROWNING. NO, HE HAD DROWNED. HE WAS sure *of it. He had let the raging sea drag him and his beloved* Santa Cristina *to their watery deaths. But somehow, inexplicably, he was drowning. Again. Drowning still.*

Could it be this was the price he was doomed to pay? Had the good Lord considered his final act not one of sacrifice, but one of suicide? Was this hell? Was he condemned to relive his last moments again and—

"Breathe, Captain!" a voice from afar yelled. A hard hand landed on his back with the force of a kicking mule and suddenly…

"Uhhhh!" He dragged in a ragged breath, coughing and hacking up great mouthfuls of seawater when someone pushed him onto his side. For a moment, his whole existence revolved around breathing, sucking in lungfuls of delicious salt-tinged air, expelling the lingering water from his chest and throat. Breathing, coughing, breathing…And then, little by little, the world came back to him. And it was a world of chaos, of madness. A world being ripped apart at the seams.

The wind shrieked like a crazed demon, howling in his ears until he wanted to raise his hands and cover them. The smell of briny water and stirred-up silt mixed with the sour pungency of sweat and fear on his skin. He opened his eyes to see waves roaring to shore, hurtling themselves over the sand like great frothing beasts. A clump of palm trees near the beach lay over on their sides, struggling to retain their grip on terra firma as el huracán *refused to give them quarter. One, then another was ripped from its precarious perch, and they surrendered themselves to the sea, rolling and breaking against the force of the waves.*

His coat was missing, as was his dagger. A deep, agonizing burn told him he had sustained a wound to his thigh. A shooting pain when he dragged in another breath made it clear he had cracked a rib. But he was alive. Blessedly alive. Gracias a Dios! *And so was Rosario…*

He blinked the rain and salt spray from his eyes and saw his brave midshipman bending over him. "How many made the shore?" he yelled. The manic gale grabbed his words and flung them out to sea.

"Thirty-six!" Rosario screamed, pointing.

Bartolome looked in the direction of his finger and saw through the sheets of horizontal rain the small group of men gathered near the tree line. They were bedraggled, bleeding from various wounds sustained during the breakup of the ship and the swim across the cutting coral of the reef. Some of them were so broken they were being carried by the others. But there were thirty-six who had survived the mighty wreck of the Santa Cristina.

Thirty-six…

Which meant 188 had not. And those lives were lost because he had not been prepared to face Mother Ocean's wrath so early in the season. Because he was arrogant and had not taken shelter sooner. He felt the weight of their deaths like a lodestone on his soul. He should not be alive. He was the captain. He was meant to go down with the ship. All the warmth of his momentary joy at being alive froze solid inside him.

Grabbing the front of Rosario's shirt, he yanked the man down until they were face-to-face. "Why did you save me?" he bellowed as sand flew around them, stinging exposed skin. "You should have let me die with my ship! With my men!"

"Look, Captain!" Rosario shouted, pointing anew. When Bartolome followed the line of his finger past the frothing lagoon to where huge breakers exploded over the reef, he saw it. The Santa Cristina's *main mast. It jutted from the sea like a triumphant finger, pointing to the heavens as if beckoning to God. "You did it! She can be salvaged! All is not lost!"*

And as Bartolome allowed his midshipman to pull him to his feet, satisfaction flickered to life inside the cold stone that was his heart. The great treasure of the Santa Cristina *would rise again.* For king and country!

Acknowledgments

I have to give major props to my husband, who didn't bat a lash when I told him we needed to move to Key West for two months so I could do research for my new series. He just smiled, packed his bags, and put his life on hold to support the next step in my career. Thank you for your continuous and unquestioning encouragement, sweetheart. I don't know what I'd do without you!

A shout-out goes to the Wayward Souls crew—Sean, Whitney, John D., and my own sweet hubby. I said, "I need to know what it's like to sail around the Caribbean," and you all gamely hopped on board a rented catamaran for a weeklong adventure of epic proportions. Sunburns were sustained. A foot was broken. And bouts of seasickness were stoically withstood. Thanks, guys! This book is a far richer, far truer account of life at sea than it would have been otherwise.

I have to thank my agent, Nicole Resciniti, who encouraged me to start this series and then worked her ass off to make sure it was as good as it could be. Nic, I'm the luckiest author in the world to have you in my corner, throwing punches when I need you to and taking hits so I don't have to. You rock!

And thanks to the residents of Key West. For two months at the beginning of 2014, you took me in, eagerly shared your stories and experiences (and boat drinks and chicken wings), and made me feel right at home. Cheers!

About the Author

Julie Ann Walker is the *New York Times* and *USA Today* bestselling author of award-winning romantic suspense. She has won the Book Buyers Best Award and has been nominated for the National Readers Choice Award, the Australian Romance Reader Awards, and the Romance Writers of America's prestigious RITA award. Her latest release was named a Top Ten Romance of 2014 by *Booklist*. Her books have been described as "alpha, edgy, and downright hot." Most days you can find Julie on her bicycle along the lakeshore in Chicago or blasting away at her keyboard, trying to wrangle her capricious imagination into submission.

Be sure to sign up for Julie's occasional newsletter at: www.julieannwalker.com.

And to learn more about Julie, follow her on Facebook: www.facebook.com/jawalkerauthor and/or Twitter: @JAWalkerAuthor.